The Last Summer of Innocence

THE LAST SUMMER
OF INNOCENCE

Linda Sole

St. Martin's Press
New York

THE LAST SUMMER OF INNOCENCE. Copyright © 1991 by Linda Sole. All rights reserved.
Printed in the United States of America. No part of this book may be used or reproduced
in any manner without written permission except in the case of brief quotations embodied
in critical articles or reviews. For information, address St. Martin's Press, 175 Fifth Avenue,
New York, N.Y. 10010.

Library of Congress Cataloging-in-Publication Data

Sole, Linda.
    The last summer of innocence / Linda Sole.
        p.   cm.
    ISBN 0-312-07150-2
    I. Title.
    PR6069.038L37   1992
    823'.914—dc20

91-34908
CIP

First published in Great Britain by Random Century Group.

10   9   8   7   6   5   4   3   2

The Last Summer of Innocence

PROLOGUE

The love between a mother and her daughter is a sacred thing. It's a special love, perhaps the most intimate and precious of all, something to be treasured throughout life. That was how it seemed to me in those early years of my childhood, when a kind of innocence surrounded us like a shining aura. Because a mother's love is so special, it's difficult to believe that it can turn to jealousy, bitterness and perhaps even hatred.

How could a mother deliberately lie in order to deceive her daughter? How could a mother conceive a cruel plot she knows will cause her only child the most terrible pain, in order to satisfy her own desires?

Already I hear an outcry – no mother could do such a thing! Mothers are the most unselfish of creatures, always ready to sacrifice themselves for their offspring. In the wild nursing females will fight to the death to protect their young. Human mothers have been known to starve rather than let their beloved children go hungry. Surely no mother would voluntarily hurt her only child?

I don't blame you if you refuse to believe me. In my innocence, I believed totally in my mother's love. Not once in my formative years did I ever suspect that she might resent me, or feel that I was a burden, preventing her from leading the kind of life that would bring her personal happiness. I loved with all my heart, and I believed myself loved. Perhaps that's why it was all such a shock to me, why, when I discovered the extent of her betrayal, I felt so devastated.

If I couldn't trust my mother, who could I trust? It was that first lie that began it all. A seemingly insignificant thing in itself, but destined to shape and almost destroy my life. Because of that lie, I have been brought to the depths of despair.

Now, as I sit looking out of my window, I know that I must make a decision. I'm at the crossroads of my life; I must take one road or the other, but whatever I do, I may cause others distress. The choice is unavoidable. Memories seem to crowd my mind, binding me to the past, and I'm caught in a web of pain. Yet I know I must break free. I must make this decision that I find so difficult.

The river winds past my window, through gently sloping banks fronded with willows. Water rats burrow in the mud at the shallow edge, fish inhabit the dark secret underworld, while a swallow swoops low over the surface to catch the flies that are its food. And I'm caught, too, held by a feeling of nostalgia that brings both a smile and a tear to my eyes.

Was the hurt and the grief I experienced my own fault for being too innocent? Perhaps some would say that I was the architect of my own fate. I can't think clearly. I must choose between the past and the present, but it's too difficult. I turn away, seeking the solace of my rocking chair – yet even that has its share of painful memories. It's the chair that Harry bought for me.

Memories bring tears to my eyes. For a moment my grief is almost too much to bear, but then, gradually, the action of rocking begins to soothe me and I let my thoughts drift back.

I've tried to shut out the past, but perhaps now I have to remember. Only by facing the truth can I decide where the future lies. So I let my thoughts return to that summer. The last summer of my innocence. . . .

PART ONE

CHAPTER ONE

My earliest memories were of a woman endlessly sewing. From my high chair in the corner of the kitchen, I would watch as she worked, her dark hair glistening in the gentle glow of the gaslight. Her hair was a glossy brown that sometimes had hints of auburn, and she was very beautiful. I felt that she was special even when I was no higher than her knee. Even then, I was aware that she was somehow different from our neighbours, that she had come from another world, another class perhaps, if a child can understand such things. She didn't belong in the drabness of the tiny cottage we called home. In my mind I saw her as a princess cast out of the palace that was her rightful home, but I was always a fanciful child. That was my mother's fault. It was she who filled my head with pictures and dreams. Dreams of faraway places and people. So perhaps I should have been warned from the first. It seems now that I was blind – perhaps wilfully so.

Some people would consider that we were poor, my mother and I, but there are riches that cannot be counted in columns of ink on paper, and we had an abundance of these. The food on our table might have been plain fare, but there was always sufficient, and for all the notice we took as we ate, it could have been a feast. My mother's very considerable skill was constantly in demand and she sometimes charged as much as three guineas for making a dress. In an age when bare-footed children starved on the streets of London and women worked as sweated labour, earning sixpence for making a fine blouse that would sell for twenty-five shillings in the shops, we were surely rich enough. Not that I was ever aware of such evils. I was protected, wrapped in the cocoon of my mother's love.

Supper was the best meal of the day; it was our special time, when my mother's work was done and we could talk. When I was small, she would talk while I listened. She read me rhymes from Edward Lear's *Book of Nonsense*, and told me stories of an enchanted world where there was always laughter and music. I never questioned how she knew such things; she was my mother and a princess in disguise, naturally she would know. As I grew older, we talked of the lessons I'd learned at school, the books we had read, and the places we would one day visit – the day when money was no longer a problem, and my mother was freed from her sewing machine. That infernal, troublesome, blessed machine with which she earned her living and mine.

'When we're rich, Kate,' she suddenly said to me once as we ate our supper of bread and the soft creamy cheese that we bought from the farm across the way, 'when we're rich, we'll have all the things I can't afford to buy you now. You'll have pretty dresses purchased from stores in London and Paris. I'll have furs and jewels and. . . .'

'But where shall we find the money?' I asked, laughing as I saw the bright glow of her sea-green eyes. This was a game of make-believe she liked to play, but it was only meant in fun – or so I thought then. 'You'll never be able to earn so much with your sewing.'

'Oh, Kate, my darling little girl,' she answered, her lashes sweeping against the pale rose of her cheeks. 'My poor, innocent baby. Don't think your mother intends to spend all her life in this cottage. I've got plans, my pet. You'll see. We'll have money – and then I'll have my revenge.'

'Your revenge?' I stared at her in surprise.

'Did I say that?' She shook her head. 'You heard me wrong, Kate. I said we'd have our reward – for all our hard work.' In another minute she was on her feet, clearing the table. 'Help me with the washing-up, Kate. I've a dress to finish this evening.'

What did she mean by revenge? I was sure I hadn't heard her wrongly. There had been a gleam in her eyes when she said it that I knew of old. When? Why? And whom? The questions were in my mind but I couldn't demand answers. She was my mother and I loved her. I obeyed her instinctively. How could I have guessed that even then she was beginning to plot her revenge? How could I have known what an effect it would have on my life?

If only I'd refused to accept the answer she gave me so carelessly then! I should have asked her what she meant, probed and insisted on the truth – but I had no reason to disbelieve her, no reason to suspect that she would lie to me. Why should she lie over such a small thing? I could never have guessed then what was hidden behind those simple words. Instead of doubting her, I was on my feet, anxious to save her.

'I'll wash up alone,' I said. 'You get on with your work.'

It worried me that my mother had to work so hard. Her name was Emma Linton, and she was a widow. She'd been married for only three years when my father died from an infected boil on the neck and she was left with a young child to bring up alone.

'Richard was hardly ill at all,' she'd said to me once, holding the photograph of a handsome young man in her hand. 'It was such a silly little thing. A boil on the neck. Who would have thought it could kill a strong man like your father?'

'It's very sad,' I said, but my sadness was for her because she had lost a husband. My concern was for her, not my father. It was his untimely death that had forced her to leave their home and come to this cottage, which was a step downwards for her. She had been used to a better environment and the change in circumstances had been hard for her. Over the years she'd had to sell many of her treasured possessions to supplement her income.

Being a seamstress wasn't easy, though she had a wonderful talent for making beautiful clothes. She sat for hours at a black iron treadle machine, her foot moving rhythmically as she guided endless lengths of cloth beneath that relentless needle.

'It's hard work, Kate,' she'd said to me often. 'But it's all I can do. I'm not clever enough to be a teacher. You're the clever one. You're the one who's going to do all the things I planned to do. We shan't stay in this house for ever. We don't belong here. We'll have money one day – you'll see.'

I smiled at her indulgently. It seemed to me that she was such a loving mother. I thought that all her ambition was for me. She'd worked so hard, never complaining, putting up with her surroundings to bring me up decently. I didn't mind that we were poor and I tried to tell her so, but she only shook her head, her eyes gleaming as she insisted that she would overcome the fate that had tried to drag her down. I knew that she was still clinging to her dreams and I wished that she would understand that I was content with my life. We were poor but we held our heads high and hung on to our respectability; I didn't want her to work too hard for my sake.

Most of her customers came to the house to be fitted for their clothes, so there was usually someone in our small parlour with its horsehair sofa and its collection of knick-knacks on top of the piano. We heard all the news of our little community as it happened, and there was often a wedding gown to be made, a child's first party dress or sometimes a gown of black bombazine for a grieving widow.

Life didn't pass us by in our tiny terraced cottage. It flowed about us, sweeping us along at such a pace that we didn't notice the passing of time until it overtook us. I remember the day when a neighbour came to tell us that a man called Blériot had made the first crossing of the Channel by aeroplane. That was in 1909, when my life was still blissfully happy and untroubled; when as a child I played on the banks of the River Ouse – just a short distance from our home in Willow Walk – and watched the eel fishermen taking in their lines in the early mornings. I heard and was amazed at the wonders of the modern world when Doctor Crippen was arrested at sea by the miracle of the radio, as did the other citizens of Ely, yet the events in the wider world seemed to me to be outside my own little sphere. Looking back now, I see that we were sheltered from reality. We saw, tasted and experienced life as it was lived by others, but we had a charmed circle of our own, perhaps because there was no man to break it.

My happiness was to last for a year or so yet; until I was fifteen. It was 1912. I was still at school, though I could have left on my fourteenth birthday. My mother wanted me to be properly educated, and had insisted on the extra year despite my pleas to be allowed to leave school and find a job.

'Most of the girls in my class are leaving,' I said. 'Clara has a job in the brewery, and Peggy. . . . '

'They can do as they please.' My mother frowned at me. 'I've managed this long. I can go on a while longer. I didn't make sacrifices to have you end up in a factory, Katie. You're a bright girl. You can make something of your life. I want you to have a better life than this. God knows, I've found it hard enough!'

'But we have a good life,' I protested. 'We have friends and we're happy – what more could we want?'

A strange look came into her eyes, and her mouth twisted in bitterness. 'You can ask me that? When I was your age I wanted so much. Maybe that was why. . . . ' She shook her head, seeming angry. 'Don't you want to do all the things we've talked about? Wouldn't you like to travel?' She coughed into her handkerchief. I'd noticed her do that once or twice recently.

As I stared at her, puzzled, her eyes began to glow with excitement. She seemed different, as if she had a secret that gave her immense pleasure.

'But we can't afford to travel – I don't suppose we ever shall.'

'Don't be so sure about that.' She laughed as I looked doubtful. 'I'm not ready to talk about it yet – but I've been making plans.'

'I thought I might like to be a teacher.'

'I don't think so, Kate.'

'Mrs Burrows says I'd be good at it. I might be able to win a scholarship to college.'

'Mrs Burrows should mind her own business. If things work out the way.... Well, I want you to stay on at school for at least the next few months, until I'm certain. Besides, you help me and that means I can work longer hours.'

I wanted to protest that she worked far too much. She looked so tired sometimes that I wondered if she were ill. I wanted to ask, but there was a secret side to my mother, things that she had never told me, and I was afraid to push her too far for fear of hurting her.

It was on a Sunday that I first became aware of changes in our lives. I'd always loved Sunday. It was the one day that Mother never worked. In the mornings we went to church, walking home along the river bank and sometimes stopping to talk to our friends or watch the swans glide effortlessly over the stretch of silver-grey water. After lunch we would read the books I'd fetched from the library the previous day – Rider Haggard's *She*, which had first been serialized in the *Graphic* magazine in 1887, was one of our favourites – relaxing by the fire or in the tiny garden at the end of the yard if the weather was fine. In the evenings Mother would play the piano in the parlour and sing for me. I loved it when she sang, for she had a pretty voice.

That first Sunday in March 1912 was different. It was different because, when we were on our way home from church, my mother was in a hurry. She seemed excited about something, and there was a secret smile on her lips. Our meal had been slowly cooking in the little black oven fuelled by the fire while we were in church, and as my mother stripped off her white cotton gloves to serve the food, I noticed that her hands trembled. She seemed in a rush, as if she could not wait for the ritual of Sunday lunch to be over, eating hardly anything herself. When she'd finished, she jumped up, hurrying upstairs. I began to clear the dishes, and I was in the wash-house up to my elbows in soda and hot water when she returned. I was surprised to see her wearing a pale green silk dress that I'd never seen before.

'I'm going out, Kate,' she said, and her voice was breathy with excitement. 'I have to see someone.'

'I've nearly finished,' I replied, puzzled by her manner. 'Where are you going?'

'I'm visiting a client at home. I haven't worked for Mrs Madison before and it may bring me a lot of business. I'll be using only the finest materials. Mrs Madison was in the habit of buying her clothes from Worth but she can't get out much any more so she wants me to make her gowns from now on.' Mother stuck a long hat pin through the straw boater she'd placed on her head and stared at her reflection anxiously. 'Do I look all right?'

'You look the same as usual,' I said sulkily. 'Why all this fuss if you're only going to see a client?'

'Mrs Madison is special,' she said, but her eyes slid away from mine.

'What shall I do?'

'Don't be such a baby, Kate. You're perfectly capable of amusing yourself for a few hours. I shan't be that long – besides, I'm doing this for you. The extra money will help – you can have those new shoes you wanted.'

There was an odd look in her eyes, but I couldn't decide whether it was guilt, annoyance or impatience. It made me feel like a spoilt wretch when she said I could have the new shoes, as if it were my fault that she had to work on a Sunday.

'I'm sorry,' I apologized, feeling remorse. 'But I look forward to Sundays.' As she opened her arms, I rushed to hug her, breathing in the scent of lavender water. 'I do love you so – and you look lovely. Your dress is beautiful. Did you make it?'

She glanced at herself in the mirror of the carved oak sideboard, and I saw her blush, her expression shy and unsure. 'No, it was given to me . . . by Mrs Madison. Her – her daughter lives in France and it came from an expensive modiste. It didn't suit her so she left it with her mother to throw away. Mrs Madison thought I might like it.'

Mother's explanation was delivered in an oddly muffled voice. She avoided looking at me, as if she were ashamed of something. I wondered why.

'That was generous of her,' I remarked. 'It looks as if it might have been made for you.'

'Yes, doesn't it. I'll probably be back for tea, but if not, you'll find all you need in the pantry.'

She was out of the door in a flash. As it closed behind her, I had the feeling that I'd been lied to several times. It was as if she would have said or done anything to get away quickly. I felt resentful, and then ashamed. My mother wouldn't lie to me! We had a wonderful, special relationship.

Left to myself that afternoon, I studied the photograph of my father on the sideboard. He'd been a handsome man with dark, curling hair and serious eyes I'd been told were grey. I'd often looked for some likeness to myself, but never found one. I looked like my mother, except that my hair was much darker and my eyes were bluer. Now I wondered what our lives might have been like if my father had lived.

'Richard was working in a drapery store to pay his way when I first met him,' Mother had told me once. 'He was studying in his spare time to become a lawyer, and I knew he would make a success of his life. He didn't have much money, but he was clever and funny – and he would have been rich one day if it hadn't been for that boil.'

There was such sadness in her voice then. I never liked to ask too many questions, because I sensed that there was something secret about that part of her life; things she didn't wish to talk about. Because I loved her, I never asked for more than she was ready to tell me. Yet that afternoon, I found myself wishing that I knew more about my father and his family.

The longcase clock in the parlour was striking seven when Mother at last came in. She glanced at the table set for tea and frowned.

'You should have eaten, Kate.'

'I waited for you.'

'I've had my tea.' She coloured slightly. 'But I'll drink a cup with you now.'

I was resentful as she put the kettle on the hob. 'Surely it doesn't take that long to measure someone for a dress?'

'It wasn't just one dress. If you must know, I didn't come straight home. I went out to tea with a friend.'

'A friend?'

'He – he's a friend of Mrs Madison, really. He brought me home and we went to the Lamb Hotel for tea.' The hotel was in the High Street, not far from the cathedral and we only ever went there on special occasions. She frowned as my eyes widened. 'Don't look at me like that. You're so selfish. It's years since I've had any fun.'

'I'm not selfish,' I cried. 'Sunday is our day. I hated being alone all the time.'

'How do you imagine I feel? I have to spend day after day in this wretched little house. I'm a prisoner of that sewing machine, never seeing anyone – anyone who matters. Before I had you, I was never in the house. I went to parties and. . . . Oh, I'm sorry, Kate.' She looked horrified as she realized what she'd said. 'No, I didn't mean that. I've never regretted having you.'

She'd never even hinted at such a thing before. Was I a burden to her? 'I'm sorry,' I said in a small voice. 'I hadn't thought how it must be for you. . . . '

She came rushing round the table to sweep me up in her arms and hug me. She smelt of a sharp, strong scent that was unlike any perfume she'd ever worn. There was something vaguely masculine about it.

'Don't look so hurt,' she begged. 'I love you, of course I do. Everything I do is for you, Kate.'

She sounded as if she were trying to convince herself.

'I'm the one who should be sorry,' I mumbled. 'You work too hard. You should have time to yourself.'

She smiled ruefully. 'But I shouldn't have left you on a Sunday afternoon, should I? Next time . . . I'll make other arrangements.'

Mother didn't desert me again on a Sunday afternoon, but the changes had begun. Often in the evening I came home from school to find the house empty and a note on the kitchen table telling me what to have for supper. She would arrive home at around seven, her eyes glowing and her cheeks reddened with the rouge she'd started to use very discreetly. She'd started to hide things from me, too. When I walked into the room unexpectedly there would be a little flurry of activity as something was stuffed under a cushion. She seemed to have more money for luxuries like perfume, shoes and hats. Once I caught sight of a pale blue envelope. She'd never had many letters until now. I was curious to know what was in it, but she was careful not to leave it lying around, and I wouldn't have dreamed of prying into my mother's drawers. So I was curious but I knew nothing – nothing except what my instinct told me. It was as if she had come to life after a long sleep, her eyes full of secret dreams from which I was excluded.

And so the summer came and went. In April the unsinkable ship that was the pride of the British company which owned her went to a watery grave. A neighbour came to tell us the terrible news of the sinking of the *Titanic*. Mother and I cried when we heard how many lives had been so cruelly lost, but our tears dried and our lives went on. Things were changing all that summer, though not sufficiently for me to suspect what was to come. Then it was autumn and I sensed a new mood in my mother. She was always on edge, as if she

12

was waiting for something . . . something that never came. At times when she looked at me, there was a coldness in her eyes and I felt that she was blaming me for . . . I didn't know what. . . .

At Christmas a card arrived for her; a special card that she didn't put on the mantel with the others. Her mood improved and I thought I must have imagined that look in her eyes. Now it was winter she had ceased to go out in the afternoons. Her cough had begun again, seeming worse than the previous year. Now she was at home when I returned from school, and it was almost as it had always been though she no longer smiled as often as she had once.

It was spring again when I arrived home one day to see an expensive automobile outside in the lane. I looked at it curiously, admiring the big brass headlamps and shiny coachwork. We rarely had cars in our lane, no one could afford them; they were a rich man's toy and I wondered who was driving this one. Hurrying into the house, I stopped and stared in surprise at the stranger sitting on the sofa in our small parlour. Clearly the owner of the automobile outside, he looked out of place in our house. He must be a client, I thought, and Mother was upstairs fetching something from the spare room.

'Is my mother fetching something for you?' I asked, startled into foolish speech.

'You must be Katie,' he said, his dark eyes glinting with a secret amusement. 'Emma was summoned urgently to a neighbour's house. I don't imagine she will be long – there was an argument of some kind.'

I nodded, understanding the hint of laughter in his eyes. Our neighbours were a noisy, quarrelsome family. Coming through the covered passage at the side of our house into the shared yard we all used, I'd noticed that Mrs Peacock had some washing on the line. Her red flannel petticoat hung next to her husband's combinations, and it looked as if she'd washed them together, causing the long-johns to turn pink. Mr Peacock wouldn't have been pleased when he came home from his job in the brewery. Living as close as we did, it was impossible to ignore all the arguments that went on around us. Mother had forbidden me to listen or to repeat the language I heard next door. We might have to live in a similar house, but we didn't have to sink to our neighbours' level. We had been used to better things, though I couldn't remember that far back, but Mother did. She always kept herself a little aloof, and some of our neighbours thought she put on airs.

I gazed at the stranger's face, thinking how different he was from

13

any other man I'd ever met. Most of the men I knew only ever wore a suit on Sundays, spending their lives in working clothes with their shirt-sleeves rolled up to the elbows. His clothes were obviously made by the finest tailors, his shoes so shiny that he must be able to see his face in them, and his dark cloth coat had a curly fur collar. His hat, cane and gloves lay on the table, all of them of the best quality – and there had been something different about the way he spoke. Suddenly, I realized that he was laughing at me now; I'd been staring rudely.

'Can I help you?' I remembered my manners. 'Have you come for a fitting?'

'No,' he said, and I knew what was different. He had an accent. His voice was soft and husky and I found it attractive. 'I've come to collect something for Grace Madison.'

'Mrs Madison?' I frowned, recalling the name. 'My mother made some dresses for her last year.'

'Yes. . . . ' A little smile played at the corners of his mouth. 'Now she's going to make some more.'

'Oh. . . . ' I wondered about his accent and the question just popped out. 'Are you French?'

'How did you guess?' The dark eyes were mocking me.

'Was it rude of me to ask?' Colour stained my cheeks and I felt foolish. 'It's just that I've never met a Frenchman before.'

'And now – what is your opinion?'

As he spoke, he got to his feet and I was aware of an odd, clutching sensation in my stomach. I gazed up at him, feeling nervous.

'You – you're very tall,' I squeaked.

'And you're quite delightful, Katie.' He smiled down at me. 'Almost sixteen, I think your mother said?'

He smelt of a strong, sharp scent that I vaguely recalled from somewhere. Not only was he tall, he was broad in the shoulders and there was something frighteningly male about him. It was the first time I'd ever been aware of masculinity as a threat, and I took a step backwards, my heart beginning to thump.

'Surely you're not frightened of me?'

'No. Why should I be?' I asked, lying through my teeth. I'd never been this close to a man before. He was scaring me to death, but I stood my ground, too proud to let him see it.

'Why indeed?' His eyes moved slowly over my face and my body, making me blush. No-one had ever looked at me that way before,

14

and it shocked me. I felt a little peculiar. 'Your mother said that you were still a child, but I think you are a young woman, Katie.'

'What do you mean?' I was beginning to tremble.

'Shall I tell you?' He was smiling, teasing me a little as his hand reached out to touch my hair. I tingled with fright, knowing instinctively that I should run to my mother, but feeling unable to move. His eyes seemed to hold me so that when the side of his hand smoothed across my jawline, his thumb moving up to trace the fullness of my bottom lip, I was mesmerized.

'I should like to kiss you,' he said, his brows arching as if testing my willingness.

'Why?' I was curious now. 'Why should you want to kiss me? You don't know me.'

'Because your lips are soft and tempting,' he murmured, laughter in his voice as though he mocked us both. 'Because I am a man and you're not quite a woman. Because you make me think of rosebuds and snowflakes, and because your hair has the sheen of a bird's wing, and your skin smells like heaven.'

'How do you know what heaven smells like?' The sensation in my stomach returned, and I was alerted to danger again. I wasn't sure that I liked this man with the compelling eyes. 'Don't look at me like that.'

'Not look at you, Katie?' His fingers moved to the nape of my neck, stroking me. It made my skin tingle and I jumped as if I'd been stung. 'You can't deny me that pleasure, surely?' His eyes were speculative. 'I wonder what you would do if I kissed you?'

A part of me was shocked at the very suggestion. Properly brought up young ladies didn't allow men to kiss them! Wasn't that how babies were made? All I really knew about such things were the whispers I'd heard at school, but I'd had practical experience of kittens being born in the garden shed so I suspected there was a little more to it. I was nervous and a trifle indignant at the mocking look in his eyes yet, as he bent his head to mine, curiosity overcame any feelings of outrage I might have felt. His lips were warm and soft, infinitely gentle as they began to move caressingly across mine, touching at one corner and then the other until they covered my mouth. Surprised, I discovered that kissing was a pleasant experience that made me feel a little light-headed, and I closed my eyes, letting myself relax. I was drifting towards him when I heard a tiny sound behind me.

I gasped and pulled away from him, swinging round to find my mother staring at me. Her eyes were blazing with anger, and there was a strange expression on her face that could almost have been jealousy.

'What do you think you're doing, Kate?' she asked coldly.

'I – I don't know,' I faltered, frightened. I glanced at the stranger as if expecting him to help me. 'I wasn't doing anything. . . . '

'It was only a speck of dust in your eye, Mademoiselle Linton,' he said. 'I hope I didn't hurt you when I removed it?'

I blinked rapidly in surprise, wondering why he'd lied for me. My mother was still staring at me angrily, but there was less certainty in her eyes now, as if she were not quite sure of what she'd seen.

'I . . . No, you didn't hurt me,' I said and rubbed at my eye. 'It's better now, thank you.'

'My pleasure,' he replied with a faint smile, then, to my mother: 'You've settled your neighbour's dispute, yes?'

A little blush came to her cheeks. She seemed to hold back for a moment as if resisting the charm of his smile, then she laughed. It was a light, flirtatious laugh and she fluttered her eyelashes at him.

'A storm in a teacup,' she said. 'Forgive me for keeping you waiting, Monsieur de Bernay. I'll fetch Mrs Madison's gown at once.'

'Please don't apologize, Madame Linton,' he replied, a sparkle in his eyes. 'As you've seen, I've met the delightful Katie. The time wasn't wasted, I assure you.'

My mother's gaze came back to me, and I sensed the undercurrent beneath the teasing banter. Once again I was aware of anger and another, more complex emotion that I couldn't name.

'Shall I set the table?' I asked nervously.

'Not just yet, Kate. Go up to the spare room and bring down the blue silk dress you'll find in the wardrobe.'

I obeyed instantly, relieved to escape from the stranger's mocking gaze and my mother's anger. I was sure she'd seen him kissing me and I trembled inside. It was a wicked sin and I knew she would punish me when he'd gone – and what must he be thinking of me? I'd let a complete stranger kiss me! I felt hot and ashamed. I must be like Belle Woodruffe – the strange, unkempt woman who lived by the river. Men visited her sometimes when it grew dark, but hardly a woman in the place would speak to her. They whispered things about her and said that no one knew who had fathered her brood of dirty children. I wasn't quite sure what they meant, but I knew it wasn't very nice.

There was a door at the bottom of our stairs. I left it open because there wasn't much light on the landing above, but my mother closed it after me. I could hear the sound of voices from the parlour, and laughter. I wondered if they were talking about me and my cheeks burned.

The blue silk dress was hanging at the front of the wardrobe. It looked as if it might have fitted me, and I was tempted to try it, but my mother was waiting.

To my surprise she didn't seem to be waiting for me at all. When I returned, she and Monsieur de Bernay were drinking sherry from the best glasses. She was laughing up at him, relaxed and somehow different. He gave me an indulgent look and my mother smiled, though it didn't quite reach her eyes. I sensed something between them, a special intimacy that seemed to shut me out. I laid the dress on the table and Mother wrapped it in brown paper.

'I hope Mrs Madison will be pleased,' she said.

'I'm sure she will.' Monsieur de Bernay inclined his head. 'You'll bring the other dress at the end of the week?' She nodded and his eyes flicked to me. '*Au revoir, mademoiselle*. I hope we shall meet again one day.'

My lips were frozen. I couldn't smile or speak, standing silently as he picked up the parcel and went out. My mother was frowning but she didn't speak until after we heard the sound of the car engine, then all she said was, 'Set the table, Kate.'

My heart raced as I spread a white linen cloth on the scrubbed pine table, fetching bread, cheese, jam and freshly baked scones from the pantry. At any moment there might be an outburst. She'd warned me to be careful of the local lads, she would surely be angry with me for behaving so badly. Instead of giving me a lecture, however, she sat by the range, staring into the fire.

'Is something wrong?' I asked at last, unable to bear the suspense. 'Are you ill?'

She looked up then and I caught a glimpse of a strange emotion in her eyes; it was sadness, pain and acceptance all at once. 'I have to make a decision, Kate,' she said quietly. 'And it isn't easy. . . . Believe me, it isn't easy. . . . '

I knelt at her feet, looking up. Her face showed signs of tiredness. 'Can I help?'

'No, there's nothing you can do. I. . . . ' She broke off as a fit of coughing overtook her. 'This wretched cough. It just won't clear up.'

'You should go to the doctor.'

17

'I will tomorrow.' She sat back in her chair, gazing at me intently. 'What did you think of Monsieur de Bernay, then?'

'I – I don't know.' Was she going to be angry with me now? 'He – he seems nice.'

She laughed as if that amused her. 'The last thing I would call him is nice – he's handsome, charming, a little wicked, perhaps. . . .'

The look in her eyes made me wonder. I thought that perhaps she liked him very much. 'Is – is he the friend who took you to tea last year?'

Her eyes narrowed and she was no longer smiling. 'Did he say anything – about me?'

'Only that you'd gone next door. I just wondered – I mean, he knows Mrs Madison and it was her friend who brought you home, wasn't it?'

She stared at me, her expression sending a shiver down my spine. She was struggling to control her emotions. For a moment longer she looked at me in silence, on the verge of speaking, then she shook her head.

'No. No, he wasn't the one. As a matter of fact, I only met him for the first time today. . . . '

'Oh, good,' I said, relief surging. 'I thought you might be planning to marry him. I'm glad you're not. I didn't really like him.'

Getting to my feet, I went back to the table.

CHAPTER TWO

'Kate, is that you?' I heard my mother calling as I came in with my basket full of shopping. 'I want you. Come up to the spare room.'

I guessed that she had a client with her. Running upstairs, I heard the sound of voices and, going into the bedroom, I saw my mother on her knees pinning up the hem of a dress.

'Oh, there you are,' she said, looking harassed. 'I've got to finish this by this evening. I'd promised to deliver Mrs Madison's gown today, but I can't manage it now. You'll have to take it for me – it's packed and ready on the kitchen table.'

I was surprised. I often delivered things for her, but she'd always been so particular about taking Mrs Madison's things herself. I'd never even been allowed to go with her, though I knew where the house was and I was only prevaricating when I said, 'That's the white house about a mile down the Stuntney road, isn't it?'

'You know it is.' Mother frowned, her eyes flashing. 'You can borrow my bicycle if you promise to take care of it.'

Her bicycle was her most precious possession after the sewing machine, and I knew how fussy she was over it. 'I'll walk,' I said. 'It's not cold; I'll come back by the river.'

'Don't dawdle on the way there.' She shot me a searching glance. 'You're to come straight back, Kate. If Mrs Madison pays you, be careful not to lose the money.'

'Anyone would think I was a child,' I said, irritated by her manner. She'd been acting oddly all week, alternating between moods of affection and coldness. 'I shan't lose anything.' A look of contrition came into her eyes as she saw my expression.

'Sorry,' she apologized. 'I don't know whether I'm on my head or my heels today – and I didn't sleep much last night.'

'It was the wind, I expect,' her customer said as I turned away. 'It kept me awake half the night – do you think that's the right length or shall we take it up another inch?'

Hearing my mother's sigh of exasperation as she began to remove the pins once more, I hurried down to the kitchen to collect the parcel. My mother was coughing harshly. She'd been coughing in the night, too. I'd heard her and I was worried by the dark shadows beneath her eyes. She hadn't been herself all week, sometimes staring into space for half an hour or more, and she'd got behind with her work. I'd sensed that she was worrying about something, but when I asked her what was wrong, she told me to get on with whatever I was doing. It seemed as if I couldn't do anything right for her these days.

Small white clouds scurried across the sky as I left the house and walked to the end of our lane with its little rows of terraced cottages, the slaughter yard at the far end and, almost opposite our house, the farm where we bought fresh creamy milk straight from the churns, ladled into a jug by little copper measures. Many of the residents of Willow Walk worked in the local breweries, though some of them were basket makers and had been for generations.

Eric Potter waved to me from the back of his coal cart and I waved back. Most of our neighbours were friendly, though I knew some of them thought that my mother put on airs, pretending to be better than she was, but Eric always treated her as if she was a lady. He was a big, burly man with coarse features and dark, grizzled hair. A widower himself, Eric obliged my mother by delivering the coke for our kitchen range right to the back door, saving us the trouble of fetching it from the yard in Broad Street, and without charging for the service. He'd had an eye for my mother for years but, though she invited him in for a cup of tea now and then, she'd never encouraged him to think of marriage.

'If ever I marry again it won't be to someone like Eric,' she'd told me once after he left us. 'Mind you, he's not short of a few pounds. If ever I was in trouble, I might reconsider.'

I was thinking about some of my mother's recent odd remarks as I walked down Bull Lane and turned towards Broad Street, past the sweet shop on the corner, across the road and past the brewery gardens and the little lane that led down to the maltings. Her remark about marriage had been made a few days earlier, and it made me wonder. Yet as far as I knew, there wasn't a special man in her life. Most of our neighbours were married. Eric was the only available male of our acquaintance. Apart from the fact that his big hands were always ingrained with coal dust – even after he'd scrubbed them for church on Sundays – I could find nothing disagreeable about him. At least Mother wouldn't have to work so hard if she was his wife. Besides, there wasn't anyone else . . . unless she'd lied about the stranger. . . .

Thinking about Monsieur de Bernay brought a frown to my fore-head. I wasn't sure why I'd taken an instinctive dislike to him, or why I felt that he posed some kind of a threat to me personally. Unless of course my mother was in love with him. Yet she had only met him recently, she'd said so – and why should she lie? Even if she did want to marry him, I would be churlish to let my own feelings blight her happiness. Other girls had step-fathers; my mother was perhaps unusual in having made her own living so successfully all these years – why should I make a fuss? Though I'd rather she chose someone more like Eric.

Busy with my own thoughts, I hadn't realized how far I'd come, and before I knew it I was standing outside the gate of the white house. It was called the Laurels and there were shiny, spotted-leaved laurel bushes at either side of the gravel drive. Although Mrs Madison was generally considered wealthy, my mother had told me it wasn't a huge house.

'It's really rather ugly,' she'd said. 'A square, early Victorian house with four reception rooms and seven bedrooms.'

Mother might not think that large, though it sounded huge to me, and I felt nervous as a black-gowned maid admitted me to the front parlour and told me to wait. The room had a suite of hard horsehair sofa, armchairs and matching, straight-backed dining chairs. They were covered with a pale green striped material and looked too immaculate to sit on, so I stood clutching my parcel in front of my chest and staring out of the window at the untidy garden – untidy because it was a riot of climbing roses, lupins that had seeded haphaz-ardly and clumps of Grandmother's Bonnets.

'Kate! This is a surprise.'

I jumped, swinging round at the sound of the man's voice. I hadn't expected to see him here, and as he'd been so recently in my mind, the shock was even greater. 'Monsieur de Bernay. . . . ' I blushed. 'You startled me.' A large diamond pin sparkled from his neck tie. Dressed in a pale grey striped suit and white shirt, he looked even more attractive than the first time we'd met. His expression was distinctly amused.

'Forgive me. When the maid said you were here, I expected your mother.' His smile faded to concern. 'I hope nothing is wrong?'

'She was too busy to come – someone wanted a dress finished urgently.'

'Your mother works too hard, Kate.'

'I know.' I gazed up into his face, clutching my parcel defensively and remembering our last encounter with resentment. 'I didn't know you would be here. You don't live in Ely, do you?'

'No. I spend much of my time travelling: France, Italy and England. . . . ' Now he seemed to sense my resentment. 'Is there some reason why I shouldn't visit my good friend Grace Madison, Kate? Have you an objection, perhaps?'

My cheeks burned. Why was it he always managed to make me feel like a gauche schoolgirl. 'I just wondered. Have you known Mrs Madison long?'

'For many years. We were brought together by a mutual acquaintance.' His eyes narrowed as he seemed to read my mind. 'Just what is going on in that suspicious little. . . . '

He stopped as a woman came in, her silk gown whispering about her ankles. She was tall, thin and white-haired, her cheeks lined with soft wrinkles that only enhanced her remarkable beauty, remarkable for a woman of her age. Although clearly in her sixties, she carried herself erect and with pride.

'Forgive me for keeping you waiting,' she said, her voice sweet and gentle. 'You must be Kate, of course. Emma has told me so much about you, my dear. I see Paul has been looking after you. His grandmother and I were friends long ago, and he takes pity on me now and then.' She smiled at him, offering her cheek for his kiss. I saw a look of understanding pass between them. 'More often of late, I must admit.' Her eyes sparkled with mischief and then she turned to me. 'You've brought my dress. How kind of you.'

'My mother couldn't come,' I mumbled, feeling foolish. I'd suspected a love affair between Paul and the mysterious Mrs Madison; now I saw that I was wrong. 'If there are any adjustments, she will do them next time.'

'I'm sure the dress will be perfect. I shall give you some money for Emma. Will you ask her to come and see me next week?' She took two guineas from her purse and handed them to me. 'I rely on her so completely now that I can't get up to town. She has such flair. I've told her that she should have her own business in London – not that I wish to lose her services.' She glanced at Paul and again I caught that hint of mischief. 'But I mustn't interfere. . . . ' She laughed as if amused at some secret they shared.

I accepted the money and said my mother would call, then turned to leave.

'You must have walked all this way,' she said suddenly. 'Paul, we can't let her walk home. Won't you take her in your car, my dear?'

22

'I should be delighted – if she will allow me the pleasure?'

His brows rose in inquiry. I stood mutely, not wanting to accept his offer, but knowing that to refuse would offend them both.

'You – you're very kind,' I said reluctantly.

'It's no trouble, I assure you.' He turned from me, taking the old lady's hand to kiss it. 'I shall leave you now, but expect me next week.'

She nodded, her eyes thoughtful as she looked at him. 'You're a wicked boy – but I love you.'

'Hardly a boy at twenty-nine,' he replied with a smile.

'But certainly a rogue,' she cried, flirting with him madly. 'If I were sixteen I too should be on my guard, but you are a charmer for all that.'

My cheeks burned as I caught the drift of their conversation and knew they were talking of me. Before Mrs Madison arrived, I'd suspected Paul de Bernay of being – I wasn't sure what, but something less than respectable.

I tried not to notice as they both glanced in my direction and whispered things that obviously amused them. I guessed that Monsieur de Bernay was deliberately making me wait because I'd been ungracious about accepting his offer.

A smile lurked in his eyes when he at last came to me. 'Ready, Kate?'

'Yes, Monsieur.'

I followed him outside. His car was parked at the back of the house, out of sight of the front entrance. He opened the passenger door for me, but I hung back uncertainly.

'What are you waiting for?'

'I'd rather ride in the back.'

He glared at me. 'Ridiculous child! Because of that foolish kiss, I suppose? I'm not going to ravish you, Kate. All I want is to become better acquainted with you.'

'Why?' I stared miserably.

'My reasons are not in the least sinister – but I've given my word to say nothing for the moment.' He stared pointedly at the front passenger seat.

Reluctantly, I climbed in, sitting stiff and straight as he swung the handle to start the engine and then got in beside me. I moved away from him as far as possible, drawing an impatient glance.

'Now what's wrong?'

'I'm not like Belle Woodruffe.'

'Who is she?'

'Men visit her at night. She lives by the river and no one knows who fathered her children.'

He chuckled as if highly amused. 'Depend upon it, Kate, someone knows.' His face became serious again as I continued to sit with my knees pressed tightly together. 'Ridiculous girl! I kissed you on a whim. A moment's madness I've since regretted. If I wanted to make love with someone, I should choose a woman, not a child. Perhaps a woman of my own age – or slightly older.' He looked at me then as if he thought I should find that significant. 'I have perhaps not always been as circumspect as I should have been, but I was taught a harsh lesson. I promise you you are quite safe with me. Now stop this nonsense and I'll take you out for cream cakes and tea.'

'No, thank you.' I couldn't look at him. My cheeks were on fire and I was mortified. 'Mother will worry if I'm late.'

He sighed in exasperation, then released the long handbrake at the side of the automobile. We began to move forwards. 'Perhaps you're right. I just thought it might make things easier if we were friends.'

'Why should we be friends?'

He was silent, and I turned my head to look at him. A little nerve was twitching in his neck, and I thought that he was about to tell me something, then he appeared to change his mind.

'I don't suppose it matters,' he said.

'Did I hear a car engine?' My mother looked up as I entered and began to pull out the black tacking cotton from the seam she'd just finished. 'Thank goodness this is almost done. I'd forgotten that I'd promised Jenny it would be ready tonight.'

'You work too hard. And you're not well. Monsieur de Bernay asked me how you were.'

'Paul?' She gave me a sharp look. 'What else did he say?'

'Only that you work too hard.'

Her eyes narrowed in suspicion. 'I did hear a car in the lane, didn't I? Did Paul bring you home? Tell me the truth, Kate.'

Suddenly she was on her feet and I realized that she was very angry. Staring, too surprised to answer, I was silent as she came round the table and grabbed me by the shoulders.

'Answer me, girl!'

'Mrs Madison suggested it.' I gasped as she slapped me. 'I didn't do anything wrong – why did you hit me? It's because of him. . . . You're in love with him, aren't you?'

24

'Don't you dare cheek me!' she cried furiously. 'I've told you not to talk to men when I send you on an errand. Men are not to be trusted, especially men like Paul de Bernay.'

'He just brought me home,' I said, tears burning as I rubbed my cheek. She'd never hit me before. She'd hardly ever raised her voice to me until these past months, now she looked as if she hated me. 'You never used to be like this – what have I done to make you turn against me?'

She stared at me, her face working with some strange emotion that might have been anything, then she began to cough, turning away as I reached out to her. 'No, leave me alone.' She took out her handkerchief and wiped her mouth. I caught a glimpse of brown stains before she pushed it into her pocket. 'I haven't turned against you, Kate, but you're not a child now. You have to learn that life isn't a dream. I've sheltered and protected you because I didn't want you to suffer as I have.'

'What do you mean? How have you suffered?'

'Perhaps I should tell you,' she said, looking thoughtful. 'Perhaps it's time.'

'Tell me what?' I knew her life hadn't been easy but now I suspected something far more serious.

She hesitated, then shook her head. 'Not now, Kate. I'm too tired. Set the table, there's a good girl. I'm sorry if I was harsh with you, but you must be careful. I know I haven't spelt it out to you, but you've studied biology at school. Surely you've heard enough gossip about girls who are no better than they should be? You don't want to lose your reputation, do you? You have no father to protect you, no family behind you. Paul is a very charming man, but. . . . '

'You don't have to warn me,' I said defensively. 'I don't want to end up like Belle Woodruffe.'

A little smile flickered over her lips. 'So you're not a complete innocent, then. Well, I shan't say any more, but if any man asks you to go for a ride in his car alone with him, say no. And I don't want you talking to Paul – do you understand?'

'Yes.' I turned away, avoiding her eyes. What would she say if she knew Paul had kissed me that first day?

Afraid of provoking her again, I didn't press her for answers to the questions that crowded my mind. I'd always sensed that there was a secret in my mother's past; now I was sure of it. She'd obviously suffered more than I'd realized; it made me feel protective towards her and anxious not to upset her.

25

As the days passed, I noticed that my mother was coughing more often. Sometimes in the mornings it was so bad that I feared she might choke.

'You must go to the doctor,' I said one morning before I left for school. 'That cough is getting worse.'

'I went last week,' she replied, with an odd look that I couldn't read. 'He's doing some tests.'

'Tests?' I stared at her anxiously. 'That sounds serious.'

'Don't worry about it, Kate,' she said, not quite meeting my eyes. 'I'm not sure yet. It may be nothing.'

'You're not hiding something from me?'

'I'll tell you if I think it necessary.' She suddenly kissed my cheek. 'You're a good girl, Katie. I wish. . . . '

'What do you wish?'

She hesitated, then shook her head. 'Nothing. Go to school now, or you'll be late.'

It was yet another unexplained incident that made me aware of the changes in our lives.

It was May now and my sixteenth birthday was imminent. I'd always looked forward to birthdays because they were special occasions for us, but this year things were different. I would soon be leaving school and I didn't know what I was going to do with myself in the future. My headmistress wanted me to stay on as a student teacher. She said I had a flair for languages, and it was true that I'd picked up French easily enough, partly because Mother and I had sometimes used it at home for fun, pretending that we were dining in Paris. It was one of our little games of make-believe. I also had good grades in Latin and English literature. Mrs Burrows wanted me to apply for a scholarship that would take me to college, but I knew my mother was against it. She had other plans for me; she'd hinted at something several times, but I still had no idea what was in her mind.

On the morning of my birthday, Mother presented me with a new dress. It was a thick, dark green wool and it had a narrow-fitting bodice and sleeves with long tight cuffs and puffed shoulders, the full skirts just flirting above my ankles. It was the smartest dress I'd ever owned, and I was delighted. I hugged my mother, knowing how hard she must have worked to fit it into her busy schedule.

'It's lovely,' I cried. 'Really elegant.'

She looked me up and down with satisfaction. 'Yes, it does suit you, Kate. I wasn't sure when I bought the material, but now I like it.'

'Thank you.' I kissed her cheek. 'I'm so lucky to have you for a mother.'

A shadow of something like guilt passed across her face and she turned away. 'The dress is only a part of your present. I've a surprise for you, but I'm keeping it until this evening. Don't be late. We'll have a special tea tonight.'

Sometimes I lingered by the river on my way home from school. I would stand at the quayside and watch the punts quanted up from the Cresswells, which was as far as the horse-drawn barges could reach, the horses being walked up through the town to be reharnessed. For years the barges had brought goods all the way from King's Lynn, Cambridge, or Bury St Edmunds, but the trade which had once made the merchants of Waterside so prosperous and supplied customers for all the inns situated along the river bank was gradually dying, replaced by the railways. It was now something of an event to see what had once been an everyday occurrence.

Water had always held a special fascination for me. I loved the sound of it lapping against the banks, and the gentle plopping of moorhens as they dived beneath the surface. I could watch forever when the breeze sent little wavelets rippling across the river, and I loved to swim in its coolness in summer, though my mother would have been furious if she'd ever guessed that I and some of the other local children had learned to swim wearing nothing but the bathing suits God had given us. We were a lawless band, my friends and I, often stealing the punts that were tied up at the quay and taking them out into mid-river, laughing as we saw their owners waving frustrated fists at us from the bank. Yet it was innocent fun, and we never did any real harm, growing out of our mischief as we left childhood behind.

That evening I didn't tarry, the thought of my special tea and the present carrying me swiftly homeward. As I turned into our lane, I heard the noise of a car engine and caught sight of the tail-end disappearing past the slaughter house and round the corner. Few cars ever came our way and I wondered if Paul de Bernay had been to the house again.

As I was about to turn into our passageway, Eric Potter shouted to me. I waited as he came hurrying towards me, waving a small

27

parcel. He was puffing and panting as he reached me, his face and neck quite red.

'I wanted to give you this, Kate,' he said, a shy smile on his lips. 'I know it's your birthday and I'd intended to take it into your mother this afternoon – but she had a visitor and I didn't like to intrude.'

'A visitor? You mean a client, I suppose?'

'No.' He scratched his head. 'I don't know, lass. Whoever it was, they came in an expensive car. One I've never seen here before.'

'Then it must've been Monsieur de Bernay. He sometimes collects things for Mrs Madison.'

'I've seen him before,' said Eric, a frown of disapproval on his face. 'This was a different sort of car altogether.'

While he was speaking I'd opened his parcel. Inside was a box of chocolates in fancy wrapping with ribbons and bows. I gave a cry of pleasure; it was the first real box of chocolates I'd ever received.

'Thank you so much,' I said. 'These look delicious.'

'It's nothing,' he grunted. 'I just wanted to give you something.'

Impulsively, I reached up to kiss his cheek. He made an alarmed, grunting sound. 'You didn't ought to have done that. Now look at your face. You've got coal dust all over you.'

'It will come off,' I said, rubbing at my cheek.

'You're a good lass,' he muttered gruffly. 'There was a time when I thought I might be able to be a father to you. . . . '

As he stopped awkwardly I felt a kind of sadness. 'I'd have liked that, Eric,' I said. 'I must go now.' I turned quickly as I saw the tears in his eyes, feeling angry. Obviously he believed his chance of marrying my mother had gone.

I was thoughtful as I went in the back door, calling out to my mother. There was no answer, yet I was sure she was home. The kitchen table was bare. No effort had been made to set it for tea. Mother was sitting in the wooden rocking chair by the fire, her eyes closed as if she was asleep. At first my disappointment was so sharp that I could only stand and stare – where was my special tea? Then I noticed how still she was and I was frightened. I ran to touch her hand, feeling relieved to find that it wasn't icy cold. She was still alive!

'Are you ill?' I cried.

She opened her eyes and looked at me then, and there was a queer blind expression in them that made my blood run cold. 'So you're home, then,' she said. 'I've been waiting for you.'

'I came straight home.' I felt oddly defensive. 'Besides, you've had a visitor. I saw the car.'

'Did you?' She smiled slightly. 'I've been waiting for you, because I've something to tell you, Kate.'

Resentment stirred in me. I was sure I knew what she was going to say and I didn't want to hear it.

'Come here,' she said as I turned away. 'Don't make it more difficult for me.'

'Is something wrong?'

'Yes, I'm afraid it is. Do you remember those tests the doctor was doing?'

'Tests?' A chill ran down my spine. I'd thought she was going to tell me she was getting married. 'What about them?'

'You asked me if I was ill. . . . ' She paused and I dug my nails into the palms of my hands. 'Well, I'm afraid I am quite ill, Kate. I'm in the first stage of consumption.'

'Consumption?' I stared at her in disbelief. I'd heard her coughing, and I'd worried about it, but surely a little cough didn't mean. . . . I stared at her in horror. 'No! No, I don't believe it.'

She caught my hand and held it tightly. 'Calm down, Kate. I'm only in the first stages as yet. The doctor told me I might get better – especially if I can go away somewhere. There's a special clinic in Switzerland where the air is very pure. People who go there live quite long lives. . . . '

I gazed into her face, trying to make sense of what she was telling me. My mother couldn't be dying. She'd always been so full of energy. Yet as I looked into her eyes, I could see that she was hiding something from me. There were faint shadows beneath her eyes, and her skin was very pale, but her hair was the same glossy brown it had always been. How blind I must have been not to realize that she was desperately ill!

I felt a choking sensation in my throat and my chest hurt. All this time I'd suspected her of building up towards telling me she was to marry, and now she was gently breaking it to me that she had received what amounted to a death sentence. Tears were burning behind my eyes. I wanted to throw myself into her arms and weep, but I knew I mustn't cry. She needed me to be strong now. All my life I'd taken her strength for granted, now she was ill. She was slowly dying and she had no one but me.

I knelt down on the peg-rag rug we had made together from bits of cloth left over from her sewing, taking her hand and holding it gently. 'I won't wait until the end of term,' I said. 'I'll leave school and find a job now. Maybe we can find the money to send you to Switzerland.'

'No, Kate,' she said. 'Don't even think of it. You could never earn enough to pay for the treatment I'd need, let alone anything else. I know you mean well, but I'm never going to get better. I would have to stay there for years. . . . '

'But we have to do something!' I protested, desperately searching for an answer in the gathering gloom of that kitchen. The daylight was fading and we hadn't yet lit the gaslamps, but I could see the huge carved dresser, the ugly day-bed against the wall, and the copper warming-pan. All of these things must be worth something. 'We'll sell everything. I'll move into lodgings and. . . . '

'It still wouldn't be the answer. I've thought of everything, Kate. I shall have to stay in England. . . . '

'We could ask Eric for the money,' I cried. 'I know he would help you.'

'No!' It was a scream of desperation. 'If you so much as mention my illness to him I'll never forgive you.' She gripped my wrist, her fingers digging into my flesh. 'Leave me some dignity, Kate. I'll find someone to look after me until I need to go into the infirmary.'

'Let me take care of you.' My throat ached with the need to cry but I fought my tears.

'You won't be here either.' She leaned forward, moving the kettle on to the fire. I noticed that the range looked dull as though it hadn't been blacked recently. She'd always been so house-proud! I should have known she was ill. She smiled a little sadly. 'It's time I got your tea ready. I'm sorry I didn't get round to baking your cake, but the ham is in the pantry and there's plenty of bottled fruit. Choose what you want.'

I sprang to take the cloth from the dresser drawer, anxious to save her. 'Why shan't I be here? Even if I stay on until the end of term, it's not that long. I can get a job helping Mrs Burrows.'

She waited until I'd finished smoothing the cloth, then, 'I had a visitor today, as you said.' She sighed. 'It's been quite a day, one way and another.'

I sensed that I was about to learn much of what had puzzled me this past year, and I waited patiently. There were memories in her eyes, and some of them must have been happy, for she no longer looked haunted. It was as if she had crossed a bridge in her mind, as if telling me that she was ill had somehow made it easier.

30

'I wrote to Gerald some weeks ago – Sir Gerald Redfern, that is,' she added, making sure that I understood. 'You've heard of him, Kate?'

'Wasn't it his wife who was arrested for chaining herself to the railings outside Buckingham Palace? There was a picture of her in the *Cambridge Evening News*.'

Sir Gerald Redfern was a justice of the peace, and his country home was near St Ives in Huntingdon, a distance of some twenty miles or so from Ely. His wife's escapades as a suffragette had caused some gossip in our town and all the surrounding villages, though since her release from prison she seemed to have been less eager in her support of Mrs Pankhurst and her band of protestors. Perhaps the harsh treatment that was meted out to those brave women had been too much for her.

Mother smiled a little grimly. 'Yes, that's her. Selina Redfern was always a determined woman. It caused me trouble in the past, but now I may have reason to bless it.'

'What do you mean?'

She seemed not to hear. I set out the cutlery, realizing that this tale was not to be told in a hurry. I'd finished laying the table by the time my mother had come out of her reverie sufficiently to continue. She raised her eyes to look at me as I sat down.

'You won't be here, Kate, because Lady Redfern has invited you to stay at Brockmere. She was my visitor today. For the time being you will share a governess with her daughter.'

'Why?' I was taken completely off guard. 'Why should she ask me to stay?'

My mother sat forward, drawing the bread board towards her. 'She considers it to be her duty. You see, I anticipated the results of my tests a little. I told Gerald I was ill, and asked him to do something for you. It seems that he showed the letter to his wife and she agreed that you should live with them.'

Mother smiled to herself as she sliced the bread, obviously pleased. I felt a horrible sinking sensation in my stomach. My world was fast crumbling around me. My mother was gravely ill – a fact I'd not yet had time to take in – and now she was calmly telling me that I was to live with strangers.

'I won't go,' I said stubbornly. 'I don't want charity from strangers. I want to stay with you.'

'I'm going away myself. I shall sell everything, as you suggested. The doctor said the next best thing to Switzerland was sea air. I'll

31

find a room in a boarding house in Devon until. . . . We'll see what happens.'

She'd thought it all out. She must have been planning it for weeks, working out every detail without asking me what I wanted or how I felt about anything. It wasn't fair! We'd always been so close; I couldn't bear the thought of her in some awful little room, slowly getting worse and worse, alone and with no one to care for her.

'You can't,' I cried, and the tears I'd fought ran down my cheeks. 'I love you. You can't leave me. I don't want to live with strangers.'

'Come here,' she said, opening her arms. 'Come here, my Katie.'

It was ages since she'd spoken so lovingly to me. I went to her and she held me, rocking me back and forth until the storm had passed. She was my rock again, and I'd so wanted to be strong for her – but how could I bear to lose her? She was all I had in the world. She was my mother and I loved her so much. When I had quieted, she began to stroke my hair while I squatted on a stool at her feet.

'You have lovely hair,' she murmured. 'So thick and black. I've often wondered where it came from. Not from me – or your father.'

'He had dark hair and so have you.' I glanced at my father's picture on the sideboard. Mother was looking at it, too. She looked so beautiful with that soft, dreaming expression in her eyes. In the gentle gaslight, she seemed young and healthy. She couldn't be so terribly ill. It was all a mistake. In a minute I would wake up and realize it was all a nightmare.

'Yes, Richard had dark hair,' she said. 'But I think your hair must have come from way back in the past – perhaps from one of your Redfern ancestors.'

'My what?' I felt the shock tingle inside me. 'What did you say?'

Mother smiled oddly. 'I'm sorry it has to come as such a shock, Kate. I know I should've told you long ago – but I was angry. Angry and bitter. I never forgave Gerald for not standing by me when I ran away.'

'When you ran away?' I was bewildered. 'I don't understand any of this. Where did you run away from? Why? Was someone unkind to you?'

'It's a long story!' Something flickered in her eyes, but I couldn't tell whether it was anger, fear or a kind of triumph. 'Gerald's father was my mother's cousin. Our great, great grandfather was Sir Harold Redfern; my mother's name was Redfern before she married. The families were very close once, but when my mother chose to wed a curate she was considered to have married beneath her, and when she and my father died within weeks of each other, Sir Mortimer Redfern – Gerald's father – took me in. I went to live at Brockmere when I was fifteen, but something happened and I ran away just after my seventeenth birthday. I married Richard Linton a few weeks later. When Richard died I was desperate, but I never went back, I never asked for help. If I hadn't offered to make a dress for a friend, we might have had to go on the parish.' She laughed harshly. 'I could have got work in a factory, but I'd rather have starved.' It was her pride again, but I thought she meant it.

'Why haven't you told me any of this before?'

'I was angry and bitter for a long time,' she said. 'I just wanted to forget – then I met Gerald one market day and he promised to help me if I was ever that desperate again. I was too proud to take his money then. . . . It might have been different if. . . . ' She was silent and thoughtful. 'Never mind that now, it's all in the past. Things are different now.'

'Why? Why should you want me to live with these people? You couldn't have been happy there or you wouldn't have run away.'

'I had my reasons for that,' she said, her eyes glittering. 'I was wronged and this is my chance to get back what was owed me. I was happy when I first went there. It's a beautiful house, Kate. The Redferns are rich. You'll have a better life with them than I could give you.'

'But what made you run away?'

'Something happened that I'd rather not talk about. You don't need to know, Kate. It was so long ago.' There was a strange look in her eyes and I didn't press her.

The ham was beginning to curl on our plates. Neither of us had eaten a thing. I felt as if the food would choke me, and I pushed my plate away. She looked at me oddly.

'I'm sorry about your cake, Kate.'

'It doesn't matter.' Emotion welled up in me suddenly. 'Please don't send me away. I want to stay with you.'

'No, Kate,' she said firmly. 'I don't want you to see me suffer. It would make it worse for me. Besides, I want to be alone. I'll write to you, but you must do as I ask. You must do this for me. Please?'

As I hesitated, she began to cough. She put a white handkerchief to her mouth and, though she tried to hide them, I saw the dark stains. She was bringing up blood! It had been happening for weeks. I'd thought it was just a little cough; I'd even suspected she put it on just to make me do what she wanted. Now I knew the truth and I was crushed with remorse. What a selfish, ungrateful child I was! She'd known she was ill but she'd said nothing until she was sure I would be taken care of. How could I refuse her? I wanted to shout and scream, to revile a cruel God who had let this happen, but I could only nod dumbly in agreement. I saw the triumph in her eyes but then it was gone.

'You're a good girl, Kate,' she said. 'I'm sorry it had to be this way.'

I felt as if I was being torn apart, but all I did was get up and start clearing the dishes. When I'd finished the washing-up, I found a small parcel on the table. It was the surprise Mother had promised. Inside was a thin gold bangle. It was my mother's, given to her by my father on their wedding day. It was beautiful and I'd often admired it. I pushed it towards her.

'You should keep this. You can sell it.'

'I want you to have it, Katie,' she said, her eyes flicking away from mine. 'Perhaps it will make up. . . . ' She faltered. 'Well, I want you to have it anyway.'

It had been arranged that Eric Potter should take me to the railway station, and that Sir Gerald would meet me at St Ives himself. On the last morning I felt so sick that I couldn't keep my breakfast down. I was fighting my tears very hard, but in the end they beat me and I began to weep silently. Mother kissed me and handed me a clean handkerchief.

'That's enough, Kate,' she said. 'You must be strong. Always remember that I've done this for you.'

She sounded strange and her face was very white. We were standing outside in the lane, and I could see the curtains twitching at our neighbours' windows. My box was already stowed on Eric's cart.

'I can't go,' I gulped. 'I can't leave you like this.'

Suddenly I began to sob desperately. I threw myself at her, wailing like a child of five and clinging to her as though my heart would break. For a moment she held me to her and I felt a deep shudder run through her.

'Oh, Kate,' she muttered resentfully. 'Don't do this to me. I have to go. It's my last chance. I can't give it up for you. I can't! I've given you the best years. Let me go now. Let me go!'

All at once she pushed me from her violently. As I gazed into her eyes, I saw that they had become hard and cold. She seemed determined to cast me off no matter how much it hurt us both.

I shivered, seeing something akin to hatred in her face, as if she were blaming me for this parting. As I stood motionless, Eric came to me, taking my arm and pushing me towards his cart.

'Come away, lass,' he said, and there was a harsh note in his voice. 'Don't hurt yourself. There's no going back. Her mind's made up.'

I wiped my sleeve across my face, gulping down my tears. Looking at him, I saw the expression on his face as he glanced at my mother. She turned even paler, taking a step back and gasping as if she understood something I did not.

'What is it?' I asked, gazing up at him in bewilderment. 'Are you angry with me, Eric?'

'Not with you, lass.' He smiled at me kindly. 'There's some as are too selfish for their own good.'

'You can't mean my mother,' I said as he shook the reins and his horse moved forward. 'You don't know what she's done for me – the sacrifices she's made for my sake.'

'No, I don't,' he said grimly.

I turned to wave to my mother. I waved all the way to the end of the lane. I thought she looked lost and lonely, a brave figure facing a bleak future alone.

'I wanted to be with her,' I said chokingly. 'She will be so wretched, and she's only got a few pounds. I don't know how she'll manage.'

'I expect she'll get by.'

Again there was that note of disapproval in his voice. I saw the grim set of his mouth. He'd always liked my mother – why had he turned against her? 'What do you mean?'

He glanced at me, seeming as if he wanted to speak, then set his mouth firmly. 'It's not for me to say,' he muttered. 'But I don't hold with what she's done, and that's a fact.'

'But she did it for me,' I said. 'Don't you see, Eric? She did it all for me. . . . '

CHAPTER THREE

The year was 1881. From her high-barred cot in the corner of the large, warm kitchen, a child watched. At the table her mother spread a clean sheet and then took a flat-iron from the fire, testing it for the correct heat before beginning to smooth it over the sheet. The smell of fresh washing permeated the air, giving the child a sense of comfort and peace. She stuck her thumb in her mouth and climbed up on chubby, unsteady legs to watch intently as her mother took up the first of a pile of the special starched collars Papa always wore.

Even as she worked the woman was happy, singing softly, unaware of the child's green eyes on her back. She had dark red hair, a creamy complexion and a face so beautiful that even her dull grey gown with its modest neckline and neat lace collar could not make it commonplace. Her eyes were clear, untroubled, as bright as they had been the day she'd cast aside home and family for love. Reared in the strictest propriety, she'd committed the unforgivable sin of falling in love with a poor man, and the even more heinous crime of daring to be happy against all expectation.

Hearing a man's heavy tread in the hall, both woman and child looked up expectantly. He came into the room, tall, bewhiskered and handsome in his black frock coat, immediately dominating the scene, too large a personality for his humble surroundings.

'Still working, Mary?' His voice was softly disapproving. 'Where's the girl I hired for you?'

'Her mother was ill, Walter. She wanted to leave early so I. . . . '

'You let her go.' Now his tone was harsher. 'You mustn't let these girls play on your sympathy, my dear. Leave the ironing until the morning. She can do it when she comes – and I shall have something to say to her.'

Watching, the child saw a flicker of some emotion she couldn't understand in her mother's eyes. Was Mama upset about something?

'Put that iron down, Mary.' Walter's voice had a curiously persuasive note. 'Come here, my dear.'

He drew Mary into his arms, holding her crushed against him as he kissed her. The child whimpered uneasily, half frightened by some fierce undercurrent she sensed between them. An involuntary wail of fear issued from her lips.

'Walter,' her mother said. 'She's crying – perhaps I should. . . . '

'Leave her,' he answered gruffly. 'Discipline, that's what she needs. Spare the rod and she'll become wilful. Come, Mary, I want you now.'

Taking her hand firmly in his, Walter drew Mary from the room. The child could hear the wooden stairs creaking and then her mother laughing with her father. They were together and she was abandoned to the flickering light of the kitchen fire. Her cries subsided to a whimper and then ceased suddenly, as if she knew that to continue would be useless.

Curling up into a ball, she began to suck her thumb.

She was six years old now; a thin, pretty girl with an inquiring mind. In many ways, she was older than her years. Independence had been forced on her from the day she could walk. It was easier to reach for what she wanted than to cry uselessly in a corner.

Snow had been falling all day. She stood with her face pressed up against the window pane of the draughty old house, filled with a sense of wonder and delight as she followed the twirling descent of a snowflake. How pretty it looked, she thought, and how much she would have liked to go outside into that world of white. But her mother had forbidden it. Mary was afraid of her only child taking a chill. So she could only look at the snow.

It was gently covering the bushes and treetops like a thick blanket, changing the garden she knew into a magical scene. Imaginative and too much alone, she often took refuge in dreams. In the stories she invented in her head, no one ever shouted at her in anger. No one ever looked at her with eyes that snapped with impatience. She was always loved, always warm.

'Are you looking for your Papa, darling?' Mary went to the window, standing beside her daughter to look out at the snow.

How she loved her mother. She loved the warm smell of her flesh as she was held in those comforting arms and lulled to sleep with the songs her mother sang in her low, musical voice. Those were the times she loved best, when they were alone in the house and the birds had gone to roost, before her father came home from evensong. It was a time of peace and quiet and her mother was all hers.

She was a little afraid of her father. He was too large, too over-powering and his laughter was too loud. Sometimes he would look

37

at her as if he thought she was some sort of changeling, and she had heard him complaining to her mother that she was stubborn and undisciplined. The trouble was that she found him too stern, too unforgiving. She loved Papa, but she felt instinctively that Papa did not really love her.

And she knew he was jealous of the little attention her mother gave her. That was unfair, because her mother adored him. Whenever he was there Mary seemed to glow as if she had a lighted candle inside her. The girl was too young to understand that look or their talk, but she knew that her mother was no longer hers.

'Walter is late. I wonder what can be keeping him?'

Mary was always anxious when her husband was away. He was the centre of her world and she could not bear to think of a life without him. When he was in the house, she was aware of him all the time, ready to grant his slightest whim. Walter demanded so much of her, but she gave willingly.

And Walter never spared himself. He worked tirelessly for the village folk, often coming home soaked to the skin because he had gone out when others would have stayed at home. He was visiting a dying woman now and she knew he would not return until he was satisfied his parishioner's soul was at peace, but the weather was treacherous and she found the waiting almost unendurable.

'Papa will be cold and tired when he comes home. We must bank up the fire, Lily.' She turned to the girl who came in from the village to help her daily. 'And then you must go home. I just hope Walter won't be too long.'

'Papa will be home for supper, Mama.'

The young girl looked up at her mother, sensing her unease. It made her feel protective. Papa worked so hard himself, he never noticed that his demands on his wife were wearing her out. He didn't see as she did the dark shadows beneath Mary's eyes or hear her coughing when the damp November mists came curling across the flat countryside of the fens, shrouding the big old rectory in a bitter cold dampness that brought agues and painful, swollen joints. When he looked at Mary he saw only the beautiful young girl he had married, his eyes blind to the toll three miscarriages and years of hard work had wrought.

She never doubted that her father loved her mother. But he was so strong, so full of life himself that he couldn't see what his demands were doing to the wife he loved. Young as she was, the girl was aware that her mother's strength was failing and she felt a deep tearing

38

grief inside when she saw the tiredness in that still beautiful face. Mama worried so much.

Suddenly she saw the strong, powerful figure of her father battling his way through the drifts of snow and her heart gladdened. It was the end of her special time, but at least now her mother would stop worrying.

The spring had come at last. Primroses were growing in the lane next to the church and the birds had begun gathering moss to line their nests. Leaving the vast, echoing coldness of the church, where she had been polishing her father's pulpit, she felt the welcoming warmth of the sun and began to sing softly as she walked the short distance to her home.

She was growing up now. It was 1893. At fourteen, she was blossoming into a very pretty girl. People told her that she looked like her mother. That always made her happy, even though Mary's beauty was beginning to fade. She smiled less these days, but the glow was still there whenever Walter walked through the door. It was when she thought herself unobserved that Mary let her tiredness show.

Reaching the house, the girl was thinking of how much she was looking forward to reading the book the verger had lent her. It was R L Stevenson's *Treasure Island*, and she could hardly wait to begin.

As she went into the kitchen, she heard her mother coughing. It was a dreadful, harsh sound. Mary had a handkerchief pressed to her mouth. She turned as she heard the girl come in, and there were bright red stains on the white cloth. The girl stared in horror, starting forward.

'Mama – you're ill!'

'It's nothing, darling.' Mary hastily stuffed the handkerchief into her pocket.

'But I saw. . . . '

'You saw nothing.' Mary frowned at her daughter. 'Not a word to your father. You must promise me, darling. I don't want him to worry.'

She stared at her mother, the tears burning behind her eyes. It was Mary who worried. Walter bestrode his world like a Colossus. Nothing could touch him.

The girl wanted to protest. The anger mounted inside her, but she held it back for her mother's sake. Seeing Mary struggling to lift a heavy stewpan from the range, she went to take it from her.

'I'll do that,' she said. 'Sit and rest for a while.'

'But there's the ironing and the baking. And Papa can't afford to hire a girl to help me any more.'

'I'm young and strong. From now on, I shall do all the heavy work.' As her mother looked anxious, she smiled. 'There's no need for Papa to know. We don't want to worry him. . . . '

The young woman stood at the window, staring out at the rain. She was dressed in a severe black gown without hoops or even a scrap of ribbon. Behind her, the voice was droning on and on, telling her what she already knew. She would have to leave the house that had been her home for the first fifteen years of her life; the rectory belonged to the church and the new encumbent would be arriving shortly. She tried to block the voice out, bringing back to mind the faces of her parents – the faces she would never see again. She tried and failed. Blinking back her tears, she turned to look at the man who was speaking. Dressed all in black, he was a formidable sight. A man of property and rank; a man of authority who was not used to being disobeyed. She was aware of disquiet within her as she saw his bushy brows meet in a frown. He frightened her much more than her father ever had. He was her mother's cousin; the head of the family from which Mary had been cast out so cruelly for daring to seek happiness by marrying a poor clergyman.

The girl knew a moment of anger as she realized that a little help from this man when her mother was alive might have saved the lives of both her parents.

'Were you listening to me at all?' he asked, his eyes grey and flinty. 'I'm offering you a home. Indeed, I insist that you come with me. You have no alternative, none that would not bring disgrace on our name. Your mother let the family down by marrying beneath her, but I'm willing to forgive that for your sake.'

'You are generous, sir.'

He stared at her, suspicious of her meekness.

'Well, girl, I'm waiting for your answer.'

What choice did she have? In death her parents were united just as they had been in life. Surprising everyone who knew him, her large, bewhiskered, selfish father had suddenly succumbed to an inflammation of the lungs that carried him off in the space of a few days. Distraught with grief and worn out with worry, Mary had soon followed her beloved Walter to a communal grave. The girl felt that they had abandoned her to her fate, as she had been abandoned so many times before. They had loved her, but they had loved each other more. Sometimes in her loneliness she had wondered if they really knew she existed, except as a mouth to feed and a body to clothe. Now they were together again and she was left to the mercy of this man with the hard eyes and cruel mouth. She turned at last, head up, eyes proud, knowing that she had no choice.

'Thank you, sir,' she said in a proud, clear tone. 'If you will allow me a few moments to collect my things, I shall be ready to come with you.'

He inclined his head, grunting his assent. She walked slowly, regally from the room. Her tears were well hidden now. She had faced the worst and nothing could ever hurt this much again. A wry smile touched her mouth. Nothing had really changed. She had always been alone. . . .

CHAPTER FOUR

It was only the second time I'd ever been on a train in my life, but for me the journey was never more than a blur of trees, fields and the shining streak of the river in the distance. My mind clung stubbornly to memories of home. I didn't even open the magazines Eric had given me as a farewell gift, even though I normally enjoyed the mystery stories in *The Strand*. I didn't want to go to this new world that would begin when I reached St Ives. I wanted to run back to the shelter of my mother's arms. Already I missed her so desperately that it was like a physical pain in my breast.

When we arrived at the station, I alighted with the other passengers. St Ives was a busy junction of three lines, leading to Cambridge, Huntingdon and March, with a branch link to Ely, and people came in to shop from all the surrounding villages. It was market day and the platform was crowded with farmers and their wives; crates of live chickens were being unloaded and the noise of their frightened clucking added to the sense of chaos. The sound of the engine letting off steam made me jump. I was seized by a feeling of panic. Supposing I didn't like the Redferns. Worse still, they might hate me on sight. Surely Lady Selina couldn't really want her husband's poor relation under her roof? No one had helped my mother when she was desperate; why should they offer to take me in now?

I stood on the platform anxiously looking for a man who resembled my mother's description of Sir Gerald, but I couldn't see anyone who could possibly have been him.

'You'll know him at once,' Mother had said. 'He's an upright man with light brown hair and hazel eyes.'

The guard had deposited my trunk on the platform. I waited beside it as the crowd gradually dispersed, feeling like a piece of unwanted baggage and staring desperately into the face of every passer-by. The guard was waving his little flag as the train prepared to leave the station. After what seemed an eternity to me a man wearing a neat brown suit and dusty brown boots came hurrying up to me. He tipped his bowler hat apologetically.

'You must be Miss Katherine Linton. I'm sorry to be late, miss, but the Ford wouldn't start and Lady Selina had taken the Daimler.

I had to bring the pony and trap. It will be a bit breezy, but it won't take us long to get home.'

I gave him a hostile look. 'Who are you? I was expecting to be met by Sir Gerald Redfern.'

'I'm Bates, miss.' His smile was still warm. 'Sir Gerald's man, and his chauffeur. Sir Gerald doesn't drive. Not like Mr Harry; he's the one for automobiles.'

He seemed to think I should know who Mr Harry was; at that moment I didn't care. All I wanted was to go home. It was obvious that I wasn't welcome. Sir Gerald hadn't even bothered to meet me.

'Is this all your luggage?' Bates asked, tucking my trunk under one arm as I nodded. 'Follow me then, miss.'

I obeyed without speaking or smiling. Resentment was building inside me. So the Redferns didn't want me: well, I didn't want to live with them either!

I sat stiff and straight as we drove through the busy market town, uninterested even though the streets were packed with people milling about the gaily covered stalls in the square. We went through the town and over the old bridge that Bates told me dated from the fifteenth century, with the Manor House on the left, a Temperance Hotel on the right and the river shining and glittering in a gleam of sunshine. My ears and nose felt cold and my eyes stung, but not with tears. It was the wind. Only the wind. I was so sunk in my own misery that I had no idea of how long we had been driving when Bates turned to glance at me.

'This is Brockmere, miss.'

I looked for a house, but all I could see were trees and fields with cattle grazing as before. 'I thought Brockmere was the name of a house?'

'It's the name of Sir Gerald's estate.'

'You mean he owns all this land?'

'Yes, miss.'

'Oh. . . . ' I digested this in silence. 'He must be very rich, then.'

'Yes, you could say that.' A chuckle escaped Bates. 'We're just coming to the Folly now, miss.'

As he spoke, my eyes were drawn to a strange building to our right. Set on a slight rise, it looked almost like a medieval tower, yet its grey stone walls were too new-looking to be several hundred years old.

'What a strange place,' I said. 'Could we stop for a moment, Mr Bates?'

43

'Sir Gerald's grandfather built it,' Bates said, slowing the horses obligingly. 'It was after his first wife died: some say as he was a bit touched in the head.'

'What is it used for?'

'Nothing. Never has been. I suppose that's why they call it the Folly.' He glanced at me. 'Why don't you take a peep inside? It's never locked.'

I stared at him, and then I realized that he had sensed my growing unease and was offering me a chance to delay my arrival at the house. I knew that it was what I needed; my emotions had been building inside me ever since I got on the train and I could scarcely contain them.

'Is it far to the house?'

He shook his head, smiling gently. 'Not more than half an hour's walk.'

'Would you take my trunk on and say I needed a little exercise?'

'I'll do that for you, miss.'

He helped me down and I stood watching as he drove off, feeling relieved that my ordeal had been put off for a while. Then I turned to look at the Folly. There was an air of mystery about it that caught my imagination. I wanted a closer look.

As I ran towards the mound on which it was built, I saw that there were steps cut into the earth. I began to climb eagerly but as I neared the top I had a peculiar feeling of oppression. From the ground it had looked intriguing but now it seemed suddenly sinister and I almost turned back. It had after all been built by a man half out of his mind with grief over his wife's death. At the door I hesitated, feeling that it would be an intrusion to go inside, yet something drew me on.

Inside, it was dark and cold, the only windows tiny slits that let in little light or air. To one side was a stone stairway that wound upwards to the top of the building, and presumably on to the mock battlements that had caught my eye from below. I moved towards it, but as I did so something crunched beneath my foot. I bent down to pick up whatever I'd trodden on and saw that it was a tortoiseshell comb, the kind that women often wore in their hair. It was broken and spoiled now. I stared at it, wondering how it had come to be in this deserted place and a little shiver went through me as I remembered the tower was a shrine to a dead wife. Suddenly, I couldn't wait to get back into the fresh air. I dropped the broken comb and ran outside.

44

Bates had disappeared into the distance. It was quite cold now and I realized that I'd been foolish. Delaying my arrival wouldn't change anything. All I'd done was to give myself a long walk. I was behaving like an idiot. If I found it impossible to fit into this household, I could simply go back to Ely and ask Mrs Burrows for a job as a student teacher.

Feeling slightly better, I began to walk in the direction Bates had taken. I'd been nervous about meeting my new relations but now I was determined not to be intimidated. What did it matter if Sir Gerald hadn't kept his promise. . . .

Suddenly hearing the sound of hoofbeats, I swung round. A horseman was approaching fast and I was standing directly in his path. Bemused, I stood as if turned to stone, unable to move. He cursed loudly as he tugged on the reins, causing his horse to rear up and almost unseat him. For a few seconds confusion reigned as I came to life and dodged out of the way of thrashing hooves, while he fought to regain control. Then, as the horse quietened, I became aware of cold grey eyes staring down at me.

'What the hell did you think you were doing?' the rider demanded angrily. 'Why didn't you get out of the way?'

'I – I couldn't,' I stuttered. 'I – I was too shocked to move. You came at me so fast round that bend and I wasn't thinking.'

'Then you damn well should have been. You could have caused a nasty accident.'

'It wouldn't have happened if you hadn't been riding like a madman!'

'Nor would it have happened if you hadn't been where you shouldn't. This is private property, you know. The servants don't normally come this way and, if they do, they've the sense to get out of the way when they hear a horse coming.'

I stared up at him indignantly. How arrogant he was, with that proud, aristocratic face of his, and how I hated him! His hair was a lightish brown and very thick and straight, as were the brows above those glaring eyes. His mouth was tight with temper, his nostrils slightly flaring as he waited imperiously for my reply.

'Who do you think you are?' I demanded. 'I'm not a servant, and I won't be spoken to as though I am!'

His eyes narrowed as if he'd suddenly remembered something. 'Good lord! You're not Father's lame dog, are you? The daughter of some dim and distant cousin he's taken pity on. . . . '

'You beast!' I cried, furious now. 'Well, I didn't want to come

45

here, and as soon as Bates can take me back to the station, I'm leaving.'

Laughter lit the slate grey eyes. 'Temper, temper,' he chided. 'So you're Katherine Linton, are you?' His searching gaze swept over me. 'Better than I'd expected, anyway. So what's all this about not wanting to come, then?' He frowned down at me. 'And what are you doing wandering about on your own? Where's Bates? I thought he was picking you up.'

'He did. . . . ' I bit my lip. No way was I going to confess to this arrogant brute that I'd been afraid of going up to the house. 'I wanted to look inside the Folly, so I asked him to drop me here.'

'And the damned idiot left you to walk back!' His eyes glittered. 'I'll have something to say to him later. The Folly isn't safe. Father discovered cracks in the walls weeks ago. I thought it had been sealed up.' He looked thoughtful. 'It's a long walk to the house. Give me your hand and I'll help you up.'

'Ride with you?' I was horrified. 'I don't even know who you are. Besides, I've never been on a horse before.'

'I'm Harry Redfern,' he said, grinning now. 'Sir Gerald's son. Wait a minute, then; if you've never ridden, I'd better lift you up myself.'

I backed away as he dismounted, shaking my head. 'No, thank you. I'd rather walk.'

'Don't be an idiot.'

'I don't trust you – or your horse!'

'That's ridiculous.' His eyes flashed with annoyance. 'Come here and do as I say.' He grabbed my wrist, pulling me towards him and encircling my waist with one arm. I struggled but he was too strong and I couldn't break free. 'That's better,' he said as I ceased to struggle. 'There's no need for this, Katherine. I shan't hurt you.'

'My name is Kate,' I retorted. 'How do I know I can trust you?'

'Because I say so.' He smiled wryly as my eyes challenged. 'You'll just have to believe me. We are cousins of a sort, after all.'

'You – you won't let me fall?'

'You have my solemn promise.' His eyes danced with mischief.

'I'll have to trust you then, won't I?'

'Good girl.' In a flash his hands were encircling my waist and he grinned as he hoisted me up and mounted behind me. 'Light as a feather. Relax, Kate. I've got you now.'

He flicked the reins and the horse began to walk steadily forward. His arms were around me, holding me securely, though I felt a bit awkward at first and the swaying motion was very strange. I glanced over my shoulder and he nodded.

'Not as bad as you thought?'

'No – not at this pace.'

'This is just the beginning. Hold on to Rustic's mane if you feel insecure.'

Alarm flared in me as he kicked his heels and urged the horse on. 'You promised,' I cried, clutching at the horse's neck as I felt the sudden surge of speed. 'Oh, I hate you!'

Harry's laughter echoed in my ears as the horse rushed madly on. Everything was a blur as we galloped across the park, leaving the road to plunge through the trees at breakneck speed. 'This is a short cut,' he said. 'Trust me, Kate. I won't let you fall.'

There was such arrogance in his statement that I wanted to hit him, but I dared not let go of Rustic's mane. The wind was taking my breath away, blowing my hair about my face and into my eyes. I was terrified but also excited; I'd never experienced anything as thrilling before, and suddenly I was no longer afraid. Laughing, I turned my head to look at the man who held me so securely in his arms.

'I knew you'd love it,' he said. 'I'll teach you to ride by yourself, Kate.'

I was sorry when I saw the great looming sprawl of the house before us. Gradually, Harry lessened the horse's pace until we were trotting gently along a sweeping drive lined by beech trees. I stared at the house in growing dismay. It was so huge, rambling over a large area of land, impressive, beautiful and daunting. Parts of it were obviously several centuries old, though it had been added to and was a hotchpotch of styles that somehow merged to form a pleasing whole. The rays of the spring sunshine were shining on its long windows, turning its faded red bricks to a fiery rose.

'Is that just one house?' I asked, feeling butterflies in my stomach. 'Surely one family can't need all that?'

Hearing Harry's laughter, I craned round to look at him. There was a touch of mockery in his eyes. 'There's plenty of room for one more, but the house is usually full. We've twenty or more servants, and my mother likes to entertain. Every weekend we have guests and then it hardly seems big enough – especially if you want some privacy.' He tugged on the reins and Rustic came to an obedient halt. 'Don't worry, Kate. You'll soon get used to it.'

At that moment I felt that I would never get used to living in such a house. I was tense and nervous as Harry lifted me down. He'd been arrogant and overbearing, though not actually unkind. Would the rest of his family be as tolerant, or would they look down their noses at me?

Harry snapped his fingers and a groom came running to take his horse. 'Give him a rub down, John,' he said, 'and tell Bates I want to see him.' He gripped my arm. 'Come on, Kate.'

'What are you going to say to Bates – you won't tell him off, will you? I asked him to leave me at the Folly.'

'I want to make sure he knows the Folly is unsafe.' Harry's frown relaxed. 'You look a mess; I'll get Miss Grant to take you up to your room.'

'Who is she?'

'Maggie Grant is my sister's governess, though Prue doesn't really need her any more. She's just a general dogsbody these days. I wonder why she stays – but then the poor woman has nowhere else to go.' He took hold of my hand. 'We'll sneak upstairs so that you can tidy yourself before anyone sees you.'

He put his finger to his lips and I was shaken by an urgent desire to giggle. I thought I might like Harry after all. We crept up the stairs like two naughty children. From somewhere below us came the sound of laughter and voices. Harry tugged at my hand and we fled down the corridor as several people came out of a room to the right of the hall and stood talking in little groups. I heard the high-pitched shrill of a girl's laughter.

'In here, quickly!' Harry threw open a door and dragged me inside. A woman had been sitting in a chair by the window, but she jumped to her feet, looking alarmed. Harry grinned at her. 'Don't worry, Maggie. I'm not sneaking in one of my light o'loves. This is Kate Linton. Bates dropped her at the Folly and I chanced on her walking back. I practically kidnapped the poor girl and as a result her hair looks disgraceful – will you see that she gets to her room without being seen?'

'Of course I will.' The look she gave him was almost adoring. 'Is she expected in the drawing room? Only, I wasn't sure what her position here was meant to. . . . '

'What nonsense are you suggesting? Kate is our cousin. At least she and I had the same great great grandfather or some such thing. She's part of the family, of course.'

Maggie looked crushed. 'I wasn't suggesting anything, sir.'

'Father wouldn't have brought her here if he hadn't meant to do the decent thing,' Harry said loftily. He smiled at me. 'Go with Maggie and make yourself presentable.'

'Where – where is Sir Gerald?' I asked. 'He was going to meet me at the station.'

'He had to go into Cambridge unexpectedly. You'll see him soon enough. Don't keep Maggie waiting.'

Once again I was plagued with doubts, but I thanked him for the ride.

'My pleasure – but best keep it to yourself.' He winked at me and went out.

As the door closed behind him, I became aware of Maggie Grant's assessing look. 'You'd better follow me, Miss Kate. Your room is on the next floor.'

'Couldn't you just call me Kate?' I asked, following her down the hall and up a short flight of stairs at the end. 'What should I call you?'

'Miss Grant – and I shall call you Miss Kate. If you're to be a member of the family. . . . ' She sniffed and looked at me oddly.

'What makes you question it? I'm a sort of cousin, aren't I?'

We were walking down a passage; it was softly carpeted, the walls panelled with mellow oak and hung at intervals with pictures. Some looked like family portraits, others were of dogs, horses and landscapes. There was a feeling of permanence, of time having no sway, as if the Redferns had and always would live here. It made me feel like an intruder.

'I'm sure I don't know who you are, miss,' Maggie said. 'I've only been told that someone was coming to live here, nothing more.'

She seemed a little put out that she hadn't received more information, and I looked at her curiously. She was a tall woman, thin and pale with dark hair neatly coiled in a bun in the nape of her neck. Her dress was a dull grey, simply cut with a fitted bodice and a high, plain neck that she'd fastened decorously with a small silver brooch. Yet there was something about her that didn't accord well with the picture she presented of a meek governess. I had a feeling that there was more to Maggie Grant than she would have me believe.

The room into which I was shown amazed me. It had a soft blue carpet, blue curtains and a large bed with a carved post at each corner. The furniture was all dark mahogany with shining polished surfaces and brass handles on the drawers of the chest. There were embroidered mats on the dressing table, silver and glass pots and a tray with brushes and combs. An arrangement of dried flowers in a large porcelain urn, painted with Chinese figures, stood in one corner and there was a picture of a woman in Elizabethan dress on the wall. It was an attractive, luxurious room.

'This is beautiful,' I exclaimed, looking round with pleasure. 'I never expected anything like this.'

Maggie sniffed. 'It isn't the best guest chamber, but I suppose it's more than you're used to.'

I stared at her. 'Why don't you like me?'

She flushed. 'I don't dislike you. It's just that someone in my position has to be very careful.'

Despite her denial, I caught a flicker of resentment in her eyes, but I decided to let it go. She looked uncomfortable and walked across to the window.

'Look, Mrs Bates has left you a tray on this table in case you were hungry when you arrived. Wasn't that thoughtful of her?'

'Mrs Bates?' I frowned. 'That must be Mr Bates's wife. Is she the housekeeper here?'

'Yes.' Maggie nodded. 'Then there's Mr Frobisher – he's the butler, and all the usual maids, gardeners, a footman and the boot boy – and me, of course.'

'You're not really a servant, surely?' I stared at her, suddenly understanding her resentment of me. 'I thought governesses were somewhere in between the servants and the family?'

'It might be better if it were not like that,' she said, sighing. 'It makes one so unsure, gives one ideas. Makes one think that with a little push one could be. . . . ' She faltered as if she had said too much. 'I thought you might be in the same situation yourself. In some households poor relations are treated little better than the servants.'

'So you think I shouldn't go down to the drawing room then?'

'If I were you, I should wait until Lady Selina sends.' She shrugged her shoulders. 'But you must please yourself. I really don't know.'

She went out, leaving me alone in the room that was at least twice as large as my bedroom at home. My trunk had been brought up, but I didn't feel like unpacking. I wasn't sure that I wanted to stay. I wandered over to the window, investigating the contents of the covered dishes on the table. There were several dainty sandwiches garnished with watercress and tomatoes. Tasting one, I discovered that I was hungry and ate the lot.

As I ate, I gazed out of the window. My room was at the back of

50

the house, and the view was of smooth lawns leading through a shrubbery to what appeared to be an orchard beyond. It was a pleasant outlook, peaceful and inviting. So inviting that I thought I should like to explore. Finishing the last sandwich, I got to my feet, preparing to leave the room when the door was suddenly thrown open. A girl of about eighteen stood on the threshold. She was of a similar height and build to me, but her hair was a mousy brown and pulled back from her face in a style that looked too severe for her rather plain face. Her eyes were an insipid blue and her pale complexion was made almost sallow by the sludge-blue shade of her gown. Flounced and frilled with satin ribbons, it looked too fussy and had no style.

'So you're Daddy's little waif,' she said, a slight hint of resentment in her tone. 'We'd begun to think you'd got lost *en route*. What on earth made you want to walk up to the house?'

'I like walking!' I said defensively.

'I prefer to ride in the carriage – or in the car if Bates is driving. But not with Harry!' She laughed suddenly and shrugged her shoulders in a slightly mannish way. 'Takes all sorts, I suppose. I'm Prunella, by the way. Everyone calls me Prue, except Mother. I suppose we ought to be friends.'

'I'm Kate,' I said. 'You're Harry's sister, aren't you?'

'So you've met my brother, have you?' she asked, an odd expression in her eyes. 'I suppose you've fallen madly in love with him? All the girls do – be warned, Kate, you'll regret it if you do.'

She wasn't really unfriendly, but her brusque manner rubbed on the raw. 'I haven't fallen in love with him. Why should I?'

'They all do and they all end up in tears. Besides, Mummy has plans for you. Obviously you've a lot to learn, but we'll teach you. Miss Grant's very good at French, music, things like that.'

'I can speak French,' I said, bristling because she so obviously thought me an idiot. 'But I can't play the piano.'

'But you must learn. You have to do all these things well if you want to find a suitable husband.'

'A. . . . ' I stared at her. 'I'm going to be a teacher.'

She seemed amused. 'I don't think so. That's not what Mummy has in mind – or your mother, either. They want you to marry so that you'll have security. It's really the only way for girls like us, you know. Working for a living is so . . . well, you know.' She looked at me without malice. 'You're quite pretty. Mummy will find you someone; she's awfully good at that sort of thing – she'll probably find

51

me someone in the end.' She pulled a self-deprecating face. 'It's one's duty to catch a husband, of course. I only wish I'd been a man.'

'Why?' I looked at her curiously and she frowned.

'I'd give anything to be in Harry's shoes.' She shook her head as I questioned. 'You'd better hurry and change. Mummy's back and she wants you in the drawing room.'

'This is my best dress.'

'Oh, I hadn't realized.' She looked startled. 'We thought as your mother was a seamstress you would have plenty of clothes. Don't worry, I've loads of dresses from last year that I never wear. I'll sort them out and get one of the maids to bring them along.'

'Thank you, but I prefer my own things.'

'Well, tell me if you change your mind.' She moved towards the door. 'When you've stopped sulking, you'll find us in the green drawing room – that's the one we always use in the afternoons. Ask one of the servants if you don't know where it is.'

I stared defiantly at the door after she'd left. Were all the Redferns as bossy as the two I'd already met? I felt resentment against them burning inside me again. How dare she criticize my dress? It was the one Mother had made for my last birthday and it suited me very well. Prue was just being snobbish, putting me in my place.

I washed my face and combed my hair, brushing the skirt of my dress free of mud. I didn't feel ashamed of my clothes or of my mother's profession, and no one was going to make me. Prue might think it was common for a woman to work, but my mother had been forced into it by circumstances beyond her control and I was proud of her! Sticking my head in the air, I went downstairs. I hadn't a clue where I should go, but I could hear the sound of laughing voices and it drew me on.

The door of the green drawing room was open. I could see several people inside. Harry was standing by the window with a pretty woman who had green eyes and honey-blonde hair, and Prue was sitting on the sofa next to a middle-aged man. He had a weak chin, pale eyes and hair the colour of sand. Opposite the sofa, an older woman presided over the tea-tray, and I realized that she must be Lady Selina; she was very like her daughter in colouring and looks. She was dressed in a simpler style that somehow had more elegance, and there was a regal air about her. She frowned as she saw me, then beckoned me forward.

'Katherine,' she said coolly. 'How good of you to come down. I was about to send Prunella to fetch you.'

My heart drummed as I went to her. She looked so formidable that I wondered if I should curtsey, then she held out her hand and I shook it. I'd almost made a fool of myself again.

'I – I'm pleased to meet you, Lady Selina.'

'Lady Selina is so formal,' she said. 'Since my husband has asked that you should make your home with us, I think we should be more comfortable. We're cousins of a sort – but that isn't entirely suitable.'

'May I call you Aunt Selina?'

I held my breath as her brows met in concentration, then she nodded, smiling slightly. 'Yes, I think that might be best. Now, let me introduce you to everyone. You've met Harry and Prunella, I know. The lady with my son is Mrs Helen Forrest. Her husband Philip is sitting next to Prunella. And this is. . . . ' She went on to introduce me to all her guests.

I smiled and whispered greetings, desperately trying to remember their names. Philip Forrest stood up, indicating that I should take his place on the sofa.

'Sit down, Kate. I'm sure you could do with a cup of tea,' he said, going to stand by the fireplace.

'Sugar, Kate?' Lady Selina asked.

'Yes, please, and milk.' I took the fragile cup she offered. 'Thank you.'

'My husband was sorry not to be here to greet you,' she said. 'He was called away but will return this evening.'

Prue offered me a plate of tiny cakes but I refused them. I wasn't sure I could balance a tea-plate and the cup. I sat holding it carefully, taking tiny sips and listening to the conversation as it flowed around us.

'Mother's going up to town next week,' Philip Forrest said. 'Helen and I may join her. We should be delighted if Prue could stay with us for a few days.'

'Do say I may,' Prue cried. 'I need some new clothes and Helen has such marvellous taste.'

'I see no reason why not. More tea, Philip?' Lady Selina frowned at her son. 'Pass Helen's cup, Harry.'

'You could go to the ballet,' Harry said, grinning at his sister. 'Or a music hall – Vesta Tilley and Maud Allen are in. . . . '

'Harry!' His mother frowned at him. 'Helen and Philip wouldn't dream of doing anything so vulgar. Another cake, Mr Henderson?'

'Vulgar, Mother?' Harry's brows went up. 'Vesta Tilley was a great success with their Majesties in the Command Performance at the Palace Theatre last year. The King's favourite is Harry Lauder, I believe. . . . '

Lady Selina frowned at him but said nothing.

'Did you see that perfectly frightful dress Sally Fields was wearing the other evening?' Prue asked of no one in particular. 'She swore it came from Worth, but I think she got some little seamstress to make it up for her on the cheap.'

There was a sudden deathly hush and Prue blushed. Then everyone began to talk at once. I sat clutching my half-drunk cup of cold tea, hardly daring to move. I wasn't sure whether Prue had said it simply to embarrass me.

'Let me take that for you.' I glanced up and saw Harry bending over me. He took the cup and set it down. 'Come and talk to Helen. She's dying to meet you.'

He grasped my hand, pulling me to my feet and leading me to the window. Helen Forrest was leaning against the deep stone sill, her pale green silk tea-gown just short enough to reveal a pair of pretty ankles in pale silk stockings. She smiled and there was sympathy in her eyes.

'So you're Kate,' she said. 'Did you have a good journey?'

'To be honest I can't remember much of it.'

She laughed merrily. 'Oh, you're like me, Kate. I can't bear travelling. It always seems such a waste of time. I want to get where I'm going in five minutes.'

'Helen is always the same,' Harry said, a look of affection in his eyes. 'Impatience is her middle name. That's why I always beat her at croquet, tennis or cards.'

She pulled a face. 'Harry Redfern! Sometimes I quite detest you. You're such an arrogant beast. Don't you know a gentleman always lets a lady win?'

'And what would you do if I did? You'd accuse me of being condescending and sulk for days.'

'The trouble is he's right,' Helen said, pouting at me. 'I'm afraid he's far too clever for his own good. He has never yet been crossed in love. I'm praying that someone will teach him a severe lesson.'

I could see that they enjoyed arguing, and I enjoyed listening to them. I wasn't brave enough to join in much yet, but they made me laugh, as they talked about the comedian Little Titch, the famous actress Sarah Bernhardt, and a cricket match at Lords in which Jack

54

Hobbs had scored several sixes. Jack Hobbs was of course a local hero, having begun his career for Cambridgeshire. Drawn by the talk of cricket, Helen's husband joined us, adding his mite to the general conversation. He so obviously adored his wife that I warmed to him, gradually forgetting to be shy. I'd just begun to relax when Lady Selina sent the tray away and the guests began to disperse.

Helen took my arm as she prepared to leave. 'Come to the door with me,' she said. 'I know you've only just come to live here and you must feel a little strange, but I should like to get to know you. If I invite you to lunch, will you come?'

'I'd like that,' I answered shyly. 'Do you think Lady Selina would let me?'

'Of course. I'll tell Harry he must bring you.' She squeezed my arm. 'You were very brave walking into the lions' den alone. Keep your chin up, my dear.'

She laughed again, then let go of my arm and walked out to join her husband by their car. I turned to find Prue watching me.

'Helen Forrest seems to like you,' she said. 'But then, she likes everyone.' She walked off, her skirt swishing about her ankles.

I watched her go, realizing that I'd somehow upset her again. Perhaps she thought of Helen as her special friend and was jealous because I'd been invited to visit. It was so difficult trying to fit into this new life when I really had no idea what was expected of me. It was all so strange and different from what I'd been accustomed to. How I wished I could go home! But that was impossible. Sighing, I went up to my room. I'd been told I would be summoned for dinner, and in the meantime I might as well unpack.

I was buttoning the cuffs of my second-best dress, a pale blue linen that had faded slightly in the wash, when someone knocked at my door. I thought it might be Prue, but the voice, when it came, was a man's.

'May I come in, Miss Linton?'

'Who is it?'

There was a short silence, then: 'It's Sir Gerald Redfern.'

I felt flustered, glancing anxiously at my reflection and smoothing a wisp of hair. 'Come in, sir.'

The door opened and he stood there looking at me. He was a tall man, upright and distinguished-looking, just as my mother had said. I was surprised that there was so little resemblance between him and Harry, though both were handsome men. His hair was much darker than his son's, but not black like mine, and it was going grey at the temples; his eyes were hazel brown and gentle, and he had a small moustache. For a moment he studied me as intently as I did him, then he nodded.

'You're very like your mother, Kate. She was beautiful, too.'

I felt suddenly shy. It was something to do with the expression in his eyes; an intimate yet wistful look that puzzled me. 'You're exactly as she described you, sir.'

'And just what did she say about me, Kate?'

'Only that your father and her mother were cousins. And that you offered to help her if she was ever in trouble, but only when she had managed to make a life for herself.'

'You sound bitter, Kate?'

'If I am it's for my mother's sake. If she hadn't had to work so hard. . . . ' I choked on the words.

'I understand. She told you she was not treated well here –' He hesitated, then, 'I was upset when she ran away. I blamed myself.' There was a strange look in his eyes.

'Why did she run away? She never told me that.'

'To marry Richard Linton,' he said, his eyes avoiding mine. 'I blamed myself because I introduced them. It wasn't considered a suitable marriage.'

'I see,' I said, but I had the feeling that he was still hiding something from me.

'I want you to know that you will be very welcome here. Your mother asked me to help because she's ill – had she asked before I would have been willing to do much more.'

Tears stung my eyes. 'Could you help her? She hasn't asked you for money, but she needs to live in the mountains where the air is pure.'

'She refused my offer, Kate. All she wanted was a chance for you.'

'I know.' I bit my lip. 'I'm not sure I belong in a house like this. If I had the train fare, I could go back to Ely and become a student teacher.'

'Is that what you want?'

I blushed, feeling ungrateful. 'I'm not sure – but I would rather not be a burden to you or your family.'

His thick brows lowered. 'I trust no one has implied that you aren't welcome here?'

'Oh no! Everyone has been kind.' It was almost true.

'Naturally you miss your mother, but I hope we shall be able to

56

ease your grief in time. Give yourself time, Kate. I ask for your mother's sake. She wants you to have a chance in life. Let me give you the things I was never able to give her.'

'I – I will try,' I promised, my eyes stinging.

There was a reflective look in his eyes as they went over me. 'That dress suits you. You will, of course, have an allowance for clothes, just as Prue does. Selina will take you into St Ives another day and help you choose some dresses – but she is better than I am at these things.'

Obviously, someone had spoken to him about my clothes. I was embarrassed but I managed to mumble my thanks. Understanding, he nodded and offered me his arm.

'Shall we go down, Kate?'

I took his arm, gazing up at him. 'My mother was only fifteen when she came here, wasn't she?'

He nodded, his expression thoughtful. 'I was thirty-two. I'd been married for seven years. Harry was five then. Prue was born a few months after Emma left. There's only a couple of years between you.'

Again I noticed something odd in his manner, and once again it made me wonder exactly why my mother had run away.

CHAPTER FIVE

It had rained throughout the carriage drive. She sat opposite the man she had already begun to call the Demon King in her thoughts. It amused her to turn him into a fairytale character; it was a way of taking secret revenge on him for all the unhappiness she knew he had caused her mother. Her father had never known how hurt Mary was by the continuing coldness her family had shown towards her, but she knew and it had made her angry as she heard her mother weeping over the return of her letters begging for help.

She would never ask for help from anyone!

Sensing the gradual slowing of the carriage, she glanced out of the window, giving way at last to the curiosity she had tried to suppress. She hadn't wanted to show any interest in her new home. That would be to let him win. There was inside her a growing desire to make him suffer as her mother had suffered, but she knew it was unlikely that she would ever be able to influence this man's life. He had the coldest eyes she had ever seen, and she knew instinctively that he despised her. She had sensed it from the moment their eyes met and it had made her determined never to let him see into her heart.

Suddenly, she saw the house up ahead of them. For a moment she was so struck that she relaxed her guard. It was beautiful – like a palace. She could scarcely believe that she was going to live there. Her heart gladdened, and then she remembered that it belonged to him.

'Remember,' he said. 'You will be expected to behave circumspectly at all times. Your mother brought shame to this house. Because of that, I shall demand absolute obedience from you.'

'Yes, sir.' Outwardly meek, the anger raged inside her. How she hated him!

The carriage door was opened and a servant came to help her down. She smiled and thanked him, and saw the Demon King frown. Of course. He would take such a service as his due. Defiantly, she lifted her chin – and then she saw *him* and her heart somersaulted.

He was walking towards them. Tall and handsome, he looked exactly as she had imagined the princes in her storybooks. He smiled at her and held out his hand.

'Welcome to your new home,' he said. 'I hope Father has looked after you and that your journey wasn't too uncomfortable?'

He was the Demon King's son, but so different. The words he spoke were simple, but his expression was so kind that she responded immediately. She had been starved of affection and something inside her reached out to him.

'Thank you,' she whispered, giving him a shy smile. 'The journey was very comfortable.'

'I'm glad,' he said. 'Come, let me take you into the house so that you can meet everyone.'

He offered his arm, and she took it, her pulse racing. How charming he was. Perhaps her new life wasn't going to be so very bad after all. Then she glanced at the Demon King and saw that he was frowning. . . .

She watched from her vantage point in the branches of an apple tree. He was walking towards her, unaware that she was watching. He was so handsome, so kind and gentle. She had responded to him from that very first moment. Because of his kindess she had found happiness here. For the first time in her life a man had taken a real interest in her, and her spirit unfolded under his care like the petals of a rose opening to the sun. She was Cinderella and he was her prince . . . except that Prince Charming already had a wife.

She remembered the shock she had felt when he introduced her to his wife. For a moment she had been unable to speak and she was afraid that she had given herself away, but they had taken her silence for shyness and the danger had passed.

In the days and weeks that followed, she had tried to fight the growing jealousy she felt towards his wife, and the foolish passion she felt for him. Such a love could never come to anything. She knew it in her heart, and yet she couldn't stop herself dreaming of what might be if. . . . if she had the courage to carry out her plan.

She knew that he returned her love. She had seen him looking at her and she knew instinctively that he was drawn to her as strongly as she was to him.

Suddenly making up her mind, she slithered from the tree, landing on the ground a few feet from him. He looked startled and then he smiled, reaching forward to wipe a smear of dirt from her cheek.

'Climbing trees?' he asked with an indulgent lift of his brows. 'You should have been a boy.'

'Should I?'

She caught her breath, all at once shockingly aware of what she was about to do, her heart beating wildly beneath the demure bodice of her white gown. Alone in her room, caught in dreams of romance, her head filled with daring stories of princes and knights in shining armour, it had all seemed perfectly simple. She knew he loved her. . . . She knew he wanted something from her; his eyes gave it away. She'd seen her father look at her mother too often not to know what it meant. Had she the courage to go through with her plan? It was dangerous. The Demon King had warned her of his anger if she dared to stray from the role he had set her, and yet perhaps that was a part of it. It was a way of taking revenge for her mother's suffering. Only a part though, for she did love Prince Charming. And she was sure that he loved her.

She looked up at him, eyes glowing, her tongue moving slowly over lips that were already soft and moist. 'Would you like me as much if I were a boy?'

He stared and his breath quickened. Could he really have understood her message? Excitement pulsed through his body, making the blood pound in his veins. He experienced a fierce surge of desire, an almost desperate longing to possess the beautiful creature who stood before him. She was so young, many years his junior, a child still, except that this girl had never been that. Her eyes held an age-old knowledge, a secret sureness that made him suspect she was fully aware of the effect her words were having on him. His resolve was weakening. He was a man who needed the physical side of love; a man with a hunger his wife would never be able to satisfy. Yet this girl was so young, and under his father's protection; if anyone even suspected what was in his mind there would be a terrible outcry, both he and she would be ostracized, shunned by decent society. It was too dangerous, too outrageous even to contemplate. He took a deep breath, preparing to turn away.

'Don't go,' she cried, catching at his arm. 'Please. Stay and talk to me. You're the only one I can talk to – the only one who cares whether I live or die.'

'That's nonsense,' he began, sounding harsh because it was so difficult to deny her. 'You know that isn't true. . . . '

She stared up at him, her eyes filling with tears. He had rejected her and she wanted to die. Turning, she fled away across the lawn, feeling as though her heart would break.

It was raining again. She stared out of the window, feeling as though

60

she would die if she had to stay cooped up in this room for much longer. Since Prince Charming's rejection of her love, she had ceased her walks in the gardens, not wanting to run the risk of meeting him alone. His words of dismissal had hurt her deeply and she was reduced to misery once more. There was no one she could turn to.

Suddenly realizing that now was the perfect time to escape into the gardens – no one else would walk in the rain – she got to her feet, grabbed a large shawl and ran. She would welcome a drenching for the sake of freedom. And what harm could a little rain do?

She walked for hours, letting her tears mingle with the raindrops. Her gown and shawl were soaked through and she was shivering with cold, but she felt exhilarated. She began to make plans for leaving, for beginning a new life of her own somewhere else. She would not stay here. Why should she? She was strong and perfectly capable of earning her own living. Even if she had to scrub pots and pans in the kitchen, it would be better than living here as something to be looked down on and despised.

'What on earth are you doing out here?' His voice made her heart jerk. She turned slowly to look at him, waiting as he strode towards her. 'You're soaked to the skin. How long have you been out here?'

'I don't know.' She faced him defiantly.

'You'll catch your death of cold.'

'Why should you care?'

'Why. . . . ' He looked into her proud young face and felt himself being swept away by a surge of desire. 'My darling. . . . ' His voice was husky with passion and she looked up at him in surprise. 'Of course I care. How could you think I didn't? It was only for your sake. . . . '

She gave a little moan and almost fell.

'You're overwrought,' he said, and swept her up into his arms. 'I know somewhere we can go. . . . '

Smiling up at him, she curled her arms about his neck. 'I love you,' she whispered.

He looked into her eyes and felt himself drowning, losing control. She was so lovely, so sweet . . . and so obviously willing.

They were in the summerhouse that was their secret place. It was there that they had become lovers on that rainy day many weeks ago. She smiled at him, voicing the thoughts that were uppermost in her mind of late. He was more in love with her than ever. Now was the time to tell him what she expected.

61

'Divorce my wife?' He looked at her in horror. 'But you couldn't have thought that I. . . . ' As he saw her stubborn look, he felt uneasy. She was such a passionate, impulsive girl. You could never tell quite what she might do. 'I couldn't hurt her. . . . You told me that nothing mattered except the way we felt about each other. . . . '

His eyes seemed to plead with her. She was fast discovering that her idol was not the strong, godlike creature she had imagined. Yet she knew how much he wanted her, she knew how easily her kisses set him on fire. When they lay together he was ready to promise her anything.

'But you love me,' she said, looking up at him. 'You do love me, don't you?'

'You know I do . . . but divorce. . . . ' He cursed himself silently for ever letting it go this far. 'Can't you see how impossible it is? For one thing, my father would never allow it.'

Her face was stubborn as she gazed up at him. 'If you won't marry me, I'll find someone who will.'

He reached out for her, trying to draw her into his arms. 'You know I love you. I shall always love you but. . . . '

She withdrew from him proudly. 'If you loved me you would do anything to be with me.'

'You had no right to expect marriage.' He was defensive in his nervousness.

'No right?' Her lovely face was scornful as she looked up at him. 'You said that you adored me, that your wife had never made you happy. You said that you wished you were free to marry me.'

'And so I do, but. . . . '

Her eyes glittered angrily. 'Then I'll find someone else and one day, I'll make you sorry. I promise you that.'

She walked away, her head high.

She had met the man she thought she might marry. He wasn't Prince Charming and he didn't live in a palace, but he had warm, laughing eyes and he made no secret of the fact that he adored her. She called him her dearest frog, teasing him as he ran after her like a puppy, the first to fetch her a glass of wine or anything else she desired.

'Take me driving in the phaeton, Frog,' she would command, and he would obey. 'Fetch my shawl, carry my netting box . . . Bring me snowdrops, bring me roses. . . . ' If they could be found he would do it, his misty eyes adoring her. 'Dance with me, Froggie dear.'

Sometimes he begged her to tell him why she called him her frog, but she only shook her head and laughed. In the fairytale the princess kissed the frog and he turned into a prince. If she couldn't marry Prince Charming, then she would make her frog into a prince. He was handsome, intelligent and kind. She knew that she had only to say the word and he would ask her to marry him.

She was considering it, but for the moment she enjoyed keeping him on her string. She liked to see the jealousy in Prince Charming's eyes when he saw them together. Since their argument, she had refused to let him touch her. Now she kept her smiles for Froggie. She gave *him* cold looks and colder words, knowing that she was driving him mad. It was a sweet revenge and yet she still loved him. She still wanted to be in his arms. Revenge was bittersweet. She wanted to hurt him, but in doing so she was hurting herself.

His wife was carrying a child. Sometimes she dreamed that she had died and he was free to marry her. Women did die in childbed all too often. It was wicked to want someone to die, to want it so badly that she hurt.

It might happen. She knew that he would marry her if he were free. She had seen the misery in his eyes when he looked at her. She would wait for a while. She wasn't ready to turn the frog into a prince just yet. Perhaps she wouldn't need to. . . .

'I have to see you.' He caught her arm as she tried to pass him in the hallway. 'Please – meet me in the summerhouse. I've missed you so badly.'

She heard the pleading in his voice and her heart softened towards him. 'After tea,' she whispered, glancing over her shoulder as the Demon King came out into the hall. 'I'll slip away after tea.'

Throughout tea she saw him watching her. His look was so intense that she thought he would give himself away. She smiled at him and saw the way his eyes lit up, and her heart quickened. He had discovered that he could not live without her. He loved her as much as she loved him. He was going to tell her that he would do as she asked. He was going to ask his wife for a divorce.

It would be difficult, she knew. It would cause a terrible scandal and people would be hurt, but his wife didn't love him. She was a quiet, dignified girl who showed no affection for her husband. She would probably be glad to go away and live peacefully in retirement, perhaps abroad.

It was all going to work out as she'd hoped. Against all odds, she'd won!

Slipping away from the house, she walked across the lawns. The sun was warm on her head and she could hear a storm-cock singing from the branches of a blossom tree. It made her want to shout with joy. Prince Charming was going to be hers. She would be able to live in this wonderful house as its mistress and the Demon King would have to be nice to her. It was all going to be wonderful – a dream come true.

She ran the last few yards to the summerhouse, her heart pounding with excitement. She could hardly wait to be in his arms, to feel his mouth on hers and. . . . She threw open the door and then stopped in surprise as she saw him standing there. The Demon King – here in the summerhouse. Where was her lover?

'You need not look for help from my son.' His first words were like a death knell. 'He will not come. His wife has made sure of that.'

'I – I don't know what you mean.'

'Don't lie to me!'

She raised her head in defiance, waiting.

'Your behaviour fills me with disgust!'

She was trembling inwardly as she saw the anger in his face. He'd frightened her from the very beginning, but now he was terrifying. He looked as if he would like to kill her, but she refused to be cowed.

'What have I done that was so very terrible?'

'You ask me that? Are you totally without shame? You have seduced my son from his duty to his wife. You have brought disgrace on this family – and you ask me what you have done!'

Her face was pale and she felt sick, but she wouldn't let him see her fear. 'We've hurt no one.'

'Wanton hussy!' He slapped her face. She recoiled but stood firm, her head unbowed. Her very defiance enraged him. 'Have you no regret? No respect for the feelings of others? My son has a wife and son – what of them?'

'She doesn't love him. She never did. She could go away somewhere and in time he. . . . '

'My son divorce his wife and marry you?' His laughter was harsh and derisive. 'If that's what you'd hoped, you can put all such thoughts from your mind. There will be no divorce, no scandal.'

She bit her lip, beginning to wilt before his righteous anger, to understand the enormity of what she had done. Foolishly, she had confused dreams with reality, and now she must pay the price. She would be disgraced in the eyes of the world, a fallen woman. How had she ever hoped to win against such a powerful enemy? She should have known that Prince Charming could never stand up to the Demon King. Lifting her shoulders in a little shrug of defeat, she stared up at her conqueror, accepting, waiting passively.

'You must be prevented from causing further trouble,' he said, his eyes colder than ice. 'There are places for girls like you – girls who have proved wilful and headstrong. Institutions that know how to deal with mindless indecency. . . . '

'What do you mean? What kind of places?'

'You need correction for your own sake,' he said, his face impassive. 'Obviously you are not in your right senses. Your mind has become unhinged.'

'No. . . . ' She shrank away from him, her eyes wide with disbelief. No one could be that cruel, that cold and calculating. 'An insane asylum – you can't. I'm not mad. I'm as sane as you or. . . . '

He smiled pityingly. 'The asylums are full of poor insane creatures claiming to be misunderstood, my dear child. You mustn't be afraid. You will be well cared for. . . . '

'No!'

She screamed and backed away from him, suddenly running from the summerhouse in pure terror. He would carry out his threat, she knew it instinctively. She would be locked away in an insane asylym until she was broken in spirit and body. Until she could no longer be a threat to him, to the good name he prided above all things. She might be left there to rot and die. It would not be the first time a wilful girl had been put away for her own good – or that of her family.

Terror clouded her mind. She was desperate as she ran towards the house. What could she do? Where could she go that he would not find her? Would Prince Charming save her from the Demon King? She saw his gentle, slightly weak face in her mind's eye and knew it would be useless to ask. There was only one escape and it must be now. She must go now, this minute, before it was too late. . . .

CHAPTER SIX

Although a formal affair, dinner that first evening wasn't the ordeal I'd expected. There was only the immediate family and Maggie Grant at table. From remarks she made, I gathered she wasn't always invited, and I wondered if her presence was meant to make me feel at ease. In actual fact, Sir Gerald and Lady Selina were soon deep in a heated discussion about various measures put forward by Asquith – who wasn't her favourite politician, I gathered, because of his negative attitude towards the suffragettes – and his Chancellor, the fiery Welshman David Lloyd George, leaving Harry and Prue free to talk about Isadora Duncan, a dancer who was now much admired for her spirited performance despite some scandal concerning her private life. Their exchange was lively and informed, making me feel like an ignoramus.

'She has given the ballet a whole new meaning,' Harry said. 'I could watch her forever.'

'Don't let Mother hear you say that,' Prue said. 'You know she doesn't approve.'

'Mother seldom approves of anything I do or say.' Harry scowled at his sister.

I sat listening to their conversation, aware that I was out of my depth. The bewildering array of cutlery had at first made my heart sink, but common sense prevailed and I watched Harry. There were so many courses of rich food that towards the end I began to feel very full and a little sick. I was relieved when Lady Selina rose and led the way into the drawing room. Prue, Lady Selina and Sir Gerald played cards, but Harry set himself to amusing me with a childish game of snakes and ladders.

At nine-thirty, Lady Selina told me it was time for me to go up. 'You may read for a while if you wish,' she said.

I hesitated and then went to kiss her cheek. 'Goodnight,' I said. 'And thank you.'

A cool smile flickered on her lips, but I couldn't tell if she was pleased or not. Except for a few moments at dinner when she had denounced the practice of force feeding women who had gone on hunger strike in prison for the sake of their cause, her tone had remained calm and emotionless, showing no particular affection for either her children or her husband. She seemed to me a very reserved woman, almost as if she was afraid to show her feelings too much and deliberately held them in check.

'Goodnight, Kate,' she said. 'In the morning we shall discuss your routine.'

I went up to my room, feeling tired. It had been a long day, and my emotions were rather raw. The lamps had been lit and the bed was turned back. A lump came to my throat as I began to undress. It all seemed so strange, so different from what I was used to. The big house was silent and I missed the comforting whir of my mother's sewing machine. Fighting my tears, I went to the window to look out at the moon, too restless to sleep. A light tap at my door made me turn in surprise.

Prue came in. She was carrying a book and she looked at me awkwardly. 'I brought you this to read,' she said. 'It's *Anne of Green Gables* – I don't know if you've read it?'

'I borrowed it from the library when it came out the other year,' I said. 'But I wouldn't mind reading it again. Thank you.'

She smiled oddly. 'It's a peace offering. I suppose I was a bit off with you earlier.'

'It was probably my fault,' I admitted. 'I'm feeling a bit miserable.'

She nodded agreement. 'Yes, I expect so. You'll settle in eventually. Goodnight, then.'

'Goodnight.'

I stared at the closed door for several seconds and then sighed. Prue had done her best to be friendly, but I still had the feeling that she didn't really want me here. I'd been accepted on sufferance because my mother had asked Sir Gerald for help. I didn't belong here, any more than she did. I turned towards the bed, wishing I knew why my mother had run away from this house, and why she hadn't told me about my relatives for all these years. If I'd known of their existence before this, I might not have felt so much out of place in their home.

The next morning one of the maids woke me with a pot of tea on a tray. I'd slept soundly after a restless start, and I was surprised by the sudden light as the curtains were drawn. I sat up, blinking.

'Good morning, Miss Kate,' the girl said. 'Mrs Bates sent me to wake you. Breakfast is served from eight until nine in the breakfast parlour – that's across the hall from the green drawing room. Lady

Selina usually takes hers at eight-thirty. She likes to see her family there.'

'Thank you for telling me,' I said. 'Who are you exactly?'

'I'm Rosie, Miss. Mrs Bates's niece.' She smiled at me. 'I'm going to be looking after you while you're here. So anything you want, you just ask me.'

'Thank you,' I looked at her gratefully. 'I will.'

After she'd gone, I washed and dressed in the dark grey skirt and white blouse I'd worn for school. It wasn't very fashionable, but the material was good. Mother had wanted it to last.

I found my way to the breakfast room easily, but only because Rosie had bothered to tell me where it was. The house was so large and rambling that if I'd taken a wrong turning, I could have wandered around for ages.

Lady Selina was pouring tea into her cup when I entered. She gave me an approving look. 'You're the first down,' she said. 'Except for Harry. But he's always out with the horses before the rest of us are awake.' She waved her hand towards a row of silver chafing dishes on the sideboard. 'We help ourselves to breakfast when we're alone. It's so much easier. Choose whatever you like.'

I peeped beneath the heavy covers, finally helping myself to a little scrambled egg. Lady Selina glanced at my plate.

'Aren't you hungry?'

'I ate too much last night. I'm not used to so many courses at dinner.'

'No, I suppose not.' She frowned and sipped her tea. 'You're sixteen, Kate – is that right?'

'I was sixteen in May.'

'A little young to be brought out just yet. I think we'll introduce you to society gradually. This summer you can take lessons in the mornings with Miss Grant and join us in the afternoons for tea so that you become accustomed to company. You will have dinner with the family, but you will not attend evening parties or dances just yet. When we're entertaining, you may dine with Miss Grant in her rooms. Next summer we shall hold a dance for you, and then you will be properly out.' She looked at me across the table. 'Does that sound reasonable to you?'

'I – I don't wish to be a nuisance to you. . . . '

'I shall not allow you to become a nuisance, Kate. If you conduct yourself as any decent young woman should, we shall get along very well together.'

Despite her level tone, I felt that I was being warned. I might be here because Sir Gerald had requested it, but she was the mistress of Brockmere. She glanced at my skirt and blouse.

'Very sensible for mornings, Kate, but it won't do for tea. You will wear the green dress you had on yesterday until other arrangements can be made. This evening you will wear a grey silk dress which you will find in your wardrobe when you return to your room. It was made for Prue two summers ago, but she has never worn it. As soon as I have time, we shall attend to the matter of your clothes.'

Her words were final, and not a matter for discussion. I ate my breakfast, replying only when an answer was required. Lady Selina mapped out a routine for my days and nights, making it clear that I was expected to amuse myself with books or sewing when I was not invited to join her in the drawing room.

When I was at last allowed to leave the breakfast table, I was aware of how much my life had changed. Mother had been strict over certain things, but I'd had far more freedom than I'd realized and it made my feeling of loss even sharper. I was going to miss my mother in so many ways!

The schoolroom was in the right wing of the house, adjoining Maggie Grant's own sitting room. I took one false turning, which led me to a room full of guns, shooting sticks and boots. Closing the door, I started back the way I'd come, bumping suddenly into Sir Gerald.

'What are you doing, Kate?' he asked, seeming startled.

'I was on my way to Miss Grant's sitting room,' I said. 'I took a wrong turning somewhere.'

'It's a little early for lessons, isn't it?'

'Lady Selina thought I could discuss my programme with Miss Grant before Prue arrives.'

'I see.' He nodded thoughtfully. 'The schoolroom is the first door down there to your right. If I were you I should wait there until Miss Grant is ready for you.'

Thanking him, I continued on my way. I supposed that he must be going to the gun room, though he seemed to have come from the direction of the governess's suite. I wondered what he could have had to discuss with Miss Grant at this hour.

The schoolroom had a pleasant, sunny aspect and overlooked the front drive. It was a big room with a long oak table in the centre, several chairs and bookcases and a piano. Accustomed to the over-crowded, noisy classes of my school, where there was always a shortage of desks and equipment, I found it strange that all this should be for just one or two pupils. I'd enjoyed the companionship of my friends and I felt rather sorry for Prue. It must be lonely at times for her, I thought, although now of course she mixed with her mother's guests. Wondering what it must have been like to be brought up in this house, I curled up on a little window seat and looked out at the gardens, thinking how beautiful the roses were, massed along the old stone walls. There would certainly be compensations in living here.

I'd been waiting for only a few seconds when I heard an odd choking sound coming from the room next door. I listened as I heard it again, realizing that it was the sound of someone crying. Hesitating for a moment, I went to the connecting door and knocked.

'Miss Grant,' I called. 'This is Kate Linton. Are you all right? Can I help you?'

There was silence, then she replied in a muffled voice. 'I shall be with you in five minutes. Please find yourself a French grammar book and begin the first exercise.'

I moved away from the door. Looking through the bookcase, I found a suitable book and took it to the table. Selecting a sheet of paper and a pencil, I began to work. It was so simple that I'd progressed to the third exercise by the time Maggie came into the room. She had obviously washed her face, but her eyes were still red from crying.

'You're early,' she said, glancing at the marble clock on the mantel. 'Miss Prue won't be here for another half an hour.'

'I'm sorry if I disturbed you.'

'I was gargling. It's good for the throat.'

'Sir Gerald said I should wait for you. . . . '

'You spoke to him?' She looked alarmed. 'When did you see him?'

'He was on his way to the gun room. Just after he left you, I expect.'

'Sir Gerald has not been here. You are mistaken if you think otherwise.' Her tone was sharp, with alarm I thought.

'I'm sorry. I assumed he had come from this direction.'

'Why should he come here?' She frowned. 'It doesn't do to assume too much.'

Why was she so agitated because I'd jumped to conclusions? It seemed to me that she was lying, but why should she lie over such a little thing? She looked over my shoulder at my work.

'This is very good.'

'I've always had a flair for languages.' I sighed as I looked at the piano. 'My mother could play, but I think I'm tone deaf.'

She smiled slightly. 'Well, we can't be good at everything, can we? Perhaps you should give me a demonstration while we're alone?'

I went over to the piano, lifting the lid reluctantly. Sitting down, I flexed my fingers nervously. As the first discordant notes assailed our ears, the door of the schoolroom was flung open. Harry stood on the threshold, dressed in riding breeches, boots and a black wool jacket over a thin silk shirt. His hair was windblown, his skin glowing from the fresh air.

'There you are, Kate,' he said. 'What a dreadful noise. You're not much of a musician, are you?'

I laughed and shook my head. 'I've got to try, though. Prue says it's important.'

'If, like my sister, you've had your head stuffed with nonsense about marriage, then perhaps it is. I hope you've got more sense, Kate.'

'If you have to play well to marry well, I expect I'll be a spinster all my life.'

He threw back his head and roared with laughter. 'Why bother then? Come on, I'm going to give you your first riding lesson. That's far more important.'

'But I'm not dressed for riding. Besides, your mother said I'm to spend my mornings with Miss Grant.'

'Maggie won't tell on you.' He gave her a brilliant smile. 'That skirt will do for today, then we'll get you fixed up. Don't worry, Kate, I'll arrange it with Mother.'

He grabbed my wrist, pulling me to my feet. I was propelled from the room by my eager captor, but I didn't fight very hard. The prospect of a riding lesson was more tempting than labouring over a piano.

Harry hurried me out of the house, striding across the courtyard towards the stables. He walked swiftly, forcing me to take little running steps to keep up with him.

'Do you do everything at this speed?' I asked, breathless.

'Almost everything. There's so much I want to do – and life is so short.'

'You're only twenty-five or so – why the hurry?'

For a moment his eyes were shadowed, then he laughed. 'I don't know. I've always been afraid that if I don't fill every hour I might not have time for all I want to do – I expect it's just impatience.'

71

As we reached the stables, I saw a groom leading a horse towards us. He touched his cap to Harry.

'Firefly's ready, sir. She needed a bit of settling, but you shouldn't have any trouble with her.'

As he spoke, the mare snorted and tossed her head. She was a pretty little horse with a chestnut coat and a white, silky mane, clearly high-spirited. Her eyes seemed to glint as if she knew that I was a novice and resented it.

'She looks as if she doesn't like me. Haven't you got a more docile horse?'

'She's as gentle as a mouse,' Harry said, a mocking note in his voice. 'You don't want an old nag, Kate. Start as you mean to go on. Today I'm only going to show you how to sit and hold the reins. There's nothing to worry about. I'll have a leading rein on her. Don't be such a coward. Either you want to ride or you don't.'

His words stung my pride and my chin went up. 'I was only asking. How do I get up then? I want to do it properly.'

'I'll give you a hand. Put your foot here and let yourself go when I throw you up.'

I did as I was told. The saddle was different from the one he'd used the previous day and I felt as if I was slipping off. I gave a cry of protest and he slapped my leg.

'Sit up straight and bring this leg forward. That's better, you can't fall now. You're going to ride like a lady by the time I've finished with you.'

'Can't I ride astride the way you do?'

'Not in that skirt. Mother would have a fit.' There was mischief in his eyes as he looked at me. 'You could if you wore breeches.'

'Then I'll wear them next time.'

A calculating expression came into his eyes. 'I'll bet you change your mind. You wouldn't dare.'

What he was suggesting was outrageous. I knew it but provoked by his mockery, I threw caution to the winds. 'You wait and see.' I gave him a challenging look. 'I'll meet you here at seven tomorrow morning. We'll ride before breakfast, then it won't interfere with my lessons.'

'You're on,' he said. 'But if you don't wear breeches, you'll have to pay a forfeit.'

'What kind of forfeit?'

'I don't know yet. I'll tell you if you go back on your word.'

'That's not fair!'

'Getting cold feet already?'

'No.' My chin went up. 'I shan't have to pay your forfeit, because I'll be wearing breeches.' I didn't know how I was going to manage it, but I'd had enough of his superiority and I was determined to win my bet.

I wondered if Lady Selina might pay a surprise visit to the schoolroom while I was absent. Harry had promised to talk to her about my riding lessons, but I knew she would be very annoyed if she guessed I'd disobeyed her on my first day. Fortunately, Maggie was still alone when I got back.

'Miss Prue is late,' she said, glancing at the clock. 'I can't understand it. Perhaps we should run through the scales again while we're waiting.'

Obediently, I took my place at the piano. I could feel the stiffness in my shoulders and an ache in the small of my back, but I held myself straight as I ran my fingers over the keys.

'You know your scales,' Maggie Grant said. 'It's when you try to translate them into music that you go wrong. I think you need to. . . .'

The door opened and Prue came in. She looked disgruntled and there was a downturn to her mouth. 'I'm sorry to be late, Miss Grant,' she said, ignoring me. 'I've been with Mother.' Obviously, the interview had been less than pleasant. It seemed that Lady Selina was every bit as strict with her daughter as she was with me.

Maggie nodded. 'What would you like to do this morning? French, music or poetry?'

'I'll play the piece you set me,' Prue said. 'If you've finished with Kate?' She seemed to become aware of me suddenly and flushed.

'Miss Kate can go back to the French exercises she was doing earlier. It will do her good to hear you play; you have such a sure touch.'

As Prue moved to the piano, I sat down at the table, but I made no effort to start work. Prue's playing was little short of magical, and I sat spellbound as her fingers stroked and coaxed sweet music from the keys. Her face wore a dreamy expression as if she was lost in her music, and she looked almost beautiful. When she'd finished, I clapped enthusiastically.

'You're so clever,' I said. 'My mother can play, but not like you.'

She smiled distantly. 'It's a gift, I know. Do you want to continue your lesson?'

'I'd rather not. Perhaps tomorrow.'

73

She glanced at the book I was using. 'Oh, you're only at the beginning; I'm halfway through.'

None of the exercises would prove difficult for me, but I held my tongue. I was the intruder here; I saw no sense in competing with her.

Maggie Grant smiled brightly. 'Why don't we read some poetry instead? We could try Robert Browning. . . . '

I looked at the grey silk dress in my wardrobe. It was very plain with a high neck and a lace collar and cuffs. The skirt was panelled at the front and I could see why Prue had refused to wear it. One of the seams was slightly puckered and because of that the front didn't hang quite as it should. I felt pleased. It wouldn't be hard to remove the pucker. I was about to start when the door opened and Rosie came in.

'I didn't know you were here, miss. I came to see if there was any laundry.'

'Just some underwear. I put it in the basket in the bathroom. I hope that's right?'

'I'll find it wherever you leave it. Miss Prue leaves hers on the floor. So does Mr Harry.'

I followed her to the door of the adjoining bathroom. 'Could you get me a pair of breeches, Rosie? Something suitable for riding that would fit me?'

Her mouth fell open. 'What would you be wanting breeches for?'

'To go riding with Harry. I don't like being perched on a side-saddle.'

She stared at me for a moment longer, doubt warring with a kind of admiration in her eyes, then she grinned. 'You'll catch it if the mistress sees you! My young brother has a spare pair. He works for the Hunt Master and he has to exercise the horses.'

'Can you get them for the morning?'

'Not for tomorrow. It's my night on duty – but the next day I'll have them.'

'That will do. I can't pay for them yet, but when I get my allowance. . . . '

'Bless you, miss. Rob has outgrown them. He'll not want anything for them.'

'I want to be up early every morning in future. I'm going riding at seven.'

'I'll wake you at six-thirty, then.' Rosie smiled. 'I'd best get back or Aunt Mary will think I've got lost.'

'Thank you – and you won't tell about the breeches?'

She crossed her heart. 'I wouldn't tell a soul. I think you're ever so daring, miss, and that's a fact.'

I knew it was terribly forward, perhaps even a little fast. It hadn't bothered me when I'd taken up Harry's challenge, but I knew it would make Lady Selina very angry that I should flout the laws of propriety so brazenly. My heart fluttered at the thought of her displeasure, but then the memory of Harry's mocking smile returned to bolster my courage. I wasn't going to let him win!

After Rosie had gone, I concentrated on my sewing. Mother had given me her basket as a parting gift, saying that she wouldn't need it any more. It was full of different coloured threads and I found one to match the dress. I'd been taught to sew properly and the alteration didn't take long. I was pleased with my industry as I returned the dress to the wardrobe, then I glanced at the clock. It was a quarter to four. Tea was at half-past three!

I shot out of the room without bothering to check my appearance. There wasn't time to change. I was late, and Lady Selina had stressed that I must be prompt to meals.

'You're late.' She was clearly annoyed. 'And you haven't changed.'

'I was sewing,' I apologized. 'I'm sorry. It won't happen again.'

'See that it doesn't.' She poured me a cup of tea. 'We were discussing Ascot. It's next week, though I'm not sure I shall go this year. Harry said you would enjoy it, but I was doubtful.'

'It's horse racing, Kate.' Harry grinned at me. 'We all dress up for it and the King will be there. You'd like that, wouldn't you?'

'Yes, I think so.' I glared at him. 'I did know about Ascot; I've seen pictures of the Royal family there. When King Edward died the papers were full of them.'

Harry grinned wickedly, and I realized that he'd been deliberating baiting me again.

'Harry, show a little restraint if you please,' his mother said, frowning at us both. 'Well, we'll see. If Kate shows me she can behave herself, I may allow her to come.'

'Mother has agreed to the riding lessons,' Harry said, winking at me as his mother turned to Prue.

'Have you written those letters, Prunella?'

'Yes, Mother.' She flushed and looked at her hands. 'I don't want to stay with the Barlows – do I have to?'

'They've asked you for Henley and I think you should go. Ernest Barlow is an excellent young man, and he likes you, Prunella.'

'But I don't like him.' Prue scowled. 'He's horse mad and you know I don't enjoy riding.'

'You ride perfectly well. The Barlows are a good family, and you won't get many more suitable offers.' Her mother frowned at her and then turned to me. 'I think the lessons are a splendid idea, Kate. I was considered a good horsewoman when I was a girl. Prunella does not take after me in that way.'

'I hate horses,' Prue said, looking miserable. 'Nasty, smelly brutes.'

Lady Selina looked at her coldly. 'I thought I asked you to tell Miss Grant I would like her to take tea with us?'

'She wasn't in her room.'

'How very annoying. She knows that I require her to join us when we do not have visitors.'

'Maggie must have some free time, Mother,' Harry put in mildly. 'She runs errands for you, arranges the flowers and sews, besides giving Prue her lessons.'

'I hope you're not suggesting I make too many demands on her?'

'No, of course not.'

'She's been a bit odd recently,' Prue said.

'What do you mean?' Lady Selina looked at her sharply.

'She keeps talking about what she'll do when she leaves us.'

'I hope she isn't planning to leave. We shall need her until at least next summer.'

'Perhaps you should tell her that,' Harry said. 'She's probably worried about losing her job when Prue marries.'

'If I ever do,' Prue muttered with a dark glance at her mother, but Lady Selina was looking at her son.

'Naturally she will have an excellent reference. I could find her another employer tomorrow.'

'If she wants one,' Prue said.

'Speak plainly, Prunella.'

Prue shrugged. 'You should ask Harry. He's the one she trusts. I think she's in love with him.'

'Is this true?' Lady Selina looked shocked.

'You should know better than to listen to Prue when she's in one of her moods,' Harry replied easily. 'I've been kind to the woman a few times and she tends to blush when I speak to her, but I haven't seduced her if that's what you mean.'

'Harry!' His mother frowned at him. 'If you've been upsetting

76

Miss Grant I shall be cross with you. You may think it's amusing to flirt with every woman who comes your way, but. . . . '

Harry put down his cup. 'Excuse me, Mother. I've an appointment. I'll see you this evening.'

'Harry. . . . '

Lady Selina stared after him, annoyance in her face. I saw that Prue was pleased with herself, and I realized that she'd deliberately tried to cause trouble for her brother. I wondered why. . . .

Lady Selina kept me with her for almost an hour. She asked me lots of questions about my school and my life before I came to Brockmere, but she didn't mention my mother or her illness, and for that I was grateful. I couldn't stop thinking about my mother, longing for the sight of her face and the sound of her voice. I kept wondering where she was and what she was doing. Was she feeling very ill? Was she missing me?

Leaving the drawing room at last, I wasn't sure what to do. There was an hour before I need change for dinner, and I decided to go for a walk. As yet I hadn't explored the gardens.

The shrubberies were delightful. Little winding walks between huge rhododendrons with mauve and pink blossoms; there were creamy camellias, too, and fine spiky sprays of a tiny white flower I didn't recognize. Roses grew in abundance, and there were old trees with gnarled trunks and protruding roots. It was all very beautiful and I wished that my mother could have seen it.

I found a wooden bench and sat down, watching a thrush hunting for worms beneath a pile of dried moss. When she was successful, she made a soft clucking in her throat and a fledgling with a short stubby tail came hopping out of the bushes towards her, opening its beak and flapping its wings. It was a charming, peaceful setting, but it made me even more aware of my loneliness. I didn't belong here. I missed the noise and chatter of our communal yard. It was so quiet. I'd never lived right out in the country before, and I knew I would miss Ely itself, with its magnificent cathedral, its historic associations with Hereward the Wake and Oliver Cromwell, and its busy market days. I would miss my friends and, worst of all, my mother. Already I felt isolated. I could never be a member of this family – nor did they really want me. A tear slid down my cheek and off my chin. I wiped it away, annoyed at myself, but it was followed by another and another. I bent my head, covering my face with my hands as I wept.

'Crying isn't going to solve anything.' Harry's voice startled me. 'I thought you had more spirit.'

I glanced up, dismayed that he had found me. 'What do you want?'

'I happened to come this way.' He frowned down at me. 'What's wrong?'

'I don't belong here.'

'And you're not going to make an effort to fit in, are you?'

'What do you mean?' I asked indignantly.

'You're behaving like a spoilt baby. Crying out here alone in the garden.'

'My mother is dying of consumption – did you know that?'

'You're crying for. . . . ' Harry looked contrite. 'I thought you were just sulking. I'm sorry, Kate.'

'And so you should be.' I got to my feet with dignity and walked away, leaving him staring after me in dismay.

Deciding to pay a visit to the governess before dinner, I slipped in at the back entrance, hurrying up to her room. There was no immediate answer to my knock and I was turning away when the door opened.

'What do you want?'

I blinked at her abrupt manner. 'I wanted to talk to you, but I see I shouldn't have come.'

She called me back as I walked away. 'Don't go. I'm sorry.' She gave me a weak smile. 'Please come in.'

'I don't wish to intrude.'

'You aren't. I'm upset about something, but it's not your fault.'

I followed her inside. Her room was comfortably furnished with two deep armchairs, a writing desk and chair, several occasional tables, a stool and a bookcase. A large vase of spring flowers stood on the windowsill and there were writing materials on the desk, and lots of books. A newspaper lay open on the table and I saw that she had been reading about Emily Davison, the suffragette who had died of the injuries sustained by throwing herself in front of the King's horse at the Derby; the inquest had returned a verdict of misadventure. But there was nothing personal lying around, nothing that might make a statement about Maggie as a person. No photographs, no little knick-knacks. It could have been anyone's room.

'Would you like a cup of tea?' she asked suddenly. 'I have my own spirit kettle.'

'I had tea in the drawing room.' I looked at her uncertainly. 'You were expected for tea today. Prue said you weren't in your room when she came to fetch you.'

Maggie frowned and fiddled with her hair, pushing the tortoiseshell comb back into place. 'It's so difficult to know when I'm wanted. If there are guests I'm not required. I went for a walk after lunch. I had some thinking to do.'

'Are you thinking of leaving?'

'Why do you ask?' She looked startled.

'It was something Prue said at tea.'

'What else did she say?'

I bit my lip. 'I think it was just to annoy her brother.'

'You might as well tell me.' Maggie's eyes were wary. 'That is why you came, isn't it?'

'I suppose it is. I thought you should be warned in case Lady Selina speaks to you – Prue said you were in love with Harry.' As I spoke, I realized that I'd had reasons of my own for coming.

To my surprise she laughed. 'Was Lady Selina very annoyed?'

'She wasn't pleased. She told Harry she would be cross with him if he'd been upsetting you, because she doesn't want you to leave before next summer.'

'She actually said that?' Maggie smiled as I nodded. 'Thank you for telling me. It was kind of you to bother, Miss Kate.'

'Couldn't you call me Kate when we're by ourselves? We're to dine together when the family entertains. You see, like you, I'm not always required.'

She was thoughtful for a moment, then nodded. 'I'm sorry if I've been stiff with you. I – I've been worrying about something.'

'Is there anything I can do?'

'No. It was a false alarm, nothing to worry about.' She shook her head. 'Let's talk of something else. Your French is better than I'd expected. I'll have to find you something more stretching than those exercises. Would you like to read Molière?'

'Very much – but in my own time. I'd rather not compete with Prue.'

'Very wise. She's an odd girl, moody and difficult at times. We'll concentrate on your music and reading. I have full access to Sir Gerald's library.'

'I'll need something to fill my time. I had some sewing today but I anticipate many hours of idleness.'

She laughed wryly. 'If you like sewing you can help me. I was once unwise enough to offer my services to Lady Selina. Since then she has found me endless repairs.'

'Perhaps I could come after lunch for an hour?'

'I like to walk then.'

'Then I'll come after tea when I can.'

'You mustn't feel obliged to help me.'

'I don't mind – besides, it will make me feel as if I'm repaying a little of what the Redferns are doing for me.'

'You're being given nothing that isn't owed you.'

I stared at her doubtfully. 'I'm only a distant cousin. Sir Gerald had no need to help me.'

She shrugged. 'Perhaps you're right.' She got up and took a mending basket from a cupboard. 'We may as well work as we talk. . . . '

I was already awake when Rosie brought my tea the next morning. I drank it quickly, anxious to be on my way. So eager was I that I reached the stables before the groom had finished saddling my horse. Harry was waiting for me even though I was early. He looked disappointed when he saw I was wearing my skirt.

'I thought you'd change your mind,' he said. 'I suppose you're scared of Mother?'

'I haven't changed my mind. I'll have the breeches for tomorrow.'

'Our wager was for today.' His eyes glinted with mischief. 'You owe me a forfeit.'

'That's not fair. I couldn't get them today.'

'You only had to ask me. I have some I wore before I went to college at Cambridge. They'd fit you.'

'You didn't tell me.'

'You didn't ask. Why should I help you win?'

'All right, I'll pay your forfeit,' I said crossly. 'But if I wear the breeches tomorrow, you'll owe me a forfeit.'

'Agreed.' He laughed with genuine amusement. 'Come on then, up with you. We'll use the leading rein for a start, then you can try walking Firefly up and down the yard yourself.'

'You haven't told me what my forfeit is yet.'

'No, I haven't, have I?' he said. 'Don't worry about it now, Kate. I'll think of something. . . . '

CHAPTER SEVEN

She seemed to have been walking forever. It was dark now and, despite having been given a lift on a haycart for part of the way, it had taken her the whole of one day and a night to reach her destination. She had not dared to re-enter the house. She had no money, no clothes apart from those she was wearing, and she was hungry. Her feet were sore and she was desperately tired, but nothing would have made her stop now. She had to find him, the one person in the world she knew would help her.

She knew exactly where he lived. He had described the village and his cottage at the end of the lane by the church. It was easy to find the church, even though she had only the light of a crescent moon. Shivering with cold, she stood at the bottom of the lane and looked towards his cottage. A light was burning in the window. It was late and she'd been afraid he would be asleep. Now that she was here, she was almost afraid to disturb him. Afraid that he would reject her. Then she remembered the way he had held her hand the last time they met.

'Always remember that I would do anything for you,' he'd said, and he had sounded sincere. 'I love you. I loved you from the moment we met.'

Prince Charming had sworn he loved her, too. She was exhausted, frightened, near to collapse. She was afraid to go on, but there was no turning back. Taking a deep breath, she began to walk up the lane. She had to force one foot after the other, her strength almost gone, her stomach rumbling with hunger. His light drew her on, renewing her hope. At least he would give her something to eat, she thought.

She knocked once, swaying with tiredness. If he rejected her she didn't know what she would do. The door opened, light streaming out onto her face. For a moment he stared in disbelief, then he moved towards her, sweeping her up in his arms and carrying her inside. He laid her gently on the sofa and when she would have spoken, he shook his head.

'Wait, my darling,' he said. 'You need rest and something to warm you. You're exhausted.'

Tears sprang to her eyes. 'You're so good to me,' she whispered. 'I love you,' he said.

He fetched brandy and made her drink it though it scolded her throat, causing her to choke. Then he brought her a bowl of hot soup and some crusty bread. She ate ravenously, feeling the warmth spreading through her. Weak and overcome with gratitude, she lay back and smiled at him.

Later, when she had recovered a little, she told him her story. He listened in silence, asking no questions but accepting all she said. Then, when she had finished, he sat beside her on the sofa and, taking her hand, asked her to marry him.

'But you can't want to marry me now?' She looked up at him. 'You did understand, Froggie? You did. . . . '

He stopped her with a kiss. 'That was before you came to me,' he said. 'That was the past, the future begins now.'

She wept then and he held her in his arms, stroking her hair and whispering words of love and comfort. But she was so tired that her eyes kept closing. He smiled and said that they would talk again in the morning. She slept in his bed while he sat in the tiny living room making plans, and in the morning he told her what he meant to do.

'I shall see him,' he said, looking grim. 'I shall ask for his permission to marry you.'

She clutched at his hands, her eyes dark with fear. 'You mustn't tell him where I am. He will take me away. He will shut me up in that place. . . . '

'No one will take you anywhere,' he said, and the look in his eyes was so fierce that she was silenced.

He had fetched a young girl to sit with her while he was gone. She had stayed in bed, sleeping and crying in turn, certain that the Demon King would snatch her away from her dearest Froggie.

She had underestimated him. When he returned he was triumphant. He had faced the enemy fearlessly, and when he was laughed to scorn, threatened and finally turned away, he'd come back to her, his resolution unshaken.

'Don't worry, my darling,' he said as he held her in his arms. 'We'll go away. He shan't hurt you. I give you my word.'

'But if he refuses his permission?' She looked up at him doubtfully. 'He's still my guardian. The law is on his side. He could force me to go with him. He could have me locked away in that terrible place.' A shudder of revulsion and fear ran through her.

He touched her cheek and smiled. He was so strong and so sure of himself that her trembling ceased. 'If you are my wife he can do nothing.'

She was puzzled by his apparent unconcern. 'How can we marry without his permission?'

'In England we couldn't,' he agreed, smiling a little at her wide-eyed look. How beautiful she was, and how clear those sea-green eyes. No one must ever hurt her again. He would have killed for her if need be, and he had said as much to her guardian. 'Haven't you heard of Gretna Green?'

'But . . . I've heard of runaway lovers being married across the anvil, but I thought the law had been changed?'

He smiled and kissed the tip of her nose. How sweet and innocent she looked at that moment. 'In 1856 it became necessary to live in Scotland for three weeks before the marriage, but after that it's perfectly legal.' He watched the dawning delight in her eyes and nodded. 'I thought that might appeal to you. Shall I sweep you up on my white charger and ride off into the night?'

Her eyes were bright as she gazed up at him. 'How well you know me.' Again she was struck by doubt. 'Are you sure you want to marry me?'

She did not know what she would do if he changed his mind, but she had to ask. She wasn't in love with Froggie, but she liked him and she liked being made to feel like a princess.

'I've never been more certain of anything.' He brushed her lips gently with his own as she would have spoken. 'I know much more than you imagine, my darling. I can't give you all the things he might have given you had circumstances been different, but I'll work for you. I'll do all I can to make you happy. I swear it.'

'We'll be happy together, Froggie dearest,' she whispered, lifting her face for his kiss.

They spent three weeks together in Scotland. Froggie had given up his job and cottage for her sake.

'We'll start a new life together,' he said when she worried that he was sacrificing too much for her sake. 'I can find another job some-where else.'

He'd managed to bring some of her clothes from the house, but she had no money of her own. She felt that she was a heavy burden to him, though he would have died rather than admit it. An orphan himself, he had always had to struggle for what he wanted. He was hard-working, dedicated and she knew that his dream of becoming a lawyer was very dear to him. He had been saving for a chance to put himself through college but now his plans would have to wait.

'I can study at home,' he said when she looked uncertain. 'Perhaps I can find a job as a clerk in chambers and work my way up from there. When we can afford it, I can take my exams.'

She knew that he had very little money. Most of it would be needed to pay for their expenses in Scotland and the move to a new house when they returned. He was sure that he would find a job easily, but money was going to be tight. She felt guilty, knowing that she'd had no right to expect so much from him. Yet he had given his love freely and he was forever telling her how happy he was that she had come to him.

They walked a great deal while they were waiting for the three weeks to pass, getting to know one another. He told her that in childhood he had suffered an illness that might make him unable to be a father.

'I've been to see a doctor,' he said as he looked down into her face. 'It isn't impossible, darling, but we have to face the fact that we may not have a child.'

'It doesn't matter,' she said, reaching up to kiss him. 'We shall have each other.'

She hid her disappointment from him. She had wanted a houseful of children. It was something she had dreamed of when she was so often alone, but he had given her sanctuary and she was grateful. She was becoming fond of him, though in her heart she knew that she didn't love him, not in the way she had loved Prince Charming.

He did not try to make love to her until after they were married. When they were at last alone together in the big, old-fashioned bed with its feather mattress and piles of pillows, he was gentle and considerate, taking her as carefully as if she had been a virgin. Afterwards, as he lay sleeping by her side, she was wakeful. She had felt nothing. Froggie was tender and kind, but she had felt no answering response to his passion. Now there was just emptiness.

Tears slid down her cheek. She wanted to love him. She wanted to feel that fierce singing in her breast. She wanted him to drive all the memories away, but they were still there. Despite everything, she still loved Prince Charming. It made her feel disloyal and she was aware of a restlessness within her.

'Must you work again tonight, Froggie?' She sighed with discontent as her young husband spread out his law books on the parlour table.

84

He worked every night, studying until his eyes ached and the candles were guttering. She had tried to accept it as a necessary evil, but she was so bored. 'Couldn't we go to the Bradshaw's party tomorrow – just for a little while?'

He looked up, his grey eyes clouding with anxiety. Her mouth was sulky, drooping at the corners. At first she had seemed happy enough, spending her time cleaning and cooking, but of late she had become moody. It worried him to see her unhappy.

'You know why I need to study,' he said quietly. 'It's for your sake, so that I can make a decent life for us. I don't want us always to be poor, but I have to work every night if I'm ever going to pass my exams.'

'But you never have time for me,' she said. 'You don't talk to me. We never go anywhere.'

She did not add that he was so tired when he climbed into bed beside her that he seldom wanted more than a kiss before he turned on his side to sleep. When he did make love to her it was usually over in a very few minutes, leaving her unsatisfied and wanting more. She did not really blame him. He worked so hard, and she knew it was for her sake, but she couldn't help wishing that he would be the devoted slave he had been before they were married. Froggie had settled for marriage and the dull routine it brought so easily. She wasn't like him. She longed for laughter and excitement and the kind of love that made her tingle with joy.

'You have your friends.' He frowned. 'You're hardly ever in the house.'

'But I can't go to evening parties without an escort, can I? Please take me. Please, Froggie darling.' Once he had been so eager to please her. Now he only had time for work.

'I just haven't time.' He sighed deeply. 'Can't you go with those friends – the ones who took you to Devon for a holiday?'

'Madeline and Freddy?' She tried to keep the excitement from her voice. 'They did say they would take me – if you wouldn't mind?'

'Of course I don't mind.' He hated it when she went out with her friends, returning to the house long after he'd closed his books, blown out the candle and gone to bed, but he could hardly keep her a prisoner against her will. She was so young and so full of life. She needed excitement and gaiety. He knew that he was too dull for her, but he didn't know what else to do. He had to work or they would never escape from the poverty that she hated so much. 'Go with Madeline and Freddy if you want to.'

'Dearest Frog!' She wrapped her arms around his neck, brushing her lips lightly against his cheek so that he caught a tantalizing whiff of her perfume. 'Thank you. Thank you.'

'Now can I get on?' He looked at her indulgently, as if she were a child to be petted and spoiled.

She pouted at him. 'I suppose you must. Anyway, I want to restyle my dress for tomorrow. Madeline is sure to have a new one.'

'You're so clever with your clothes,' he said. 'I'm sorry I can't afford to buy you more.'

'It doesn't matter.' The smile she gave him was brilliant. 'I know exactly what I want to do. I saw a dress in a shop in St Ives that's exactly right – and I can make it out of some oddments and my yellow silk.'

'I didn't know you had been to St Ives.' He frowned slightly. 'When was this?'

She turned away, reaching for her sewing box, hiding her blushes. 'Didn't I tell you? Madeline took me last week. She wanted to do some shopping.'

'I should have thought you would stay well clear of St Ives. It's too near. . . . '

She frowned and then shook her head. 'He never goes into town – the Demon King. He – he's had some kind of a seizure and he's confined to the house.'

'Who told you?'

She hesitated, bending her head over her work. 'I'm not sure. It might have been Freddie. Why? Does it matter?' Her heart beat wildly as she lied. If he knew that she had seen Prince Charming, he would be angry and then he might not let her go to the party.

Froggie saw the faint flush in her cheeks. 'No, I don't suppose it does,' he said, and looked down at his books.

Her heart was skittering with fright. She kept looking over her shoulder as she walked, wondering if anyone was watching her. It was her guilty conscience, of course. She had lain awake half the night, listening to her husband's gentle breathing, going over and over it in her mind. Surely it wasn't so very wrong just to have tea with him? She'd justified it a thousand times during her restless night, but the guilt was still there. Froggie was so good to her. He worked so hard for her sake, and he had helped her when she was in trouble. She ought not to have agreed to meet the other one again; it could only lead to unhappiness. The first time they had bumped into each other by accident and she had felt her heart flutter as she looked up into his handsome face. That had been quite innocent, but this time it was an assignation.

No one could know that, of course. Anyone looking at her would think she was simply going shopping. Pausing to look at herself in a shop window, she was pleased with what she saw. Her dress was the new narrow shape, without hoops or a bustle, skimming over her slender hips to flare flirtatiously above her ankles. She had seen one or two older women look at her disapprovingly, but it was the latest fashion and she didn't care what they thought. At least, she wasn't going to let it stop her wearing whatever she liked. It suited her well, she knew that. The waist was nipped in tightly with a wide sash that she had tied to one side in a daringly large bow, and the high neckline had a frill of lace.

She was the Edwardian ideal of womanhood, with her hour-glass figure and slightly rakish elegance, her long hair swept up from the neck to a tumble of curls, on which she had perched a wide-brimmed hat trimmed with rosettes to match her sash. She carried a pretty parasol in her white-gloved hands, and a little beaded purse hung from her wrist. She looked every bit as young and lovely as she had before her marriage – but would he think so? Prince Charming. . . .

He was standing in front of the new Temperance Hotel. Dressed in a striped blazer, white shirt and white flannels, and wearing a jaunty straw boater, he was as handsome as ever and her heart leaped with excitement. He had a large red carnation in his lapel and he was carrying a posy of them – for her, she realized. Her heart turned over and she was remembering the touch of his mouth on hers. The way her body had surged into pulsing life as soon as he began to caress her – but she was married now. She had a home and a husband; friends who would be shocked if they knew she was meeting another man.

For a moment she hesitated. It wasn't too late to turn back. She could go home now and no one would ever know. She paused, battling with her conscience, knowing that what she was about to do was terribly disloyal. Then he turned and saw her, a smile of welcome in his eyes. Her heart began to race wildly. She wanted to be with him so much. Just this once, she promised herself. She wouldn't do anything wrong. She just wanted to talk to him – to laugh for a little while. Just this once and then she would never see him again. She lifted her hand in answer to his smile; then, crushing her feelings of guilt, she walked to meet him.

It did not stop there. He owned a small cottage behind the coalyard. It was usually let to a tenant but the last one had moved out and it was empty. He suggested that they should go there after tea. She had known it was wrong. Even as she agreed to his suggestion, the guilt had been eating at her. She had seen a neighbour looking at her as she slipped inside the little house and it made her uneasy.

They had made love quickly and furtively. It was not as she had remembered in the summerhouse. That had been a magical dream. She had kept it enshrined in her memory. Now it was destroyed and she felt betrayed. This was not what she had longed for. She felt dirty and used, and she was angry. She dressed quickly afterwards, wanting to get away. He came to her, putting his arms about her waist and kissing the back of her neck.

'Will you come again next week?' he asked.

She turned to look at him, doubtful and ashamed. 'I'm not sure. We shouldn't have come here. It isn't fair to Froggie.'

'You don't love him,' he said. 'I know he married you – but if you'd told me. If you'd come to me. . . . '

'What would you have done?'

Meeting her challenging eyes, he was unable to answer at once. Then he frowned, saying, 'I would never have let Father put you in an asylum. You must have known that. I was ready to ask her for a divorce. You must believe me.' His voice was impassioned. 'I love you so much.'

Her heart jerked and she swayed towards him. Perhaps it had been her fault that their loving had seemed so sordid and empty. She remembered how often she had lain beside Froggie, wanting to be with this man, and she wavered.

'Perhaps I could come next week,' she said.

'Where have you been?' He took a big silver watch from his waistcoat pocket, his eyes like flint. 'I've been waiting for over an hour.'

Her heart lurched and she was suddenly frightened. Froggie had never looked at her like that. He knew! But that wasn't possible. He couldn't know. She'd been so careful not to let him guess that she was meeting someone. Her panic subsided a little.

'I've been shopping with Madeline.'

'Don't lie to me.' His eyes seemed to pierce her. 'Madeline was here a few minutes ago. She wondered if you were ill. She hasn't seen much of you recently.'

She turned away, fear striking her dumb. How could she have

been such a fool? What had she done? Why had she lied to him? It would have been easy to say she'd been shopping alone, but her guilt had betrayed her. She felt wretched. Soiled. Her mind was numbed. She could think of nothing to say . . . nothing that he would believe.

'You've been seeing him, haven't you?'

She didn't answer at once. The pain lanced through her and she wanted to curl up and die. How could she have betrayed him for a few minutes of physical pleasure? She was afraid to look at him. Ashamed. She hadn't meant to hurt him. She didn't want to hurt him. She loved him! The realization hit her as she turned and saw the agony in his eyes. She loved him. Guilt and regret twisted in her like the blade of a knife. She had been so selfish, so wrapped up in her own boredom that she hadn't thought what it must be like for him, working all day in an office and then coming home to study all night. It was no wonder that he was too tired to make love to her, and she hadn't helped him. She had lain stiffly beneath him, longing for something that no longer existed. Now, when it was too late, she knew that her love for Prince Charming had been an infatuation. She had made him a prince but now she knew that he was simply a rather selfish man.

'It's over,' she said. 'I promise you. I saw him three times, but I shan't see him again. I give you my word.'

He came towards her, and she was frightened by the look in his eyes. He was tormented. In Hell. She watched as he fought for control and in that moment she wished that he would strike out at her. She wanted him to hurt her. She wished she could die rather than see that look in his eyes. Then the agony gradually faded from his eyes and they went cold.

'Have I your promise that you won't see him again?'

'Yes.' She tried to put her heart into her eyes, willing him to see how sorry she was. 'Forgive me, Froggie. Please.'

'Don't call me that,' he said, and his voice almost cracked. 'I've a perfectly good name. Oblige me by using it.'

'Yes, Richard,' she whispered. 'I'm sorry. So very sorry.'

He looked at her for a moment longer and she saw his disappointment and hurt, then he nodded. 'So am I,' he said. 'So am I. . . . '

CHAPTER EIGHT

When the family were lunching informally, a cold buffet was laid in the breakfast room for twelve-thirty. I arrived one minute late to find both Prue and Lady Selina being served by Rosie.

'I'm not late, am I?'

'Please sit down, Kate.' I received a slight frown.

Rosie asked me what I wanted, then served me with cold chicken and potato salad. I ate in silence, listening to Prue's conversation with her mother.

'Helen said she would call for me on Monday. It's a pity you can't come, too, Mother.'

'I have guests for the weekend. You'll be perfectly happy with Helen.'

'I was thinking of you.'

'I want to take Kate shopping next week. It will give us time to get to know one another.'

Prue shot me a jealous look. 'Poor Mummy. I know how you love the theatres in town . . . and it's Ascot week.'

Sir Gerald came in then. 'Sorry to be late, m'dear.' He bent to kiss his wife's cheek but she turned away. 'Rosie, you may serve me the game pie, please.' He looked round the table. 'Has anyone seen Harry?'

'He went into Huntingdon,' Prue said.

'I wish he'd checked with me first. Old Reeder's been complaining about the roof of his barn, and that new stallion is being shod this afternoon. The brute is the very devil to control. I'd have liked Harry to be there.'

'You should have spoken to him this morning,' Lady Selina said frostily. 'Harry can't be expected to read your mind.'

'Of course not.'

She stood up. 'Excuse me; I have a headache.'

He frowned as she walked from the room. They seemed to have had some sort of a quarrel. I hoped it wasn't about me. He was silent for a moment, then smiled at Prue.

'So what are you going to do this afternoon?' His brows rose when she didn't answer. 'Why don't you take Kate round the gardens? You might even go down to the river.'

'I suppose we could.' She glanced at me uncertainly. 'If Kate wants to?'

'I'd like that – if you don't mind?'

'Of course she doesn't,' her father said. 'Whatever you do, don't go near the Folly. Harry says it's dangerous.'

I frowned, seeming to remember that Harry said his father had discovered the cracks in the wall.

'I shall have it locked,' Sir Gerald went on. 'It's not worth repairing. No one goes there.'

'Miss Grant does,' Prue said. 'I've seen her coming out.'

'And when was that?'

'Oh, weeks ago.'

'Well, in future, you're to stay away from there. Do you understand me?'

'Yes, sir.'

His frown lightened. 'So you're off to town then, miss? I suppose you've spent all your allowance this quarter?' He smiled indulgently as she nodded. 'Come and see me in the study before dinner and I'll see what I can do.'

Prue gave a cry of delight, jumped to her feet and ran round the table to embrace him. 'You spoil me, dearest Papa. Thank you so much.'

'Don't strangle me then.' His tone was gruff but he looked pleased.

It was obvious that he was fond of her. I was less sure about his relationship with his wife.

Perhaps because of her father's generosity, Prue was in a good mood as we set out for our walk. She talked animatedly about the coming visit to London, and what a wonderful time she was going to have with Helen.

'She's such good fun, and she knows all the best places to shop.' Prue sighed. 'Helen and Harry are the same age, you know. For years everyone expected them to marry, but last year she met Philip and they married almost at once.'

'He seems very fond of her.'

'He adores her.' Prue pulled a face. 'Anyone can see why he married her – but why did she marry him?'

'Perhaps she loves him.'

Prue shook her head. 'How could she? I expect it's because he's rich. Harry lives on the allowance Father gives him. He has Grand-father's trust, of course, but that's tied up until next year. Perhaps Helen didn't want to wait. Philip has bought her such beautiful. . . . Look at that, Kate! It must be the new stallion.'

A riderless horse was galloping wildly through the park. We watched as it disappeared from sight, staring at each other in dismay.

'What can have happened?'

Prue shook her head. 'No one but Harry can control the thing – Father's going to be furious.'

'Do you think anyone's hurt? Should we go and see?'

'It's only one of the grooms. It's nearly time for tea; I'm going back.'

'It came from the direction of the Folly. I'll walk a little way and investigate.'

'You'll be late.'

'Not if I run all the way back.'

'Please yourself, then.'

As Prue swung away, I began to walk swiftly in the direction from which the horse had come. I wasn't sure why I was bothering, but I suppose I was half afraid that I might find Harry unconscious or in pain. Prue said he'd gone into Huntingdon, but he might have returned and decided to visit the stables. In any case, I hated to think of anyone lying hurt after a fall. I walked hastily, looking for signs of an accident, but my search appeared to be a waste of time, just as Prue had said it would be.

The Folly was just ahead. Remembering Sir Gerald's warning, I hesitated to go nearer. As I stood wondering what to do next, the door of the Folly opened and a woman came out. She glanced about her in a rather furtive manner, then took a key from her pocket and locked the door. Instinctively, I drew back as she came towards me.

If the Folly was in a dangerous condition, what was Maggie Grant doing there – and how did she come to be in possession of the key?

I ran all the way back to the house. It was twenty minutes past the hour when I reached my room. I threw off my skirt and blouse, hastily pulling on the green dress. There was no time to do more than drag a brush through my hair and make a dash for the drawing room. I was one minute late. Prue was sitting on a little gilt sofa near the window, but Lady Selina hadn't arrived.

'Did you see anyone?' Prue asked. 'Father's furious. They caught the stallion eventually, but it has cut its leg and. . . . ' She broke off as we heard the sound of voices.

'I hold Harry responsible for this. If he'd been here where he should have. . . . '

'You're being unreasonable, Gerald.'

'Why did he have to go into Huntingdon this afternoon?'

'He probably has a perfectly good explanation. . . . '

They stopped talking as they saw us. Sir Gerald was clearly very angry. He stood by the fireplace, glowering at us all as the maids carried in the large silver tea-tray.

'If Patterson hadn't been so quick-thinking that horse could've damaged itself. We might have had to have it put down, and it would have cost a small fortune.'

'Well, it didn't happen,' Lady Selina said. 'Please calm yourself, Gerald.'

'You accuse me of being unreasonable – surely I've the right to expect some respect from my own son?' Sir Gerald grumbled on. 'He's so thoughtless.'

'I always find Harry extremely thoughtful.'

'Naturally, he would do anything for you. It's me he disregards. Sometimes I wonder how I ever fathered such a son!'

Lady Selina's face paled, and I noticed that her hand shook as she poured tea into a cup. 'So much fuss over a horse.'

'I've a great deal on my mind.' He shook his head as she offered the cup. 'Excuse me. I've business to attend to.'

Her eyes glinted with annoyance as he strode from the room. She was quiet and thoughtful and tea was soon over.

Dismissed, I made my way towards the governess's room, wondering if she'd returned yet. Should I warn her about the dangerous state of the Folly, or would she think I'd been spying on her if I said that I'd seen her there? I wondered why she wanted to go to such a gloomy place.

I knocked at Maggie's door, half expecting to be turned away, but it was opened promptly and I was invited to enter. She was clearly in a good mood, her skin glowing from the fresh air. She looked almost pretty.

'Did you enjoy your walk?' I asked.

She looked at me speculatively, then nodded. 'I won't ask how you knew I'd been walking – but yes, I did enjoy it very much.'

'You said you always walk after lunch.'

'So I did.' She smiled to herself. 'You don't forget anything, do you? I shall have to watch what I say to you. Shall we get on with our sewing?' She brought out a pile of mending. 'Lady Selina visited me this morning to ask if I was happy here. I told her I was and that I would be staying on until Miss Prue marries.'

'That's all right then, isn't it?'

'Yes.' Her eyes were bright with a secret amusement. 'I think perhaps it will be now.'

Once again I felt that there was more behind the meek façade that Maggie showed to the world than she wanted anyone to know, but I didn't ask any questions. She was entitled to her secrets.

After leaving the governess, I ran up to my own room. Maggie had given me several books to read and I was looking forward to some time alone before dinner. Throwing open the door of my bedroom, I gasped in surprise as I saw Harry standing by the dressing table. He was looking at a photograph of my mother.

'What are you doing?' I asked, a little annoyed that he should pry into my personal things.

'Waiting for you,' he replied easily. 'Your mother is a beautiful woman, Kate. You're very like her.'

'She is beautiful, isn't she?' I noticed some boxes on my bed. 'What are those?'

'Helen helped me choose so they should fit.' He laughed as I stared. 'Open them, then. It's a riding habit.'

I looked at him and then at the large brown box, hesitating. In my ignorance, I wasn't sure what a riding habit consisted of. Gingerly, I untied the strings, very much aware of Harry's amused eyes watching me as I lifted the layers of tissue inside. On the top was a plain white silk blouse with tiny pearls for buttons, and a matching stock edged with exquisite lace. I touched it reverently, lifting it out onto the bed. Next came a fitted jacket in a fine black wool; it was severely tailored and quite plain, but even to my inexperienced eyes it was clearly the creation of an expert. The matching skirt was equally well made but I was puzzled by the design. It appeared to divide at the back and I wasn't sure how it fastened.

'You wear these under it, Kate.'

He delved under the last layer of tissue and brought out a pair of softly fitting breeches. I gaped as he tossed them on the bed.

'Your boots, hat and gloves are in those boxes.' He pointed to more parcels. 'Everything should fit. . . . Why are you looking at me like that?'

94

'Why didn't you tell me?' I demanded. 'You let me make a fool of myself – that stupid wager and then this. You must have been laughing at me. I didn't know, Harry. I didn't know women wore trousers under the skirt.'

'Ah, but that's entirely different.' His eyes gleamed.

'You rotten beast!' I flew at him in sudden anger but he caught my wrists before I could hit him. 'I think I hate you.'

His laughter infuriated me and I struggled violently, trying to strike him. It was useless. He was so much stronger than I.

'Little vixen,' he said when I at last gave up. 'I wasn't laughing at your ignorance, Kate. Wearing men's breeches and riding astride is an entirely different thing. Mother would think it shocking, believe me. It's just as well you didn't do it. You won't need to now you've got the proper clothes. Besides, you're already getting the hang of it, though your style is awful.' His eyes sparkled. 'You haven't thanked me yet – and I went into Huntingdon especially. . . . '

'It was thoughtful of you,' I said, biting my lip. 'But you shouldn't have done it.'

'Why – don't you like them?'

'Everything is beautiful. . . . ' I stared at him. 'Haven't you heard what happened to the new stallion? Your father's so angry.'

'I came straight up here – what happened, then?'

I explained quickly and he frowned. 'So you see, your father blames you. . . . '

'He should've told me,' Harry said, annoyed. 'I'm supposed to be in charge of the stables. He shouldn't interfere.'

'Your mother said something similar to him.'

'Did she now?' His brows went up. 'That's unusual – it's normally the other way around.'

'What do you mean?'

Harry shook his head. 'It doesn't matter. I must go – but first I'll take my forfeit.'

'What kind of forfeit?' I was wary now.

Grinning, he picked up a pair of scissors from the dressing table. 'A lock of your hair. I'll take it from the back so that it doesn't show. Turn round and lift up your hair.'

I hesitated, then obeyed, gathering up the mass of my thick hair and holding it on top of my head. I waited, sensing his closeness. The unexpected touch of his lips on the tender skin at the nape of my neck made me jump. I jerked away, glancing back at him.

'Don't do that!'

'I couldn't resist it. Stand still and don't make so much fuss.' I felt the coldness of metal and heard a snipping sound. 'There, it's done. You can relax now.'

I stared at the strand of dark hair in his hand. 'What will you do with it?'

'Twist it into a little plait and put it somewhere safe, probably in my watch fob. Don't worry, Kate. No one will know.'

'I wasn't worrying. We've done nothing wrong.'

We hadn't, but even the fact that he was here in my room would be enough to arouse Lady Selina's censure.

He nodded, reading my mind. 'I'd better go before our luck runs out. I just wanted to give you the riding habit.'

As he turned to leave, I ran after him. Impulsively, I kissed his cheek. 'Thank you. It's the most beautiful thing I've ever owned,' I said hastily. 'I want to thank you, not just for the habit – but for bothering with me.'

'I wanted to apologize for what I said in the garden. I spoke too hastily. Please forgive me.'

'I already have,' I said. 'But it's nice when someone has the decency to say sorry. I – I'm sorry, too, Harry.'

He gazed down at me and I was shaken by the sudden blaze in his eyes. I felt breathless, uncertain and a little frightened. Then just as suddenly the look faded and he was laughing.

'You interest me, Kate. It's a pity I shan't see you in those breeches now.'

My chin went up. 'Our wager for tomorrow is still on. I'll learn to ride like a lady for you, Harry, but sometimes I want to ride the way you do.'

'It's a bargain,' he said. 'If you've the courage, I'll take you riding in the park tomorrow.'

'I'll be there,' I promised.

He smiled and went out. For a moment I stood unmoving, laughing inwardly. This battle between us was exhilarating. Then I turned back to the bed, lifting the silk blouse to drape it against my body. The material was so soft and tempting, I couldn't wait to try it on. Eagerly, I threw off my clothes, putting on the blouse, then the breeches and skirt, and finally the waist-hugging jacket. Remembering the boots and hat, I tore open the remaining parcels, hopping on one foot as I struggled with the long boots. At last I turned to the mirror, my transformation complete.

'Oh, Harry . . . ' I whispered in disbelief. 'What have you done to me?'

The young woman in the mirror stared back at me with haughty pride. She was tall, slender and elegant – it couldn't be me! It certainly wasn't the Kate Linton I knew.

I stared at myself for a long time before I took off the clothes and hung them carefully in the wardrobe. If the girl in the mirror wasn't me, who was she? Was I already beginning to change? Was I in danger of forgetting so soon? All at once a wave of grief swept over me. How could I take pleasure in my new clothes when somewhere my mother was alone and ill?

I flung myself down on the bed and began to weep.

That night I had a terrible dream. I saw my mother lying on a bed in a filthy little room, the sheets and pillowcases stained with blood. She was coughing and choking as she cried my name.

I started up, waking from the nightmare with sweat soaking my body. It had been so real! For a moment I lay shivering, frightened and miserable. What was I doing in this house? I should be with my mother, wherever she was.

I knew it would be ages before I could sleep, and I got out of bed, shrugging on a warm robe as I wandered over to the window and pulled back the curtains. It was a bright, moonlit night. Everything looked silver, even the grass and the branches of the trees. I was tempted to go out into the gardens. It was mild and a walk might clear my head of those terrible pictures. Just as I was about to turn away, I saw two figures emerge from the shrubbery. They stood for a moment in the moonlight embracing, looking like a marble statue turned to silver. Then they parted and the woman ran across the lawns towards the house; the man went back into the shrubberies. I could see neither of them clearly enough to be sure of their identities, but I thought it must have been one of the maids with a lover.

Clearly it had been a clandestine meeting. Lady Selina would be strict about such things, and if she guessed what was going on, the girl would be dismissed. I was glad I hadn't seen exactly who it was. The prospect of a walk no longer appealed. I drew my curtains and went back to bed.

I was still asleep when Rosie came to wake me. I yawned and stretched, feeling heavy-eyed as I got out of bed.

'These should fit you,' she said, laying a pair of freshly laundered riding breeches on the bed. 'But I'm afraid Rob's jackets are worn out.'

'All I need is the breeches,' I said.

'I thought perhaps you were going to hide your hair under a cap and hope to pass for a boy?'

'I hadn't thought of that. Anyway, I haven't got a man's cap or a jacket, so I'll have to go as I am.'

'Are you sure you want to do this? Wouldn't you rather wear that lovely habit Mr Harry bought you?'

I looked at the clothes hanging in the wardrobe as Rosie opened the door temptingly, then shook my head. 'Harry's promised to let me ride the way he does if I wear these. So I'm going to, even if it's only this once.'

'Let's hope Lady Selina doesn't see you.'

'She can't kill me, can she?' I asked with an air of bravado. 'It's a wager, Rosie. I have to risk it. Besides, it will be fun.'

'She might stop you having riding lessons.'

'She wouldn't!' I stared at Rosie in horror. 'She would, though, wouldn't she? You'd better keep your fingers crossed for me.'

'If I were you, I'd use the servants' entrance at the back. She's not likely to see you then — nor are any of the others.'

'Clever you,' I cried, laughing. 'Wish me luck.'

'Hurry, before someone catches you,' she said. 'I'll make sure no one is about.' She looked out into the hall. 'Run for it, Miss Kate!'

Giggling, I scampered down the passage and the back stairs. It was a great adventure. I felt terribly daring in my breeches, which fitted me like a glove. I wasn't the first woman ever to wear them, but Lady Selina would consider it very shocking. She might believe that women were entitled to the vote, but she was strict in all matters of etiquette, and she'd made no secret of the fact that she disapproved of the bold young women who had begun smashing windows in Piccadilly in the name of their cause.

'They go too far,' she'd said recently. 'Women should behave decently even in the face of provocation.'

What would she say to my breeches, then?

My heart was in my mouth as I made my escape, running across the back courtyard to the stables as fast as I could. The early morning air was crisp but not cold, and already I could tell that it was going to be a beautiful day. I was out of breath when I reached the row of red brick stables, my heart thumping. Although it was early, there was an air of activity, with stable lads busy at their tasks. I stopped

98

suddenly as I saw Harry talking to a groom, my courage almost failing me as I wondered what he would think of me. I stood hesitant, poised for flight, when Harry seemed to realize I was there and swung round to look at me. He stared long and hard, that sudden blaze of fire in his eyes again. I felt shy and awkward, wanting the anonymity of my skirts and wishing I could disappear through the floor. Then he smiled and came towards me.

'You look wonderful, Kate,' he said. 'If only people realized how sensible it is, other women would soon follow your example.'

'You don't think I'm terribly wicked, then? Rosie nearly had a fit.'

'I don't care if you're wicked or not.' He took my hand and led me forward. 'I brought you a jacket and cap. The jacket may be a little too big, but I think you should wear it. Ned here is in our little secret, but we don't want anyone running to Mother with tales, do we? Here, let me help you.' He held the jacket for me. 'Now put the cap on. Tuck your hair up.'

I did as I was told and his eyes went over me critically. 'She makes a good stable lad, don't you think so, Ned?'

The groom nodded, carefully controlling the grin that was trying to break through. 'The image of my young brother, I'd say, sir.'

'And you'd better swear to it if anyone asks,' Harry warned, turning to me with a satisfied nod. 'You'll pass muster from a distance – and if anyone tries to get a closer look, run for it. Do you hear, Kate?'

'I'll remember,' I promised. 'Let's go. You said we could ride in the park today.'

'Impatient miss,' he replied. 'Ned's saddling Rustic for you.'

'Is something wrong with Firefly?'

'You'll ride her when you use the side-saddle. It will only confuse her if you chop and change.'

I glanced up, eyes bright. 'So you'll let me ride this way again?'

'Providing you work at riding properly – and that you don't get caught.'

'I'm going to sneak in and out the back way.'

'Little minx! If I didn't find this amusing, I'd tell Mother to give you a birching.'

'You wouldn't really – would you?' I asked doubtfully.

'Good lord! What do you think I am?'

'I'm never sure when you're joking.'

He towered over me, his face grim. 'If ever I'm angry with you, you'll know it.'

'Then I'll just have to be careful, won't I?'

There was a letter beside my breakfast plate. I seized it at once, my heart racing as I recognized the writing. I read it swiftly, then popped it into my pocket. I would read it more carefully later.

'A letter from your mother?' Lady Selina asked.

'Yes.' I smiled. 'She's on her way to Devon and she says she feels a little better.'

'Good.' She nodded her satisfaction. 'Did you enjoy your ride?'

'Yes, thank you.' My heart pounded – was she about to denounce me as a brazen hussy for wearing breeches? I'd thought I'd got away with it.

She glanced at Harry, frowning, and then at me. 'My son tells me he has provided you with a habit. I'd intended to look one out for you until something could be arranged.'

'It was very kind of Harry.'

'Yes – though I understand Helen did most of the work. You must write and thank her, Kate.'

'She's asked Kate to lunch today,' Harry said, surprising me. 'She wants to get to know her.'

'I have guests for lunch myself, Harry.'

'Surely it can't matter if Kate is there or not?' Harry smiled persuasively. 'Helen is looking forward to it.'

Lady Selina sighed. 'Kate can meet my friends another day. You may ask Miss Grant to excuse you early, Kate. Prunella, I shall want you promptly in the dining room at twelve-thirty.'

Harry winked at me as his mother left the room. 'Well, that's got you out of that, Kate. It's some of Mother's suffragette friends – those old harridans scare the life out of me.'

'Trust you to get out of it,' Prue said resentfully. 'I think you're very rude about Mother's friends. Actually, some of them are young and pretty – and brave.'

'If you think it's brave to smash shop windows and get yourself thrown in prison, then I think you're mad.' Harry snorted. 'It's all a load of nonsense. Give women the vote and you're asking for trouble.'

'You're an arrogant beast,' Prue cried. 'No wonder Helen preferred Philip.'

I saw a flicker of something in Harry's eyes. 'Leave Helen out of this,' he muttered. 'Sometimes I despair of you, Prue. I pity the poor man who marries you – if anyone can be persuaded into it. . . . '

100

'Oh, leave her alone, Harry,' I said, as I saw the miserable flush in her cheeks. 'I know you're only teasing, but Prue doesn't like it.'

'I don't need you to defend me,' she shouted, then jumped up and ran from the room.

'Take no notice of her,' Harry said. 'She's just jealous because you've been invited to Helen's and she hasn't.'

'Perhaps I shouldn't go, then.'

'I arranged this with Helen – and I don't want my sister along.' Harry frowned as his father came in. 'I'll be waiting at twelve sharp. If you're not there I'll go without you.'

'Harry,' Sir Gerald said. 'I'd like a word later.'

'I'll be at the stables, sir.'

Sir Gerald frowned as his son walked by, then looked at me. 'Everyone's in a mood this morning. You'll stay and have a cup of tea with me, Kate?'

'Yes, of course,' I said. 'I'm going to lunch with Helen Forrest today – and I've had a letter from my mother.'

'That's good news.' He smiled at me, seeming in a sunny humour himself. 'I want you to enjoy yourself here, Kate. I was saying to Selina that as she's going to miss Ascot this year, we ought to take a little trip up to London soon. Just to do some shopping and visit a few friends – would you like that?'

'It sounds wonderful, sir.'

'Then we'll see,' he said, heaping bacon, eggs and mushrooms on to his plate. 'Now tell me how you're getting on with your riding. . . .'

Harry was waiting for me when I arrived at five minutes before twelve. He looked at me approvingly and opened the door of Sir Gerald's Daimler.

'Next time I'll take you for a spin in one of my cars,' he said, grinning.

I laughed as I saw the sparkle in his eyes. He'd already told me about his collection of marques that dated from the early 1860's, including one of the first Peugeots, a Bugatti and an Adams V-8 phaeton. Restoring automobiles that had fallen into disrepair was one of his hobbies and he'd discovered many of his finds rusting in barns.

'I'll look forward to that,' I said and laughed. 'I think. . . . '

'Prue's been talking, I see. Don't worry, Kate. I'll drive carefully today. Father was in a good mood this morning. I don't want to upset him again by pranging his car.'

We laughed together. It was a lovely sunny day, and I enjoyed the drive along country roads that were bright with summer greenery. The hedges had white blossom and the horse chestnuts were still in flower. I was excited at being in the car with Harry, and looking forward to meeting his friend again. The countryside was fairly flat with a slight rise here and there, villages tucked into the hollows; stands of trees broke the flatness and isolated cottages or farms appeared out of nowhere. Huge black crows flew up from the side of the road as we passed, and a hare went bounding across a field.

Helen lived in Earith in a pretty Queen Anne house set back in extensive gardens and hidden from the road by trees. We drove up a long, sheltered approach, stopping in front of the stone terraces bordered with roses and clumps of pinks. Helen came out on to the steps to greet us, wearing a dress of some filmy material that clung seductively to her hips as she walked towards us, her waist nipped in so tightly that it gave her a perfect hour-glass figure. Her hair was swept up into a froth of curls over her brow and she looked beautiful and elegant. She kissed both Harry and me on the cheek before taking us inside.

'It was sweet of you to keep me company today, Kate,' she said, tucking her arm through mine. 'Philip went into Huntingdon on business and I hate being alone.'

'I'm glad you asked me.' I glanced round the elegant room we had entered, struck by the soft pinks and greens of the décor and the pretty furniture, much of which was inlaid with pale yellow woods in designs of birds, musical instruments and flowers. 'Oh, what a lovely room!'

'Yes, most of the furniture is French,' Helen said, pleased. 'Philip gave me *carte blance* when we married. I'm afraid I was rather extravagant.' She laughed, unrepentant. 'Help yourself to a drink, Harry, while I take Kate upstairs.'

She took me to her bedroom. It was equally as luxurious as the rooms downstairs. The wardrobes were of polished walnut with ormolu mountings and large mirrors, and stretched the length of one wall. Her dressing table was strewn with silver-topped pots and brushes, and there were fluffy white rugs scattered on a soft green carpet.

Helen patted her immaculate hair in front of the mirror. 'The bathroom is through there, Kate. Help yourself to my scent if you like.'

'Thank you.' I smiled at her. 'I thought my room at Brockmere was pretty – but this is all so beautiful.'

'Yes, I'm very lucky. I'll leave you. You can find your own way back, can't you?'

I assured her that I could. Helen's house was lovely but nowhere near as big as Brockmere.

After she'd gone, I went to the bathroom, combed my hair and sprayed myself liberally with her perfume. It was rather strong and I coughed as I replaced the cut-glass bottle. Satisfied with my appearance, I went downstairs.

The door of Helen's drawing room was open. I halted abruptly as I saw the couple embracing by the window. Helen had her arms around Harry's neck and they were kissing passionately. I drew back so that I could not see them, my cheeks flushed with embarrassment. I felt a fierce surge of anger against Harry. How could he? How could he kiss another man's wife? Closing my eyes, I counted to thirty then cleared my throat. When I entered the room, Harry was standing by the fireplace and Helen was pouring sherry from a decanter.

'Would you like a drink, Kate?' she asked, turning to smile at me. I thought her eyes looked red, as though she'd been crying.

'May I have just a small one?' I said, trying desperately to hide my feelings. 'I hope I wasn't too long upstairs?'

'Of course not. I was just saying to Harry that it's a pity you can't come with us next week.'

'Mother wouldn't agree,' Harry said. 'Kate hasn't anything to wear yet. Besides, we're all going up in a few weeks time.'

'It was just a suggestion.' She shrugged her shoulders. 'Shall we have lunch?'

Harry stopped the car at the side of the road and turned to look at me, his brows knitted in a frown.

'You saw, didn't you?' he said. 'I know because of the way you've been behaving ever since.'

I couldn't meet his eyes. 'I don't know what you mean.'

'Yes, you do. I hate liars, Kate, so don't pretend. You saw me kissing Helen, didn't you?'

'Yes.' I bit my lip. 'It's nothing to do with me.'

'No, it isn't, but it wasn't what you thought, so don't sulk. Helen was feeling low because she'd had a row with Philip. I tried to comfort her and it went too far.'

'You don't have to explain to me.'

'I didn't want you thinking I'd only taken you there so I could make love to Philip's wife.' He glared at me as I was silent. 'I'm not a saint. I've had affairs with women, and most of them were married – but it meant nothing to them or me. When you're older, you'll understand.'

'I'm not a child.'

'Then don't act like one.' He looked annoyed. 'It happens a lot in our circles, Kate. I'm not excusing myself, but I've never – well, I was never in any danger of ruining a marriage.'

I stared at him, feeling shocked and indignant. I was reminded of a similar conversation with Paul de Bernay when he'd taken me home from Mrs Madison's in his car. Paul had accused me of being a child just because I didn't like him kissing me. And now Harry was talking as though that kiss he'd given Helen was something that didn't matter. Well, it did to me! He might be used to such behaviour, but I certainly wasn't. Where I'd come from decent women had high moral standards, and they didn't conduct their affairs behind their husbands' backs. In our little community, women were either respectable – or the other kind. I liked Helen and witnessing her fall from grace had made me uncomfortable. I avoided looking at Harry as I said, 'Philip adores Helen.'

'It was just a kiss on the spur of the moment. It hasn't gone any further and it won't. I rather like old Philip.'

'You don't have to tell me all this.'

'No, I don't,' he said. 'And if you're going to behave like a silly child, I shall treat you like one. If you want to live with us, you have to accept us as we are.'

'Don't go on about it,' I said, glaring at him. 'I know these things happen. I just don't want to think about it.'

'Then we'll forget it,' he said, and started the car again.

Relations were strained between us for a couple of days, and then I forgot it. I was beginning to enjoy myself at Brockmere. My heart ached when I thought of my mother, and that was every day, but my time was filled to capacity. I had my riding and the lessons with Maggie, and after that I took walks in the park. When there were guests in the afternoons, I was often invited to play tennis or croquet. I wasn't very good at either of them, and so Harry started coaching me whenever he had the time, though he was busy too.

Besides being an expert horseman, Harry had a passion for automobiles. He drove them fast and he had a racing model that he sometimes took down to Brooklands. His main task was the care of the stables and the breeding mares. Sir Gerald had a reputation for good horses, and he liked to race them at Newmarket and Ascot. He and Harry always seemed to be in a discussions about mares, foals and bloodlines. Whenever Harry wasn't involved with the horses or dealing with the complaints of various tenants, he could be found lying flat on his back tinkering with one of his beloved cars.

Once I'd discovered that he was mostly at the barn that housed his collection in the early afternoon, I developed the habit of walking that way so that I could watch him. Sometimes, if he was in a good mood, he would crawl out from under whichever car he was working on and talk to me. Thus I learned the various names of the automobiles, and a great deal about Harry.

While Prue was in London, Sir Gerald and Harry went up to Ascot to watch one of their horses race and Lady Selina took me into St Ives; it was a pretty, ancient town that had stood at the river crossing since medieval times. From the quaint, narrow bridge we could see the quayside and the wide, sweeping bend of the river. Here, I was told, the local sportsmen were often to be seen in long rowing boats, competing in a regatta or simply indulging in a popular pastime. Monday was market day, and we had deliberately chosen a quieter day, but the town was still busy, the streets thronged with wagons, horses and the occasional car.

We spent the whole day there, talking to friends Lady Selina chanced to meet, gazing into the shop windows and debating what to buy. We had lunch at the Crown Inn. After that, we called in at a little grocer's shop to leave an order for six tins of Palmer's biscuits and a supply of Hudson's best tea that had somehow failed to be delivered with our usual order; then Lady Selina said it was time to buy my new clothes.

There was a small dress shop near the old clock tower in Bridge Street that she had patronized before, and there we bought nine dresses: three very simple ones for mornings, three elegant tea-gowns, and three evening dresses. We also bought shoes, hats, underwear, silk stockings, and a white cotton skirt and loose top with a sailor collar for playing tennis, that we were assured was the latest thing. The annual lawn tennis championships were soon to be held at Wimbledon in London, and Brockmere always had its own tennis parties at the same time.

'You can play, I hope?' Lady Selina asked.

'Not very well, I'm afraid,' I replied. 'But I can learn.'

She nodded, frowning slightly. 'Perhaps Harry will teach you. He really ought to take the game more seriously; he's very good at it – but Harry never takes anything seriously.'

'It was kind of you to buy me all these clothes,' I said, avoiding her eyes. The back of the car was piled high with parcels. 'I've never owned so many dresses!'

'These will do until you're properly out,' she replied. 'The styles are a little provincial, of course, but the material is good.'

When Prue returned from London, she brought back a trunkful of new clothes. She took me to her room to show me, but I wasn't jealous. I was satisfied with my new wardrobe, even though the dresses were much plainer than Prue's. Besides, Harry approved of what I'd chosen and that was all that mattered to me.

I'd had another letter from my mother. She said that the sea air had done her good and she might be going abroad for a holiday. A friend had lent her some money and she was going to travel, so I wasn't to be anxious if I didn't hear from her for a while.

'I'll be thinking of you,' she'd written. 'And I'll be happy imagining all the wonderful things you must be doing. I know there will be lots of parties, so you must just enjoy yourself and not worry about me. I'm really feeling very much better. All my love, dearest. Your loving mother.'

I wondered who could have lent her the money. Could it be Sir Gerald after all, or perhaps Eric Potter. His manner had been a bit strange when he drove me to the station. I remembered thinking that he was angry with Mother, but perhaps I'd been mistaken. She'd once told me she would go to him if she were ever in trouble.

I tied her letters in blue ribbon and put them in a drawer. I could read them whenever I was feeling homesick.

CHAPTER NINE

She lay in the darkness beside her husband, wakeful as he slept. Surely it couldn't be true. She had always been so regular. . . . Oh, please don't let it be true! It would mean that she would never be certain. She would never know for sure. . . .

Richard had made love to her two nights before she met the other one. Since his discovery of her betrayal, he had not touched her once. She wondered if he ever would again. She had hurt him so badly. He hardly spoke to her these days unless it was absolutely necessary, and he never smiled. It was like living with a stranger. Sometimes she could hardly bear it and she longed for the return of the old Froggie. How could she have been such a fool!

She would have to tell him soon. Supposing he was angry? Supposing he threw her out? She could find work if necessary, but she wanted to be with him. She wanted him to love her.

Turning towards him, she put her arms around him, beginning to kiss his neck, then sliding down the bed to kiss and lick his body, willing him to wake up. He stirred and she felt him stiffen, but he made no attempt to stop her as she continued to arouse him. She felt him grow hard beneath her teasing lips and took him into her mouth, sucking delicately and licking the soft tip until he groaned.

Without speaking, he rolled her beneath him in the bed, taking her fiercely and in silence. For the first time he awoke an answering response in her, making her cry out as she climaxed beneath him.

Afterwards, as he left her, she tried to hold him to her. 'That was wonderful,' she whispered.

'Go to sleep,' he said coldly, and turned over on his side.

She lay with the tears on her cheeks, making no sound as she stared into the darkness once more. She had lost him. He still wanted her but he didn't love her.

Richard looked at the tiny scrap of humanity in the cradle and a surge of love entered the heart he'd thought was dead. She was a miniature version of the woman he had adored, but she was innocent. She hadn't lied to him and deceived him.

His eyes moved to the woman in the bed. Her hair was spread on

107

the pillow. Streaked with sweat and tangled, it was still that glorious chestnut brown he had first admired. She was still the woman he had fallen in love with, the woman who had broken his heart. And she had almost died giving birth to this child. He'd held her hands while she writhed in agony, giving her the strength to endure the long hours of pain. He felt the ice cracking around his heart and some of his own pain was washed away in the flood of emotion. He would never again adore her blindly, but he still cared for the woman she was. Sitting beside her on the bed, he reached for her hand and smiled. Her fingers curled about his gratefully, and she summoned a weak smile.

'Richard?'

'Yes?'

'She's beautiful, isn't she? Your daughter . . . '

'Is she mine?' There was no bitterness, no accusation in his voice. It was merely a question.

'Of course she is. I swear it.'

'You wouldn't lie to me?'

'I swear it on her life – on my own.'

'Then I believe you.' He bent to kiss her lips, then, turning to the crib, he took the child in his arms. 'What shall we call her?'

'You choose.' She watched from the bed, saw the tenderness in his face and a tear slid from the corner of her eye as she realized how much she had lost. Richard had once loved her like that, but her betrayal had killed something in him. A surge of regret went through her. She would give anything to turn back the clock and start again, but it was too late.

Richard glanced at his wife. Was she lying about the child being his? Would he ever be sure? Did it really matter? The child was his by right and already he adored her. His life had a new purpose and he knew just what he was going to call her . . .

'What's the matter with your neck, Richard?' She saw him run his finger beneath his starched collar and wince. 'Is something bothering you?'

'It's just a little boil,' he said, dismissing her concern. It had been irritating him for a few days now. He pushed his plate away, annoyed with himself for letting it get on top of him. He had too much to do to be hampered by such a small thing. 'I'm not hungry this evening. I think I'll sit quietly for a while and then go to bed early.'

'Let me look at it for you.' She got up and came round the table, noticing with surprise the flushed look in his face. 'Should I fetch a doctor? Do you feel ill?'

'Fetch a doctor for a little boil on the neck?' He smiled and shook his head. 'Why waste the money? I expect I'm just tired. I'll be better in the morning.'

She looked at him anxiously. It wasn't like Richard to give in to illness. He went to work whether he had colds or not. If he wasn't any better, she would get the doctor in the morning.

Waking in the night, she heard Richard moaning and calling out. She lit a candle and bent over him, shocked as she saw that he was delirious. Placing a hand on his brow, she discovered that he was burning up with a fever. She got out of bed, going to the washstand to pour cool water into a bowl.

The sponging seemed to ease him for a while. He quietened and slept. She was relieved but she didn't return to bed. It would soon be morning. She might as well get ahead with the washing. Going downstairs, she lit the fire under the copper and put some sheets in to boil, then she woke her daughter, gave her some milk and went back up to Richard. As she reached their bedroom, she heard him cry out. He was tossing and turning, throwing off the bedclothes in his restlessness.

Hurrying downstairs, she scooped the child up in her arms and took her across the road to a neighbour, then she ran all the way to the doctor's house, her heart beating wildly. Richard was really ill. The boil on his neck was oozing yellow pus and smelt dreadful. It had obviously become infected and must have been that way for some time. Richard had just refused to give in to the pain.

'Oh, God,' she prayed as she pounded on the doctor's door. 'Please don't let him die. I swear I'll never complain of being bored or poor again. I swear I'll never grumble about anything ever again, if only he lives. . . . '

If Richard died she couldn't bear it. She loved him. She loved him so much, and she had never told him.

She was dressed in black from head to toe, a little veil over her face to hide the ravages of her tears – those hard, soul-destroying, useless tears she'd shed beside her husband's coffin before they took him away. Now he was buried six feet under the soft black earth and she would never see him again, never hear his voice, never feel the touch of his hand.

Staring out of the window, she saw that it was raining. How bleak and cold the world looked to her now, how empty without her dearest Richard. She'd really lost him long ago, she thought, before the child was born. It had never been the same between them after she. . . . Her thoughts brought such pain that she gave a little cry.

'Richard! Why did you have to die?' A sob broke from her. 'I was winning you back. I was . . . I was. . . . '

She heard the child crying in its cot, and her eyes closed to prevent her own tears. If Richard had begun to come back to her, it was because of his love for their child . . . hers and Richard's. . . . At least he'd died believing that. He had believed it. She couldn't bear to think that he had doubted it, because his little girl meant so much to him. And she wanted the child to be his.

What a fool she had been. She had thrown away true love for a stupid dream. Anger throbbed in her, making her want to strike out at something. Prince Charming had feet of clay; he made empty promises that he never kept. She wouldn't go to him or his family for help. She would find a way of making her own living. She would go away somewhere, find a little house she could afford to rent. . . .

'Oh, Richard.' She blinked away her tears. 'I hate being alone. Why did you have to leave me? A boil on the neck. A stupid little boil! How could you die of it? How could you?'

It had been blood poisoning of course, and the doctors were helpless against it. He had died hard and in pain. The memory of his last hours was like a stone in her heart. At the end she had simply held him in her arms, trying to ease him.

Now, hearing the child's cries again, she sighed. She wasn't alone. She had a child to care for. Two mouths to feed instead of one. . . .

'Four shillings a week, you say?' She looked at the terraced cottage, her heart sinking at the sight of the communal yard and the washing flapping on a rope line. Had it really come to this? Had she sunk so low? 'Let me think about it for a while. I'm not sure if it's what I want.'

'Well, don't take too long. There's plenty of others who won't turn up their noses.' The landlord stared at her hard. 'I'm doing you a favour, and that's a fact.'

It had come as a shock to learn that Richard was in debt. She'd had to sell all his books, his silver watch and chain and even his clothes to pay the funeral expenses. Most of the furniture had gone, too.

In her desperation she'd written to the Demon King, asking for help. Her letter had been returned unopened. Her pride wouldn't let her approach Him. Prince Charming. She believed that to him she had just been a pleasant diversion. He hadn't even called or written to say that he was sorry about Richard's death. She hadn't seen him since the day Richard made her promise not to. She was angry and bitter, and in her heart she blamed him. He hadn't been a prince at all. Her dearest Frog had been the prince all the time, and she'd been too blind to see it.

Tears stung her eyes but she dashed them away. Crying wouldn't help her. It never had, not even when she was a child. She'd always been alone – except for the brief time that she'd been with Richard – and she would manage. Pride made her lift her head. She wasn't going to pity herself. She'd had a little time of happiness and now she had her child.

This place wasn't so bad. Looking out of the parlour window into the lane, she saw that the houses opposite were draped with black flags as a mark of respect for Queen Victoria, who had recently passed away. At least the people were decent and honest, and the cottage could be made respectable. It would do until she could find somewhere better.

And she would! One day she would have all the things she'd always longed for. Pretty clothes that she hadn't made herself, jewels, furs and a beautiful house. Yes, she would have them one day, but for now this would have to do. She smiled at the sour-faced landlord.

'I've made up my mind – when can I move in?'

CHAPTER TEN

At Wimbledon that year, Dorothea Chambers beat Slocock McNair in the ladies' finals, and at Brockmere Harry and Helen Forrest emerged as the winners of all their matches. They stood with their arms about each other's waists to have their photograph taken with the small silver trophy presented by Sir Gerald. Watching them together, I couldn't help remembering that passionate kiss I'd witnessed, but there was nothing lover-like in their behaviour and Philip didn't seem in the least jealous – so perhaps I'd made too much of it.

When the guests had gone, it was decided we should all go up to town. My first visit to London was so exciting. It was mid-July and the weather was perfect for exploring. I loved the hustle and bustle of the busy streets, and I walked as often as possible, eager to see as many of the sights as I could: Westminster, the Tower and Buckingham Palace were first on my list, closely followed by the Zoological Gardens in Regent's Park, Madame Tussaud's, Kew Gardens and the State Apartments at Kensington Palace. Lady Selina had decreed that I couldn't attend the theatre or the evening parties given by her friends, but there was so much to see and do during the day that I was too exhausted to want to do anything more than retire early with a book. It was usually Harry who took me on these pleasure trips, spending hours hiding his yawns as I dragged him to endless museums and art galleries. Sometimes we walked in the parks or took a trip on the river, but often we simply wandered about the city, discovering something new on every corner.

'London is so beautiful,' I said as we strolled along the Victoria Embankment. I looked at the swirling columns of the lampposts and the carved stone lions' heads, swinging round to laugh up at Harry. 'There's so much to see and do – and we're going home tomorrow.'

'And you call me impatient,' he said, smiling indulgently. 'You'll come back next year and then you'll be really busy – out to parties morning, noon and night.'

'I'm not sure I'll enjoy that as much as I've enjoyed being with you.'

'You'll have so many admirers that you'll forget all about me.'

'No, I shan't.' I pulled a face at him. 'What you mean is that you'll have more time to spend at your club or. . . . '

'Or what?' He frowned as I shook my head. 'Or have affairs with married women, is that it, Kate?'

'It's none of my business.'

'You're damned right it isn't – but for your information, I don't have half a dozen light o'loves, or even a mistress.' He grabbed my arm, forcing me across the road in front of a heavy dray cart. The driver swore and shook his fist at us, but Harry ignored him. He stopped outside a tobacconist's shop. 'I want to buy something here. They sell Passing Cloud cigarettes and you can't get them at home; they're Father's favourites. I'll order a dozen boxes for his birthday. You needn't come in, Kate. Stay here in the doorway, and don't go wandering off. I'll only be a few minutes.'

Annoyed by his tone, I began to wander up the street as soon as he disappeared into the dark interior of the shop. I was brooding about something Harry had said earlier, and I stared at the elegantly-dressed woman who had just come out of an exclusive gown emporium for several seconds before I realized who it was. A shock ran through me and I was stunned by sheer disbelief. For a moment I couldn't move, then I saw she was about to get into the back of a chauffeur-driven car and I jerked suddenly into action.

'Mother!' I yelled. 'Please wait! It's me, Kate!'

Shoppers passing by gave me odd looks as I began to wave both hands above my head and run towards the woman, still calling out at the top of my voice. She turned to look at me and I saw her face clearly. I was certain it was my mother, but looking younger and more beautiful than I'd ever seen her. I waved again, excitement making my heart thump wildly. She had to see me. She had to! She looked at me, hesitated and then got into the car. It drove off as I reached the spot where she'd been standing a moment ago. Her head was turned away, the large hat she was wearing preventing me from getting a closer look at her face, but I didn't need to. There was no doubt in my mind that it had been my mother.

Disappointment swept over me. I was overcome with emotion, and I began to cry. I stood in the middle of the busy pavement, tears rolling silently down my cheeks. Then I felt someone grip my arm and I turned to Harry with a sob, throwing myself against his chest. He held me tightly for a moment, then gave me a little shake.

'What's the matter, Kate? Why did you go charging off like that?'

I lifted my tearful face to gaze up at him. 'I saw her, Harry. It was my mother. She came out of that dress shop and drove away in a big black car.'

'Are you sure? That's a very expensive shop, Kate. They sell what look like Paul Poiret evening designs – look at that ridiculous hobble skirt in the window!'

'It was her,' I said, ignoring his attempt to divert my thoughts but accepting his handkerchief. 'She saw me but she wouldn't wait. She just got in the car and drove off.'

'Either it wasn't her or she didn't see you.' Harry frowned. 'Think about it sensibly. She isn't well and she doesn't have much money. Is it likely that she would be shopping at an exclusive store in London? It was someone who resembled your mother, Kate. That's why she didn't stop to speak to you. She was probably embarrassed.'

'I know it was her. I'm going to ask inside.'

'You're in too much of a state. Leave it to me. Just wait here while I inquire – and don't go running off again.'

I waited while he went inside the shop. I was certain I had seen my mother, no matter what anyone said. Harry was out again within a few minutes. He shook his head as I went to him eagerly.

'They don't know a Mrs Emma Linton,' he said. 'The only client to leave within the last twenty minutes was a Frenchwoman. You must have been mistaken.'

'Are you sure?'

'Of course. You don't think I'd lie to you?'

I glanced up at him, seeing the annoyance in his face. 'No, I don't. I'm sorry, Harry – but I was so sure.'

He smiled and took my hand to squeeze it gently. 'She looked like your mother, Kate. Because you were so desperate to see Emma, you saw what you wanted to see.'

'Yes, I suppose so.' I bit my lip. 'It's like having a nightmare while you're awake.'

'Have you had nightmares about her?'

'Only one.' I gazed up at him. 'I think about her all the time, Harry. I can't forget.'

'That's only natural.' He smiled understandingly. 'Come on, I want to buy you a present – what shall it be?'

'You don't have to buy me anything.'

'No, but I want to.' He tucked my arm through his. 'We'll go to Liberty. I saw some pretty Art Nouveau trinkets there the other day.'

'What would I do without you?' I asked, giving him a watery smile.

He flicked my cheek with his finger. 'Well, someone has to look after you . . . '

The visit to London over, life fell into its gentle pattern at Brockmere once more. Almost every week there were house guests, especially during the shooting season. Harry was busy then, organizing the shoots and looking after the guests. Most of the men brought their wives with them; I couldn't help noticing that there was a certain amount of whispering going on and a few clandestine meetings. When I asked her, Rosie admitted that she sometimes saw a gentleman sneaking furtively along the passage to the room of another man's wife.

'After tea is the time they seem to like best,' she said. 'But we're not supposed to notice – so don't you let on I've told you.'

'Of course not.' I wrinkled my brow at her. 'Why do they do it, Rosie? I thought you got married because you loved someone?'

Rosie laughed. 'Not this lot. It's more likely to be a beneficial arrangement – a title for money, if you see what I mean. One or two of them probably did care about each other once – and they have their own rules. No messing about until the wife has provided a son and heir. That's the worst thing a wife can do, to present her husband with a bastard before the succession is secured. That's a crime punishable by death.' She winked at me as she went out.

I wasn't sure whether to believe all she said or not. I remembered the passionate kiss I'd witnessed in Helen's sitting room and wondered. One evening I went into the library to find a book to take up with me and found Harry and the wife of one of the guests in what looked to me like an intimate situation. I apologized and withdrew quickly. The next day Harry was moody and hardly spoke to me when we went riding. I thought he was angry with me for intruding and I tried to tell him I was sorry, but he cut me off abruptly.

'You're too young to understand,' he said.

I was hurt, but the next day his mood had gone and he was his normal self, teasing me in the lordly manner he always used towards me.

And so the autumn passed and the mornings became more chilly. In Germany the world's largest airship had exploded with the loss of all life on board; at Brooklands thousands of people watched a French pilot loop-the-loop, and Lady Selina lost her temper when she read about Almoth Wright's anti-women's suffrage book. But for me life centred on my riding lessons with Harry. I was slowly making progress, and I was learning what was expected of me in the Redfern's household. The rules might be relaxed for married women, but for young girls like me they were very strict. I was expected to behave correctly at all times, and whenever we went on the river or played games, there had to be a group of us together. The only man I was ever alone with was Harry, because he was almost like a brother. I'd become quite popular with the young men who came to stay, and I was no longer as shy of the guests, holding my own in the sharp, sometimes slightly malicious exchanges at tea.

I hadn't heard from my mother since the letter that told me she might be going abroad, and some nights I lay awake worrying about where she was and what she was doing. I'd accepted that Harry was right; the woman I'd seen in London couldn't have been her – but where was she and why didn't she write to me?

Christmas was coming and there was an atmosphere of excitement at Brockmere. The Redferns were invited to lots of parties; I was allowed to attend only luncheons and tea-parties, but in the evening I was left to my own devices. I spent many of them with Maggie. She had begun to open out a little, telling me of her life before she came to Brockmere.

'My father was a vicar,' she said as we sat sewing. 'My mother died soon after I was born and he brought me up single-handed.'

'You must have been very close,' I said.

She shook her head. 'He was such a cold man. I had to be quiet all the time, even when I was tiny. When I grew up, I had to study for hours, and was never allowed to play with other children. If I disobeyed, he whipped me.'

'That's awful. I was so lucky. My mother was hardly ever cross with me . . . until she was ill.'

Maggie nodded. 'You were lucky. I never knew what it was to feel loved. As soon as I could, I found myself a post as a governess, vowing never to return.' Her eyes clouded. 'Brockmere is the best place I've had. If I had to leave . . . '

'Lady Selina would give you a good reference. You'll find another job.'

She laughed harshly. 'Is that all you think I want? What about a home, children and a man to love me?'

'Perhaps you'll find them too one day.'

'At my age?' Her mouth twisted sourly. 'Not much chance of that,

116

is there? Sometimes I think I'd be better off dead. There's just no place for a woman like me. . . . '

'Oh, Maggie! Please don't say that.'

I looked at her, noticing the shadows beneath her eyes. Was she very unhappy? She saw me looking and shook her head.

'Forget what I said, Kate. It isn't your fault. You're young and the world seems a good place to you – make the most of it while you can. Innocence goes too fast. . . . '

It was a week before Christmas. Prue was excited about the dance being held at Brockmere. She showed me her new dress – a creation of pink satin and tulle – and talked about the guests who were coming.

'Helen's cousins are staying with her, so they'll be here,' she said. 'And Philip's younger brother. We'll have about twenty guests to sleep overnight.'

Even Rosie had caught the mood of anticipation. 'The ballroom looks so pretty now that it's decorated,' she said. 'It's a shame you can't go down. It wouldn't have hurt for one night.'

'I'm not allowed to go to dances yet,' I sighed.

'There's no reason you shouldn't take a peep from the minstrels' gallery if you stay behind the screens.'

I laughed at the mischief in her eyes. Rosie was firmly on my side, an ally in my continuing deception once a week. I'd had several narrow escapes returning to the house in my breeches, and if it hadn't been for her I would surely have been caught before this.

'That's a good idea,' I said. 'I can watch if I can't join in.'

And so that evening I crept down to hide in the gallery, watching as the guests arrived. Some of the ladies wore superb gowns, bought from the salons of Worth, Lanvin or Patou. I'd seen similar gowns in the fashion magazines Prue borrowed from Helen. She had *Harper's Bazaar* every month, and less frequently, *Le Journal des Dames et des Modes*, a French magazine with illustrations of clothes and informative articles. As the music began to float up from the room below, my foot tapped to the rhythm. I closed my eyes, swaying as I imagined myself dancing.

'Poor Kate,' a voice said behind me, making me jump. 'It's unfair that you should miss out on all the fun.'

I smiled at Harry as he came to stand beside me. 'How did you know I was here?'

'I popped up to your room to bring you some food and Rosie told me you were here.'

'Rosie sent Maggie and me a little taste of everything.'

He looked at me quizzically. 'As long as you're not feeling left out?'

'Well, to be truthful I am, but I know it's silly.' I gazed wistfully at the couples dancing below. 'It looks so much fun.'

Harry laughed with gentle mockery. He was very handsome in his evening suit and crisp white shirt. 'It's terrible to be sixteen, isn't it, Kate? You're not quite a woman but you don't feel like a child.'

His words stirred a memory. Someone else had once said something similar to me. I recalled the day Paul de Bernay had come to my mother's cottage. He'd teased me and kissed me, and then my mother had come in. After that, everything seemed to go wrong. Where was my mother? It was months since I'd had a letter. I wasn't even sure if she was still alive – and I missed her so terribly.

Harry saw the tears in my eyes. 'You're not crying because you can't come to the dance?'

I blinked rapidly. 'I was thinking of my mother. It's almost Christmas and I don't even know where she is.'

'You can't do anything for her, Kate.'

'I know – but I can't stop loving her.'

'I didn't say that you should.' He took my hand. 'Come on, I'll teach you to dance. This one is a waltz. Now pay attention.' As Harry's voice chided me I was somehow comforted. He drew me against him. 'Follow my lead.'

We were enclosed in our own little world as we danced in the shadows of the gallery. The music seemed to come from a long way away. I leaned my head against his shoulder, letting my body move with his. He was so strong and sure of himself. He made me feel that nothing could really be that bad. The hurt drained out of me and I was strangely happy, as if this moment was something special I should always remember. I wanted it to go on forever.

When the music ended I was sorry. I wanted to stay in his arms, and an involuntary protest escaped my lips as he let me go. I stood gazing up at him, still caught by the enchantment of the moment. I saw that he too was held by this feeling between us, then his eyes darkened and he frowned.

'I must join our guests, Kate. Mother will be wondering where I've got to, and I think perhaps it's time you went to bed. You have to be up early in the morning. It's our day for riding in the park – but wear your habit in case some of the guests are about.'

I watched as he walked away. Sometimes he was so good to me, then his mood would change and he would dismiss me summarily. It was almost as if he were on his guard. As if he didn't want to like me too much. . . .

On Christmas Eve there was a special dinner for intimate friends, to which both Maggie and I were bidden. Everyone received a present from Sir Gerald: mine was a delicate gold cross and chain. After dinner we retired to the drawing room, and Maggie played the piano while we all sang Christmas songs. There were no card games that evening, nor any form of gambling, and at half-past eleven the cars were brought round to take us to church for midnight mass. It was cold and our breath made little white clouds on the frosty air.

Inside the church candles were burning brightly from brass sconces, the flickering light giving new meaning to the stained glass windows portraying scenes from Christ's life. I prayed for my mother, my new family and myself.

After the service we returned to the house and were served a hot, spicy punch before retiring. I walked part of the way upstairs with Maggie, who seemed quiet and thoughtful, though she thanked me for the scarf I'd given her.

'And thank you for my copy of Shakespeare's sonnets.'

She smiled and we parted. I wondered if I would see her on Christmas Day. She had been invited to the celebration dinner, but would probably eat alone on the day itself. Hers was a strange existence, and I thought she must often be lonely. I decided I would take the time to visit her during the day.

Breakfast on Christmas Morning was the same as usual, except for the custom of leaving small gifts beside each plate. For once everyone was there when I arrived. I was thanked politely by Lady Selina and Prue for my presents to them. Harry only smiled, but I noticed he was wearing the cravat I'd bought him. They all watched as I opened the parcels beside my place.

From Prue there was a box of embroidered handkerchiefs; from Lady Selina a silver photograph frame from Liberty of London, and from Harry a gold stock pin with a horse's head on the bar.

'It's lovely,' I said, smiling at him. 'Thank you, Harry – thank you all for my presents.'

I tried not to feel disappointed that nothing had come from my mother, not even a card or a letter. I tried, but it hurt. In the midst of all the celebrations, I couldn't help wondering where she was. Was she enjoying Christmas, or was she ill and miserable in some lonely little room?

After tea I popped up to see Maggie. She didn't answer the door immediately, and when she did, I saw that her face was flushed.

'Oh, it's you,' she said. 'I didn't expect you today.'

'I brought some chocolates.'

She smiled oddly. 'How thoughtful of you. Come in, then. . . . '
She gestured towards a bottle of sherry on the table. 'I was just having a drink – would you like one?'

'I'd better not. I had some wine at lunch.'

'So did I,' she said and hiccupped. 'Pardon. Shocking manners – but what can you expect? I'm only a servant after all. Not good enough to join the family, not good enough to marry. . . . Only good for. . . . ' Suddenly she stopped, putting a finger to her lips. 'I forgot. Have to be careful when you're around, don't I, Kate?'

Surprised, I realized that she was just the tiniest bit drunk. 'I wouldn't tell tales,' I said. 'We're friends, aren't we?'

'Friends?' She looked as if she might burst into tears. 'Too late for that now.'

'What do you mean?'

'Nothing.' She poured another sherry. 'Go away, Kate. Go back to your family and leave me alone. . . . '

I stared at her for a moment, then I turned and went out.

Boxing Day was even colder than Christmas Eve. Looking out of my window, I saw the white rings of frost on the trees and wondered if it would be too cold to ride. It was still very early as I dressed in my breeches and slipped out of the house. Rosie had the day off and I'd told her not to bother with my tea-tray.

'If you're sure, miss. I can get away earlier.'

'I'm quite sure.'

I was eager for my ride with Harry. Because of the bad weather we hadn't been out as often as usual, and I'd had to be careful with guests staying on after the dance. They had all gone now, and Harry had promised we could escape for a while.

He was waiting, talking to Ned, his back towards me. He turned, smiling as I ran the last few yards.

'I thought it might be too cold for you?'

'Only snow would stop me.'

'Good girl. Come on then; I've been looking forward to this.'

He helped me to mount. We cantered out of the yard, the horses' hooves ringing on the hard ground. It was a cold, crisp morning, but the sun was shining as we rode through the park. The air had an invigorating freshness that made us feel very much alive. There was an unspoken rapport between us, and somehow I wasn't surprised when Harry turned to me.

'You're ready now, Kate. Give Rustic his head. I'll race you to the Folly – but I'll give you a start.'

I laughed, gripping with my knees and flicking the reins. 'Go on, Rustic,' I cried. 'Let's show him we don't need a start!'

As the horse suddenly surged forward, I felt a thrill of excitement. The sheer speed took me by surprise and my nerves tingled. It was frightening, and yet it was the most wonderful sensation. Everything became a blur and I was aware only of being at one with the horse and the exhilaration of speed. Then, all at once, I realized that Harry was beside me, his horse and mine matching stride for stride.

'It's wonderful!'

'You're wonderful, Kate.'

I'd never been so happy. Nothing else seemed to matter. We were in a world of our own, a world of cold, glittering sunlight, air that tasted like wine and trees that shone with the diamonds of Jack Frost. I felt as if I could go on forever. The Folly was in sight when Harry called a halt.

'Let's walk for a while,' he said. 'I want to talk to you.'

I was surprised, but nodded agreement and dismounted. 'What do you want to talk about, Harry?'

He didn't answer immediately and we walked in silence, leading the horses, then, 'I want to talk about you, Kate. About us – myself.'

I was alarmed. 'Have I done something wrong?'

'Of course not.' He stopped walking and stared down at me. 'You weren't happy when you first came to Brockmere – have things improved?'

'I still feel a bit strange, and neither Prue or your mother have really accepted me – but I'm happy enough. Why?'

'Father said you had thoughts of becoming a teacher.'

'That was before I got used to being here. I would like to stay now – unless my mother needs me.'

'She wanted you to come here.'

'I know. I'm worried about her, Harry. She hasn't written for ages.'

'She probably thinks it would only upset you again. You have a new life now.'

'I just wish she would write – but most of the time I'm content.'

'Then you like living here?'

'Yes. Especially when I'm with you. That's the best part of it.'

His mouth relaxed into a smile. 'Oh, Kate, you're so young and innocent.'

'I'm nearly seventeen,' I retorted indignantly.

'I'm twenty-five, eight years older than you.'

'So what?' I pulled a face. 'I can't see any grey hairs yet.'

'Minx!' He laughed as I raised my brows. 'What I'm trying to say is. . . .'

'Harry!' I grabbed his arm. 'What's that on the ground by the Folly? It looks like . . . ' I stared at him in horror. 'It looks like a woman's body. . . . '

'My God!' He was shocked. 'I think you're right. Stay here while I take a closer look.'

'I'll come with you. I – I think it's Maggie.'

He looked again. 'Damnation! What the hell has happened to her?'

We left the horses to graze as we hurried to the body lying at the foot of the Folly. It was as I'd feared, a woman, and she was sprawled in an ungainly heap as if she'd fallen from a great height. There was no doubt of her identity now, and as I looked at Maggie's white face, my throat closed with emotion. The look in her eyes was so terrible! Harry glanced up at the battlements of the pseudo medieval tower, and I guessed what he was thinking.

'She must have been looking over the top and fallen,' I said. 'She is dead, isn't she?'

Harry was holding her wrist. 'I can't feel a pulse and she's very cold. I should think she's been dead for a while.'

'I visited her after tea yesterday. She – she had been drinking sherry and she seemed a little odd.'

'Do you mean she was drunk?' Harry stared at me hard. 'If you know something, Kate, you must tell me.'

'I don't, not really.'

'What does that mean?'

'When I first came here I saw her crying – and I've seen her locking the Folly after she'd left it. Why should she have a key if it's unsafe?'

'Yes, that is odd.' He looked grim. 'Is that all?'

'Yes – except that she'd been very unhappy recently. She said there was no place for a woman like her, and spoke of being better off dead.'

'The poor woman; I'd no idea.' His frown deepened. 'This is a mess. The last thing we needed just now was a scandal.'

'I don't understand.'

'It doesn't matter. It was something I wanted – but it will have to wait. Mother's going to be upset enough as it is.'

He was obviously deeply troubled. So was I – I hadn't known Maggie long but I'd felt a kind of bond with her.

'We'd better get back. I'll get some of the men to fetch her – and perhaps we should call the police.'

'We can't just leave her. I'll stay here until someone comes.'

'In those clothes?' Harry shook his head. 'No, you won't, Kate. Mother would be sure to hear. Besides, you can't help Maggie now.'

'No . . . ' Tears stung my eyes. 'She was so lonely, Harry. She had no one who really cared about her.' A sob escaped me. 'Poor, poor Maggie.'

Harry nodded, his face grave. 'She couldn't have had much of a life – but to end it like this . . . ' He looked at me. 'Come on, we'd better get back.'

We rode at a quick trot. The magic of the morning had gone. Harry's mood was grim and I felt guilty. Something must have driven Maggie back to the Folly again and again. Some secret fascination with the place itself. . . . Unless she had gone there to meet someone. I remembered the night I'd seen the lovers embracing in the shrubbery and I wondered.

At the stables we parted in haste. Harry talking to the shocked grooms as I ran back to the house. I was shocked and shaken by my first close encounter with death. Running up the back stairs, I threw open my bedroom door and froze in shock as I saw Lady Selina sitting in a chair by the window.

'So I was not mistaken,' she said coldly. 'What have you to say for yourself?'

I glanced down at my breeches. 'Is it so disgraceful? I find it easier to ride astride.'

She looked outraged. 'Have you no sense of decency? No self-respecting woman would ride in that outfit – it shows every line of your body.'

My cheeks were flaming as I heard the scorn in her voice. 'Harry thought they were sensible.'

'My son is dear to me, but I do not delude myself. He is a man and all men have their baser sides. No doubt he found it very entertaining. I expect that every groom in the stables is laughing at you. Do you really wish to be the butt of questionable jests by persons of that order, Kate?'

I hung my head. 'I hadn't thought of it like that.'

'I don't suppose you had. It's not that I don't understand how easy it is to be carried away by a young man's smile . . . ' She stopped herself suddenly. 'But you should have more pride in yourself. I'm disappointed in you, Kate. I'd had such good reports of you from Miss Grant. . . . '

She'd given me a sharp reminder. 'Maggie's dead,' I blurted out. 'Harry and I found her. It looks as if she fell from the Folly.'

Her faced paled. 'Dead? But she can't be – when did this happen?'

'Harry said he thought she must have been dead some hours.'

'But I saw her last evening.'

'I visited her after tea.'

'You visited her yesterday – why?'

'Because I felt sorry for her. She was very lonely.'

'You seem to know a great deal about her. Is there anything else I should know?'

I hesitated, then shook my head. It would be best to keep my suspicions about Maggie's visits to the Folly to myself.

Lady Selina stared at me hard, then nodded. 'I should punish you for your wilful behaviour, Kate. You deliberately deceived me.'

'I'm sorry. It started as a joke and I saw no harm in it.'

'You must promise never to do it again, otherwise I might have to cancel your riding lessons.'

'Please don't do that.'

'Then give me your word, Kate.'

I drew a deep breath. If I gave my word I must keep it, and I should miss the freedom those rides had given me, but I had no choice.

'I give you my word I shall not ride like this again while you are my guardian.'

'That is sufficient. I know you will keep your promise.'

'Thank you.'

She smiled slightly. 'You are not a wicked girl, Kate, just a little impulsive. I remember your mother was much the same as a girl.'

'Do you know why she ran away from Brockmere?'

'To marry your father, I presume. Sir Gerald's father didn't approve of the young man – though I'm sure he was decent enough. He did marry your mother after all.'

'What do you mean?'

She shook her head. 'Nothing – except that it is not always wise to trust in men, Kate. I know Harry is very charming, but he doesn't always think of the trouble his actions cause other people.' She sighed deeply. 'He's never been quite the same since Helen married Philip Forrest.'

I swallowed hard. 'Was – was Harry in love with Helen?'

'He still is, my dear. He's far too proud to let anyone guess, but he can't hide it from me. As a child he adored her, and when he left college we expected them to become engaged, but something went wrong and then Helen met Philip. Harry hardly spoke to anyone for a month.'

'I – I see. Thank you for telling me.'

'It is best that you know the truth. I'm sure Harry is fond of you as a cousin, but it won't do to fill your head with silly dreams!'

'I – I hadn't even thought of anything else.'

'Then you're a sensible girl.' She looked at me approvingly. 'I shall say no more about this nonsense. In the circumstances, you are bound to be upset by Maggie's unfortunate death. Don't forget what I've said, Kate.'

As the door shut behind her, I closed my eyes, letting the humiliation wash over me. She was right, of course, she was right. Harry had found it amusing, that's why he'd encouraged me to flout convention. I'd thought he was interested in me because I was special to him, but all the time he'd been laughing at me. The only reason he'd bothered with me was because he couldn't be with the woman he really wanted.

It wasn't until much later that I wondered exactly what Lady Selina had meant about everyone being allowed one mistake. Had she once done something that she bitterly regretted?

I didn't see Harry alone for almost a week. The weather was too bad to ride and besides, Maggie's death had cast a shadow over the house. The police came and took details, questioning both Harry and me about the way in which we'd found her. Then they interviewed all the servants. It seemed they didn't believe Maggie had accidentally fallen to her death. It was in fact almost impossible. She would have had to lean out right over the edge. Rosie told me the police believed it was suicide.

'They think she threw herself over?' I asked. 'But why should she?'

'I'm sure I don't know, miss. Maybe it will come out after the inquest.'

I was shocked and stunned – had Maggie been that unhappy? I felt very guilty. I should have tried to help her more.

The result of the post-mortem stunned everyone. Maggie had been nearly three months gone with child. I could hardly believe it, and Lady Selina was furiously angry.

'To think it was going on under my nose,' she said to Sir Gerald. 'What will people say? It's scandalous.'

'It's unfortunate,' he agreed. 'I wonder that she did not come to you, my dear.'

'If she had, I should have dismissed her at once. There's no place in decent society for a woman like that. With her reputation gone, she would never have found work as a governess again – and in my opinion quite rightly so.'

'That is not worthy of you, Selina. Don't you think. . . . '

'She knew what she was doing, Gerald. If a woman breaks the laws of society, she has to be prepared to take the consequences. Or she must find a way out of her predicament. . . . '

I heard no more as they closed the library door. Maggie would never have dared confess her secret to her employer. As I recalled the last time I'd seen her, I understood how desperate she'd become. If the father of her child wouldn't – or couldn't – marry her, she might well have felt there was no point in going on. As an unmarried woman with a child, she would find it difficult to secure a respectable position, and might have been forced into menial work; she'd preferred to take her own life.

The question on everyone's lips was – who was Maggie's lover? If anyone knew, no one was telling. Lady Selina interrogated all the servants herself, but no one would admit to knowing anything. I thought perhaps Rosie might have her suspicions, but when I asked, a closed expression came over her face and she only shook her head.

A verdict of suicide while under stress was given by the magistrates, but at Brockmere an atmosphere of gloom and unease prevailed. Lady Selina went around with a permanent frown, and Sir Gerald spent most of his time alone in his library. The snow was falling in earnest now, and Harry seemed moody. When Lady Selina told me that Helen was expecting a baby, I thought I understood the reason for Harry's long face.

Imprisoned by the winter weather, Prue and I were thrown into each other's company more than before. Now that Maggie was dead there could be no more lessons. Since neither of us wanted to use the schoolroom, which seemed haunted by ghosts, if only of the mind, we practised playing the piano in the drawing room and Prue tried to help me improve my technique, without much success. We were not exactly friends, but she didn't seem to resent me as much as before.

The bad weather dragged on for weeks. When the snow had gone it rained continuously, turning the rides to slush and mud. Even the papers were full of gloom: Lloyd George called the build-up of arms in Western Europe sheer lunacy, nine million people were reported to be starving in the north-east of Japan, and in London almost twenty thousand builders had decided to strike. In comparison my troubles were small, but I missed my exercise and I missed being with Harry. By the end of February, I was restless and miserable.

CHAPTER ELEVEN

She was trembling with excitement as she let herself into the house. It had happened at last! She had begun to think that it was too late, that she would be trapped forever on the treadmill she had made for herself. There had been days and weeks when she was driven mad by the enforced hours of loneliness, when the endless whirr of her sewing machine stretched her nerves to breaking point and she longed for something to happen. She had thought she would grow old in this miserable cottage, but now she felt the first faint flicker of hope.

She had met a man. A man unlike any other she had met in the long years of her widowhood. He liked her. She had seen the sudden interest in his eyes when they were introduced, and felt the slight pressure of his fingers as he held her hand a moment longer than necessary. He wasn't the first man to look at her in all this time, but he was the first to make her heart beat faster – the first to make her feel young again.

She studied herself in the mirror of the big, carved oak sideboard – were there tiny lines at the corners of her eyes? She wasn't old, only thirty-three. That wasn't really old, was it? He was younger, of course. Young, handsome and from that other world, the world to which she truly belonged. He could take her there if he wished, back to that carefree life she had tasted so briefly. He could give her all the things her soul craved – but would he? How interested was he?

She knew he wanted her. She'd seen the gleam of sudden desire, the inquiring lift of his brows, and she had known. She'd sensed that she was on the brink of a love-affair, but she was a little frightened. She had made a life for herself. She was respected and she had friends. If she gave all that up for a brief moment of passion. . . . She was no longer a young girl. The years had taught her caution – and she had her daughter to think of. She couldn't afford gossip. And yet he really liked her. Was it too much to hope for marriage? Other men had looked at her over the years. She could have married if she'd wished, but she'd waited, waited for the right man, the right moment. Now perhaps it had come.

The back door opened and a voice called out to her. 'I'm home, Mother.'

She turned to meet her daughter with a welcoming smile, trying to suppress her excitement. It could mean a wonderful new life for them both. She would be able to give her child all the things she had been unable to afford. It was for both of them, but she mustn't say anything just yet. It was too soon. It was her secret. She wanted to hold it inside her, to let it warm her, to feel it washing away the loneliness of the years.

No, she wouldn't say anything just yet. . . .

She had had tea with him. He bought her tiny sandwiches and cream cakes at the best hotel in town, and then he'd taken her home in his car. She had seen the neighbour across the road watching from behind the curtains, and she knew that people would talk if she asked him in. So she just smiled and thanked him for a lovely afternoon.

'We must do it again some time,' he said. 'Perhaps when I come back.'

'Are you going away?'

Her heart sank as he nodded. 'As you know, I like to travel. It may be several months before I return.'

'How lovely for you,' she said, feeling the bitter disappointment inside. 'I always envy people who are free to travel as much as they like.'

His dark eyes sparkled with amusement. 'Perhaps you would like to accompany me sometime?'

'Oh no, I couldn't!' The words were out before she could stop them. She blushed. 'I mean . . . what would people say?'

He chuckled deep in his throat. 'Who cares what your neighbours think? You would never have to come back here, unless you wanted to.'

'What – what do you mean?' Her heart beat wildly. Was he asking her to marry him?

'I mean what you think I mean, my dear.' He smiled at her wickedly. 'Think about it. We'll talk more when I come back in the spring.'

She got out of the car, feeling confused. Had she lost him? Had her hesitation made him think it was not worthwhile pursuing her?

'Will you write to me?' she asked, suddenly desperate.

'Perhaps,' he said. 'Think about what I've said.'

She stared after him as he drove away.

The winter had never seemed longer or more lonely. She felt trapped by her work, trapped by the stupid conventions that had made her hesitate. If he never came back. . . . When she realized that he would probably forget all about her she wanted to scream and shout at the unfairness of life. Her one chance of some happiness and she had let it slip through her fingers. And for what? Because some old busybody down the road might talk about her behind her back!

'Let him come back,' she prayed, though her prayer was only in her head, never uttered. 'I can't stand it if he doesn't come back.'

She was snapping at her daughter too much. It wasn't the girl's fault. She was a good girl and she loved her, but she was one more chain binding her to a life she hated. She hadn't told him about her daughter yet, but he probably knew. He was so intelligent, so confident and full of joy. She couldn't stop thinking about him.

It was ages before he wrote, and the letter was very brief. He described a village in northern Italy, telling her he thought she would love it. So he hadn't forgotten her. Her heart leaped and she was filled with hope again, but then the days and weeks passed and there were no more letters, just a card at Christmas. A card she didn't put on the shelf with the others.

She could hardly wait for spring. Please let him come back. Please. . . .

He wanted her to go away with him! He knew she had a fifteen-year-old daughter. He said it didn't matter.

'She can come with us,' he'd said with that smile, the smile that could make her heart sing. 'We'll go to my château in Provence. You'll love it there, and so will the child. The sunshine will do you so much good – and my house will be a home again.'

'I'm not sure.' She prevaricated, hoping that he would ask her to marry him, but knowing that if he didn't she would go anyway. She would go anywhere, do anything he asked. She was in love, wildly, madly in love. 'I'm older than you. Are you sure you want me to come?'

He kissed her hand, delicately sucking each fingertip, catching them playfully between his strong white teeth, nibbling them. His touch aroused a fierce, overwhelming desire in her. It was so long since a man had touched her, so long since she had felt the warmth of love. She couldn't let anything stand in her way. Even if it did mean that she could never return to her home, it didn't matter. She had to seize her one chance of life.

'Shall I show you, *ma chère?*' he asked, teasing her. 'Shall I show you how much I want you?'

She trembled as he took her in his arms, feeling the heat of his flesh against hers. No one had ever made love to her like this, no one had ever made her feel this alive. She was seventeen again, her body supple and soft as she yielded to him, her mouth opening beneath his as the petals of a flower to a bee, drawing him in. She gave a little cry of ecstasy, jerking spasmodically beneath him.

'I love you,' she whispered. 'I love you. I love you. . . . '

Clinging to him as he brought her to a swift climax, she knew that nothing had ever mattered to her this much. She would go anywhere, sacrifice anything to be with him. . . .

She had seen him kissing her daughter. He had come to the cottage to collect something and she was called away. When she returned he was kissing her child. . . . But she wasn't a child any more, was she? Looking at her, she saw that the girl was almost a young woman and very lovely. Jealousy struck at her. She felt it worming away inside her, eating at her guts. She loved him but she didn't trust him. She knew that she wasn't the first woman in his life, and there would be others. But not her daughter.

She could imagine what might happen when they were all at the château. She could see the girl growing lovelier and lovelier, while she grew older. She could see him making comparisons, and then one day . . . but she couldn't let that happen. It mustn't happen.

It wasn't because she was jealous, she told herself, knowing that she lied. It was for the girl's sake. It was one thing for her to throw away her respectability, but quite another for her daughter. She was young, pretty and clever. She could have a wonderful future ahead of her, especially if. . . . She laughed aloud at the perfect solution to her problem.

It was the revenge she had always promised herself. And it would be good for the girl. She would have a wonderful life, and . . . she would be free to go with him. Perhaps if they were alone she might be able to persuade him to marry her. Even if she didn't, she would make it last for as long as she could.

But first she had to find a way of persuading her daughter that she should do as she was asked. The girl had a very stubborn streak in her. If she merely suggested that it was a good idea. . . . Her thoughts were suspended as she had a fit of coughing. She took her handkerchief from her pocket and looked at it. There were brown

131

stains on it. Where had they come from? Was she bringing up blood? A memory from long ago flashed into her mind. Then she remembered how the blood had come to be on her hanky. But the memory lingered on in her mind, tantalizing her.

Suddenly, the idea came to her. It was terrible. Cruel. No, she couldn't do it. But what was the alternative? Surely there was some other way. . . .

She knew she was going to do it. It was the one sure way of making certain her daughter would do as she asked. It was the worst thing she had ever done in her life, and she had been through hell this past week, first making up her mind and then changing it again. Now she was certain. It was the only way.

He had seen the girl again. He had brought her home in his car. If she allowed it to go on, it could only end in disaster for them all. He wouldn't touch her yet, of course. She was too young. The kiss had been just a whim. She knew him so well. He probably wasn't even aware that he was physically attracted to the girl, but it would happen. She could refuse to go with him, send him away, out of her life – or she could go ahead with her plans. But she couldn't give him up. She just couldn't.

It would take careful planning. She mustn't be too obvious or her daughter would suspect. She would let the suspicion build slowly and then. . . . But first there was something else she must do.

Getting up, she took paper, pen and ink from a drawer of the sideboard, then she sat down to write a letter.

She looked at herself in the dressing mirror. Surely she ought to look different? She had just broken her only child's heart, and in doing so, had almost broken her own. Pressing her trembling fingers to her lips, she took a deep breath, steadying herself. It was done now. It was over. And she had done it for the girl.

For a moment her own reflection seemed to mist and she saw a picture from the past. Froggie was bending over a cot. He picked up the child and turned to look at her.

'Is she mine?' he asked.

As the picture faded and she could see her own very white face again, she took a deep breath.

'I'm sorry, Froggie,' she whispered. 'But I did it for the best. Truly I did. . . . '

It seemed to her then that she could see his grey eyes looking at

132

her with reproach. Covering her face with her hands, she turned away from the mirror and sat down on the bed. For several minutes she could scarcely stop shaking, then she pulled herself together, and her head went up.

The past was dead and gone. She was alive.

She stood looking at the view from the château terrace. It was beautiful beyond anything she had ever imagined, with the setting sun turning the sloping valley to reds, purples and gold – so beautiful that it tore her heart in two just to look at it. She was happy, happier than she had ever been, happier than she deserved to be, perhaps. A tiny thorn of guilt pricked at her conscience. She still felt that she had acted wrongly, yet she'd had no choice. She'd been forced into it against her will. She hadn't wanted it to be this way. . . .

Hearing the man's step behind her, she glanced over her shoulder, a little shiver of anticipation running through her as she felt his lips against her throat and his arms close about her. She smiled, moving closer, turning her face for his kiss, her body thrilling to his touch. His arms tightened, holding her to him. She arched into his body, her breath quickening.

Already she was aching for him, wanting the hardness of him inside her. She groaned as she felt the moisture run between her thighs. Her desire for him was almost like a sickness, a fever that throbbed in her veins, turning her into a mindless being who lived only for those moments when she lay writhing beneath him. She was shameless where he was concerned, utterly shameless, never satisfied even after their loving, never able to get enough of him. She sometimes thought she must be like that spider that devours her mate after copulation. She wanted to swallow him up so that he would always be inside her.

She heard him laugh deep in his throat. '*Mon Dieu*, you're insatiable,' he murmured as he swept her up into his arms, carrying her inside.

She avoided his eyes as he handed her the fragile glass, her fingers trembling on the twisted stem. He was angry. She knew his moods now and she could see it in his face and the set of his mouth. She'd provoked him too often recently, and he was finding her behaviour tiresome. He wouldn't put up with it for long. There was no reason why he should. They had agreed how it would be before she came to Provence, and it was useless to go on asking for the one thing she knew he would not give her. Knowing what she was risking, she pressed him yet again.

'I still don't see why we can't be married,' she said, her tone sulky. 'You say you care for me. . . . '

'I do care for you,' he said, eyes glittering. 'I should not otherwise have brought you here to my home – but marriage is out of the question. You knew that from the start.'

He had told her. She had thought she could accept this situation, but now she wanted more.

'I know you said your marriage was no marriage – so why can't you divorce her, Paul? It wouldn't hurt her. She doesn't even know you when you visit her . . . '

'Be quiet!' he commanded, and she faltered as she saw the cold, deep anger she had aroused. 'My reasons are my own. I refuse to discuss them with you.'

He turned away from her, staring blindly at the magnificent view from the salon windows, seeing only the pictures in his mind. A girl was running barefoot across the château lawns, her long, pale hair blowing about her laughing face. She was young and beautiful, hardly more than a child. She waved to him, blowing a kiss. He half lifted his hand to wave back and then he remembered.

The pictured faded abruptly and his eyes darkened as he thought of Marianne as he had last seen her, her beautiful hair lank and dull, her eyes empty as she sat staring mindlessly into space. . . . And he had turned her into that pitiful creature! It was his fault and his alone. The agony ground relentlessly inside him, making him groan aloud. Swinging round to face the woman in whose arms he had thought to find some comfort, his face was suddenly hard.

'I shall never divorce Marianne,' he said coldly. 'And if I did, I would not marry you. You could never take her place. She was so young, so sweet and innocent . . . rather like your own daughter in a way. . . . ' A smile of reminiscence touched his lips. 'Yes, she reminded me of Marianne when I saw her. . . . '

'Don't!' she cried, flinching. 'Please, Paul, don't say that.'

He stared at her, his dark eyes brooding and distant. 'I don't want to hurt you. We have a satisfactory relationship and I've no wish to end it. I shall never marry again. We're good for each other. Can't you be content with that? You won't lose by it, I give you my word. When it's over, I'll see you have enough money to live in comfort for the rest of your life.'

'Stop!' she cried, jumping to her feet. 'I don't want to hear this.'

She flung herself at him, pressing herself against his body, her eyes wild. 'Please,' she whispered brokenly. 'Don't say any more. I can't bear it. I can't. . . . '

He looked down at her, sadness replacing the anger. 'Don't cry, *ma chère*. We're the same you and I – we hurt others without meaning to and then we regret it.'

She gazed up at him, the tears arrested. 'How do you know that I. . . . '

His mouth twisted wryly. 'It's in your eyes,' he said softly. 'I understand because I too have been alone in the wilderness. . . . '

She had never felt as wretched as she did now. It was almost over, she sensed it as surely as she knew that day followed night, and it was her own fault. They had quarrelled too often of late, and Paul was bored by her petulance. She cursed herself for being a fool. She had always known that it would take skill to hold his interest and she had thrown it all away. She knew that it was ridiculous to let herself become so obsessed with Paul, but there was nothing she could do about it, no way she could ease the ache inside her. She had given up so much for him. Her home, her friends, respectability . . . and the love of her daughter. She had thought them all dispensable, but for a while now she had begun to realize just what she had done. She had begun to feel lost without her daughter. To regret the companionship they had always shared, to think of the grandchildren she would never see . . .

The sun was warm on her head as she walked across the lawns towards the summerhouse. She hadn't seen Paul since he had flung out of the room the previous night, his face rigid with anger. Why had she provoked him once again? Why had she pressed for the one thing she knew he wouldn't give her? He was so generous in every other way. She had all the clothes she could want, jewellery and money of her own to spend as she wished, and yet she couldn't be satisfied. She wanted more, so much more than he was willing to give. And inside her was that nagging little doubt, that hurtful, stupid jealousy that would not let her be.

She had almost reached the summerhouse. Paul's horse was tethered nearby. She hadn't really been looking for him, but she was eager to see him, anxious to apologize. Her heart raced and she felt nervous as she thought of the careful words she meant to use. She mustn't upset him by being too emotional; he didn't like that. She would smile and shrug her shoulders as she promised that she would never behave so stupidly again, that she would accept the situation for what it was. Surely it was enough that Paul cared for her sufficiently to bring her here? It had to be, because she couldn't bear to lose him entirely and she knew that she was very close to doing just that.

As she ran lightly up the steps to the summerhouse, she heard the sound of voices from inside and her blood froze. Someone was with Paul – a woman! She stood as if turned to stone, a warning voice in her head telling her to leave at once. She must not go in there! She must turn around and walk back the way she had come. . . .

The need to know, the need to see with her own eyes drove her on. Sweat trickled over her breasts and between her thighs as she pushed the door open – and then her heart caught and in a moment of terrible pain, she thought she would die.

They had not heard her come in. They were too absorbed in each other to be aware of her even while she watched them. Only the girl's white legs were visible from this angle, and her arms, wound around Paul's neck as she clung to him. She was moaning as he drove into her, her little panting cries making the woman sick with envy. Even while she hated him for his betrayal, she would have given her soul to change places with the girl. And she was only eighteen or nineteen. . . .

She backed away as the misery swept over her, unable to take her eyes from the smooth tanned skin of the man's back and the paler shade of his buttocks. Then the girl's eyes widened and she said something to him. He turned his head and saw her and his face was shocked. He spoke her name but the spell was broken. She gave a cry of despair, then turned and fled back across the lawns to the house.

She sat outside the little open-air café in Montparnasse, staring blindly in front of her as the stream of colourful Parisian life swirled about her. She hadn't touched the tiny cup of black coffee on the table in front of her, nor was she really aware of the scent of flowers from the baskets of the sellers or the warmth of the sun on her face. She was deadened, numbed, drained of all emotion. She would never, ever feel anything again. Her life was over. He didn't love her. He had never loved her.

She wanted to end it all. She had to stop this gnawing pain inside her. Where had it all gone wrong? What had she done? Her head pounded, throbbing as the desperate thoughts went round and round in circles. She closed her eyes, trying to shut out the truth, but it would not be denied. She had demanded too much. Always, she asked for more than they were willing to give: her parents, Gerald, Richard, Paul. . . . Paul. Her heart felt as if it was breaking. She couldn't bear the absolute emptiness inside her.

She had to stop thinking about him. A picture of a girl's grief-stricken face flashed into her mind. She pressed a hand to her eyes, trying to scrub out the memory. She hadn't meant to hurt Kate like that. She hadn't meant to destroy the one person who had really loved her. . . . She remembered that chance meeting in London, when Kate had suddenly come rushing along the street, screaming at the top of her voice. She had panicked, getting into Paul's car and ordering the chauffeur to drive off immediately. She had sat in the car, trembling and overcome with guilt at what she had done. How could she have lied to her only child – and for what? Paul had tired of her anyway. She had thrown it all away for nothing.

She got to her feet, the world whirling dizzily around her. She ought never to have drunk all that champagne. A spasm of disgust shook her as she remembered waking in a strange room, in a strange bed and with a man she had never seen before sleeping beside her. He was almost young enough to be her son. She had felt the sickness swirling inside her as she grabbed her clothes and fled. Outside, she had vomited in the gutters.

She had no idea why she had done it. It hadn't helped in the least. She just felt ashamed.

Her head was throbbing. She felt that she couldn't go on. She had nothing to live for. She rose unsteadily to her feet and took a step forward, staggering and crashing into the tables as she fell.

CHAPTER TWELVE

Spring came at last. Lady Selina put aside whatever had been worrying her and began entertaining again. We had twenty guests coming for lunch, including Helen Forrest and her husband, who had recently returned from the South of France. I was dressing for lunch when someone came to my door. I called out that I wasn't quite ready, but the door opened and Prue came in.

I looked at her in surprise. 'Did you want something, Prue?'

'I've heard something,' she said awkwardly. 'But I don't know whether I should say or not.'

'Is it to do with my mother?' She nodded, her cheeks flushed. 'Please tell me, Prue. You have to – you must!'

'Someone saw her in France . . . '

'In France?' I was stunned. 'How was she? Was she well? How did they know it was her?'

Prue moved uncomfortably from one foot to the other. 'You're going to hate me for saying this . . . she was in a nightclub and she was laughing a lot, drinking and flirting with all the men. . . . '

'I don't believe you. It couldn't have been her!'

'Helen says she noticed a resemblance to you and she asked someone who the woman was. They said her name was Linton. . . . '

'There must be other women with that name.'

'Helen spoke to her in the powder room later, and she deliberately mentioned your name. She says the woman turned very pale and rushed off without answering – don't you think that's rather strange?'

'What are you implying?' But I knew what she was saying and it made me angry. 'My mother wouldn't do that. She's ill. It's all a horrible lie.'

Prue shrugged her shoulders. 'Well, you asked me to tell you and I did.'

I turned away as she went out, the sickness sweeping over me. It wasn't true. It couldn't be! It would mean that my mother had lied to me . . . to us all. Why should she do something so utterly cruel?

Helen looked at me uncomfortably as I demanded the truth, and I had a sinking feeling.

138

'What made you think she might be my mother?' I asked.

'You showed me a photograph once,' she replied uneasily. 'We happened to visit the powder room at the same time and I thought I'd ask if she were any relation to you. . . . '

'What happened then?'

'She turned pale, mumbled something and left.' Helen attempted a smile. 'I shouldn't have told anyone. I'm sorry, Kate, but it seemed so peculiar.'

'You said she was drunk?'

Helen blushed. 'She was having a good time, but I didn't say that, I promise you.'

I held out a photograph to her. 'Was that her?'

'I can't be sure. She looked different – better dressed.'

I remembered the mystery woman I'd seen in London and frowned. Harry had said she was French and yet Helen had been told the woman's name was Linton. It was unsettling to be told such things and not know for certain.

After lunch I escaped into the gardens to be alone. I felt confused, deeply hurt and frustrated. What should I believe? My mother was ill. She'd asked Sir Gerald to take me in because she couldn't look after me . . . but supposing she'd lied to everyone? Why – why would she do such a thing?

I missed her so! I was tormented with pictures of her lying ill and alone in a miserable little room in a boarding house – but if she were alive and dancing in a nightclub. . . .

Suddenly, a rush of grief came over me. I didn't want my mother to be ill, but if she had lied just to be rid of me, it meant that she had never really loved me – and that hurt. It hurt so much that I felt devastated. Burying my face in my hands, I rocked back and forth on my stone bench. I'd prayed for a miracle; I'd longed for my mother to come back to me well and happy. Now I didn't know what to think. I just felt very much alone, unwanted and unloved.

'What's the matter?' I heard the voice but didn't look up. 'I can't bear to see you like this, my darling.'

In another moment Harry was beside me on the bench. His arms went round me and he drew me close, his lips whispering against my hair.

'My poor little love,' he said. 'Can't you tell me?'

I looked up then. 'But you don't really care for me. I'm just a poor relation you tolerate because I amused you. You don't love me,

Harry . . . do you?' My voice cracked as I saw the flame leap in his eyes. 'Harry. . . . '

Whatever I might have said was lost as he groaned and pulled me against him, his lips crushing mine in a hard, demanding kiss that conveyed desperation. When at last he let me go, I stared at him, frightened yet elated by the look in his eyes.

'Not love you,' he said in a queer, strangled voice. 'You should know better, Kate. Not love you – my God! I've been fighting my feelings for you from the moment we met. You're so young. . . . '

'You do love me?' I stared at him in wonder. 'Then why have you been avoiding me?'

'I might have asked the same of you,' he said. 'You could have restarted your riding lessons weeks ago.'

I flushed as he looked at me hard. 'I didn't like to ask. You've seemed so moody lately. I thought. . . . '

'Just what did you think, Kate? You haven't been the same since Maggie – hell! You didn't imagine that I was her lover?'

'Of course not.' I looked into his searching eyes. 'Your mother was waiting for me when I got back to my room that morning. She forbade me to ride astride again – and she said you were just amusing yourself – that everyone was laughing at me.'

'You didn't believe her?' Harry looked grim. 'But of course you did. She can be very convincing.' He studied my face. 'That wasn't all, was it? Tell me what else she said to you.'

'She said you were still in love with Helen and that I shouldn't hope for anything.'

'Damn her interference!' he cried angrily. 'I thought you were blaming me for what happened to Maggie.'

'That wasn't your fault. I blamed myself as much as anyone. I knew she was unhappy.'

'I'd no idea she was that desperate.' Harry frowned. 'I suppose we shall never know the truth of it.' He took my hand, smiling gently. 'Mother was wrong, Kate. I've always been fond of Helen – but I've never wanted to marry her. It was the other way around. Helen assumed that we would become engaged when I left Cambridge. I told her I wasn't ready to marry and she said she'd known it in her heart, and then she married Philip. We're friends – but despite that kiss you saw, there's no more to it. Do you believe me?'

I gazed up at him for a few seconds, then nodded. 'Yes, I believe you.'

'Good.' He took my hand and kissed it. 'I was trying to tell you the morning we found Maggie. I wanted to find out how you felt about things.'

'What do you mean?'

'About living here for the rest of your life. I'm the heir to Brockmere, Kate. I have a kind of love-hate relationship with the place. Sometimes I feel as though I'm trapped, yet I couldn't desert my duty. If you married me, you'd be trapped too.'

'If I married you?' My heart raced wildly. 'Are you asking me to marry you, Harry?'

'I'm asking you to think about it.' He smiled tenderly. 'You're very young, Kate. It's a lot to ask of you. You wouldn't just be taking me on – and I'm not the easiest person in the world! – you'd be taking on Brockmere and Mother. She's formidable, I know. It would be years before you were mistress of the house. She wouldn't be pleased with the marriage, and she could make it difficult for you.'

'But I love you, Harry,' I said, my eyes searching his. 'Does anything else really matter?'

'Bless you, my darling.' He reached out to stroke my cheek. 'You're so young and sweet and innocent. You don't understand how awkward Mother could make things for you.'

'Oh, I think I do, Harry. Do you think she will let us marry?'

'We shall have to win her over gradually. It won't be easy. Of course my father is your legal guardian while your mother isn't here. If he's happy with the idea, Mother will come round eventually.'

'When will you speak to him?'

'Not until the end of the summer.' Harry laughed as I pulled a face. 'My impatient Kate, how I love you when you look like that. Don't think I don't want to get it all settled. I wish we could be married tomorrow – but it's only fair that you should have one season. I know Father would say the same.'

'September seems so far away.' I sighed. 'I'm almost seventeen, Harry. I know my own mind. I think I fell in love with you that very first day – when you yelled at me for being in your way.'

'Did you, my sweet?' He grinned. 'I confess I wasn't sure until I saw you in those breeches. . . . '

'Beast!' I glared at him. 'Sometimes I – no, I don't. I love you so much, Harry. I've missed being with you these past weeks.'

'Well, there's no reason why we shouldn't continue your riding lessons – but we must be careful. If it came to a choice between Brockmere and you, I'd choose you, but I'm not sure where we'd go or what we'd do.'

'This place means a lot to you, doesn't it?'

'It's my heritage, Kate. It's in my blood. There have been Redferns here for centuries. If I turned my back on them, I would feel that I was letting them all down.' He touched my cheek. 'But I would still choose you.'

He was so confident, so determined, but I could sense just how much Brockmere really meant to Harry. He might talk of choosing me, and I had no doubt that he was strong enough to do it, but it would tear him apart.

'Then we'll be very careful, Harry. We won't let anyone guess how we feel until you think it's time – and by then your Mother will be so pleased with me that she won't object to our marriage. I'll be so good that she'll think I'm the perfect wife for you.'

'Don't let her change you too much. I love you the way you are.'

'Oh, Harry,' I sighed. 'I wish. . . . '

'I know,' he said. 'You wish your mother was here, but she isn't. You just have to accept it – and ignore what anyone else says.' He took my hand and pulled me to my feet. 'Come on, let's go on the river.'

I dreamed that night of a woman who was my mother and yet not my mother. She had the same face and hair, but her eyes were different. Cold and icy, they looked through me when I called to her.

'Mother . . . ' I cried despairingly, holding out my arms to her. 'Please come back. . . . Oh, please come back to me.'

She was dancing with a man, laughing up at him, her face young and beautiful. She danced right by me, turning to glance at me once, but not seeing me. It was as if she was a stranger.

'Mother,' I said again. 'Don't you know me?'

She and her partner danced away into the mist. I awoke with tears on my cheeks.

It was a beautiful spring morning. Harry was waiting for me as I left the breakfast room.

'I've a new car,' he said, his eyes sparkling. 'It's a Barré 3-litre sports and I'm going to race it at Brooklands next month. Come on, Kate. I'll show you how fast it will go – if you dare?'

'What do you mean – if I dare?'

'That's my Kate!' He tugged at my hand, hurrying me through the gardens. 'Until you've driven with me at speed, you've never lived.'

'Such arrogance,' I said, laughing. 'We'll see.'

His car was an open-topped sports model with flat running-boards over the wire wheels, and its bonnet was tied down with a leather strap. It was clearly intended for racing and not for comfort. Harry reached into the back and handed me a huge, enveloping coat.

'You'd better put this dustcoat on or you'll spoil your dress,' he said.

I climbed into the car, watching as he cranked the engine to roaring life before jumping in beside me. 'You asked for it,' he said, a demon smile spreading over his mouth as he pulled on his leather skull cap and goggles. 'Hold on, Kate.'

The coarse gravel rattled beneath the wheels as he started off. I hung onto the side of the car, realizing I'd provoked him into a show of dare-devilry. We roared through the estate, out into country lanes that had been built for the slow progress of horse-drawn vehicles, far exceeding the speed limit enforced on all roads. I was sure he couldn't have stopped if we'd met any other traffic, but it seemed as if the gods were with us, for we saw no one as we sped through the brilliance of that early spring morning. It was an exhilarating experience that took my breath away, but I wasn't frightened. Instead, I laughed, urging Harry on and on, faster and faster. He grinned at me, pushing the car to its full speed before gradually slowing to a saner pace.

When at last we stopped, I was covered in a fine, powdery dust. Harry helped me down and I took off the dustcoat. He shook it for me and brushed the dust from my hair, wiping my face with a large white handkerchief. I stood absolutely still, my eyes bright as I looked up at him.

'You win,' he said, and grinned.

'It wasn't a contest,' I murmured. 'It was fun. I enjoyed it so. . . .' My words were stilled as I saw the look in his eyes. 'Harry, we mustn't. . . . '

He caught me to him and, as his mouth covered mine, I surrendered to the clamouring of my heart, clinging to him urgently. I was swept away on a tide of sensation, feeling as though I would melt for the sheer pleasure of being in his arms. When he let me go I was trembling and so was he.

'I'm going to speak to Father,' he said breathlessly. 'I can't go on like this.'

'Yes, yes,' I said eagerly. 'I do love you so, Harry.'

He smiled at me. 'We'll explore for a while,' he said, 'then I'll take you to lunch – and when we get home I'll tell Father we're going to get married.'

'Your mother has guests for lunch,' I reminded him. 'She'll be expecting me.'

'It's time my mother learnt that she can't have it all her own way.' Harry took my hand. 'Come on, Kate, let's go exploring. . . . '

We walked into the house hand in hand. We could hear voices coming from the drawing room. Harry let go of my hand. I saw that he was slightly apprehensive.

'I want to talk to Father first,' he said. 'Don't say anything for the moment.'

I nodded, smiling. 'I promise.'

Prue, Lady Selina and Sir Gerald were all together. There was no sign of the luncheon guests and I presumed they had gone. Glancing at Lady Selina, I saw that her face was serious and I trembled inwardly. She was going to be very angry because I'd missed lunch.

'So there you are, Kate,' she said, and I was surprised at the gentleness of her tone. 'I've been waiting for you.'

'It's my fault, Mother,' Harry said quickly. 'I kidnapped Kate for a drive in my new car. You mustn't be angry with her.'

'I'm not angry,' Lady Selina said. She looked at me and something in her face made me feel frightened. 'I'm sorry, Kate. There's no way I can soften the blow. I'm afraid I have to tell you that your mother is dead.'

I felt as if she'd punched me in the stomach. 'No . . . ' I gasped. 'I don't believe you . . . she can't be. . . . '

'I've had a letter,' she said. 'And documents. Your mother died in France about three weeks ago.'

'No. . . . ' I shook my head, feeling the hysteria sweep over me. 'It isn't true. It isn't! It isn't. . . . '

I stared wildly about me, looking for some escape from the nightmare her words had evoked.

'Oh, Harry. . . . ' I turned to him instinctively as the pain struck. 'Harry, tell me it isn't true. Tell me this is all a lie.'

His face was ashen. He stared at his mother and then reached out to take me in his arms, holding me and stroking my hair.

'I'm sorry, darling,' he said. 'Truly sorry.'

'But it can't be true,' I sobbed, looking up at him. 'Her last letter said she was feeling better.' I was shaking, my eyes wild as I begged him to tell me it wasn't really happening.

'Kate,' he said uncertainly. 'My mother wouldn't lie to you about something like this.'

'She would!' I cried, losing all control and pounding at his chest with my fists. 'You know she doesn't like me. It can't be true. I can't bear it. I can't!'

'Calm down, Kate,' Harry said, his voice sounding harsh to me. 'You knew it had to happen – perhaps it's for the best. . . . '

'For the best?' I stared at him in stunned disbelief. 'How could you say that? How could you?' He took a step towards me and I backed away, shaking my head. 'NO! Don't come near me. Don't touch me.'

'Kate,' he cried. 'I didn't mean it that way. . . . '

I whirled and ran from the room, taking the stairs two at a time in my haste to get away. How could Harry say such a terrible thing? I'd always known he didn't really approve of my mother but he knew how much she meant to me.

I raced into my room and locked the door. Harry was seconds behind me. He pounded on the door, begging to be let in.

'I'm sorry, Kate. I didn't mean to hurt you, you know I didn't. I only meant that now the worst was over, you would be able to forget. . . . '

'I'll never forget her,' I cried. 'How could you think that I would?' I leant my back against the door, tears streaming down my cheeks. 'Go away, Harry. I don't want to talk to you. I shall never forgive you.'

'Don't say that, Kate. I love you.'

'Go away. Go away. Go away!'

I ran to the bed and threw myself down, sobbing as my heart shattered into a thousand tiny pieces.

I stayed in my room for two days, eating nothing and drinking only water from the bathroom. I wouldn't let anyone in and I wouldn't answer Harry when he pleaded with me to let him in. On the evening of the second day, he came to my door again.

'Forgive me, Kate. I didn't mean to hurt you.'

'I can't forgive you.'

'I'm going away for a while.' I didn't answer. 'I haven't spoken to Father; there's no point until you let me talk to you. I'm going down to Brooklands to race the car, and I'll stay with some friends for a week or two.' He paused, then: 'Kate, are you listening?'

'Yes.'

'I won't go if you don't want me to.'

'Go, Harry. Please go.'

'All right. Try to forgive me, Kate. Please.'

I didn't answer and after a few minutes he went away.

'Kate.' Lady Selina knocked at the door. 'Let me in, Kate. I have to talk to you. It's no good being silly. You have to eat or you'll be ill.'

I didn't answer and she rattled the door handle.

'Is Harry with you?'

'No. He's gone to stay with friends. He spoke thoughtlessly, Kate, but he didn't intend to hurt you.'

'I know,' I said and opened the door. 'I'm all right now. I was coming down soon.'

'You look terrible. Rosie can bring you a light meal on a tray. You can come down in the morning.'

'As you say,' I agreed meekly. 'I'm sorry I accused you of lying. Of course I know you wouldn't.'

'It was a terrible shock for you. Death is never easy to accept, however inevitable it is.' She looked at me oddly. 'Before I married Sir Gerald there was someone I loved very much. I knew that he was dying of an incurable illness, but when the end came it nearly destroyed me.'

'I'm so sorry.' I stared at her. It must have cost her something to tell me that.

'So you see, Kate, you are not the only one who has known sorrow.'

'I know. It was just that Harry sounded so – so callous.'

She nodded, frowning. 'I'm very angry with Harry. He was thoughtless – though he was actually thinking of you.'

'I know that,' I said. 'I – I suppose there's no doubt it is true?'

'I have all the documents. A woman had been with her until the end. She said it was quick and that Emma didn't suffer.'

'I see – was she buried in France?'

'You would've liked to have seen her grave?' Lady Selina frowned as I nodded. 'Perhaps we can arrange it at a future date.'

'Thank you.' I bit my lip. 'I'm sorry I made such a fuss.'

'It was quite understandable. You've been under a strain. Harry was right when he said you may begin to feel better now.'

'Yes, I've realized that now. He only said it because he cares about me.'

Lady Selina looked thoughtful. 'Yes,' she said. 'I think you are right.'

After she had gone, I thought about what she had told me. There were hidden depths to Lady Selina that I had never suspected.

In the days that followed, Lady Selina and Prue were both very considerate. I was allowed to do what I liked. For a week or two I avoided being in company, but then I found that the ache in my heart eased a little when I was with a group of young people, and I realized I couldn't go on grieving alone. I had to accept that my mother was dead. I had to make a new life for myself. I'd begun to miss Harry and wish that he would come home. I should never have sent him away.

It was early summer now and there was always a dinner-party or guests for luncheon and tea at Brockmere. We went to visit Lady Selina's friends, and they came to us. Gradually, I was being introduced to all the young men of the neighbourhood, and to my surprise I found that I was becoming popular. I never went out with any of the young men alone, of course, that wouldn't have been proper, but whenever a special entertainment was planned, I was always invited.

Lady Selina had decided against my going into mourning. 'You're young, Kate,' she said. 'And your mother's death isn't generally known amongst our friends. You will do better to mix with young people than spend your time moping alone.'

My seventeenth birthday arrived. Harry sent me a present and a card, but his message was brief and formal. I felt a little hurt, though in my heart I knew our quarrel had been my fault. He had tried to apologize but in my grief I had refused to listen. Now that I'd had time to think, I realized how foolish I had been. I missed Harry so much. I hadn't known, until he went away, how big a part he played in my life. I missed that feeling of having someone special to share jokes with. We had always been able to communicate with just a look or a smile. It just wasn't the same without him. I began to look for him every day and listen for his voice, to long for his return.

The house was always full of people. Lady Selina seemed determined to keep Prue and me busy. We were always going somewhere. We went to Ascot dressed in our best, picnicked on the banks of the river at Henley, cheering for the Cambridge Blues and drinking champagne from crystal glasses. I thought we might see Harry there, supporting his old college team, but if he went he didn't come near us. I was beginning to wonder if he would ever come home.

PART TWO

'If you've finished your breakfast, we may as well do it now. Come into the sitting room and I'll give you the note.' She glanced at Prue. 'You'll have to ring Mrs Bates if everything is cold. I haven't time to see to it. Why can't you be bright and early like Kate?'

Prue didn't say anything, but she gave me a look of dislike, as if she were blaming me for her mother's coolness towards her.

In the sitting room, Lady Selina wrote a brief note and handed it to me. 'I hope you don't mind obliging me, Kate?'

'A walk in the fresh air will do me good.'

She nodded. 'You look a little peaky. We want you looking your best next week, don't we? I know all your admirers will be anxious to greet you.'

My cheeks burned. 'I don't have any.'

'But I think you do, Kate. There was that nice Mr Havers – good family though not much money – and Philip's younger brother, he was very taken with you, I know. And Mr Goodman. . . . '

'But he's old enough to be my grandfather.'

'But wealthy, and such a nice man. You could do worse, Kate.' Annoyance flickered in her eyes. 'Haven't you met anyone you particularly like?'

'I like lots of people, but I don't want to marry them.'

She frowned at me. 'I hope you're not going to be difficult, too. I really don't know what's got into Prunella lately.' She tapped her fingers impatiently on the desk, seeming to have forgotten me for the moment.

'Shall I take the letter now?'

She nodded, dismissing me, apparently more annoyed with her daughter than with me. I knew she had hoped to announce Prue's engagement this year, but so far Prue had formed no special attachments, or none that her mother knew of. . . .

It was very warm, but there was a pleasant breeze as I walked through the orchard and across the meadows to the Vicarage. It was quicker this way than by the road to the village, and prettier, but it still took me a good half an hour to walk it.

I paused by the river, watching a pair of swans glide majestically by. I was thinking about what Lady Selina had said at breakfast – was Harry really courting this other girl? He hadn't exactly lived like a monk, but the other women in his life had all been married. If he was paying attention to Miss Brockley it could mean only one thing. And yet he'd sworn he loved me.

I spent over an hour at the Vicarage listening to Mrs Bridge gossip. On the return journey I had no time to stand and stare at the muddy waters of the river; I mustn't be late for lunch as Lady Selina wasn't in the best of moods. I walked swiftly through the orchard, which was alive with the sound of birdsong, through the arched gateway and into the shrubberies. The scent of roses and honeysuckle was borne to me on the breeze, and then I saw the man coming across the lawns to meet me.

'Kate,' he called, his stride lengthening. 'I saw you coming and thought I'd wait for you.'

'Good morning, monsieur,' I said. 'Where's Prue?'

'She's changing for lunch, I should imagine. Why?'

'I just wondered.' How could I explain that she would think I'd planned this meeting? That she thought of him as being her private property? 'Did you want something in particular?'

'I wanted to say goodbye. I'm returning to London this afternoon – and then to France.'

'I thought you were staying with Helen for a few more days?'

'I was, but something has happened. Lady Selina has invited me to call again when I'm in England, and I'd like to.' He looked at me as if to gauge my reaction.

'I'm sure Prue will be pleased to see you.'

'If I call it will be to see you, Kate.' His look was significant and I dropped my eyes.

'I – I don't think that's wise, monsieur.'

'Why?' he asked, a note of impatience in his voice. 'Look at me, Kate.' He reached out to take me by the shoulders, giving me a little shake. 'You must know I have a deep regard for you?'

'I don't see why you should have.' I refused to look at him and he sighed with exasperation.

'So stubborn,' he said. 'I'm going to leave you my address in both France and London. I want you to contact me if you're ever unhappy or in trouble. Promise me, Kate.'

That brought my gaze up sharply. 'Why should you want to help me?'

His expression was very odd, half guilt, half something else that I didn't understand. 'I think I owe you . . . ' he began, but even as he spoke we heard someone calling my name. We turned as a man came striding towards us. 'Your friend seems anxious to attract your attention, Kate.'

'It's Harry,' I said, my heart pounding wildly. 'Prue's brother.'

Paul saw the expression on my face and nodded. 'I see. . . . '

Harry came up to us, his face grim. Paul had been holding my arm, now he let go. We all stood silently, looking at each other.

'Won't you introduce me to your friend, Kate?' Harry's tone was icy.

'This is Monsieur Paul de Bernay,' I said, defiantly. 'So you're home, then?'

'Not a moment too soon by the looks of it.'

'What do you mean?' My cheeks flamed. His meaning was very clear and I was embarrassed. He was glaring at Paul belligerently, his fists clenched as though he wanted to knock him down.

'You know what I mean,' he snarled. 'Does my mother know you came out to meet this friend of yours?'

'I've been delivering a letter for her,' I said, indignant now. 'I met Monsieur de Bernay by accident.'

'Really?' The disbelief was written all over his face.

'I wanted to tell Kate I was leaving,' Paul said quickly. 'If there has been any impropriety, it is my fault, not hers.'

'Indeed?' Harry was bristling like a dog whose bone was under attack. 'Is it usual for a gentleman to embrace a girl he hardly knows? Or is there something I don't know about, Kate?'

'No, there isn't,' I snapped back. 'And if you'd been here these past few weeks, you'd know that.' I glared at him. 'But you've been too busy with Clara Brockley.'

'And what is that supposed to mean?' Harry glowered down at me.

'Excuse me, I think this is private.' Paul inclined his head to us and walked away, a faint smile on his lips.

Harry stared at me, still angry. 'What's this all about, Kate? You sent me away.'

'I was upset,' I admitted, 'but only for a few days. If you'd come home when you said you would, we could have talked it out – but you were having too much fun.'

'Who told you I was interested in Clara?'

'Your mother said she was exactly the kind of girl they want you to marry.'

'I might have known,' he cried, exasperated. 'She wrote to me and told me to stay away for a bit longer because you still hadn't forgiven me.'

We stared at each other, then Harry smiled ruefully. He reached out to take my hand.

'Were you courting her, Harry?'

'Have you so little faith in me?'

'I – I wasn't sure. I sent you away. I thought you might have stopped loving me.'

'And I thought you'd found someone else.' He smiled wryly. 'I'm sorry I flew into a temper, Kate. When I saw him holding you like that I thought. . . . '

'Paul knew my mother, Harry. He wanted to help me.'

'You don't need help. I'm going to look after you.' There was jealousy in his eyes. 'I love you, Kate.'

'Do you?' I asked, smiling up at him. 'I wish we hadn't quarrelled like that.'

'It was my fault. I spoke carelessly, but I only meant that the uncertainty was over. It worried you so much, not knowing. . . . ' He looked at me pleadingly. 'Forgive me, Kate.'

'I already have. Let's forget it, shall we?'

'Thank you.' He touched my hand to his lips. 'Dearest Kate.'

'Does the family know you're home?'

'No. I saw you and. . . . ' He laughed ruefully.

'We'd better go in or we'll be late for lunch.'

'That will never do. We want Mother to be in a good mood when I talk to Father about us.'

We linked arms and walked towards the house. 'Perhaps you ought to wait a few days, Harry. She'd made up her mind that you were going to marry Clara. Can't you let her down gently?'

He pulled a face. 'I expect you're right. I don't want to antagonize her – for your sake.'

'Let's leave it until we get back from town then,' I said.

I went to tidy myself before lunch. Just as I was about to leave, the door opened and Prue came in. Her face looked puffy and I guessed that she'd been crying again.

'What's wrong, Prue?' I asked.

'Don't pretend you don't know,' she said, her eyes like crystal. 'I've seen you making eyes at him – and I saw you with him in the garden the other day. How could you do it, Kate? You could have any of the men who come here; they all fall over themselves to do things for you. You knew he was the one I wanted.'

My heart sank as I realized she was talking about Paul. 'I haven't done anything to encourage Paul de Bernay,' I said. 'The other day

158

in the garden – well, I'd told him my mother was dead and it upset me. He was just trying to comfort me.'

'He put his arms round you!'

'It didn't mean anything, Prue. I promise you.'

She stared at me miserably. 'I thought he liked me the first time he came, but now he just ignores me – and I've seen him looking at you as if he wanted to gobble you up.'

'I think he just feels sorry for me.'

She hardly seemed to hear. 'I hoped he would ask me to marry him. I hoped he might speak to Father. . . . ' Her voice broke. 'What am I going to do, Kate? I think I'm in love with him.'

'Perhaps it's just too soon. He might call when we're in London.'

'Do you think so?' Her face cleared. 'Mother's been on to me about making an effort to form an attachment with someone suitable – but no one else has even looked at me. Paul was so kind to me that first day I thought. . . . ' She caught back a sob. 'Oh, why did I have to be a girl? Why couldn't I have been a man and born first? I wish I didn't have to leave Brockmere ever!'

I looked at her flushed face and saw that she was really miserable. 'You love Brockmere, don't you?' I asked.

She nodded, and her face lit up with an inner radiance that made her look almost beautiful. 'I love the house,' she said reverently. 'I love the feeling that my family have been here for generations. I love all the pictures and the Bible. . . . ' She looked at me suddenly. 'Your mother's name is in it, Kate. The whole family tree is there – you, too, and your children when you marry.'

'Will you show me one day, Prue?'

She nodded, the glow fading. Her face looked red and puffy and plain once more. 'I can't come down, Kate – will you tell Mother I have a headache?'

'Yes,' I said, feeling sorry for her as she suddenly rushed from the room. It couldn't be very pleasant to feel that you were constantly being pushed into a suitable marriage just because it was expected of you by the family.

We had three hectic weeks in London, buying clothes, visiting friends and attending lunches, dinners and dances. Lady Selina had arranged for me to be presented early in August with the daughters of some close friends, just before my own dance at Brockmere. A white satin gown was being prepared for me, and I'd already tried on the white feathers I would wear in my hair. I grumbled to Harry about all the practising I had to do for the formal curtsey I must make to Their Majesties, but he only laughed.

'It's no good moaning,' he said unsympathetically. 'It's just something all you girls have to go through.'

'Well, I just wish I didn't,' I retorted crossly. 'And if you keep on grinning like that, Harry, I shall hit you!'

I was secretly dreading the ordeal and hoping that something would happen to save me, but when it did, it was so dreadful that I felt guilty – as if by wishing for my own selfish reasons to be out of London, I'd made it happen.

It was near the end of July when the news that was to change all our lives was announced. Sir Gerald had been right; the assassination of the Archduke had been the catalyst that brought about the start of the war which had for so long been threatening to erupt in Europe.

'Austria has declared war on Serbia,' he announced over breakfast, after reading the headlines. 'The Imperial Council in Berlin has also voted for war against Russia, and that means France will be dragged into it. We can't hope to stay out of it now.'

'You're right, of course.' Lady Selina paused in the act of pouring tea from a large silver pot. 'Do you think we should go home early?'

'Yes.' He looked at me apologetically. 'This means we shall have to put off your presentation, Kate, but I'm sure all such affairs will be cancelled in the light of this news.'

'I'm quite happy to go home,' I said. 'But I hope there won't be a war.'

'I fear it's inevitable. I shall go on ahead today, and the rest of you can follow tomorrow. No doubt we shall lose half the men from the estate once the King makes it official.'

'At least it will give me a few extra days to prepare for the church garden party,' Lady Selina said, looking thoughtful. 'We may have to cancel your dance, Kate.'

'We'll see what happens,' Sir Gerald said. 'We don't want to spoil the young people's fun unless we have to.'

'Even if we go to war, it can't last long – can it?' Lady Selina frowned at him.

'With luck, it will be over by Christmas – but one never knows with these things.' He was obviously trying to reassure us. 'Where's Harry?'

'He breakfasted earlier so that he could go to look at a car, I think.'

'That son of mine is car mad!' Sir Gerald snorted.

160

Lady Selina looked at Prue and then me. 'Since this is our last day in town for a while, how would you like to spend it?'

'Shopping,' Prue replied promptly. 'I want some shoes.'

'And I need to go to Swan and Edgar,' Lady Selina said. 'What about you, Kate?' I was about to reply when Rosie came in with a small package on a silver salver. 'Is that for me?'

'No, ma'am,' Rosie replied. 'It's for Miss Kate – by special delivery.'

I took the package and thanked her. For a moment I stared at the writing on the label. 'I wonder who it's from?'

'Open it,' Lady Selina said, frowning slightly.

I obeyed. Inside was a letter and a blue velvet box. I unfolded the letter, staring at the impressive heading in surprise. 'It's from a lawyer acting on behalf of another lawyer in France. Oh. . . . ' I looked at her across the table. 'It's about a legacy from my mother. She has left me a gold locket and – and five hundred pounds.'

Lady Selina frowned. 'Are you sure, Kate? Couldn't it be fifty pounds?'

I handed her the letter and opened the box. Inside was a large but delicate gold locket worked with applied flowers and leaves in a different coloured gold, and there was an inscription inside.

'It says, "To my dearest Kate from her loving mother", isn't that lovely?' I cried, feeling the sting of tears and torn between pleasure at the gift and grief. This proved without doubt that my mother was dead. Until this moment I'd secretly hoped it was all a terrible mistake.

Lady Selina returned the letter. 'That is a considerable sum of money, Kate. You must take care of it.'

'Will you allow me to repay you for some of what you've given me?'

'Certainly not,' she replied, annoyed that I had suggested such an idea. 'It will provide an independence for you.'

'You mustn't think of repayment,' Sir Gerald said. 'Keep your money, Kate.'

'I didn't think she ever had this much money.'

'It's a small mystery,' Lady Selina agreed. She glanced at the gold watch pinned to her gown. 'Go and get ready, girls. I'll be with you shortly. I've something to discuss with Gerald.'

We had been dismissed, and Prue and I rose immediately. I thought that perhaps Lady Selina wished to discuss my unexpected legacy. It was quite a mystery.

Prue looked at me as we went upstairs. 'Don't you think that legacy was rather odd?' she asked. 'How could your mother possibly have five hundred pounds to leave you?'

'I don't know.' I wrinkled my brow.

'She didn't own the house you lived in, did she?'

'No – we rented it. She did say a friend had given her some money. Perhaps she didn't use it all.'

Disbelief was in her eyes. 'Well, it all sounds a bit fishy to me.'

'What do you mean?'

'Mother told me Paul mentioned to her that he would like to help you.'

I stared at her. 'He wouldn't do something like this! Why should he?'

She shrugged her shoulders but I could see the jealousy in her eyes. 'If he felt sorry for you he might – Helen said he's enormously wealthy. Five hundred pounds would be nothing to him.'

'That's a rotten thing to say.'

She flushed, dropping her eyes as we went our separate ways. I walked into my room, locking the door behind me. My temples were pounding and I had to fight the storm of emotion that swept over me. Why should the legacy have come from Paul? No, that was only Prue's jealous imagination. The locket was a gift from my mother and I would treasure it as such.

It was wonderful to be back at Brockmere. The last day in town had been hectic, with everyone rushing around in a frenzy, all talking about the coming war.

It was a lovely day and I'd decided to escape for a while. Prue had gone off to sulk in her room, and Harry was tinkering with his cars. It was a perfect opportunity to be alone.

I began by walking beside the river. As the afternoon wore on it became warmer and muggy, making my skin moist with sweat. I paused at a shallow spot in the river, sitting on the bank to gaze into the clear water. It looked inviting and I stared longingly before taking off my shoes and stockings to paddle. The river bed was covered with sharp sand and stones and I had a sudden urge to swim. It would be so good to feel the coolness of the water all over my body. . . . Why not? Why shouldn't I swim naked as I had years before in the river at home?

I glanced round furtively, knowing that there would be trouble if I were caught. Even though this stretch of the river was isolated, it was still risky. Supposing someone came? But everyone was busy. No one need ever know if I was careful. I could dry myself with my petticoat and then let that dry in the sun before I went back to the house. I must just be careful not to get my hair wet.

Finding a bush near the water's edge, I swiftly unbuttoned my bodice and stepped out of my dress. Throwing off my underclothes, I ran into the water, plunging in despite the sudden chill on my heated skin. It was colder than I'd expected, but it felt wonderful. I swam boldly out into mid-stream, enjoying my adventure. After months of restrictions, it was marvellous to feel so free. I knew it was sheer madness – Lady Selina would think I'd taken leave of my senses! – but it was such fun. Forgetting to be cautious, I turned over on my back. Only when I felt the water soaking into my hair did I realize what I'd done. It would take ages to dry, and I couldn't go back to the house with wet hair. I struck out for the shore, sprinting to my bush. Snatching up my petticoat, I began to dry myself, shaking out my hair so that it would have a better chance to dry. Then I heard an odd choking sound behind me and I spun round in alarm.

'Harry!' I clutched my petticoat to my naked breasts. 'I – I thought you were working on your. . . . '

My voice trailed away as I saw the longing in his eyes. He was staring at me as a man dying of thirst might stare at the mirage of an oasis. I was trembling from head to toe, unable to move as my pulse began to race wildly. I couldn't breathe properly and my head was whirling. I gave a little cry and my petticoat dropped from my nervous fingers.

'Kate . . . ' Harry groaned. 'Kate, you're so beautiful. I love you. I want you so much . . . so much. . . . '

I was in a dream. I felt as if my mind was suspended from thought, my lips parting beneath his as I gave myself up to his kiss. Then my hands were in his hair, moving feverishly on the back of his neck. I clung to him, almost swooning as I felt the touch of his lips against my throat, then my shoulders and my breasts. A shiver went through me and I arched into his body, feeling the urgent throb of desire. Instinctively, I knew that this was what love between a man and a woman was all about. It was so right and natural.

'Harry,' I whispered. 'I love you . . . I love you.'

'My darling Kate,' he muttered hoarsely. 'I've tried to be patient, but I need you, I want you.'

I felt the heat of his breath as his kisses rained on my face, my throat, my shoulders. I moaned, caught up by the force of our mutual desire. I was drowning in a sea of longing and wanting. Convention decreed that we should wait for our wedding night, but this felt so right, how could it be wrong?

Somehow Harry had struggled out of his clothes, though our lips had hardly parted. We were on fire, eager and greedy in our demands. I responded to his every touch, following his lead so that each new step seemed as natural as breathing. I wasn't frightened as Harry took me with such gentleness that I experienced only a little pain. I did not feel the exquisite pleasure that it seemed to give him when he emptied himself inside me, but my pleasure came from his. His kisses covered my body, his impassioned words making me feel so happy. I lay in his arms, contented and glowing in the warmth of his love.

Harry smiled at me tenderly. 'You're wonderful, Kate. I adore you, do you know that?'

I looked at him shyly. 'I never knew I could feel like that.'

'Didn't you?' He laughed. 'I knew it from the start. There's something special about you, Kate. No wonder I never wanted to marry any of those milk and water misses my mother kept pushing at me – I was waiting for my own little firebrand.'

'Harry!' I exclaimed, indignantly. 'You make me sound immoral.'

'Then that's the way I want you.' He stroked my face, pushing back my hair. 'We're going to be married just as soon as I can arrange it. I'm going to make sure we're never parted again – that no other man will ever have you.'

'Oh, Harry. . . . ' I gazed up at him, my eyes shining. 'When will you speak to your father?'

'This evening,' he said. 'But it doesn't matter what he says – or Mother either – I'm going to marry you, Kate.'

'Harry, I do love . . . ' I began, but his lips were on mine, shutting off the words as he drew me to him once more.

The afternoon was drawing to its close. I knew we should get back, but as Harry's hands began to stroke and caress me once more, I forgot everything, clinging to him wildly and crying out his name over and over again. . . .

CHAPTER FOURTEEN

She woke with a terrible headache in a strange room. Looking around her, she saw that it was a rather shabby room but the sheets smelt fresh and everything was neat and tidy. She sat up in bed, groaning as her senses swam. Then the door opened and a woman came in. A shock of surprise went through her – the woman was a complete stranger, and yet she knew that face. It was the face she saw every time she glanced in a mirror!

The woman laughed as she saw Emma's expression. 'So you've noticed it, too,' she said. 'I was there when you were taken ill in the square the other day, and I was struck by the resemblance between us. No one knew who you were, so I had you brought here. I hope you don't mind?' She spoke in French but her accent betrayed her. She was not a native of France.

'I'm very grateful,' Emma replied. 'I don't see why you should have. . . . '

Now that she looked closer, she saw that there were differences between them. The woman was older, and there was something about her . . . a look in the eyes that made her wonder. As the woman began to cough, turning away to press a handkerchief to her mouth, Emma knew what was wrong.

'You're ill,' she said and got out of bed. 'You're really ill, aren't you?'

It was a while before the woman was able to reply. Then she just smiled sadly. 'You've seen it before, haven't you?'

'My mother was slowly dying of consumption, then my father died and she went quickly. It was a blessing for her.'

'Yes. I often wish I could go quickly. My husband was killed in an accident two years ago. I have very little money and the doctors can't do anything for me.'

'And you've been looking after me.' Emma stared at her for a moment, then, 'You need help. I'm going to take you to my rooms – they're better than these – and I'm going to be with you until. . . .'

'Until the end?' The woman's brows went up. 'But why should you? You don't even know me.'

'You're English.' Emma smiled as she stared. 'I can tell by the way you pronounce certain words. We're both alone. Both widows. Why shouldn't we be friends?'

'No. . . . ' The woman shook her head. 'There's something more, isn't there?'

Emma hesitated and then she nodded. 'Yes, there is,' she said slowly. 'I want something from you . . . something only you can give me. . . . '

Emma stood looking down at the dead woman's face. Now that the pain had gone she looked younger, but less like Emma, somehow. The likeness had been superficial after all. Yet it was near enough to serve her purpose.

For the last few months they had changed identities. It had been simple enough, for the woman's name had been Emmeline Dubois. They had hardly noticed the difference themselves after the first few days.

At first Emmeline had been doubtful, wanting assurances that Emma had not done anything very terrible.

'I'm not a murderer,' Emma said. 'It's just that I want to leave my past behind, become someone else.'

Perhaps because she was lonely and in desperate need, Emmeline had agreed that she would be buried as Emma Linton. In return, Emma cared for her devotedly, paying for the doctor's visits and for food, lodging and fires for them both. They spent the long winter nights talking about their lives, becoming friends. At the end she had sat holding the dying woman's hand, comforting her as she slipped away. And she had wept for the loss of a friend.

Now the papers were hers. She could send them to Selina Redfern as proof of her death. She had thought it through carefully, and she knew it was for the best. She could never go back to England. It was for Kate's sake, so that she would be free. She knew Kate too well. For as long as she believed her mother was alive, she would cling to the hope of seeing her again.

It was for the best. The papers that confirmed her death were in her hand. She had to do it. . . .

She'd drunk too much champagne. Emma knew it but she didn't care. It was the only way to dull the ache inside her, the only way to forget. . . . But she would never forget him, the man for whom she had thrown everything away. She had loved Paul. She had loved him with a blind, obsessive intensity that was almost madness. It was

166

months now since they'd parted, but her body still craved his touch; it was a sickness inside her that she could ease only with the steady deadening of alcohol, and sometimes the kisses of a stranger. . . .

It had been bearable while she was caring for Emmeline. She had been able to cope with the hurt, because her friend was in pain and she had subdued her own misery, but now she was alone. She had always hated being alone. It brought too many memories. Memories of her parents, Froggie and . . . Kate. She needed another drink. . . . She looked round for the waiter and then a man came over to her table. He smiled down at her as he asked, 'Can I get you another drink?'

She looked up into the face of the stranger and her heart jerked. It wasn't Paul, but the dark eyes had that same compelling softness and the smile was almost as charming. She nodded, forcing the ghosts from her mind. They would come back, she knew. In the morning they would all be there to haunt her once more, but for now perhaps she could find forgetfulness, if only for a few hours. . . .

Her mouth felt like sawdust and her temples pounded. Her gaze travelled slowly round the untidy room. Strewn with canvases, paints and all kinds of clutter, from bits of twig, pebbles and empty wine bottles to piles of unwashed clothing, it smelt of a mixture of linseed oil, sweat and stale cooking. On the bed her current lover lay snoring, his mouth open. Their relationship had lasted for longer than most; she'd been with Armand a month now. He was a large, greedy man – greedy for life, the pleasures of the flesh and money. His paintings were flamboyant and not particularly good. When he had money he spent it recklessly, but he was more often broke. She had been supporting him for the past two weeks, and soon the money Paul had given her would be gone. She still had some of the jewellery he'd bought her, hidden in a safe place, but she would be loathe to sell it. It was time she moved on.

Moving carefully so as not to wake Armand, she began to pick up her clothes and push them into a battered suitcase. She was reaching for her shoes from beneath the bed when Armand suddenly rolled over and caught her wrist, his strong fingers bruising her flesh. A chill went through her as she stared into his bloodshot eyes.

'And where do you think you're going?' he asked.

Emma's head went up and she tried to wrench free of his grasp. 'I'm leaving.'

He slapped her hard across the mouth, pulling her down on to the bed and rolling her beneath him so that she was trapped by his weight.

'You leave when I say,' he growled, and belched in her face.

'Pig!' She spat at him and he hit her again. 'Let me go!'

'When I'm good and ready,' he muttered, his hand going beneath her skirt, forcing her legs apart as he thrust his fingers into the very centre of her, making her gasp at the sudden pain. Then he was lying on top of her, thrusting himself savagely into her, hurting her. He looked down at her face as she twisted beneath him, trying to throw him off. 'Love it, don't you' he murmured tauntingly. 'Can't get enough, can you?'

She struggled, hating him, wanting to shut out what was happening to her. She closed her eyes, blocking the sight of his mocking face and the sound of his harsh breathing from her mind. Tears trickled from the corners of her eyes as she endured the physical pain. But the mental agony was much worse – and this was the man she had thought was like Paul. . . . As the picture of his face came into her mind, she gave an animal scream and thrashed wildly, her head turning from side to side on the pillow. Then she saw the knife Armand used for scraping his palette lying on the little table beside the bed. Her fingers reached desperately and she knew a sense of triumph as they closed around the wooden handle.

Picking it up, she drove it hard into the side of his neck. . . .

Armand had taken himself off for a few hours and she was alone. She stared at herself in the mirror, seeing the dark bruises on her face and arms. Her hair was unwashed and she looked ill. A wave of misery swept over her as she reached for the wine bottle. How she wished she'd managed to kill that pig when she'd stabbed him in the neck. All she'd done was to wound him slightly and earn herself a beating.

How had she come to this? Looking at her own reflection, she felt a surge of disgust. Armand was using her and when her money had gone, he would throw her out. She ought to seize this chance to leave him, but all the fight seemed to have drained out of her. A sob broke from her and she closed her eyes, wishing she could turn back the clock. Why had she ever left England and her safe, secure little world? She'd been happy enough all those years, working at her sewing, dreaming and talking with Kate. . . .

As pictures of the girl's stricken face swam into her memory, she was stabbed with guilt. She'd sent Kate away. She'd lied to her and broken her heart. . . . She'd meant it for the best, of course she had, but there was something she ought to have told her. Something Kate ought to know in case. . . . It had begun to haunt her, this idea that she might have condemned her daughter to heartbreak and pain. Of course it was a chance in a million, but still, she ought to have warned Kate.

Perhaps it wasn't too late? She got up and began to search feverishly for paper and a pen. She would write to Kate. She would tell her the truth and beg her forgiveness. She could go home, back to England and they could start again. . . . Catching sight of herself in the mirror, a groan of despair broke from her. She couldn't go back. Emma Linton was dead; she'd sent the papers to prove it to England, and in a small, untended graveyard south of Paris there lay the body of Emmeline Dubois, a widow of English extraction, whom she had befriended in the first dark, desperate months after she'd parted from Paul.

She had wanted to disappear. She had wanted to sever all ties with the past, and she had succeeded only too well. Kate must be accustomed to living at Brockmere now. Why should she give it all up to go back to a life of poverty with the mother who had betrayed her?

She reached for the wine bottle once more, lifting it to her mouth to drain the last dregs. She couldn't go back; it was too late.

She came in from the market, her basket filled with fresh fruit, cheese and good, crusty bread. Armand was bending over her things. Seeing he had the last of her money in his hand, she gave a cry of rage and flung herself at him, trying to snatch the notes from him.

'That's mine!' she cried. 'You've no right. . . . '

'Bitch,' he snarled, hitting her across the face and throwing her backwards. 'We're finished. I'm leaving Paris before the Germans get here. If you've any sense, you'll do the same. Go back to England where you belong.'

She stared at him sullenly. 'They won't reach Paris; the British army will drive them back across the Rhine.'

'Pah!' He spat on the floor. 'The British don't know what has hit them. The Germans will flatten them and then they'll walk right into Paris. I'm getting out before they do.'

'What about your studio?'

He shrugged his shoulders. 'The rent's paid until the end of the month. Stay here if you wish.' He smiled mockingly and waved the money at her. 'A fair exchange, no?'

She watched as he picked up his easel and a satchel, saying nothing. At the door he turned to look back at her, neither of them spoke. When she realized he had finally gone, relief flooded through her. She was free of him at last; the money had been a small price to pay and she still had the jewellery hidden away.

Sitting down at the table, she began to unpack her basket. Would it be better to sell what she had and go back to England? If Armand was right and the Germans reached Paris. . . . But she had a French identity; there was no reason to panic just yet. She was free now, free to do as she pleased. But if she didn't sell the jewellery, she would need to find work. . . .

CHAPTER FIFTEEN

At dinner Harry smiled at me and my heart turned over. I thought that everyone must be able to see the intimacy of that smile and guess that we were lovers. Lovers! While the thought warmed and filled me with happiness, I was also a little shocked at my own behaviour and I dared not even think what Lady Selina would say if she knew! Yet surely it couldn't be so very wicked, when we were soon to be married.

The talk was all of the war, and opinion seemed divided. Philip said it would be a picnic and all over by Christmas, but Sir Gerald maintained it would be a far more serious affair than anyone yet realized.

'And what about you, Harry?' Philip asked. 'Shall you join if they call for volunteers?'

'War hasn't been declared yet,' Harry replied with a reassuring glance at me. 'We'll see what happens.'

'Harry will do his duty,' Sir Gerald put in with a frown. 'He's no coward.'

'War is a monstrosity,' Lady Selina said. 'Surely if, as everyone seems to think, the war won't last long, the regular army can cope?'

Sir Gerald's brows knitted. 'Men of decent background like Harry are sure to be needed.'

I wanted to scream at them to stop. I wanted to jump up and tell them all that Harry couldn't go because we were in love and we wanted to be together, but of course I did nothing of the sort. I sat in silence, longing for dinner to be over. Then, at last, Lady Selina led the ladies into the drawing room.

There were six of us in all: Helen, Prue, Lady Selina and two older women I didn't know very well. They were ladies of strong opinions and were more interested in condemning Mr Asquith than in talking of the war. Lady Selina was dispensing coffee. I moved away to the window, looking out into the darkness. The night looked cool and mysterious and I would have liked to slip away into the gardens. I could still feel the imprint of Harry's kisses on my lips. I wanted to think and feel and hold onto the memory of those precious hours by the river.

171

Prue came up to me, carrying a glass of sherry which she drained and set down. 'You seem different tonight,' she said, suspicion in her eyes.

'Do I?' I blushed and looked away. Had she seen that look Harry gave me at dinner?

'Kate, I've been wondering if there's something you ought to. . . .' She broke off as Helen came up to us.

'I hate all this talk of war, don't you?' she asked, flopping down in the chair beside me. 'Thank God Philip is too old to join up. If he does, they'll only give him a desk job in London.' She smiled winningly at Prue. 'Do get me another brandy, will you?'

'Do you think most of the men will sign up?' I asked as Prue moved away.

'You mean will Harry have to go?' Her brows rose. 'It's obvious how you two feel about each other, Kate.' She smiled as I blushed. 'I'm absolutely delighted, my dear.'

'Are you?'

She nodded. 'I was fond of Harry, but Philip spoils me. I wouldn't change him for. . . . Ah, here come the men, thank God. Those suffragette friends of Selina's are so boring. . . . '

She waved to Philip and he came over to sit with us. For a while the talk was general, then the card tables were set up. Helen went to make a four at bridge and Prue sat down at the piano. She flirted madly with Philip as he turned the music for her, and he seemed a little embarrassed. I'd noticed she'd been drinking quite a lot during dinner and afterwards, and I wondered what was wrong. She wasn't exactly drunk, but she was certainly acting oddly.

'A penny for them?'

Startled, I looked up at Harry. 'I was thinking about Prue. She seems unhappy.'

'Does she?' He frowned and glanced at his sister. 'I never know with Prue. We've never really got on; I don't know why. I've been trying to have a word with Father, but he can't talk of anything but the war.'

'Will you have to join the army?'

'I suppose it's my duty.' He shrugged. 'But there's no rush. It hasn't been made official yet.'

War was formally declared on the fourth of August, the day before the church garden party. The next day no-one could talk of anything else. Several of Sir Gerald's estate workers had already given notice.

172

'They say there were people on the streets of London all last night,' Sir Gerald said at breakfast. 'Recruiting stations are springing up all over the place and our boys are queuing up to offer their services to the Crown.' He looked significantly at Harry.

'I must speak to you, Father.'

'Not today, my boy.' Sir Gerald beamed at him. 'We all have enough to do with this affair of your mother's. I know what you want to discuss, but tomorrow will be time enough. Now, I have some business of my own to attend to.'

Harry glanced at me, obviously frustrated.

Lady Selina caught the brief exchange between us and her mouth tightened. I had the feeling that she knew something had happened between us.

'I've said nothing about your behaviour yesterday, staying out all day,' she said coldly. 'But I expect you to do your share today. And you, Harry. Just because there's going to be a war, it doesn't mean we can ignore the church restoration fund.'

'Yes, Mother.' He winked at me. 'We'll do our duty – won't we, Kate?'

By the middle of the afternoon the fête was in full swing. There were gay striped awnings over the stalls, roundabouts run by noisy steam engines for the children, darts and a coconut shy. It was well attended by women and children, though not many young men were in evidence. From the snatches of conversation I overheard as I mingled with the crowd, most of them had rushed off to join up.

'My Bob went first thing this morning. He wouldn't miss it for the world.'

'Jack was the same. Says it will be a great lark.'

'Bob was afraid it would be over before he could get out there. . . .'

I moved on to meet Harry. He was carrying a china fairing, which he showed off proudly. 'I won this on the darts. What shall I do with it?'

I laughed as I saw the ugly object. 'Give it to the white elephant stall. Someone might buy it.'

'Wait for me then. I have to talk to you.' The look he gave me set my heart racing. 'Can't we slip away for a while?'

'Do you think we dare?'

'Go down to the boathouse, Kate. I'll follow in a few minutes.'

'Don't be long.' I felt breathless as I saw the wicked glint in his eyes.

I moved unhurriedly across the lawns, feeling guilty as I slipped into the shrubberies. Lady Selina would be furious if she saw me sneaking away. She'd sent me to help with the refreshments.

The sun was warm on my head as I walked swiftly through the shrubberies and then the orchard. I could hear a lark singing above me, and my spirits rose skywards. I was a little guilty and nervous, but my heart was soaring. There might be some argument when Harry told his parents we wished to marry, but he loved me and nothing else really mattered.

It was warm and dry inside the boathouse, and there was a tang of linseed oil. The sun was streaming through a high window as I looked round at the coils of neatly stacked ropes; the oars were clamped on the walls and everything was in its place. I clambered into one of the rowing boats and sat down, lifting my face to the sun and closing my eyes.

A slight sound made me jump. 'Harry?' I said, blinking in the strong light as I opened my eyes. 'Is that you?'

'Who else would it be?' He grinned at me. 'Were you expecting your lover?'

'Yes.' I smiled and stood up. 'You.'

Harry lifted me from the boat, holding me above him for a moment before letting me slip down so that our lips were almost touching. He looked into my eyes, then moaned softly as he began to kiss me. My arms were around his neck, my fingers moving urgently in his hair.

'I love you,' he murmured. 'I love you, I love you. . . . '

'I love you,' I whispered, looking up at him in delight. 'You said you wanted to talk to me?'

'That was an excuse.' He grinned. 'What I really want is to make love to you. . . . '

'That wouldn't be wise,' a voice said from the doorway, and we turned to see Prue watching us, an odd expression in her eyes.

'What are you doing here?' Harry demanded.

'I saw you both slip away.' I sensed that she was very nervous but also triumphant. 'I thought I should follow you.'

'You might as well know that Kate and I are going to be married,' Harry said. 'I'm going to speak to Father tonight.'

Prue's laughter was shrill and very strange. 'You can't marry Kate,' she said. 'It's impossible.'

174

'What are you talking about? I know she's only seventeen, but Father. . . . '

'It's not a matter of Father's permission,' she said, her voice high with tension. 'You can't marry Kate because . . . because she's our half sister. Our father is her father. . . . '

For a moment there was complete silence, then Harry shook his head, a look of dawning horror in his eyes. 'NO! I don't believe it. You're lying, Prue.'

The sickness was swirling inside me. I stared at Prue; the triumph had gone now and she looked deflated, as though she no longer felt any pleasure in her victory over us.

'It's true,' she said in a strangled voice. 'I saw the letter your mother sent to Father, Kate. It was lying on his desk in the library and I read it.'

'No!' Harry's face was grim. 'You're making it up. You wanted to hurt me because I'm the heir to Brockmere – that's it, isn't it? You've always been jealous, and now you think you've found a way to hit back at me.'

Prue's eyes glittered with tears and I saw a flash of hatred as she looked at her brother. 'Yes, I've always been jealous,' she said bitterly. 'I've always wished that I was you – but I'm not lying. It's the truth. If you don't believe me, ask Father.'

'I intend to!' Harry yelled. 'Get out of here, Prue, or I refuse to be held responsible for my actions!'

She backed away from him, fear in her eyes. I called to her and she hesitated, poised for flight.

'If you knew, why didn't you tell me?' I asked.

She flushed guiltily. 'I wasn't sure about you and Harry . . . not until last night. I – I thought you wanted Paul and I was afraid that if. . . . ' She backed away nervously. 'I did see that letter, Kate. Honestly.'

'My mother. . . . ' I stared at Harry. 'It can't be true. She couldn't have let me come here, not knowing the truth. . . . '

His eyes were dark with shock. 'I don't know, Kate. I don't know. . . . '

'It's the truth,' Prue said again. 'Why should I lie?'

'Get out!' Harry yelled. 'If you knew you could've told us ages ago, but you let us go on thinking we were free to fall in love. At this moment I could break your ugly little neck!'

She stared at him, her face red with anger and misery, then she turned and ran out of the door.

175

When she'd gone a tense silence fell on us. We stared at each other, neither of us able to speak. The pain was almost beyond bearing, tearing at us as we struggled to understand what had happened.

'It can't be true,' I choked on the words. 'Harry. . . . '

'My half sister. . . . ' His face was ashen. 'It's like a nightmare. I can't believe it. I won't believe it. Kate, I can't bear it. I love you. I want you. . . . ' He was battling against his emotions.

'Oh, Harry.' I stared at him, feeling as if my heart were being ripped apart. 'Harry . . . not to be able to touch you or kiss you. . . .'

I saw the agony in his face and I knew he was remembering yesterday afternoon by the river when we had gloried in our love – a love that was now forbidden to us.

He moved towards me, a queer, blind look in his eyes. 'My darling Kate – what have I done to you?'

'It wasn't you,' I said. 'If Prue is telling the truth, it was my mother and your father. They knew, Harry – they knew and they didn't tell us.'

Grief gave way to anger then. 'I could kill him,' he said bitterly. 'He's my father, but if he's done this to us. . . . '

'We have to know,' I said. 'We have to ask him.'

'Yes.' The look in Harry's eyes was so murderous that I was afraid of what he might do if Prue wasn't lying.

We walked back to the house in silence, avoiding the lawns where the garden party was still going on. It seemed strange to hear the sound of laughter when our world was crumbling around us.

Harry's father was also my father. I'd made love with my own brother; that was incest and a crime against the laws of both God and Man. If it was true it was sickening, horrible – it couldn't be true. It musn't be true!

I looked at Harry and I knew my feelings hadn't changed. I still loved him; I still wanted him. I wanted to feel his body close to mine, to kiss and caress him, to be one with him. Knowing that he might be my half brother made no difference. The hunger was still there.

'Go up to your room,' Harry said. 'I'll speak to Father, then I'll tell you what he says.'

'No.' I looked him squarely in the eyes. 'I want to hear everything. I want to know why we haven't been told.'

'Please, Kate.' Harry's face was tense and grim. 'Please let me do this my way.'

I stared at him stubbornly, wanting to insist that we saw Sir Gerald together, but the cold determination in his face sapped my will.

'If that's what you want,' I said. 'I'll be in my room.'

He looked at me a moment longer, then bent to brush his lips gently over mine. 'I love you,' he said. 'Whatever happens – whatever the truth is, remember that, Kate. Remember I shall always love you. . . . '

How is it that a minute can seem like an hour, and an hour become an eternity? Time passed so slowly as I waited for Harry's return. I could hear the sound of birds singing through my open window. The sun was still shining, everything outside was as it had always been, but inside my room I'd become a prisoner in Hell, tormented and afraid.

What was happening? What were they saying to each other? Surely Harry would come back at any moment and say it was all a lie!

I paced my room like a caged lioness, anger and frustration mixing with grief. How could they do this to us? My mother and Harry's father – how could they be so cruel and unthinking? Had it never occurred to either of them that Harry and I might fall in love? Not one word of warning from Sir Gerald. Only his wife had tried to tell me not to hope for anything. Did she know I was her husband's child? Was that why she'd agreed to take me in?

I stopped my pacing as the door opened and I turned to look at Harry, my heart in my mouth. One glance was sufficient. The room seemed to spin and I felt as if I was about to faint.

'It's true, then,' I whispered. 'God help us. . . . '

Harry's eyes were like death. 'He was ashamed to tell me,' he said in a choked voice. 'He's just come out with a long, involved story about how he fell in love with your mother. . . . She wasn't even sixteen when. . . . '

'Don't!' I cried. 'I can't bear it.' I stared at him wildly. 'What shall we do? Harry. . . . '

'Don't cry, Kate.' He moved towards me. 'I hate myself for what I've done to you. I should never. . . . '

'You mustn't say it!' I pressed my fingers to his lips. 'I'm not sorry it happened – I'm glad we were together that way once. If I can never be in your arms again, I shall always remember. . . . '

'My God!' he choked. 'I wish I was dead.'

'NO!' Tears ran down my cheeks. 'Swear to me that you won't do

177

anything foolish. Swear it, Harry! If you go on living then I can just bear it, but if you die I shall die too.'

'Kate. . . . ' He gave a cry of agony. Suddenly he took me in his arms, kissing me with such a desperate hunger that I almost swooned. 'I promise,' he muttered. 'I shan't take my own life.' He broke away from me.

'Where are you going?'

He turned to look at me then, a smile flickering on his lips. 'To join the army, Kate. I shan't kill myself – but I pray to God the Germans will do it for me. . . . '

I didn't go down to dinner that night. No one came to my door, no one sent to see what was the matter. I lay alone on my bed, staring into the blackness. I'd cried until the tears were all gone, now I felt numbed and empty. I didn't know what to do with myself. I wanted to die and yet something inside me would not let me take that final step. I was close to despair, my world shattered into a thousand fragments, but there was anger in me, too, anger against the man who was my father – and anger against the mother I'd adored.

Sir Gerald had always seemed such a kind, considerate man, but such a man would never have stood by and let me fall in love with a man I could never marry. I saw now that he was weak and selfish. If he'd only told me the truth at the start. . . . And yet it had begun the moment I first saw Harry.

How could I have fallen in love with my own brother? Surely some inner instinct should have warned me!

How could I go on loving and wanting him physically now that I knew the truth?

It was the longest, most terrible night of my life, but by the morning I knew what I had to do.

The morning room had long windows that overlooked the lawns. In summer it was the first to be warmed by the sun's rays, but in the autumn it could be cool. Furnished very simply with comfortable chairs, various tables and a writing desk, it was Lady Selina's favourite place at this time of day.

She was sitting at her desk, writing a letter. She looked up as I entered, frowning slightly as she waited for me to speak.

'I've decided to become a nurse,' I said. 'I've packed my things and I shall leave today if Bates will drive me to the station.'

She was silent for a moment or two. 'You don't have to leave,

Kate. This is your home, and there are plenty of voluntary groups you can join if you want to help the war effort.'

'I want to train properly,' I said, then, 'This was never really my home, was it?'

Her eyes met mine steadily. 'Naturally you're angry. I wanted you to know from the start. Your mother asked us not to tell you – and Gerald didn't wish either Harry or Prunella to know.'

'It was Prue who told us. She read my mother's letter.'

'That was very wrong of her.' Lady Selina's mouth tightened. 'I can only apologize for her, Kate.'

'At least you tried to warn me.'

'Yes.' Her eyes didn't quite meet mine. 'That was for reasons of my own, however.' I raised my brows but she shook her head. 'I've no wish to explain them to you – nor am I at liberty to do so.'

'You've never liked me, have you? I suppose I can't blame you – most women would refuse to have their husband's bastard in the house.'

'On the contrary, I've become quite fond of you, Kate. I may not wish you to marry my son, but I've nothing against you personally.'

'Well, you needn't worry about my marrying Harry,' I said bitterly. 'Nothing could've stopped us – except this.'

Again her eyes slid away from mine, as though she was afraid to look at me. 'I'm sorry you've both been hurt. As I said, I thought you should've been told at the beginning.'

'It's too late now.' I felt the anger stir inside me.

'Perhaps it would've been better if you'd never come here.'

'Yes.' I stared at her a moment longer, then turned to leave. 'Goodbye.'

'Have you enough money?'

'I still have the inheritance from my mother.'

'Ah yes, that will be helpful. If you ever need anything, Kate, please come to me – and you will be welcome to return for a visit at any time.'

'I doubt that I shall.'

'Will you say goodbye to – to Gerald?'

'No. I might say things that are better left unsaid.'

'I understand – but he does care for you, Kate.'

'Does he?' I could taste the bitterness in my mouth. 'I'm sorry, I can't believe that.'

'You will write to me occasionally?' She sounded concerned. 'Please, Kate. Let me know how you are.'

'Perhaps.' I laughed harshly. 'Perhaps I owe you that much.'

Rosie was tearful as she helped me pack. 'I'm going to miss you, Miss Kate,' she said. 'It won't seem the same with you and Mr Harry gone.'

I kissed her cheek. 'I'll miss you, too,' I said, 'but I'll write if you like.'

'Oh yes,' she said. 'Take care of yourself, then.'

'I will.' I looked at her curiously. 'Can I ask you something?'

'Anything you like.'

'It's about Maggie – about her lover. . . . ' I paused as she frowned. 'Was it Sir Gerald, Rosie? I always felt that you knew.'

She hesitated and then nodded. 'I'd seen them leaving the Folly one after the other – you'll keep it to yourself, won't you?'

'Yes,' I promised. 'Thank you for telling me.'

I was thoughtful as I went down to the car. It seemed as if I wasn't the only one who had been let down by Sir Gerald. Just what kind of a man was he? I remembered the serious-eyed man in the photograph on my mother's sideboard and I wished with all my heart that he'd been my father as I'd always believed.

How could my mother have deceived her husband? What kind of a woman would lie to her only child the way she had? I felt very bitter as I was driven away from Brockmere. Between them, the two people who should have loved me had destroyed my life.

It seemed to me that the best place to be now that the war had actually begun was London, the best place if I wanted to be really involved. Once the fighting started, the hospitals would soon be overflowing with wounded men. I went to a large infirmary and talked to the matron about enrolling as a student nurse.

'You're just the kind of girl we're looking for,' she said. 'Sensible, intelligent and practical. It's going to be hard work, Miss Linton. Not at all romantic. If you think nursing means smoothing fevered brows, then go home now.'

'I'm not looking for romance,' I said. 'I just want to do something useful.'

'Then we shall be glad to have you.' She smiled at me. 'Here is a list of our rules. We expect unmarried girls to live in the nurses' home and be in at a reasonable time. We also expect our girls to live a decent, moral life. Study the rules and come back on Friday if you still want to join us.'

'I shan't change my mind,' I said, feeling thankful that the afternoon I'd spent on the river bank with Harry hadn't resulted in my being with child. 'I'd like to enroll now, please.'

'Come back on Friday,' she said firmly.

I shook her hand. 'I'll be here,' I said.

'What time do you call this?' An avenging angel in the shape of Sister MacKenzie pounced as I made a tardy appearance on the ward.

'I'm sorry, Sister. I couldn't seem to wake up this morning.'

She nodded, her sharp eyes surveying me with contempt. Sister MacKenzie was a dedicated professional. She'd made it quite clear what she thought of girls like me; girls with privileged backgrounds who'd come into her profession because they believed it was glamorous to nurse wounded soldiers.

'I suppose you were at a party last night.' She glared at me. 'Please try to remember that you're a member of the nursing profession now. Go to the sluice room. You can make yourself useful there.'

Hurrying to do as I was told, I was very much aware of the drabness of my surroundings. The ward was painted to waist height with dark green glossy paint and then a dull cream to the ceiling. Here and there a jug of flowers brightened the clinical coldness, but the worst thing was the smell of disinfectant and the stench of death.

The battle of Mons had resulted in an influx of wounded men on the wards. The regular army had fought brilliantly against crippling odds, holding out for twenty-four hours before retreating to make a further stand at Le Câteau. It had been a miracle that they managed to hold out so bravely in the face of overwhelming numbers. The Germans had been better prepared for war than anyone had guessed, and it would be months before Kitchener's army of volunteers was ready to back up the regulars. Even though I was still a very raw recruit to nursing, I knew that I as well as many others would be needed in the coming months.

I'd spent more than an hour at the sink when Sister came to call me. 'Haven't you finished that yet? You can help make up the beds now. We've some new patients coming in.'

Drying my hands, I hurried to obey, but by the time I reached the ward most of the beds were done. They were just transferring a patient from the trolley to a bed near the entrance, close to Sister's desk.

'Poor devil,' Jean Butts whispered as she saw me. 'They've taken off his left leg. He lost the right in an explosion, and they tried to save the other, but it was no good.'

I looked at the soldier's ashen face, feeling my throat tighten with emotion. I still hadn't got used to the appalling injuries that some of the men had suffered. 'He can't be more than twenty-two,' I said. 'Do you know what his job was before the war?'

'He was a regular.' Jean always knew all the gossip on the wards. 'Not much chance of him going back into the army, is there? Poor devil! My mother says it's them as come home are the unlucky ones. The only heroes are dead heroes.'

'Oh, Jean!'

When I'd first met Jean her outspokenness had slightly shocked me. She was one of the new breed of women that had been spawned by the suffragette movement. She believed firmly that the time of women's emancipation had finally arrived, and she refused to conform to the traditional role of women, insisting that she'd been born into a free country and would do and speak as she saw fit. Despite her sometimes shocking behaviour, I liked her very much. She'd begun her nursing training at the same time as me, so we'd become friends almost at once. She was a member of a large, hard-working family, and she had four brothers, all of whom were in the army. It was Jean's practical manner that had helped me through the early days of my training. Sister MacKenzie was unfair to accuse me of going to parties. I'd hardly been out in the evening at all since joining up – I was usually so tired that all I wanted to do was to fall into my hard bunk at the nurses' home.

'Look at it this way,' Jean had said cheerfully when I'd been close to tears after one of Sister's lectures. 'It can't get any worse so it's got to get better, right?'

It was slowly getting better. I was beginning to cope with my emotions, and I wasn't quite as tired now as at the beginning, though I still occasionally overslept in the mornings.

'What are you doing tonight, then?'

I blinked and looked at Jean. 'Nothing. I need an early night.'

She pulled a face. 'You can't stay in all the time, Kate. I was going to ask you to come to the pictures with Jack and me – and a friend of his. There's a melodrama on and a comedy with Charlie Chaplin.'

I smiled and shook my head; it wasn't the first time she'd tried to involve me with one of her many friends. Jean was very popular with the patients, and those who left hospital to return to their units were always asking her out to parties or the pictures. And they usually had a friend.

'Perhaps next time,' I said. 'I'd better have that early night. I was late again this morning.'

I was surprised when Jean told me there was a telephone call for me. The telephone was situated in a narrow landing on the first floor of the nurses' home. There were always girls coming and going and it was usually noisy. I had to cover one ear with my hand as I answered the call.

'Hello,' I said. 'Kate Linton speaking.'

'Kate? It's me, Harry.'

The sound of his voice made me dizzy with shock. I closed my eyes, close to tears. 'Harry,' I croaked. 'How are you? Where are you?'

'I'm in town,' he said. 'I have to see you.'

'Is that wise?'

'Probably not. If you don't want to come. . . . ' There was a hint of bitterness in his voice.

'Where do you want to meet and when?'

'I thought perhaps lunch or tea tomorrow – I'm not asking you to be alone with me.'

'Don't be angry, Harry.' I moved so that a girl could squeeze past me and she gave me an apologetic smile. 'It's difficult to talk here. I'm on duty tomorrow but I can probably swap with Jean – where shall I meet you for tea?'

'We'll go to the Ritz,' he said. 'I'll be waiting outside at three-thirty. You will come?'

'I'll be there,' I promised, and hung up the small black earpiece.

The tears were rolling down my cheeks as I stood there, unable to move. I'd tried so hard to put Harry out of my mind, but now all the longing and the heartache came flooding back.

'Are you all right?'

I looked at the girl who had spoken, nodding but unable to speak.

'Was it bad news?' she asked sympathetically. 'Your boyfriend been wounded, has he?'

I found my voice. 'No, nothing like that,' I said. 'Excuse me.'

I walked past her, fighting my emotions. I'd been a fool to agree to meet Harry; it could only bring us both pain. It would be much better if I didn't keep the appointment.

I smiled and waved as I saw Harry outside the hotel. The road was busy, choked with a stream of horse-drawn drays, motorbuses and trams, and I had to stand and wait for a moment before I could cross, the wind blowing my hair into my eyes. Catching a lull in the traffic, I ran to greet him. His lean, sensitive face lit up as he saw me and my heart turned over. Nothing had changed. I still loved him; I still felt that trembling inside at the sight of him.

He took my hand, his eyes seeming to devour me. 'I was afraid you would change your mind.'

'I almost did.'

'I suppose I shouldn't have phoned you – but I can't stand not seeing you, Kate.' His smile dimmed and I could see the hurt in his eyes. 'God curse my father for what he's done to us!'

'Oh, Harry my darling,' I said. 'Don't be so bitter. You mustn't hate him. We have to accept and learn to be . . . friends.'

'Friends!' His mouth twisted bitterly. 'I had to see you, Kate. Just once before. . . . '

'So you're going, then?'

'They haven't told us, but we've all been given leave.'

I nodded. 'I know you couldn't say even if you knew for sure.' I smiled at him, feeling my love swell inside me, easing the pain. 'I'm glad you rang. Really, I am.'

'Kate,' he said. For a moment the old, confident grin was there. 'No wonder I can't stop thinking about you – wanting you. . . . '

'Don't!' I blinked as tears stung my eyes. 'We can love each other but we can't be lovers. We have to accept that.'

'I have tried – believe me.' The anger was back.

'Shall we go in and have our tea?'

'Yes, of course.'

The reception area was crowded with officers talking and laughing. I guessed that, like Harry, they were saying goodbye to their girl-friends and wives. I thought we might have difficulty in getting a table, but a waiter directed us to one by the window, whisking away the reserved notice with a flourish.

'We were lucky,' I said. 'It's crowded today.'

'I booked. Besides, old Morris knows me. He's been here for years. Thank goodness he's too old for the army.'

'You sound a bit disillusioned?'

'The army's not so bad. I enjoy the training and I can stick the routine and the grind, but. . . . ' He gave me an intense look. 'You

184

know what's wrong, Kate. I can't forgive myself . . . I feel I've damaged you. . . . '

'Hush,' I said. 'We both wanted it to happen – and we were lucky. I'm not having a child.'

'I suppose that's something.' He took a cigarette from a silver case and lit it. 'It will be easier when we get out there.'

'Has the training been hard?'

'For the men – the poor devils get blisters from digging trenches, and it's impossible to get hot water at the barracks. It amazes me how cheerful they all are. Most of them are keen to get out there and do their bit.'

'That shouldn't surprise you. The recruiting stations were overrun as soon as war was declared.'

Harry smiled. 'There were almost too many at the start. They've only just got their uniforms and weapons. We had to train with sticks or pitchforks at first. One man even used to take his pet mongrel on parade with him. Still, we're getting better. Kitchener's New Army, they call us. I only hope we'll do as well as the regular boys.'

'You will.' I touched his hand. 'You'll be fine when it comes to it.'

'Oh, God,' he said, his fingers curling round mine. 'I love you so much, Kate.'

He let my hand go as our waiter returned with tea and crumpets and, when he spoke again, he had himself under control.

'Tell me about you – do you like nursing?'

'I'm not really a nurse yet. I spend most of my time making beds, scrubbing bedpans and attending lectures – but yes, I think I do like it. It's what I want to do – for the moment, anyway.'

'You've made up your mind then? You're going on with it?'

'When I've completed eighteen months of my course I can apply to be sent out to France. They're in desperate need in the field hospitals.'

Harry nodded. 'It looks as if the war will go on for a long time yet.'

'Anyone who thought otherwise has discovered how wrong they were now.'

Harry looked grim, then, 'Will you go down to Brockmere while I'm away?'

'I don't think so.' I looked at him. 'Have you been back?'

'I can't, Kate.'

'But it's your home.'

'It's only a house.'

'What about your mother?'

'I never did tell you about her, did I?'

'What do you mean?'

He smiled oddly. 'That's the trouble, I don't really know. It was just a feeling I had sometimes – that she didn't like me very much.'

'You're wrong, Harry. She loves you; I'm certain of it.'

'You're prejudiced in my favour.' He looked at me longingly. 'What am I going to do, Kate? I can't bear not seeing you, not being able to. . . .'

'We'll manage,' I said quickly. 'We have to.' I finished my tea. 'I think I'd better go. I've only got an hour. Jean covered for me, but she's going out this evening.'

Harry summoned the waiter and paid the bill. We went outside. The wind was rising and it had turned colder. I shivered as I looked at him. 'Will you write occasionally? Just to let me know how you are?'

'Yes.' He smiled and touched my cheek. 'Goodbye, my darling. I'll think of you always.'

'Kiss me,' I said. 'Just this once.'

He stared at me, then he took me into his arms. Our lips met in a sweet, gentle kiss that nearly tore my heart from my body. Letting go, he stared at me hungrily, all the anguished desire and frustration in his eyes. Then he swung away, walking swiftly as though he had to leave quickly. I stood watching as he threaded his way through the crowds.

'Goodbye, Harry,' I whispered as the tears began to fall. 'May God bless and protect you. . . .'

CHAPTER SIXTEEN

Emma stood watching the customers eating and drinking, one ear cocked for the shrill voice of her employer's wife. She had found a job in a café soon after she left Armand's studio, and a room that was small but cheap and clean. The work was hard and demanding, and by the end of the day she was so tired that all she wanted to do was to fall into bed alone and sleep. She spoke French almost like a native these days and few people ever questioned her nationality. She believed she would be safe even if the Germans broke through the Allied lines. The fighting on the bank of the Marne had been fierce, but the enemy had been driven back to the Asine and for the moment Paris was safe.

The café was full of young men in uniform. Most of them flirted with Emma, but she gave them a cool smile that warned them to keep their distance. Men were to be treated with caution. Armand had taught her that. Sometimes she remembered Paul and the pain swirled in her so that she almost ached with the longing to see him again. She thought about getting in touch with him – perhaps she had been foolish to leave that night – but always her courage failed her before she could post the letters she wrote. Paul wouldn't want to hear from her – why should he?

She recalled the face of the girl he had been making love to and the knife twisted in her heart. She was so pretty. . . .

She looked at her own face in the mirror, seeing the first lines at the corners of her eyes, the first signs of ageing. The drinking was having its effect, but she couldn't give it up entirely, even though she managed to control it while she was working. But she couldn't do without a few drinks at night. She needed them to ease her aching limbs and the emptiness inside her.

She caught sight of the face in the newspaper and almost spilled the young French officer's drink as her hand shook. He glanced up at her, concerned at the pallor cf her complexion.

'Is something wrong, Madame?' he asked politely.

'No. . . .' She smiled wearily. 'I'm a little tired and – and I thought I saw someone I once knew in your paper.'

'Please, have a look for yourself,' he said, handing it to her immediately. 'Sit down for a moment – have a glass of wine with me.'

She always refused such invitations but something in the young officer's face made her accept. She read the article eagerly, feasting her eyes on the picture of Paul. He looked as handsome as ever and she felt a surge of longing. Even after all this time she still wanted him, still loved him.

'Was it your friend?' the officer inquired.

She nodded and smiled. 'Yes, Lieutenant. He is attending an important conference in London.'

'This friend – he was important to you, yes?'

'Yes. . . . ' Her face saddened.

The lieutenant touched her hand. 'Come, drink your wine, Madame, it will ease the ache. I, Marc Normand, know what it is to lose someone you love.'

Emma felt a little flutter about her heart. For the first time since she had left Armand, she was attracted to a man. She smiled at him. 'You remind me of my friend a little, Lieutenant Normand.'

'Please,' he said. 'My name is Marc.'

'Marc,' she repeated and nodded. 'Are you on leave?'

'For two days,' he said, looking thoughtful. 'I know no one in Paris . . . would you take pity on me, Madame? Would you spend a few hours with me this evening? I ask for nothing but friendship. I give you my word.'

She hesitated and then nodded. 'Yes, Marc. I finish in an hour – will you wait for me?'

'Of course.' He smiled and her heart thumped. He was so young and handsome; it could almost have been Paul sitting there.

Marc followed her into the tiny room. She was aware of its shabbiness, and of her clothes lying strewn about the furniture. Making a laughing excuse, she began to move about, gathering things up.

'Why bother?' he asked. 'It doesn't worry me, Emmeline.'

She stopped with her arms full of clothes. Then, as he came towards her, she let them drop in a heap on the floor. She tried to suppress her shiver as he touched her, and he looked surprised.

'Someone hurt me,' she said. 'He beat me and raped me.'

Marc's eyes were soft as he looked down at her. 'Poor Emmie,' he said. 'I too have been hurt, though not in the same way. Trust me. I shan't hurt you.'

He bent his head, his lips brushing hers gently, softly, with tenderness. She felt herself responding. It was almost like being with Paul all over again. She gave a little whimper of desire, melting into his arms.

'Make love to me,' she whispered. 'Let's give each other a little happiness.'

They lay down together on the bed. Smiling and in no hurry, they undressed each other. She pushed him back onto the bed, kissing his body, licking, teasing, arousing him. Then when he was ready, she sat astride him and he took her by the hips, lifting her so that she slid down on him, and he gasped at the hot wetness of her as she fitted to him like a silk sheath. She bent over him, and he took her breasts into his mouth, sucking on the nipples until she moaned and raised herself to come down on him hard. Then he was lifting her, driving and thrusting as they both lost control. Suddenly he cried out and she felt the scalding sperm shoot into her, and she pressed down on him, her body slippery with sweat as she nuzzled his neck.

Afterwards, as they lay talking, he asked her about the man she had seen in the paper, and she told him about Paul. She waited for him to tell her his story, but he simply took her in his arms, beginning to kiss and arouse her once more.

CHAPTER SEVENTEEN

There were two letters waiting for me at the nurses' home. I picked them up eagerly, feeling disappointed that neither was from Harry. He'd sent me a postcard just after Christmas, but nothing since. One of my letters was from Rosie, the other from Lady Selina. I opened the latter immediately, my breath catching as I scanned the first few lines.

'I have both good news and bad,' she'd written. 'Harry has been wounded, not badly I'm glad to say, but sufficient for them to send him back to England. I don't yet know which hospital he's being sent to, but if you telephone me in a few days, I should have had confirmation. My other news is about Prunella. I told you she was driving an ambulance for the voluntary unit in my last letter. Well, she has become engaged to a doctor and they are to be married next month. She has asked me to invite you to the wedding, and I should be very pleased if you. . . . ' I tossed the letter aside and Jean frowned at me.

'Bad news?'

'My – my cousin is to be married. Aunt Selina wants me to go down for the wedding.'

'Will you go?' Jean looked concerned. She knew that my relationship with my family was awkward; I'd told her that I'd left Brockmere because of a quarrel, but nothing more.

'I don't know.' I bit my lip. 'Harry's been wounded, but she says it's not serious.'

'He's your cousin, too, isn't he?'

'Well, sort of.' I couldn't look at her as I lied. It was difficult to be casual when inside I was torn with worry. How badly was Harry hurt? Where was he and why hadn't he written to me? I couldn't let my emotions show and the strain was almost unbearable.

'He's the one you went to tea with, isn't he?'

'Yes,' I said stiffly.

'I suppose the family are against the marriage?' she said, guessing more than I'd told her.

'Something like that. I'd rather not talk about it.'

'All right,' she said, and grinned at me. 'Want to come to a party? Tom just happens to have a friend. . . . '

I smiled and shook my head. 'No, thanks, Jean. I'm not in the mood.'

In a way it was almost a relief to know that Harry was wounded and on his way home. The loss of life reported in the British papers was horrendous, with well over a hundred thousand casualties. I'd been so afraid that Harry was dead, but now at least I knew he would be safe for a while.

I telephoned Lady Selina the morning after her letter arrived. She told me that Harry was at St Mark's Hospital.

'He rang me last night,' she said. 'He says he'll be out in a matter of days and he doesn't want any visitors – but he'd probably be glad to see you, Kate.'

'I'll go this afternoon. I'm not on duty until later.'

'Will you let me know how he really is?'

'Of course.'

'Kate. . . . ' She hesitated. 'Paul de Bernay rang me yesterday. He asked me where you were and I gave him your address. I hope I did right?'

'You could hardly refuse,' I said, then: 'How is Prue?'

'Running around in circles. You will come down for the wedding, won't you?'

'I'm not sure if I can get the time off,' I replied awkwardly.

'You've every right to be angry – but I wish you could find it in your heart to forgive Gerald. He's very fond of both you and Harry – Harry hasn't spoken to him since that day. Perhaps if you. . . . '

'Please,' I begged. 'Don't press me. I'll think about it.'

'Very well. Let me know about Harry.'

'Yes. Goodbye.'

My hand was shaking as I replaced the receiver.

I wore a blue dress that Harry had always liked that afternoon, and a rather frivolous hat with lots of tulle and silk roses. I wanted to look pretty for him, as if the war and all the unhappiness had never been. My heart was racing wildly as I got out of the taxi I'd hired to take me to the hospital. St Mark's was a small building set in its own grounds, and I knew that Lady Selina must have pulled strings to have her son sent there rather than to one of the larger military hospitals. I was feeling nervous but hopeful as I approached the receptionist.

'May I see Lieutenant Harry Redfern, please?'

She glanced at her register. 'Room 23,' she said. 'Down the corridor to your left. Is he expecting you?'

'I'm his cousin. I think he will see me.'

'Just one moment, please. I'll ring his room.' She dialled and listened, then shook her head. 'He doesn't answer. That means he's probably in the dayroom – down there and through those doors.'

I thanked her and set off in the direction she'd indicated, finding my way easily enough. The dayroom had several hard leather chairs, a bookcase, writing desk and a telephone. A newspaper was lying on the desk, its headlines condemning the sinking of an American cruiser called the *Lusitania* off the Irish coast as the atrocities of the war reached new peaks. Two young officers were playing cards, but there was no sign of Harry. I asked if anyone had seen him and was told he'd gone for a walk in the gardens.

'You'll probably find him by the fishpond,' one of the officers said. 'He feeds them with bread.'

I went through the open French windows to the terrace, crossing the lawns to walk through a pretty shrubbery. It was certainly an attractive place, much nicer than the grounds of the hospital where I worked. Harry was standing by the pond, his back towards me. I approached slowly, my heart thumping.

'Harry?' I said softly. 'How are you?'

His shoulders stiffened and his hands curled into tight fists at his sides. For a moment he remained with his back towards me, then he turned slowly to face me. He had a red mark on his left temple and one arm was in a sling, but otherwise he looked exactly as he always had.

'I'm fine, Kate,' he said in a carefully controlled tone. 'Mother shouldn't have worried you.'

'How did it happen?'

'It was my own fault.'

'Your fault?'

'There was this chap on the wire. He'd got caught on a raid earlier that night. I went back to get him – something we've been warned not to do.'

'Oh, Harry.' I looked at him through misted eyes. 'Why did you have to be a hero?'

'I couldn't stand to hear him screaming. I just wanted some peace,' he said tersely.

'Is it unbearable out there, Harry?'

'Sometimes.' His mouth twisted in a wry smile. 'The noise when there's an attack going on is indescribable, but the funny thing is that once it all starts you lose your fear. It's the waiting that's the worst – and the thinking, especially when your thoughts are hell.'

'Oh, Harry,' I said. 'I've been so worried. You didn't write.'

His eyes were angry. 'What do you want me to write, Kate? Breezy letters about a charming château I stayed at? Perhaps you would like me to describe the dovecot in a tower over the gatepost? It was like a peaceful old house in England – except for the sound of the guns and an occasional visit from a German plane shooting up the yard.'

'Don't be bitter, Harry. I just want to hear from you sometimes, to know you're all right.'

'Do you?' He stared at me as if he hated me. 'Perhaps you can just let go,' he said icily. 'Maybe being friends is enough for you? It never will be for me. I'd rather not hear from you or see you if I can't have you.'

I recoiled as though he'd struck me. 'Don't do this to me, Harry,' I whispered. 'I love you so. . . . '

His laughter was merciless and cruel. 'You'll soon get over it, Kate.' His eyes seemed to stab me. 'Go away. Leave me alone. I don't want to see you. Ever. . . . '

Zeppelins had been used against London for the first time, but the hospital was never in any danger from the bombs. It was nearly seven o'clock in the evening as I finished my shift and began to walk home. I was tired and Harry's bitter words kept running through my head. Perhaps he was right, but even a letter from him would have been enough to lift my spirits. Never to see him again. . . . The thought was unbearable.

Tears stung my eyes but I brushed them away impatiently. I wanted to buy a bottle of sherry for Jean. It was her birthday and so far I hadn't got her a present. I dashed across the road just as the off-licence was about to close.

'I need a bottle of sherry as a birthday present,' I said to the assistant. 'I've only just come off duty.'

She looked at my uniform and nodded. 'Well, seeing as it's for a special occasion.' She wrapped the bottle and gave it to me.

I left the shop and hurried home through the gathering dusk. I

193

walked swiftly, relieved when I reached the nurses' home. Entering the room I shared with Jean, I saw my friend buttoning her best blouse.

'Going out?' I asked.

'Yes.' She smiled at me like a cat that has swallowed the cream. 'And so are you, Kate.'

'What do you mean? I don't feel like a party.'

'This is a party for two,' she said smugly. 'A friend of yours called to see you. He asked me if you were on duty tonight and I told him you would be home soon. He's going to pick you up in an hour.'

'A friend of mine?' I stared at her.

'His name is Paul de Bernay,' she said, rolling her eyes at me. 'No wonder you didn't want any of the men I tried to fix you up with! I'm never going to feel sorry for you again, Kate Linton!'

'Paul. . . . ' I stared at her. 'He's coming to pick me up in an hour . . . ?'

'To take you to dinner,' Jean said and giggled. 'So you can just put on your best dress and enjoy yourself for once!'

The restaurant was small and intimate with soft lighting and bright gingham tablecloths. Paul was greeted by the French owner, and we were given a table in a corner by the window.

'What would you like?' Paul asked, flicking through the menu.

'Something light,' I said. 'You choose for me.'

'Then I think we'll have mushroom soufflé to start and then fresh salmon with a delicate herb sauce.' He looked at me. 'How does that sound?'

'Delicious. I didn't know it was still possible to find food like that these days.'

'Ah,' he said with a smile. 'You have to know where to look.' He ordered a light, sparkling wine, and the waiter retreated. 'This decision to become a nurse was sudden, was it not?'

'It became impossible for me to go on living at Brockmere – please don't ask me why.' I looked at him. 'Can we talk of something else? What are you doing in London?'

'Liaising with your Government. Forgive me, I'm not at liberty to say more.'

'That sounds important.'

'Not really.' He shrugged his shoulders. 'I'm a very small cog in a very big wheel.' He paused as the waiter brought our wine, showing him the label. 'Yes, thank you, that will be perfect.' Then to me, 'Try this and tell me what you think?'

I sipped the wine and nodded. 'I like it.'

'Good.' His eyes were warm as he looked at me. 'I have a few days in England, Kate. May we spend some time together?'

I hesitated, then as I recalled Harry's bitter words, I shrugged my shoulders. 'Why not?'

He looked pleased. 'So this weekend we shall drive into the country, no?'

'Yes,' I said and some of the pain eased inside me. 'Yes, I would enjoy that, Paul.'

'What's the matter, Kate?' Paul looked at me across the table. 'You've been very quiet all morning. Have I done something to upset you?'

We were sitting at a little wooden table in the window of a country inn, drinking wine. Outside the sun was shining, though it was still early spring, and it was quite warm. I twirled the stem of my wine glass, not looking at him as I replied.

'I went to see Harry in the hospital.'

Paul frowned. 'Was he badly wounded?'

'He had a scratch on his temple and a shoulder wound. He seemed to be recovering well.'

Paul looked at me hard for a moment, then, 'You're in love with him, aren't you?'

'Yes.' I glanced up, tears in my eyes. 'I have to talk to someone.'

His hand covered mine on the table. 'I'm willing to listen, Kate – if you'll trust me?'

I nodded, smiling mistily. 'Yes, I do trust you now. I disliked you when we first met, because – because I thought you'd stolen my mother's love from me.'

His eyes met mine steadily. 'You were right to blame me. In a way I did exactly that.'

'What do you mean?'

'Emma told me you didn't want to come with us. She said you preferred to stay with your friends.'

I stared at him, but even though it was a shock to hear the words spoken out loud, I realized I'd always known it instinctively. 'My mother went away with you when I was sent to Brockmere. You and she were. . . .'

'Lovers?' His expression was grave. 'Yes, for a short time. She left me after a few months, when she understood finally that I wouldn't

195

marry her. It was my fault; I did something that hurt her very much. It – it was an impulse I've since regretted. Something of which I am deeply ashamed.'

'After a few months?' I frowned. 'I thought it might have been you she was with when Helen saw her in Paris.' I knew now that the woman Helen had spoken to must have been my mother. What I didn't know was why she'd denied all knowledge of me.

'We stayed for a little time in London, but most of our time together was spent at my château in the south of France. I gave Emma money when we parted – perhaps she used it to go to Paris.'

'But she was ill – I don't understand. . . . '

'She had a nasty cough, yes. It cleared up after a few weeks in the sunshine. I thought she was better.' He frowned, then, 'That's why I was so shocked when I heard she was dead. I've wondered if I was in part to blame.'

'Why should it be your fault?'

'She was angry and hurt when she left me. Angry that I wouldn't marry her – and because of something else. . . . '

'Did you promise her marriage?'

'No. I couldn't do that, Kate.'

'Why – are you already married?'

'Yes.' Pain flickered in his eyes. 'Marianne – my wife – lives in France, in a nursing home run by the nuns.'

'Is she an invalid?'

'She has not spoken since the death of our son, some five years ago. The nuns do everything for her. She has to be washed, fed and cared for like a baby.'

'Oh, Paul,' I cried. 'I'm so terribly sorry. I had no idea.'

'How could you?' He smiled sadly. 'I visit Marianne from time to time, but she doesn't know me. Emma thought I should divorce her, but I couldn't do that. You see, it's my fault that she's ill. I – I was not faithful to her when we were apart and we quarrelled. The argument resulted in her miscarriage. I am responsible for what happened, therefore I can never divorce her. Do you understand?' His eyes had a strange, haunted look that made me reach out to him in sympathy.

'Yes, yes, I do.'

'Unfortunately, Emma didn't.' He sighed deeply. 'She pretended to be happy with our arrangement at the start, but then there were quarrels. She accused me of lying to her, but that wasn't true. I made it clear from the beginning that we could have a satisfactory relationship but nothing more.'

'Thank you for explaining.'

He smiled wistfully and pressed my hand. 'I wanted to tell you that day at Brockmere, but then Harry came. He was angry and I believed he was in love with you. I thought you might marry him?'

'If only that were possible.' I raised my eyes to his, a little shudder running through me. 'Sir Gerald is also my father. He and my mother were lovers when she was married to Richard Linton. Neither Harry nor I knew. We fell in love believing we were free to marry. . . . '

'My poor Kate. That was unspeakably cruel of both Emma and Sir Gerald,' Paul said, a flash of anger in his eyes. 'One of them should have warned you.'

'Yes. It hurts me very much that my mother could do such a thing . . . even more than that she should lie about her intention of going away with you.' Tears stung my eyes as a wave of emotion went over me and the full realization of what my mother had done finally sank in. 'Why did she do it, Paul? Why didn't she just tell me the truth? Why let me think she was dying?' For a long time I'd suspected that my mother had told me several lies, but I'd managed to hold on to a little of my faith in her until now. I swallowed hard, looking at Paul with a mute appeal in my eyes.

'I don't know,' he said awkwardly, seeming consumed with a private guilt of his own. 'Believe me, Kate, I truly don't understand. I thought you were coming with us – that's why I attempted to make friends with you that day at Grace Madison's. I knew I'd annoyed you by kissing you. . . . ' He frowned suddenly. 'I wonder if. . . . '

'What?' I looked at him curiously.

'Nothing. It was just a thought.' His expression was rather odd and I sensed something hidden as he shied away from the question. 'I wish your problem with Harry was one that I could solve, Kate. I would do anything in my power to make you happy. Anything!'

My eyes dropped before the brightness of his. 'It's something I have to face alone. I know no one can change things.'

'You will face it, Kate,' he said. 'You're strong enough to cope with whatever comes. But if you need me I'll be there.'

'Thank you.' I finished my wine. 'It has helped just to be able to talk about it.'

Paul touched my hand. 'I'm often in London for a few days. Will you allow me to see you now and then?'

'Why not?' I asked. 'We could be friends, couldn't we?'

'I would be honoured to be your friend, Kate,' he said.

'Did you have a good day?' Jean asked as I walked in, her eyes bright with curiosity.

'Yes.' I laughed at the question in her eyes. 'Paul is only a friend, Jean – but it was good to get away for a while, and I did enjoy it.'

'So you're not angry with me for saying you would go out to dinner with him that first time?'

'No, of course not. Paul – Paul doesn't ask anything of me. I can relax with him. I didn't like him much when we first met, but now I do.'

Jean laughed and rolled her eyes. 'You're lucky I didn't see him first.'

'You don't really mean that. I thought you'd found someone special now?'

'Well, I might have done.' She grinned, then her smile faded. 'I took a phone call for you earlier. It was rather odd. . . . '

'Oh.' I looked at her. 'Why?'

'It was from a woman. I told her you were out and asked her name but she wouldn't leave it. She said she would ring back later.'

I stared at her, puzzled. 'Aunt Selina wouldn't . . . I should think it was Prue wanting to know if I was going to the wedding. She probably got cold feet and thought better of it. We didn't part on the best of terms.'

'I expect that's it,' Jean said, looking relieved. 'Are you going to the wedding?'

'I think I might,' I said. 'Talking to Paul today has made me realize that I have to face up to things. Yes, I think I might go after all. . . . '

Bates was waiting for me at the station. He took my cases and put them in the car. 'It's good to have you back, Miss Kate,' he said.

'Thank you, Bates. I almost didn't come.'

'Rosie said you would. We've all been worried about you. What with the influenza and all the trouble lately in London. We read about that German baker being attacked and his shop set on fire – and the crowd stoning the police. It just doesn't bear thinking about!'

'You can't really blame people for turning against Germans living in Britain after what happened to the *Lusitania*, though of course it's unpleasant and I feel sorry for the elderly chemist who was attacked – but you mustn't worry about me. I'm quite safe at the nurses' home,' I said. We drove in silence until I saw the Folly up ahead, then I tapped his shoulder. 'Will you let me out here? I'd like to walk the rest of the way.'

'Are you sure?'

'Yes.' I smiled at him. 'Don't worry. I just need a little time.'

I walked slowly towards the house, prolonging the moment of my arrival. I was remembering the way Harry had ridden up on his horse the day I first came to Brockmere. He'd been so arrogant, so sure of himself – so different from the embittered man I'd seen at the hospital. The memory brought a sharp pain and I almost wished I hadn't come.

In the spring sunshine the house had a special beauty. I stopped to stare at it, my breath catching as a man came out of the front door. He paused on the steps and for a moment I thought it was Harry. My heart began to race wildly then, as he came towards me, I saw it was Sir Gerald. I waited until he came up to me.

'Thank you for coming,' he said. 'I've wanted to tell. . . . '

'Please don't,' I said quickly. 'I've come because Lady Selina asked me to, and I'm willing to forget if I can – but I don't want to hear about you and my mother. Not ever.'

His face reflected grief and regret. 'I thought it might help you to understand – to forgive me?'

'If you'd told me when I first came here, I would have understood and forgiven you,' I said. 'What I can't forgive is what you and my mother have done to Harry and me.'

'I don't suppose you can,' he said dully, his hands moving awkwardly at his sides as if he wanted to reach out to me. 'It won't help you, but I did love your mother, Kate – and I've come to love you, too.'

'Then it's a pity you didn't show it a long time ago.' I drew back as he attempted to touch me, feeling a surge of panic. 'Excuse me, I'm a little tired. I would like to rest before I change for dinner.'

I closed the door of my room and leaned against it, shutting my eyes. I felt a little faint and I wanted to cry. Sir Gerald's mute cry for forgiveness had affected me far more than his words. It was difficult to accept that he was my father. For a moment I'd felt myself responding to him and I'd had to escape. I was determined not to weaken towards him. What he'd done was unforgivable! Yet that look in his eyes had hurt me. Perhaps it hadn't been wise to come down for Prue's wedding after all.

Sighing, I took off my hat and threw it on the bed, turning to look at myself in the mirror. The girl who looked back at me wasn't the girl who'd first come to Brockmere; I could see shadows in my eyes, shadows of a grief that sometimes threatened to destroy me.

There was a knock at my door, and I called out that whoever it was might enter. Prue came in, staring at me hesitantly.

'I didn't think you would come,' she said.

'I'm not sure I should have.'

'I don't blame you for being angry. I was rather a beast that day at the boathouse – but I was pretty miserable myself.'

'I know,' I said. 'It wasn't really your fault, Prue. I should have been told by my mother or . . . Sir Gerald.'

'Yes.' She looked uncomfortable. 'It must've been rotten for you and Harry. I don't really hate him, you know. I just wish that. . . .' Her words trailed off in a sigh.

'But you won't mind that so much now you're getting married, will you?'

'No. . . . ' She sounded hesitant. 'No, I suppose it won't matter now.'

'You are happy about the marriage, aren't you?'

'Yes, of course,' she said, rather too brightly. 'Michael is wonderful. I'm sure you'll like him, Kate. He's. . . . '

'May I come in?'

Lady Selina was at the open door. Seeing her, Prue seemed to freeze. 'I have to pick Michael up,' she said. 'I'll see you later, Kate. I'm glad you came.'

'What was Prunella saying to you?' Lady Selina asked after her daughter had gone.

'She was just telling me about Michael.'

'I do hope she will be happy.' Lady Selina frowned. 'It's difficult to tell what's in her mind these days.' She sighed and shrugged her shoulders. 'It was good of you to come, Kate.'

'Was it? I can't see why you wanted me to be here.'

She looked thoughtful, uncertain as she answered. 'It will do you good to get some country air, but I musn't make excuses – perhaps I wanted to ease my mind. We've none of us treated you very well, have we?'

'Perhaps a part of it was my own fault for being too innocent. I ought to have realized there was a reason for my being sent here.' I looked at her curiously. 'It must have been very difficult for you – to learn that your husband had a bastard child?'

200

Her eyes flicked away from mine. 'These things happen. I never expected Gerald to be entirely faithful to me. Our marriage was never a love-match. All I've ever asked of him is that there should be no scandal – it was part of a promise I made to myself a long time ago.'

'What do you mean?' There was an odd expression in her eyes that made me curious.

'I wish I could tell you, Kate. I've wished it many times – but if I speak I may do more harm than good. To keep my silence is my burden, and mine alone.'

'I don't understand.'

'No, and I'm afraid you never will,' she said, her eyes strangely sad. 'Now, Kate, let us talk of other things. . . . '

She began to talk of the wedding and I knew the subject was closed, but it made me wonder. What was it that she could tell me if she chose?

CHAPTER EIGHTEEN

She watched from the shadows as the car drew up in front of the nurses' home. She had been waiting for hours, waiting for them to return, and her feet were frozen. She rubbed her hands together, trying to warm herself. Then she was suddenly still as a man got out to open the passenger door: it was Paul! Until that moment she hadn't been sure. The girl on the telephone had been so vague.

Emma's chest was tight with tension, and she could hardly breathe as she saw him give his hand to the girl to help her out. How solicitous he was for her comfort! She could see his face clearly in the headlights and his expression was one of tenderness – if only he had looked at her that way! Then she saw the girl and her heart stopped beating for one terrible moment. Kate! It was Kate – but how different she looked! She was no longer a child, but a very beautiful young woman. She laughed up at Paul as he stood holding her hand in his.

'It was a wonderful day, Paul,' she said, her voice clear and happy. 'I can't thank you enough. You've made me feel so much better.'

He raised her hand to his lips, and the look in his eyes made Emma feel faint. He was in love with her! He wanted her, yes, that was obvious and not surprising. Paul would always be aroused by a pretty woman, it was his nature; but this was something more. Much, much more! He worshipped the girl: it was there in his eyes.

They had finished saying their goodbyes. Paul stood watching as Kate disappeared into the nurses' home, then turned and glanced in Emma's direction. She shrank back, not wanting him to see her now. She'd sold the last remaining piece of her jewellery to come to England in the hope of seeing him, but now she was twisted and torn with the bitter jealousy that had haunted her ever since they parted.

She ought never to have come. It was the young French officer who had persuaded her that she should try to make her peace with Paul. When Marc made love to her, his tenderness had broken through the hard crust she'd built around her heart. In his arms she'd found a little of the happiness that she'd known with Paul, and it had given her hope. Perhaps it wasn't too late? Perhaps Paul still wanted her? Now she knew the truth. Paul had never really wanted her, not in the way he wanted Kate. He had never loved her. Emma knew it now, and she knew why he'd been unable to love her. And that hurt, that hurt so much.

Emma remained in the shadows as Paul drove away, bitterness festering inside her as she recalled all the heart-searching that had brought her here to witness that tender little scene. She'd telephoned Brockmere, pretending to be a friend of Kate's from school, and Selina had given her the number of the nurses' home. It had taken a lot of courage finally to get round to ringing that number, but she'd wanted to see Kate, to heal some of the hurt she'd inflicted if she could. A girl called Jean Butts had answered the phone, telling her that Kate was out for the day with a friend.

'She's gone into the country with Paul,' Jean had said cheerfully. 'Who shall I say called?'

'Oh . . . it doesn't matter,' Emma faltered. 'I'll ring her again.'

She'd waited all day, not leaving her self-appointed vigil to find food or drink. She'd waited, hoping, fearing the worst – and now her fears were confirmed. Turning away, she staggered blindly into the night, the bitter anger and hatred eating into her soul.

Paul was in love with Kate. It was too late for her. Much, much too late.

CHAPTER NINETEEN

Puffy white clouds drifted across the sky as I walked through the streets of London. It was spring again – the spring of 1916 – and at Brockmere the fruit trees would be in bloom. In Europe the desperate struggle against the enemy went on as men fought and died in the trenches. In Britain a Conscription Bill had been brought in earlier that year, because volunteers were no longer enough to win the war. I had two weeks' leave due to me before being sent out to the field hospitals in France. Although my training wasn't completed, the situation out there was now so critical that anyone with the capability was being accepted for volunteer service.

'We're desperate for nurses in the field hospitals,' Matron had told me when I asked for the transfer. 'You'll find it unpleasant, exhausting work, Nurse Linton – but I don't want to discourage you. You are needed out there. Your knowledge of the language will be a big help, too.'

Jean had applied at the same time. She was delighted when we were informed that we would be going out there together.

'I'll meet you at the station,' she'd said, hugging me as she left to spend a few days with her family. 'Are you sure you won't come with me? Mum would love to have you.'

'I've been asked down to Brockmere,' I replied with a sigh, 'but I doubt if I shall go. I haven't been back since the wedding – I'd come with you, Jean, but Paul is in town and I've promised to spend a little time with him.'

I was on my way to meet Paul now. He'd telephoned the hospital earlier asking me to have lunch with him.

'I'm on duty until nearly one,' I'd said looking down at my cumbersome uniform. 'I shan't have time to change, Paul.'

'That doesn't matter.' His voice was warm with amusement over the line. 'I know just the place. It's very exclusive. Only a few people know the secret, but I assure you the food is very good – and the proprietor won't mind how you're dressed.'

I laughed. 'Then you'd better give me the address,' I said.

Paul's apartment overlooked the river. It had a long picture window that let in lots of light, and he told me that it had once been an artist's studio. The ceilings were high and had exposed beams that had been painted black. The walls were plain white and the furniture was all French, with padded velvet sofas and a pair of Empire consoles in ormolu-mounted bronze and mahogany. We sat in gilt and ebony chairs at the dining table, looking out at the waving fronds of willows that dipped down to the water's edge, and eating the delicious seafood soufflés that Paul had cooked himself.

'This is superb,' I said as the food melted in my mouth. 'I didn't know you could cook, Paul.'

'There are many things you don't know about me.' He smiled as he refilled my wine glass. 'And many things I would like to learn about you. That is the fun of life, is it not? Learning about people?'

I looked at him curiously, realizing that there was so much mystery still clinging to this man whose entry into my life had had such far-reaching effects.

'We're still strangers really, aren't we?' I said. 'I don't even know where your real home is.'

His expression was tinged with sadness. 'Like you, I was an only child. My mother died soon after giving birth to me and my father was killed in a hunting accident when I was six years old. I was brought up by my grandmother until I was seventeen and then she died very peacefully in her sleep. After that I was alone until I married at twenty. Marianne was only sixteen; it was an unsuitable match; we were both still children and she was never strong. Her parents should never have allowed it, but they wanted her to have security and I was rich, foolish and very much in love. I thought that love was all, but I soon discovered my mistake; the marriage was a disaster from the beginning. Marianne was a child; when she knew she had conceived, she turned against me, refusing to let me near her. Even the touch of my hand against her shoulder set her shuddering. . . . ' He pulled a wry face. 'I do not tell you this to excuse what I did; I blame myself very much for what happened.'

'What you did wasn't so very wrong,' I said softly. 'I think that in your place many men would have done the same, Paul. You couldn't have known that it would result in Marianne's illness.'

'No. . . . ' He inhaled deeply, seeming to force himself to smile. 'So, now you know the whole story. Since then I've travelled extensively and until the war began I left my estates in the hands of agents. The threat of invasion made me realize how much I had to lose and I am a reformed character.' He laughed at himself. 'You see before you a man dedicated to the restoration of peace and a life spent in good works. From now on there will be no more of the self-indulgent Paul de Bernay.' The self-mockery glinted in his eyes. 'And now you will tell me about yourself – no?'

'There isn't much to know about me,' I said, understanding the pain and doubt he was hiding behind his show of bravado. 'I'm a reasonably good nurse, and I like books and music – other people's music. I still can't play the piano properly. That's about all there is to know.'

He shook his head, studying my face intently. 'No, I don't believe that. This is the face you show to the world, but there's another Kate – a woman who has not yet learned to live.'

I felt the colour come into my cheeks and it was difficult to breathe. 'Are you sure she's there, Paul?'

'Oh yes, I think so.' He took a sip of his wine, his eyes holding mine, and I experienced the compelling power of the man. 'Her time has not come yet, but it will. You are not yet ready to let go of the past.'

He saw too much! My eyes dropped away. 'Does it show so plainly?'

'Only to me. I see sadness in you, Kate.' He touched my hand. 'You still love him, don't you?'

'Yes.' I gazed up at him. 'Do you find that shocking – that I should still desire a man who is my half-brother?'

A smile quirked at the corners of his mouth. 'Very little shocks me, Kate. I was never brought up according to your strict Victorian values. No, I think it was almost inevitable that it should happen, given the circumstances. You were both young and full of youth's passion. It isn't easy to put out such fires.'

'You're not that much older than Harry yourself,' I said with a wry smile.

'Did I say I was immune to foolish passions?' he asked huskily. 'Perhaps it is because of my own desires that I understand yours.'

'You are very understanding, Paul,' I said warmly. 'Without your friendship I don't know what I would have done these past months. You've been very kind to me.'

'That's because I care for you deeply. I want to help you in any way I can.'

'You have helped me – just by being there when I needed a shoulder to cry on.'

'Then I count myself fortunate.' He smiled. 'How would you like to go to a music hall tonight? I think there you will find laughter and forgetfulness for a few hours.'

Paul took me to the theatre that evening. We laughed at George Robey's comic routines and listened to Violet Loraine singing a song that was popular with thousands of soldiers and their sweethearts. Songs like hers were played over and over again in the billets in France, bringing precious memories of loved ones back home.

Afterwards, we sang the words of the songs we'd heard: *If You Were the Only Girl in the World*, *Keep the Home Fires Burning*, and Paul whistled to the tune of *St Louis Blues*.

As we drove through the darkened streets to my hotel, I felt relaxed and slightly dreamy. For a few days and nights I'd had a freedom never dreamed of at the nurses' home and, as we stood in the street outside my hotel, I looked up at Paul and I knew I didn't want to be alone that night.

'Would – would you stay with me?' I asked, my cheeks tinged with colour.

For a moment he was silent, then he took me in his arms to kiss me gently. The kiss was sweet, and yet as soon as his lips touched mine, I went cold and stiff in his arms. He let me go, shaking his head regretfully.

'No, I shall not stay tonight, Kate,' he murmured softly. 'No doubt I shall wish a thousand times that I had, but it is too soon.' He smiled and touched my cheek. 'Take care of yourself, my dearest girl.'

As he turned to get into his car, I felt a ridiculous urge to weep, yet I knew he was right. I longed for warm, comforting arms and tender kisses, but it was Harry's arms I wanted. Perhaps I always would.

I rang Lady Selina the next morning to say goodbye. She was disappointed that I wouldn't go down, but she didn't press me.

'Next time you come to Brockmere you'll see a change,' she said.

'What do you mean?'

'We're going to turn it into a home for convalescent officers. We have far more room than we need these days – and it will give me something to do.'

'I think that's a marvellous idea,' I said. 'How is Prue?'

'She's expecting her first child. I'm afraid she isn't feeling very well just at the moment.'

'I'm sorry — but the sickness should soon pass, shouldn't it?'

'Yes, of course — though I'm worried about her. It seems there may be complications.'

'Let me know how she goes on, won't you?'

'Yes — and you must let me know if there's anything you need while you're in France. I can always send out parcels through the Red Cross.'

'Yes, I will,' I promised. 'Goodbye, then.'

'Goodbye, Kate — and take care of yourself.'

As I replaced the receiver, I wondered why she seemed so much warmer towards me than she'd once been. Perhaps it was only my imagination.

Jean Butts greeted me with a scream of delight as I got on to the train. She took my case, stowing it in the rack with hers.

'Isn't this exciting?' she asked. 'I've had my instructions to report to the 23rd General when we get there — what about you?'

'It looks as if we'll be staying together, then.'

'That's good,' she said. 'How was your leave?'

'It was relaxing. How about yours? Have you heard from that lieutenant — what was his name?'

'Tom Rees.' Jean grinned, shaking out her light brown curls confidently. She took a small green envelope, the kind issued to forces overseas, and waved it triumphantly. 'It's been censored in places, but we have our own code. He's been up at the front but he's all right, and now they've sent his battalion back to base for a rest. Isn't that lucky? We'll probably be able to see one another.'

'That's wonderful, Jean. I'm so pleased for you.'

'What about you?' she asked curiously. 'Did you meet anyone? It's time you found yourself someone, Kate.'

Jean's expression made me laugh. Lady Selina would no doubt find her free manners and open way of talking very shocking, but Jean was a law unto herself. The war had given her far more freedom than she would ever have had in her own village, and she had used it to good effect, reading all the literature put out by the various women's movements and attending the open meetings at the Lyceum Club, where the language was bold, lively and often outrageous. She was typical of the new woman who was emerging in these troubled days; the woman who would refuse to accept the old restrictions when the war was over.

Christable Pankhurst's march to Whitehall at the head of thirty thousand women in July 1915 had led to women being given the right to serve, and women were now filling the vacant jobs created by their men's departure to the war; you could see their smiling, confident faces in offices, in the cabs of buses and trams and in industry. Jean and women like her had won the freedom for which their suffragette sisters had been battling for so long, simply because the country couldn't manage without them.

'I did spend some time with a man,' I said, smiling as her brows went up. 'Do you remember Paul de Bernay?'

'How could I forget?' She rolled her eyes at me. 'Well, tell me more! Are you in love with him? Did you – you know!'

'I like him a lot – and no, I didn't.' I shook my head at her evident disappointment. 'But I enjoyed myself, and next time I just might.'

Jean's eyes sparkled with interest, but our conversation was interrupted by the arrival of a group of Kitchenaires. Although Lord Kitchener had recently been reported lost at sea, with the sinking of the cruiser *Hampshire*, a loss that was mourned by the whole nation, the name given to the new recruits at the beginning of the war had stuck. This batch of young soldiers were fresh-faced, boisterous and eager, obviously on their first trip to France. They were a noisy, friendly lot and went out of their way to be gallant when they realized we were nurses, helping us with our suitcases and buying us tea when we changed trains.

Throughout the sea voyage, the troop ships were protected by the British Navy. Despite the battle of Jutland, which had resulted in several losses for both Britain and Germany, the navy was doing a good job of keeping the sea lanes open. The newspapers might talk of the importance of blocking Germany's ports around the world to prevent the Germans from obtaining the raw materials needed to help their war machine on the move, but as I saw the shores of France, I was thankful that the navy had seen us safely across the Channel.

One of the seamen told us that Boulogne was almost exactly as it had been before the war, with its Channel-steamer berths on one side, and the smelly fishquays on the other. Except that now there was evidence of troop movements everywhere: wagons and horses queued along the harbour front, with its cliff-backed hotels and the long hill leading up to the ramparts, patiently waiting to load up with barrels of fresh water and food supplies for the troops inland. It was a scene of confusion and noise, constant comings and goings.

The railway station was quite a distance to walk, and we were grateful when a young officer in a staff car offered us a lift.

'You'll be nurses going up to the hospital,' he said, grinning at us. 'You don't know how much we need you girls. Hop in, my lovelies. I'm going to the station anyway.'

We piled in gratefully, tired and hungry and slightly overawed by all the activity going on around us. War was suddenly a powerful and rather frightening reality.

At the station we had to wait several hours for a train as priority was given to the troops moving up the line. It wasn't until mid-afternoon on the following day that we finally got settled into our billets. Other nurses arriving on the same ships had got there before us, and all the available rooms in the area were taken. Jean and I were told we could share a tent with a nurse who had been out almost from the start. This turned out to be lucky, as Sandy was able to tell us what to expect.

'I was here the first Christmas,' she said, greeting us with a cheerful grin. 'Things have changed a lot since then. There was a strange kind of truce up at the line for a few hours on Christmas Day. The men actually exchanged gifts and went over to the Boche trenches. Others just walked in No Man's Land.'

'No Man's Land?'

'Between the trenches,' Sandy Jones explained. 'It was an odd experience, so they say – that was before the Flammenwerfer and the gassing, of course. You should hear the men now; they really hate the Boche after the gassing.'

Over the next few weeks, as the carnage of the Somme began, I was to see and hear things that would linger in my mind for the rest of my life. Back home I'd been used to seeing men who had received some treatment; here they were brought in straight from the casualty stations up at the front. Many of them had necessarily received only the crudest of attention; they lay screaming with pain, waiting on stretchers outside the wards because all the beds were full. Men with shattered limbs; men with half their faces blown away; men with blind, staring eyes and grey, haunted faces. Some died quickly from loss of blood, others had amputations that left them rotting with gangrene to die in slow agony. Still others had flesh wounds that would heal in time. These were the lucky ones. They joked about their 'Blighty' wounds, and the doctors patched them up, sending them back home for a well-earned rest.

I had never worked so hard in my life. Everyone was overworked and tired. Everything was in short supply; beds, medical supplies, sheets, towels and sometimes food. The endless stream of injured men seemed to increase and we heard desperate stories of fighting going on on the Somme. The terrible losses sustained by the British soldiers were rightly described as a blood-bath. I grew used to the sound of swearing from men enduring hell. They cursed and they cried, but they also laughed, inventing nicknames for the messengers of death the enemy launched at them. I heard about 'Berthing Bertha' and 'Whistling Willy' as I bound suppurating wounds and smoothed fevered brows. It was like being in the pit of hell, but I wouldn't have exchanged my life for anything. I was driven by something deep within myself, as we all were who tended the wounded in that summer of 1916. It was during those hot sweaty days and nights that I began to know the other Kate – a Kate who was no longer innocent, who faced the world with her eyes wide open.

Jean had snatched a couple of precious days at Béthune with her Tom before he was sent back to the line. They'd had a meal at a restaurant and walked in some woods, finding a quiet country inn that still had a cellar of fine wines.

'Tom looks much better than I'd expected,' she told me. 'He's asked me to marry him when this is all over.'

'That's the best news I've had in ages,' I cried, hugging her. 'I just wish I knew how Harry is. I haven't had a letter in ages, nor has his mother.'

'He's all right, Kate,' she said. 'If anything had happened, your family would have heard.'

'Yes, I suppose you're right,' I said, but I continued to look anxiously at the faces of the injured men as they were brought in, half afraid that I would find Harry amongst them. It was a chance in a million, of course; there were many other hospitals he could be taken to if he was hurt.

It would have been better if only he'd written now and then, just to say that he was alive. I tried hard to forget him, to live a normal life and put all the old regrets from my mind. Jean and Sandy were forever fixing me up with blind dates, but it was like a sickness in my blood, this longing for the one man in the world I couldn't have.

It was autumn 1917. I was in the tent that served as a canteen for the medical staff. I sipped my lukewarm tea, ignoring the headache that had been threatening all day. Having just come off duty, I had several hours before I was due on again. It would probably be best to try to get some sleep.

'I want a volunteer who can speak French.'

A young man in his early twenties, whom I recognized as a newly arrived doctor, was standing in the middle of the floor. His eyes flashed with impatience as no one answered his request, and he scowled at two male orderlies who were trying to ignore him. Not knowing why I did it, I got to my feet.

'I can speak French, sir.'

His grey eyes narrowed to sharp flints. 'This is a dangerous mission, nurse. I was hoping for a man – can't any of you men speak the lingo?' He gave a sigh of exasperation as they shook their heads, running long, sensitive fingers through his short brown hair.

I smiled as his gaze came reluctantly back to me. 'It looks as if you're stuck with me, sir.'

'Are you sure?' He frowned at me from beneath thick brows. 'I'm going up to Ypres to replace a doctor at one of the casualty stations. He was out with the wounded a couple of nights ago and bought it. I need someone to drive up there with me and bring back a truckload of men. Can you do that? I have a driver but he doesn't speak any French and we may need that to get through.'

'Yes, sir, I can manage that. I'm off duty for a few hours.'

His frown relaxed slightly, his mouth softening into a smile. 'You sound very sure of yourself, nurse. I'm Doctor David Matthews – what's your name?'

'Kate Linton.' I shook the hand he extended. 'I might even be able to help out with the driving. I've been taking lessons since I've been out here.'

'And how long is that?'

'I came out in the spring of 1916, and I've been here ever since. I could've gone home at Christmas, but I took my leave in Bethune with friends.'

There was a look of admiration in his face. 'Then it seems as if I'm in luck, Kate Linton. I've only been out a few weeks myself, and I don't really know my way about yet.'

'Don't worry, you'll soon get used to it. I found it hard at first, but now I don't even hear the guns most of the time.'

'I don't know how you girls stand it. The long hours you work, the conditions and the stench. . . . '

I grinned at him. 'Oh, that's only the easy bit,' I said. 'It's the lice and the tummy bugs that get you down.'

'Don't I know it.' He grimaced and then smiled engagingly. 'Are you ready then?'

'Yes. It won't be the first time I've helped out, though I've never been up as far as Ypres before.'

'You're risking your life, you know that, don't you? We could be shelled.'

'I understand that, sir. I'll risk it if you will. Excuse me, I'll just tell my friend where I'm going. She can explain if I'm late back. Jean will cover for me if she has to.'

'Thank you.' Doctor Matthews gave me a brilliant smile. 'You're a brave young woman.'

We didn't enter the doomed town of Ypres. As we approached, the truck was stopped by an infantry officer who advised us to take a quieter detour.

'You'll be safe in the woods,' he said. 'Shells are more dangerous in the town than in the country. Besides, you've no need to go through the town to get where you're going.'

There was destruction everywhere. I felt a tightness in my chest as I looked round at the devastation. It was one thing to hear the men talk about it, another to see it for myself. I hadn't realized it would be this bad. Villages were flattened, churches merely ruins, their glory destroyed forever, whole fields turned into mine craters. We'd passed the corpses of several dead horses, their bellies swollen and putrid, and the stench was sickening.

It was late in the evening when we neared our destination. In the distance the sky was bright red. A wood was on fire and the air was thick with smoke. As we approached the rough tumble of sheds and dug-outs that must be the depot we were looking for, the noise of the guns became deafening. I had to strain to hear what Doctor Matthews was saying as the explosions seemed to surround us on all sides.

'We'll stop here,' he told the driver. 'I'll go and inquire where we are. This should be the right place, but I'll make certain.'

The driver switched off the engine. The truck had been a delivery van for a high-class London department store before the war and it still had its name emblazoned on the side in green and gold. I wondered how it had managed to find its way out to France. Still, it was marginally better than the London buses that had been brought in to transport the troops at the start of the war. At least a few more of the wounded would be on their way back to base and a hospital bed tonight because of the enterprising Doctor Matthews.

I watched as he picked his way through the mud and clutter of the depot. It wasn't so much different from the hospital compound, except that there were more horses. A sudden explosion to the right of the van made me change my mind. I wiped my hands on my skirt. That one had been a bit too close for comfort! I began to recite one of my favourite poems, written by Rupert Brooke, a soldier and a poet who had died on active service from blood poisoning caused by a mosquito bite. The driver expelled a long breath and then grinned at me as he heard the words of *The Soldier*.

'It's a bit warm round here, ain't it, miss?'

'Yes, Wally, it is,' I said. 'Let's hope we're at the right place.'

It seemed ages before David Matthews came back, though it could only have been five or ten minutes. He came running towards us, dodging the potholes.

'This is it. Bring the truck up now. They've got several badly wounded men who can't walk. You'll be needed on the way back, Kate. Follow me – and watch out for the shells. They say this is the worst attack for a week.'

'Just our luck,' the driver said, giving me a nervous wink.

He drove carefully over ruts large enough to cause severe bumping and swaying, stopping as he reached the rough shelter that obviously served as the casualty station. A young corporal had been doing what he could for the injured, but he looked relieved to see the new doctor and surprised to see me. I jumped out and unlocked the back as soldiers began to carry out the stetchers.

'I think we can take about four stretchers,' I said. 'And twice as many who can sit or stan. . . . ' My voice trailed away as I saw an injured man coming slowly towards me. He had a thick bandage round his head and his arm was in a sling. 'Harry – oh, my God! Harry. . . . ' I ran to meet him, my throat choked with emotion as I saw that he was barely managing to keep on his feet.

He stopped and stared at me, unable to believe his eyes. 'Is it really you, Kate?' he whispered. 'What are you doing here?'

'I came with Doctor Matthews. He needed someone who could speak French.'

'You shouldn't be here.' He blinked wearily. 'It's too dangerous. You could have been killed.'

'I volunteered to help,' I said, putting my arm around his waist. 'Lean on me, Harry. You can sit in the front beside me.'

'Special treatment?' He smiled faintly but made no further protest as I led him towards the van. 'It must be my lucky night.'

214

There was something different about him. I sensed it, but I couldn't be sure just what it was. Perhaps it was because he was exhausted and in pain. Yet there was a look in his eyes that I'd never seen there before – a look of defeat. I smiled at him as I helped him into the van.

'We'll soon have you back at the hospital, Harry. It won't be long.'

He nodded but didn't answer. Doctor Matthews called to me to help with some of the others. I went to assist him, fighting the tears. Compared to some of them Harry had been lucky – but he was mine.

'Thank you for what you've done,' Doctor Matthews said as we saw the last of the wounded into the back of the van. 'I shan't forget this.'

My eyes were bright as I looked at him. 'I've been well rewarded for my trouble. One of the men – he's my cousin. . . . '

'Good Lord!' Matthews looked astonished. 'It was a chance in a million. You'd better get off now before they start shelling again. You can find your way back?'

'I can do that, sir.' The driver winked at me. 'Just as long as we don't get stopped by some interfering Froggie.'

'I'll handle it if we do,' I said. 'Don't worry. Good luck, Doctor Matthews. I'd better get back before Matron goes on the warpath. We're not supposed to leave the hospital compound without a pass from her.' I laughed as I saw the startled expression on his face. 'Well, she can't hang me, can she?'

I ran back to the van, my heart lifting as I saw Harry sitting there with his eyes closed. He was alive! He was injured but he was alive. For the moment that was enough.

'I'm very angry with you, Nurse Linton.' Matron looked across her desk at me. 'I think your behaviour was the most foolish escapade I've heard of. There was simply no need for it.'

'No one else volunteered – and Doctor Matthews had been told he would have to wait for thirty-six hours for official transport.' I bit my lip. 'I – I didn't think it could do any harm.'

'It could have done a great deal of harm,' Matron contradicted. 'You might have been killed – and I cannot afford to lose one of my best nurses. It's difficult enough to keep the hospital staffed, Nurse Linton, without girls like you putting ideas into the others' heads. You were lucky. The next foolish nurse who tries to be a heroine might not be. You're not Edith Cavell – there's no need for you to get yourself shot for the sake of saving Doctor Matthews a few hours.'

'No, Matron. I'm sorry, Matron. It won't happen again.'

'I should hope not. Leave the transport to the army, nurse. You have more important things to do.' A slight smile softened her mouth. 'Even though I'm angry with you, I do appreciate that it was done with the best intentions. Doctor Matthews was at fault. I shall have something to say to him when we meet again. Very well, you may go now. Get a few hours rest before you come back on the wards.'

'Thank you.' I swallowed hard, feeling thoroughly chastened, especially by her reference to the British nurse who had truly been a heroine, dying for her beliefs in Belgium. Edith Cavell had followed her calling to the end, nursing and helping the injured Allied soldiers despite knowing that she could be shot as a spy by the Germans. My little adventure had seemed exciting and worthwhile at the time, now I realized it had been reckless and foolish. I was a nurse, not a soldier. I walked back to my billet, feeling dejected, but as I entered the tent Jean flew at me, screaming in frustration.

'You bloody heroine,' she yelled. 'What on earth made you do it? Matron nearly had a fit – everyone's talking about it.'

'Oh, don't you start,' I muttered. 'I've just been flattened by Matron. I know it was a stupid thing to do, so don't tell me.'

'It was, of course,' Sandy said, grinning. 'But you are a heroine, Kate. Matron is an old misery. Everyone else thinks you deserve a medal.'

'Perish the thought.' I looked at her and Jean in alarm. 'Why don't you two idiots get out of here and let me get some sleep? I didn't do anything special.'

'Oh no?' Jean shook her head. 'Well, you're going to get a party, Miss Linton. We've had a collection and tonight, whether you like it or not, you're going to be fêted with wine and food! So you can just get yourself prettied up, because we're not going to take no for an answer.'

It was two days before I managed to visit Harry. He was lying with his eyes closed when I approached the bed, but he opened them and smiled at me.

'I was just thinking about you,' he said.

'I hope it was something good?'

'I hoped you would come before they shipped me home,' he said awkwardly. 'I wasn't really aware of what was going on when you brought me in.'

216

'Are you feeling better?' My heart caught as I heard the note of weariness in his voice.

'Yes, much better,' he said, but I knew that he lied.

'You'll get a good rest now, anyway.' I was making conversation as if we were strangers.

'Yes.' It was there again in his eyes, that look of defeat. He was struggling against it, but it was there. It made me want to hold him in my arms, because I knew how ill he must be. Nothing had ever defeated my Harry in his life. 'I'm sorry I was rude to you that day in London,' he said.

'I understood.' I smiled, my throat tight with emotion.

He closed his eyes. 'I'm sorry. I can't fight this tiredness. It just comes over me in waves.'

'I'll leave you to sleep,' I said softly. 'I love you, Harry. I always will.'

There was no reply. He might have been asleep.

I frowned as I finished reading my letter and replaced it in its envelope.

'Is something wrong?' Sandy asked. 'You look worried. Is your cousin worse?'

'No. . . . ' I glanced up. 'He says he should be released from hospital next week. He's going to convalesce in London instead of going home.'

'So – what's wrong with that? He probably wants to meet a girl.'

'Yes, probably.' I turned away. It was impossible to explain when she knew nothing of the circumstances surrounding my relationship with Harry. 'It's almost time for me to report back. I think I'll go and talk to some of the patients.'

'Don't you ever let up?' she groaned. 'Where do you get your energy?'

'I've no idea.'

I'd lost the habit of sleep. It was impossible for me to relax any more. I was full of a nervous energy, wanting only to block out the thoughts that tortured me when I lay restless on my hard cot.

Frowning, I went outside. It had been raining again and the hospital compound was squelching beneath my feet. I had to lift the hem of my cumbersome uniform to keep it from dragging in the mud. The dirt and the discomfort were sometimes harder to bear than the work. I'd had to ask Jean to cut my hair really short. It was impossible to keep free of lice otherwise. The men were crawling with them

217

when they came in from the trenches; they apologized for it, but it wasn't their fault. Often they went for weeks at a time without being able to take a bath or even change their clothes. When they were stood down for a rest, there were long queues for the wine vats that served as baths for the men. However, conditions had at last begun to improve behind the lines, though very slowly. There was the occasional concert party and the men themselves put on some entertainment when they could, but medical supplies were still hard to come by, as were all the little necessities that one took for granted at home. I was always distributing the parcels I received from Brockmere amongst the other girls and the patients, but it wasn't just out here that things were difficult. From Lady Selina's letters, I knew that there were shortages at home, too. Even so, she'd never yet failed to send me anything I asked for, and her letters to me had gradually become warmer and warmer. I had the feeling that she no longer thought of me as her husband's bastard, but as a friend.

It was of Harry that I was thinking most as I made my way towards the wards that wet afternoon. Was Sandy right? Had he found someone else?

I couldn't forget that look of defeat in his eyes, as though the sight of me had somehow been too much for him to bear. Perhaps he had managed to find happiness with someone else. If so he was more successful than I – my love for him still haunted my mind and I believed it always would. But I tried not to let it interfere with my work, and now I made an effort to forget my personal problems as I began my tour of the wards.

There was one particular patient that I wanted to visit. A young Canadian flier had come in the previous night. His plane had crashed when he was returning from a mission over enemy lines, and he was in a pretty bad way. I'd promised to call in before I went on duty and write a letter to his wife for him, but as I walked into the ward, I saw that his bed was being stripped.

Second Lieutenant Bieunne hadn't made it. Tears were stinging my eyes as I turned away. He couldn't have been more than twenty years old. . . .

Two months after the death of Lieutenant Bieunne I came off duty to find that it was raining yet again. I turned up the collar of my coat, feeling tired and depressed. I'd been in France for almost two years. Perhaps it was time to ask for home leave. Lady Selina had constantly pleaded with me to visit her and I thought perhaps I would. Life was too short to bear grudges. Because the rain was driving into my face and blinding me, I didn't see the man until I bumped into him.

'I'm sorry,' I said. 'I wasn't looking where I was going.'

'Not your fault. It's this blasted rain.' He laughed then. 'Aren't you Kate Linton?'

I looked up, recognizing him. 'Doctor Matthews? You got back safely, then?'

'Yes. I'm on a few days' leave.' He hesitated, then, 'Would you like to have dinner with me this evening?'

'I'd love to, Doctor Matthews,' I said, smiling. 'I was just wondering whether to kill myself or wash my hair.'

'What an alternative!' He grinned. 'Please call me David – and I hope that was a joke?'

'Just about. It's the weather, I expect.'

'It is depressing. I'll have to cheer you up this evening, won't I? We could drive into Le Touquet. I know a place that isn't overflowing with officers from the airforce.'

I laughed as he pulled a face. Le Touquet was usually full of the RFC officers. 'Anywhere you like. It will be wonderful to get away for a few hours.'

'You are down, aren't you, Kate? I'll see you at about six-thirty, then?'

'Yes.' I smiled. 'Now I really will wash my hair.'

We parted and I walked on to my billet. When I entered, Jean was sitting on the edge of the bed. She didn't seem to notice me, and I sensed that something was wrong. As I spoke, she turned towards me and a piece of paper fluttered to the floor. I gasped as I saw the look in her eyes.

'What's wrong, Jean?'

'It's Tom.' She stared at me but her eyes were looking far beyond me. 'He's been wounded, Kate. It's bad.'

'Oh, Jean,' I said. 'I'm so sorry. Where is he?'

'They've taken him to Château Thierry. I've asked for compassionate leave.' She gazed up at me, her eyes dull with misery. 'I love him, Kate. What am I going to do if he dies?'

So much for feminine independence in the face of love! I sat beside her on the bed, putting my arm about her waist. Jean had always been so strong and cheerful, now she looked frightened. 'You mustn't think like that,' I said. 'You've got to look on the positive side. You've got to be strong for Tom's sake. He's going to need you now.'

'Yes, you're right.' Her chin went up. 'I'd better pack my things. I doubt if I shall come back here. When Tom is shipped home, I shall go with him.'

'Yes, of course you must, though I shall miss you. You will write and tell me how you are, won't you?'

'Yes, I'd like to keep in touch.' Her gaze rested on my face reflectively. 'You're too thin, Kate. You work too hard, but you seem to take the patients' cares onto your own shoulders. You should apply for home leave.'

'Perhaps I will soon.' I smiled at her. 'Guess what – I've got a dinner date this evening.'

'Honestly?' She rolled her eyes. 'Now that is something! Who's the lucky man?'

'David Matthews. The doctor I drove up to Ypres with that day.'

'I remember.' She pulled a face. 'You should have got a medal for that. Well, well, do I scent a romance?'

'It's just dinner, but. . . . ' I shrugged my shoulders. 'Who knows? I've got to the stage where I don't really care what happens anymore.'

'Kate!' Jean pretended to be shocked. 'You wicked thing.' She gave me a hug. 'It's about time you had some fun.'

'Well, I intend to this evening.' My smile faded as I looked at her. 'I just hope things won't be too bad for you.'

'Wish me luck, Kate.' She grabbed my hand and held it tightly.

'You know I do,' I said. 'Lots and lots of it.'

I tried not to think about Jean's problems as I dressed for dinner that night, but it wasn't easy. She was my closest friend and I knew how much Tom meant to her. It would be so unfair if he were to die. My mind was reeling from the shock of too many deaths. I felt pressured, close to breaking point, and I just wanted to forget everything for a few hours.

Perhaps that's why I drank too much wine at dinner. I knew I was laughing too much, but I just couldn't stop. I flirted outrageously with David Matthews, touching my foot against his beneath the table and leaning against him at every opportunity.

'It's too late to go back,' I said when we left the hotel dining room. 'Why can't we stay here tonight?'

'Do you mean together?' He looked surprised but pleased.

I giggled and swayed slightly. 'Why not? Live dangerously, David. Tomorrow it might be too late.' I hiccupped as my head started to swim. I could only just manage to see David's face through the haze.

'Yes. Perhaps we'd better stay,' he said. 'You sit there on that sofa while I arrange it – and don't move.'

'Yes, David,' I murmured obediently, wondering why the floor wouldn't stay still.

He pushed me gently but firmly onto a hard sofa in the hallway. I smiled at him as he walked away. I was feeling happy, pleasantly sleepy, as I leaned my head back against the sofa. I would just close my eyes for a moment. . . .

When I opened them again it was to a blinding shaft of pain. I groaned and shut them again quickly. It took me several seconds to realize that I was in bed and that someone was with me. Gathering my courage, I opened one eye.

'Drink this, Kate,' that someone said. 'Come on, sit up. You're not dying. It's only a hangover.'

I sat up gingerly, opening both eyes. David pushed a glass that was making an obscenely loud fizzing noise into my hand. I drank obediently and pulled a face.

'I feel disgusting.'

'You look disgustingly lovely,' he said cheerfully. 'It's all your own fault, you know. You drank too much wine last night. This is the price you pay for wild nights, Kate.'

'I hate you,' I said. 'Was I terribly drunk?'

'Actually, you were endearing and rather funny.' He smiled at me gently. 'You propositioned me. I was very flattered.'

'Oh, my Lord!' I stared at him in dismay. 'I wish I was dead.'

'Thanks.' He laughed. 'My ego was high, now you've flattened it.'

'I didn't mean it that way.' I blushed. 'Did we – well, you know.'

'Regretfully, I have to say no. You passed out before we got here and I had to carry you up. Besides, I don't take advantage of lovely ladies in distress.' He smiled and shook his head. 'You didn't give any secrets away, Kate. I recognized the symptoms. I've been known to break out myself on the odd occasion. You've been under a strain for far too long, my girl. As a doctor, I recommend a spot of home leave – I'll speak to Matron for you if you like.'

'No. My leave is long overdue. I'll ask her myself.'

'See that you do.'

'I will,' I promised, then shot him a grateful look. 'Thank you, David.'

'Any time. I have broad shoulders, just right for crying on.' He grinned. 'Next time you proposition me, though, try not to drink so much. I'd like to be seduced by you, Kate – when you're feeling more yourself.'

'Maybe next time.' I threw a pillow at him as he laughed. 'Now get out of here and let me die in peace.'

'I was just on my way to breakfast. I suppose you wouldn't . . . ?'

I groaned and buried my face in the other pillow.

I ought to have spoken to Matron straight away, but when David went back to his unit I somehow got bogged down with routine chores. With Jean gone we were having to work extra hours until some new replacements came out from England. My little fling had done me good, and I wasn't feeling too desperate when Matron sent for me that morning.

'I wonder what I've done now?' I said as Sandy passed on the message. 'Would you like to read this letter from Jean? She says that Tom isn't as bad as she'd feared. They've taken his right leg off to the knee, but she thinks he'll pull through.'

'That's something,' Sandy said, taking the letter. 'I'll leave it on your bed. You'd better hurry or you'll be late.'

'What are you going to do?'

'Sleep.' Sandy yawned. 'Thank goodness those replacents are due out next week. I could do with a break.'

I nodded, smothering a sigh as I went out. I was too tired to worry about Matron's summons. If some petty little rule had been broken it was just too bad.

Matron's office was simply another tent, but inside everything was as spick and span as it would have been back home. It even had a carpet on the floor, which spoke volumes for the determination of the woman.

'Ah, there you are, Nurse Linton. Come in and sit down please.'

I sat on a wooden chair that had been commandeered from one of the farms in the district, feeling a sinking sensation in my stomach as I saw her expression.

'Is something wrong, Matron?'

'I'm afraid I have bad news for you.'

A shiver of fear went through me. 'Is it Harry?'

'Harry?' She frowned and shook her head. 'I don't understand.'

'He's my cousin. He was wounded some months back and he was ill for some time. Has he had a relapse?'

'No, nurse, it isn't your cousin.' She folded her hands on the desk in front of her. 'I believe you knew Doctor David Matthews?'

222

'David?' I stared at her in surprise. 'He was here on leave only a few days ago.'

'Yes, so I understand. Was he a friend of yours?'

'Was. . . . Oh no!' I tingled with shock. 'He can't be. . . . '

'He was killed on duty while tending the wounded; in No Man's Land, I hear. He's to be recommended for a posthumous medal.'

'No. . . . No, no, no!' I felt the scream building inside me. It was too much. 'He can't be dead. He was so good and gentle and kind. It isn't fair. . . . ' Suddenly I felt the tears pouring down my cheeks and I was sobbing out of control. 'No, it isn't true. I don't believe it. It's a lie. It's a lie!'

'Pull yourself together, nurse.' Matron came to me, giving my shoulder a little shake. 'You're obviously in a nervous state. I'm going to give you compassionate leave.'

'No. . . . ' I raised my head, wiping my hand across my face. 'I'll be all right. We're too busy. I can't go.'

Matron smiled. 'You've been a tower of strength, my dear, but we all need time to rest. I'm sending you home for a month – only a month, mind. I need you back here.'

I blinked rapidly, taking the handkerchief she gave me. 'Thank you. I'm sorry for being so silly.'

'It wasn't silly. A good cry was probably what you needed.' She nodded approvingly as I rose to my feet. 'Go home and see your family. Have some fun and enjoy yourself, then come back to us. The war isn't over yet. They say there's going to be one more big push – and you know what that means. We'll be needing all our nurses, and they'll need to be fit.'

'Thank you, Matron,' I said, blowing my nose. 'I'll be fine now.'

CHAPTER TWENTY

She stood watching the café customers without really being aware of them or of the tempting aroma of cooking from the kitchen behind her, though it was a while since she'd eaten. Her back ached and her eyes were gritty with tiredness. All she wanted was to lie down, but there were two hours until closing time, two long hours before she could crawl back to that miserable little attic room she called home. No, it could never be a home, Emma reflected bitterly. It was just somewhere to sleep . . . somewhere to drink alone.

She knew that she was drinking too much but after her return from England all those weary months ago, it had been her only refuge, the only way she coud ease the bitterness. Sometimes it burned inside her, tasting like gall in her mouth. She was aware that the war was not going well for the Allies, that the casualties on the Somme now numbered some five hundred thousand for the Allied Forces and nearer six hundred and fifty thousand Germans; she was aware that General Joffre had been replaced by General Robert Nievelle as the head of the French forces on the Somme, because the offensive had failed; she was aware that the chef had for sometime been using horsemeat as the main ingredient of most dishes in the kitchen and she'd heard that in England the price of bread had risen to an outrageous tenpence a loaf, but all these things washed over her like so many grains of sand in the surf of her own personal grief. Always the memory of that night and the look in Paul's eyes stayed with her. She could never quite rid herself of the pain, no matter how much she drank. . . .

'Madame. . . . ' The voice broke into her thoughts; she blinked at the young officer as he tried to catch her attention once more. 'If you please. . . . '

'Pardon, Monsieur,' she said. 'You wish for some wine?'

'Perhaps,' he replied, frowning and unsure. 'I'm looking for Madame Dubois – are you she?'

Emma regarded him with suspicion. 'And if I were?'

'Then you would perhaps remember a certain Lieutenant Marc Normand?'

'Marc?' She was jerked out of her reflective mood. Of course she remembered the only man to show her kindness since she came to Paris. 'Naturally, I remember – is something wrong?' She read the answer in his eyes and her heart plunged. 'Has he been wounded? Is he dead?'

'Not dead,' the officer replied and Emma was surprised at the relief flooding through her. 'But badly wounded. He named you as his next of kin, Madame. He has asked if you would visit him. . . . '

'He named me?' Emma's surprise faded as she recalled the night they had spent together. Marc had been lonely, too. She'd sensed there was some personal tragedy he'd wanted to forget; known it was the reason he'd chosen her rather than a younger woman. It was for comfort that he'd turned to her in his despair, recognizing a kindred spirit; a fellow soul in torment. Marc had given her warmth and comfort; it wasn't his fault that his advice had turned sour. Suddenly she was filled with an urgent desire to see him agin. 'Where is he?' she asked. 'Can you take me to him?'

The young officer's mouth relaxed into a smile of relief. 'Thank you,' he said fervently. 'I promised to find you if I could. We were friends and it was a pact between us – that we would look out for each other. Marc once saved my life and. . . . '

'You can tell me as we go.' Emma began to untie her apron, stiffening as she heard the harsh voice of the café owner's wife behind her.

'Where do you think you're going?'

Emma turned, facing the woman who had never liked her, knowing that she had waited for this chance, waited for Emma to make a mistake.

'A friend of mine has been wounded. I must go to him.'

'If you leave now, you needn't bother to return.' The woman's eyes glinted with spite.

'As you wish.' Emma's gaze went over her, taking in the red-veined cheeks, huge, pendulous breasts straining beneath a black gown that was far too tight, and the sour line of her mouth. 'You may send what you owe me to my lodgings.'

'You'll get nothing more from us,' the woman called after her. 'Pah!' She spat on the stret. 'We're well rid of you. Whore!'

Beside Emma, the young man stiffened, his face angry. He hesitated as though he would turn back to avenge the insult, but Emma laid a hand on his arm.

'It doesn't matter,' she said. 'Please tell me your name – and how Marc saved your life. . . . '

'My name is Jacques,' he said. 'It happened when we were on a routine patrol. I was badly wounded and. . . . '

Emma sat looking down at the man in the bed, fighting the wave of nausea that swept over her. Jacques had tried to prepare her for his friend's injuries but words were inadequate to describe the horrifying sight that met her eyes. Marc's face was terribly burned, making him unrecognizable as the handsome lieutenant she'd met so briefly in Paris. She breathed deeply, controlling her desire to weep, glad that his eyes were covered with bandages. At least he hadn't been able to see that first betraying surge of revulsion she'd been unable to hide. It had quickly turned to shame and then pity. Now, as she reached for his hand, the pity became something more, some deeper emotion that was perhaps a kind of love. He was at least ten years younger than she.

'Marc,' she said softly, her voice giving no hint of the horror she had first experienced. 'Are you awake?'

The red slit that was all that remained of a mouth that had once been so kissable tried to form a smile, but it was too much of an effort. His fingers stirred in hers and then went limp. For one heart-rending moment she thought he was dead, then she saw a leg move restlessly beneath its light covering and she whispered a prayer of thanks.

'Don't try to talk,' she said, stroking the back of his hand. Jacques had told her that the rest of Marc's body had escaped the burning that had destroyed his face, and because of that he would probably live. 'Don't worry about anything, Marc. I'm here and I'm going to stay with you for as long as you need me. I promise I won't leave you. I won't ever leave you while you need me.'

She couldn't be sure, but it seemed to Emma that this time he smiled.

It was growing dark when Emma left the hospital and began to walk across the compound. Mud squelched beneath her feet; it was raining, driving into her face and mingling with her tears.

Marc was holding his own. Sister had told her she was certain he would live; they were going to move him again very soon.

'We can't cope with long-term nursing here,' she'd explained gently. 'We do our best to patch them up when they come in. If they survive the first few weeks we send them on; to a hospital near their homes if possible, but in Lieutenant Normand's case. . . . '

226

Emma nodded, understanding the look that accompanied her words. 'Marc is going to need a great deal of care, isn't he?'

'Yes.' The Sister sighed. 'The nuns are his only real hope, Madame. In time the doctors may be able to help but. . . . '

'He'll never be handsome again – is that what you're trying to say?'

'When he sees himself for the first time. . . . '

'Yes, I understand. You think he may want to hide – and the hospice is the best place for him in the circumstances. Yes, I do see what you mean.'

'At least he has you, Madame.'

Emma nodded, a slight smile on her lips. The Sister believed she was the widow of a Frenchman and Marc's sister. Knowing that her friendly smiles would turn to veiled hostility if she guessed the truth, Emma had let her believe the small lie. It was easier for everyone and the only way she could continue to visit Marc regularly.

The move to the hospice was due to happen within a few days. Emma was to stay in a guest cottage at the convent so that she could visit Marc daily. It was a temporary arrangement, and she knew she would eventually have to find somewhere to live – somewhere for both her and Marc. At the moment she had no financial worries; Jacques had given her all Marc's possessions, including a wad of notes that represented most of his last quarter's pay. As his named representative, she supposed she was entitled to receive future payments, but she was loathe to touch any of the money. When Marc was able to think for himself it would be different, but for the time being she would use her slender savings to support them both. . . .

Suddenly Emma froze as she saw the girl crossing the compound. She looked familiar – it wasn't . . . it couldn't be! Yet instinctively she knew that it was Kate. And she was coming towards her; their paths were bound to cross! A rush of emotion made her feel as if she couldn't breathe properly. Kate was here at the same hospital! She could see her, speak to her. For a moment she was tempted, and then she remembered. Panic swept through her. She looked frantically for a way of escape, her heart beating wildly, and then the miracle happened. Kate had met a friend; she was talking to her, laughing as she turned away towards the canteen.

Breathing a sigh of relief, Emma waited until they were out of sight. She'd had no idea Kate was even out here. She would have to be careful for the next few days. Now that the first shock of seeing her daughter was over, she realized that it would have ruined everything if Kate had chanced to see her.

There had been a time when she'd been haunted with guilt for what she'd done to her daughter, a time when she'd been tempted to contact her and ask for forgiveness, but that time was over.

She'd made her plans for the future and an accidental meeting with Kate now would only confuse things. Emma Linton was dead: let her rest in peace.

CHAPTER TWENTY-ONE

'Kate! Miss Kate,' Bates called, hurrying towards me as I alighted from the train. 'God bless you, miss. Rosie and me had begun to think we would never see you again.'

He sounded quite emotional, and I was surprised to catch a glimpse of tears in his eyes. 'I haven't been away that long, have I?' I asked, smiling as he took my case.

'Too long, and that's a fact. Is this all your luggage, miss?'

'Yes. There wasn't much call for fancy frocks out there.' I shivered in the chill wind and pulled my coat collar up around my neck.

His eyes went over me anxiously and he shook his head. 'You're too thin, Miss Kate. What have they been doing to you?'

'Somehow eating doesn't seem that important when injured and dying men are being brought in every day,' I said. 'But I expect I'll make up for it now that I'm home. How is everybody? Is Mrs Bates well?'

'She gets a touch of the rheumatics now and then, but she doesn't complain. It's not been easy to get decent staff up at the house, what with the boot boys running off as soon as they're old enough to join up, and the maids leaving to work in the munitions factories. Rosie married a widower with a small child – but she'll have told you that in her letters?' I nodded and he smiled. 'If it wasn't for Rosie giving a hand now and then, I don't know how we'd manage.' He glanced at me from beneath brows that had sprouted grey hairs since I was last at Brockmere. 'Sir Gerald is very well, but the mistress. . . . Well, she's not been too good this last winter. You'll likely see a change in her.'

'Oh?' I was surprised. 'She hasn't mentioned feeling ill in her letters.'

'Well, she's not one for talking about her health, but it upset her when Miss Prue – or Mrs Marsh as I should say – lost her baby.'

'Poor Prue,' I said. 'I knew she'd had a miscarriage, but I was so busy I never really thought what it must mean for both her and her mother.' I hesitated, then, 'Did – did Harry come down for Christmas?'

'No, miss.' Bates avoided my eyes. 'We expected him but he

telephoned at the last minute to say he wouldn't be down. I think that upset the mistress badly.'

'Is he ill, Bates? He wrote when he left hospital but I haven't heard since.'

'He doesn't write home much. Sir Gerald went up to see him in January. He wasn't staying at the house in Hanover Square. Seems he'd taken lodgings and was expecting to be sent back to his unit. . . . Only they've given him some sort of a desk job in London. Something about him not being fit for duty. Not mentally fit, that is.'

I stared at him, alarmed. 'What do you mean?'

'I'm not too sure myself, miss. You'll have to ask Sir Gerald – I think they had a bit of an argument.'

I was thoughtful as I climbed into the car. I knew that Harry wouldn't be the first soldier to recover from his physical wounds and yet fail to be passed as fit for active duty. Sometimes the horrors of war in the trenches were difficult to erase from the mind. I recalled the expression I'd seen in Harry's eyes that day at the front, and the mental exhaustion he'd suffered in hospital, and I knew why he hadn't been sent back. Yet that still didn't explain why he wouldn't visit his mother. He must know it was pointless to go on holding a grudge against his father.

Bates had stopped the car a short distance from the main door. I was puzzled, then I saw an amazing sight. Two men dressed in pyjamas and dressing gowns were furiously pushing other men in similar attire in wheelchairs. They appeared to be having some sort of a race, for they came rushing madly towards us, looking as if they would crash into the car; then they suddenly split apart, passing one each side of the vehicle and disappearing round the corner of the house.

As I got out, still feeling bewildered, I could hear the sound of cheering, and glancing up, I saw several young men hanging out of an upstairs window. At that moment Prue came out of the house and walked towards me. She was wearing a pale grey dress with a high neck, and her hair was swept back from her face in a sleek chignon at the back. She looked poised and elegant, very different from the girl I'd met the first day I'd come to Brockmere. She smiled and held out her hands in welcome.

'Kate. It's good to see you again.'

'Thank you Prue. You can't imagine how good it is to be here. It's so peaceful and beautiful. . . . Or it was until a moment ago.' I looked over my shoulder at the spot from where the men in wheelchairs had recently disappeared. 'What was all that about?'

'Oh, don't take any notice of them,' she said, laughing. 'They're all quite mad. It's the relief of knowing they're getting better, I think. And Mother allows them to do whatever they like. She spoils them disgracefully – when I think of how strict she was with us. . . . ' A flicker of something that might have been pain or perhaps jealousy passed across her face and was gone. 'I've been staying for a few days because she isn't well. Besides, Michael works so hard he's never home.'

I caught a hint of bitterness in her voice and wondered – was there something not quite right with her marriage? But before I could collect my thoughts, she began to speak again.

'Perhaps Harry will come down now that you're here. I've tried telephoning him, but he always makes some excuse.' She looked at me, her eyes dark with suppressed emotion. 'It's so ridiculous to keep up this feud, Kate. I know I was a spiteful little cat that day at the boathouse, but I was going through a bad time – and I suppose I've always been jealous of Harry, because he's the heir of Brockmere. The thing is, Mother's ill. Really ill. She's had a slight heart attack, though she pretends it was just indigestion, but we all know it was her heart. She hasn't been the same since the quarrel with Harry.' Now there was a hint of the old jealousy in her eyes. 'She won't admit she's pining over him, nor will she admit she's ill – though she's given up her Red Cross work.'

'Your mother doesn't give up easily.'

'I know – that's what's worrying me. Harry ought to come down, Kate.'

'Yes.' I glanced at her thoughtfully. 'You're looking very well yourself, Prue.'

She laughed confidently. 'I am well. I don't drink too much these days, and I've stopped feeling sorry for myself.'

'I'm glad.' I smiled at her. 'How is Michael?'

'He's fine. Works too much, as I said – but that's his business.' She shrugged carelessly but I sensed something hidden. 'Whatever happens, I don't intend to go back to what I was before the war. I've been helping Mother with her committee work, and I've discovered that I like being busy. When things are back to normal, I intend to live my own life. I'm a woman, not just a wife.'

'Good for you,' I said, smiling. 'I haven't thought about what I'll do when it's all over. They say one more big offensive will do it. I pray they're right. How long can we go on before they realize what a waste it all is?'

'You've been working too hard,' Prue said, taking my arm as we went into the house. 'Mother's determined to make a fuss of you while you're here – so don't let on that I told you she's ill, will you?'

'Of course not.' I drew a deep breath as I felt the welcoming atmosphere of the house surround me. 'It's good to be back. I really missed this place while I was away.'

It was an hour before I was allowed to slip away to my room. Not the one I'd had before the war, because that was presently occupied by Major Watkins, a young officer who had lost the use of his right arm at the second Ypres. All my personal things had been moved into a much smaller space so it was rather crowded, but compared with what I'd recently been used to in France it was luxury. I looked through my wardrobe at the clothes I'd left behind, hesitating for a few seconds before choosing a pretty blue dress I'd had new just before the start of the war. I'd been wearing it the day Prue followed me to the boathouse. Making up my mind, I slipped into it; there was no point in harbouring old grudges. The dress was a little loose around the waist but otherwise fitted me perfectly.

For the first time in ages, I studied my reflection. It was true that my face was thinner, and I looked older. I thought I resembled my mother even more than I had when I was younger and I felt pleased. I'd always thought her a beautiful woman. Sighing, I turned away from the mirror. Even after all this time, the manner of our parting, the lies and the pain of her lonely death still had the power to hurt me. Sometimes I almost convinced myself that she was alive, and yet if she was, she would surely have found a way to let me know. It was foolish. I'd seen the certificate of her death. Emma Linton was dead; I had to accept that.

Frowning, my thoughts turned to the woman who had taken me into her home. Bates was right, there was a marked change in Lady Selina. Her face had lost its healthy bloom, becoming grey and drawn. Her manner wasn't as brisk as it had been, though she tried to hide her tiredness, and I'd noticed that she sometimes appeared to forget what she was saying in mid-sentence.

I'd tidied my hair and was about to leave the room when someone knocked. 'Come in,' I called, turning to see Lady Selina in the doorway. 'I'm almost ready.' I smiled and went to meet her. 'You should have sent for me. I would have come to you.'

She waved her hand in a gesture of dismissal. 'I'm not a complete invalid yet.'

'I only meant. . . . '

'I know what you meant.' She smiled at me. 'I've come to appreciate you over the years, Kate. You've been like a daughter to me – and I don't deserve it.'

I blushed and shook my head, surprised. She had certainly mellowed, but perhaps that was her illness. 'I've done nothing special. You've been very good to me. . . . '

'No,' she contradicted. 'I've wronged you, Kate. Don't look so startled. I've given you hints before this – admit it.'

'If you mean because of Sir Gerald being my. . . . '

'I've never been certain of that,' she said, sending a shock down my spine. 'I thought your mother might have lied to get her revenge on me. . . . ' A wry smile touched her mouth as my eyes opened wide. 'She had good cause, Kate. It was I who had her sent away from Brockmere. Oh yes, she was sent fleeing in terror for her very existence by my father-in-law. He was a tyrant; the coldest man I ever met, but he liked me. When I discovered that my husband had seduced a seventeen-year-old child, I told Sir Mortimer and he did the rest.'

'What do you mean?' I shivered, feeling suddenly cold.

'He threatened to have her locked away in an insane asylum. I didn't know that at the time, of course. I just wanted the affair to stop. I was horrified. After she told me how she'd suffered, I knew that I had to give you a home no matter whether you were Gerald's daughter or not.'

'But how could he have even suggested such a thing? She wasn't mad!'

'I told you, he was a tyrant. It was quite possible in those days to have a wilful girl locked up for bad behaviour. Sir Mortimer was a powerful man; he only had to say that she was uncontrollable. No one would have questioned his word.'

'But that's wicked!' I cried. 'What a terrible man he must have been. How frightened my mother must have been. No wonder she ran away.'

'He was rather a cruel man,' Lady Selina agreed. 'Not to me, of course. I brought a fortune to Brockmere when I married his son, therefore I could do no wrong. I think Gerald was a little afraid of his father – that's why Sir Mortimer despised him. I stood up to him and he admired me for it.'

'Was my mother carrying me when she ran away?'

'No, that isn't possible. I was carrying Prunella and she's well over a year older than you – so if you are Gerald's child, they must have met again after she left here.'

'And after she married my . . . Richard Linton,' I said, feeling shocked and hurt by this further revelation about my mother's character. 'What does Sir Gerald say?'

'I've never asked him.'

'But you must have wanted to know the truth?'

She shook her head. 'It wasn't important at first – and I have my own reasons for not inquiring too deeply, Kate.'

I nodded, feeling bitter. 'It suited you to believe it because you didn't want your son to marry me – that's it, isn't it?'

'Don't hate me for it, Kate. At first I was prejudiced against you because you were her daughter but now. . . . '

I was hardly listening to her. My mind was going round and round in circles. 'It must be true. Sir Gerald wouldn't have lied to Harry. Why should he? Unless he wanted to stop us marrying. . . . '

'I can't be sure, but I doubt that, Kate.' She saw the spark of hope die from my eyes and gave me an odd smile. 'My husband is a weak man. He has been unfaithful to me several times – but he likes you, Kate, and he thinks the world of Harry. I don't believe he would deliberately ruin your lives.'

'Then there's nothing we can do. The only person who knew the truth is dead.'

'Yes, I'm afraid that's right. . . . ' She hesitated, obviously unsure. 'There might be a way. . . . '

'What do you mean?' I stared at her again. What was she hiding? 'Is there some proof – something we could discover about my birth that might prove Sir Gerald isn't my father?'

'I can tell you no more for the moment,' she said. 'Please don't be angry with me, Kate. I must speak to Harry. I thought I knew what was best – but now he must choose. I haven't the right to choose for him. . . . '

I stared at her in bewilderment. 'I don't understand you. Either Sir Gerald is my father or he isn't.'

'You are angry.' She smiled again. 'I'm afraid I must endure your censure until I've spoken to Harry. Perhaps then you will understand and even forgive me.' She looked into my eyes. 'I must see Harry. I must talk to him privately. Please, Kate. You're the only one who can reach him.'

'I'm not sure that he would listen to me.'

'I'm going to die quite soon, Kate.' She held up her hand as I would have protested. 'No, my dear, don't deny the truth. I've told no-one else, but I know I have only a year or so at best – perhaps only a few months. I asked my doctor for the truth and he told me that my heart just won't hold out much longer.'

'I – I don't know what to say.' I felt my throat close with emotion. 'The doctors aren't always right. If you take care of yourself. . . . '

'And don't worry?' She laughed softly. 'I'm not afraid to die, Kate. But I must speak to my son – you do see that, don't you?'

'Yes, of course. I'll get him here,' I promised. 'If it's possible, I'll find a way.'

'I knew I could rely on you, Kate.' That strange look was in her eyes again. 'I once did something that I grew to be ashamed of. Because of it, I had to subdue all my natural feelings, and I forgot what it was to love. I've been a foolish, selfish woman – but when you know everything, you may find it in your heart to forgive me.'

As she went out, closing the door behind her, I was puzzled and confused. She seemed to be hinting that there was some secret she knew that would disprove my mother's story. And yet if Sir Gerald was convinced I was his daughter . . . ? It just didn't add up. Something was eluding me. A piece of the puzzle was missing – unless Lady Selina was just using me to persuade Harry to come home. . . .

I stayed at Brockmere for three days, then I caught the train to London. The complete relaxation of those few days had done me good. I felt rested and the awful, aching tiredness had gone at last. Staring out of the train window, I thought about Harry. He'd sounded off when I telephoned to say I was coming up and that I had something important to tell him. He hadn't refused to see me, but I'd thought there was a certain reluctance in his voice when he agreed to meet my train.

'You will be alone, Kate? Prue isn't coming with you – or Father?'

'I'll be by myself,' I promised. 'I want to see you, Harry. I've missed you.'

There was a pause and I wondered if he was still there, then: 'I've missed you too, Kate. You've no idea how much.'

It was the beginning of spring and the sun was shining as I got down from the train. The cold winds that had kept me shivering on my return from France had finally abated. I felt a lightness in my step as I followed the general exodus from the busy platform, and then I saw Harry. He was in uniform – the uniform of a captain – and my heart missed a beat as I ran to greet him. If only Lady Selina was right and there was some way of proving that we didn't have the same father!

'I didn't know you'd been promoted,' I said. 'Congratulations.' He was silent and I gazed anxiously at his face. 'Harry? Harry, what's wrong?'

For a moment he didn't answer, and in those few seconds I took in the shadows beneath his eyes and the hollows in his cheeks. Then he smiled and it was as if all the months and years of bitter regret had been swept away. We were on a river bank; it was very hot and the love between us was as strong as ever. We gazed at each other hungrily, drinking in the beloved features. I sensed the deep need in him and I held out my hands. He took them, just looking at me as if he could never bear to tear his eyes away.

'Nothing's wrong,' he said. 'Now that you're here.'

'Oh, my dearest Harry,' I whispered. 'My dearest love. I had no idea you were ill.'

He shook his head. 'I'm not ill, Kate. Not really. It's just – just the nightmares. I can't sleep. I'm afraid to sleep, Kate.'

'Let's go somewhere we can talk. Somewhere private.'

'The car's waiting outside.' He glanced at my small suitcase. 'Is that all you brought?'

'I thought I might buy a new dress while I'm in town. Most of mine are a bit young for me now – and too big.'

His eyes went over me. 'You've lost weight. You've been working too hard. All you nurses work too hard.'

'We just do what we have to do. You know what it's like out there.'

'Yes, I know.' The shadows came and went in his eyes. 'I've applied to go back, Kate. I have another medical next month. If I pass it. . . . '

'Haven't you done enough?' I gazed up into his face. 'Surely you've done your share? Why must you force yourself to go through it all again?'

'I'm not a coward, Kate.'

'I know that. You don't have to prove it to me.'

'Perhaps I need to prove it to myself.'

'But why, Harry?'

He didn't answer as we went out to the car. But I knew it was a matter of pride. I'd seen it in other young officers, a need to prove that they were strong enough to overcome the very natural fear anyone who had been badly injured had of returning to the front. I knew it, just as I knew Harry would do whatever he had to do. He had suffered terribly, but underneath he was still the same determined man I loved so much. He put my case in the boot and opened the door for me, then he looked at me. 'Are you hungry, Kate? Shall we eat before I take you to your hotel?'

He was playing for time, putting off the questions he knew I wanted to ask. For a few moments he'd been glad to see me, now he was remembering, withdrawing behind barriers. I wondered whether to tell him what his mother had hinted. It might help to banish those shadows in his eyes – but supposing it all came to nothing? That might hurt him even more.

'Yes, I'd like to have lunch,' I said. 'Where shall we go?'

'There's a pleasant little place I found recently. It's by the river and they do good, old-fashioned English food. I thought you might appreciate that after two years in France?'

'Roast beef and Yorkshire pudding,' I said, laughing up at him. 'I can almost taste it. Better still, steak and kidney pudding with lots of gravy.'

The tension went out of Harry as he smiled again. 'Still the same old Kate. Thank God,' he said. 'I'm glad you came. When you rang I almost told you not to bother, but now I'm glad you're here. I need you, Kate. There's no one else I can talk to.'

'We'll talk when you're ready,' I said. 'Let's have lunch, then we'll walk by the river – and when you feel like it, we'll talk.'

'Water always has a soothing effect on me,' I said, tucking my arm through Harry's as we strolled in the warm spring sunshine. 'I love the sound of it, don't you? That swishing, rushing noise it makes. . . .'

'Yes.' He looked at me and it was a caress. 'I often think of that afternoon we spent by the river. It was so peaceful – and you were happy, weren't you, Kate?'

'You know I was. I think about all the times we were together – the night you danced with me in the gallery; the first time you took me riding in my breeches . . . .' As he frowned I realized my mistake. The old memories were too painful for him. 'That was a gorgeous meal,' I said quickly. 'You can't get a really meaty, soggy pudding like that in France. The canteen food was awful.'

'I'm glad you enjoyed your lunch.' His eyes were far away.

We walked in silence for a few minutes, then I spotted a pair of swans with three very tiny cygnets. I pointed to them excitedly. 'Look at that, Harry. They must be early, surely?'

'Yes, I should think so . . . . ' He was silent again, then, 'Has there been anyone in France? Anyone special for you?'

'No. I had friends, of course. I usually went out with Sandy and Jean in a group. There was one man I liked very much – Doctor David Matthews – the one I was with the night I found you in Ypres. He took me to dinner. I got drunk and propositioned him.' I glanced up then. 'I think I wanted it to happen, Harry. I wanted to find someone to take away the ache – but you were always there in my mind. David wasn't the sort to take advantage, but even if he had it wouldn't have meant anything. No one was ever quite right. What about you?'

'I've tried,' he said, a little nerve twitching in his cheek. 'There have been one or two. . . . On leave in France with the other chaps, I went along to a certain house. Afterwards, I thought of you, then I wished I could die. I've never stopped wanting you, loving you, Kate. Sometimes I feel there's no point in living if I can never have you. Life just seems empty and . . . . '

'Don't, Harry.' Tears stung my eyes as I swung him round to face me. 'Don't say such terrible things. You can have me, my darling. You can have my heart and my love. They've always been yours. They always will be.'

'But I can never have all of you. I can never hold you in my arms. . . . '

I saw the pain and deep need in him. 'If you want me,' I said slowly and with great clarity, 'if you really want me, you can have me. You can have all of me.'

'Kate. . . . ' There was both shock and dawning excitement in his eyes. 'I know you don't mean it. You haven't thought it through.'

'Oh, Harry.' I laughed and shook my head. 'I've thought about it for years . . . and I don't care any more. I don't care if it's a sin. I don't care if my soul is destined to burn in hell for eternity. I love you, Harry. I love you and I want you.' I reached up to trace the fullness of his mouth with my fingertips. 'Let's go somewhere, darling. Somewhere quiet where we can be alone.'

'Are you sure about this, Kate?'

He was trying to hold back, to do the honorable thing, but I could see that it was what he wanted, needed, longed for desperately. 'Perfectly sure.' I let my fingers caress his cheek and felt the shudder run through him. 'I've thought about it carefully, Harry. I believe there's a possibility that my mother lied about my being Sir Gerald's child.'

'What do you mean?' There was a sudden glow in his eyes, a wanting to believe.

'She lied to me about so much – this could be a lie, too.'

'And if it's the truth?' The glow had faded.

'It makes no difference.' I gazed up into his eyes. 'I want to be with you, Harry. I want to love you, to kiss you and feel your body close to mine. Even if I knew for sure that we were brother and sister, it would make no difference to me.' I knew that my eyes were bright with desire as I looked at him. 'Let's take what happiness we can, now, today. Life is too short to worry about what's right and what's wrong – let's take this one moment in time for ourselves. . . . '

'And the future?' He looked at me anxiously. 'I don't want to hurt you, Kate.'

'Then give me this.' I said huskily. 'Please, Harry. It's what I want. I promise you.'

'There's a cottage just outside Cambridge my grandfather left me,' he said slowly. 'I opened it up a few weeks ago. I thought I might live there after the war. It's close to the river and quiet. You'll like it.'

'It sounds wonderful. You know I love the river.'

'I love you,' he said. 'We'll be together now, Kate. I promise you – we'll find a way, even if it means leaving England when the war is over. I need you so. . . . ' His voice was hushed as if he were making a vow.

I only smiled as he took my hand. A deep-seated warmth was spreading through my body and I knew that what I was doing was right. Our love might be a sin in the eyes of God and man, but for us it was the most beautiful thing that had ever happened. We had fought it, but now we had stopped fighting and I knew. I knew it was meant to be. No matter what the future might hold, we would have this precious time together. I would take my happiness and I wouldn't allow myself to feel guilt or shame. Shame was for others, not for us. In our hearts this love was pure. Let those who had made our love a sin feel the shame.

The cottage had crumbling red bricks and a thatched roof. Its tiny windows had leaded panes and there was an oak door with iron studs and a black knocker in the shape of a lion's head. When we went inside, I could smell polish and lavender. As Harry lit the oil lamp

239

on a table just beyond the front door, I gave a cry of surprise and delight. It was just as it might have been more than fifty years before, untouched by time.

'It's lovely,' I said. 'So warm and comfortable – as if it were waiting just for us.'

Harry turned to take me in his arms, looking at me with such tenderness that I felt tears prick my eyes. 'It is for us, Kate. When I came down the other week, I knew it was our place. I could see you here. I could almost feel your presence. I longed for you so much . . . so much. . . . '

'Harry. Harry, I love you.'

We moved together of one accord. My hands slid up his shoulders round to the back of his neck, my fingers stroking the soft skin at the nape. He bent his head and kissed me gently, then his arms closed about me and the kiss deepened with a fierce desire that awoke an instant response within me. I trembled, clinging to him as the tears wetted my cheeks. He felt the wetness on his skin and looked at me, wiping away the tears with his fingertips and arching his brow.

'No regrets, Kate?'

'They're tears of happiness, Harry. If I died tomorrow, I would die content. . . . '

'Shush!' He placed his fingers to my lips. 'We're going to live, my Kate. Even if we have to lie and hide from everyone who knows us for the rest of our lives. I can't give you up again. We'll find a way – and we'll be happy. I swear it.'

'Harry. . . . ' I whispered. 'Oh, Harry. . . . '

I cared not that his promises were straws in the wind. Giving myself up to the glory of our love, I knew exactly what I was doing. In my mind there were doubts but no fears. I was going to make love in the full knowledge that Harry might be my half-brother, but I didn't care. With my body I could ease the pain inside this man, and for me that was vindication of what I did.

Harry took me by the hand, leading me into the bedroom. I smiled as I saw the brass bed with its patchwork quilt, feather mattress and piles of pillows. I had a feeling that whoever had lived here years ago had been happy in that bed. It was in every way a homely, welcoming room, and it made me feel safe. I turned to look at my lover. If the way I was feeling at this moment was wrong, then the world was mad. Nothing had ever been more right. We were made for each other, Harry and I. All the struggling had been in vain. We had been born for this love and this time.

I began to unbutton my blouse. My eyes never left Harry's face as I slid the thin silk off my shoulders, letting it fall to the ground. My skirt slithered over my hips; I stepped out of it, standing in my clinging petticoat, waiting. Harry took one step towards me. I saw the anguish of desire in his face as he reached out for me, his lips moving hungrily on mine.

'Kate,' he murmured. 'My darling, am I dreaming?'

'If you are then so am I – and I never want to wake up.'

In the soft light of the lamp our bodies took on a golden glow as we lay side by side in that accommodating bed. For a while we lay without moving, content to look and feel each other's closeness, anticipating that joy we had so long denied ourselves. Then Harry gave a groan and pulled me towards him. As his hands began to caress my flesh, I shivered and moaned in ecstasy. My cry unleashed the passion he'd held in check. Suddenly we pressed closer, seeking urgent relief for the desire that burned so brightly in us both.

Our need was such that it was part pain, part pleasure, a swift sating of the hunger that had tormented us. Harry groaned in frustration as he spilled himself inside me far too quickly. But with kisses and caresses, his desire was renewed again and again, carrying us both through a night that we would never forget. The grief we had known was eased by an orgy of loving. If this short time was all we were ever to have, it would remain in our memories for ever. Harry asked and I gave myself completely, swept away to that dark place of enchantment that only lovers ever find. Then, at last, exhausted, we slept.

I woke suddenly as Harry jerked wildly, kicking and crying out in terror. Lighting the lamp, I bent over him, whispering his name.

'Harry,' I said gently, shaking his shoulder. 'Wake up, my love.'

He was fast asleep, obviously in the grip of a nightmare. As I watched, he began to thrash from side to side, his body arching and twitching convulsively. He moaned and sobbed, beginning to mutter something. I strained to catch the words.

'No! No, don't die,' he cried. 'Hang on, Bob. We'll get you back. . . . Oh, God . . . Oh, God. . . . Don't. . . . ' His voice rose higher and higher. 'The blood . . . the blood . . . I can't stop the blood. . . . '

I reached out, intending to shake his shoulder harder to make him wake up, but even as I did so he jerked to a sitting position, screaming. Although his eyes were now wide open, he was still dreaming, still caught in some terrible nightmare. I slapped his face several times, calling his name, forcing him to come out of that nightmare world he was inhabiting. For a moment he tried to fight me, then he came to himself, staring at me blankly before falling back against the pillows. He lay gazing up at me for a few seconds, then he reached for my hand.

'I'm sorry, Kate. It was just a bad dream.'

'I know.' I smoothed the hair from his damp forehead. 'How long have you been having these dreams, Harry?'

For a moment he didn't answer, then: 'Since I was wounded this last time. At the hospital they said it was shock. That last little affair was pretty rough. Apparently, I'm not the only one to have ... dreams.'

'Quite a few of the men have them,' I said. 'It's not something to be ashamed of, Harry. Anyone who has endured the hell of those trenches is entitled to the occasional nightmare.'

He looked at me. 'I have them all the time. It's got so bad that I'm afraid to go to sleep. Afraid of what I might see.' He sighed and ran his fingers through his hair. 'I'm not a coward, Kate – but sometimes I think I can't go on. I keep seeing the same thing over and over again – until I think I shall go mad.'

I touched his cheek. 'You're not mad, Harry. I heard some of what you were saying in your sleep. Anyone who has had to go through what you did is. . . . '

'I survived,' he said, a trace of bitterness in his voice. 'I survived because Bob saw it coming. He – he knocked me down and covered me with his own body. . . . '

'He must have been a good friend.' I felt the emotion in my throat as I saw his agony.

'The best. . . . ' Harry's eyes were bleak as he looked at me. 'He was lying on top of me and I couldn't get up. There was earth on top of us, almost burying us. I could feel something warm and sticky. . . . '

His voice had begun to quiver and he was shivering as if he was cold. I put my arms around him, drawing his head down on to my breast and stroking his hair. 'Go on, my darling,' I whispered. 'You can tell me.'

'When they finally dug us out I was covered in blood,' he said, and I felt his body retch. 'It was his mostly. When I saw him . . . the whole of the back of his head had gone. . . . '

'He must have died quickly. It wasn't your fault.'

242

'Why?' Harry asked. 'Bob had a wife and two small children, Kate. Why should he die while I. . . . '

I sensed the bitterness in the words he hadn't spoken, and they struck deep into my heart. 'Don't, Harry,' I said chokingly. 'I can't bear it.'

'I'm sorry, Kate,' he said quickly. 'Forgive me. I didn't mean to hurt you.'

'It's not your fault,' I said again. 'None of it is your fault, Harry.'

'Forgive me,' he begged. He had stopped shivering as he looked down at me. 'I shouldn't have forced you to share my nightmares.'

'I wanted to help,' I said. 'Just don't blame yourself. Your friend's death has nothing to do with us — he didn't die because of what we've. . . . '

Harry's mouth drowned out the words. We made love feverishly, needing to shut out the pain.

A long time afterwards we lay talking quietly in the darkness. Harry was calmer now. We spoke of many things. Light, inconsequential things that couldn't hurt us. Then I told him why I'd sought him out.

'You should go to see your mother,' I said. 'She's not well, Harry.'

'So my father told me.' He sounded angry again. 'I've sworn I won't go back to Brockmere, Kate. I can't forgive him — not ever. If he'd told me at the beginning. . . . '

'It might not have made any difference. I loved you from the first moment I saw you, Harry. We didn't plan it — it just happened.'

'Perhaps you're right.' He sighed deeply. 'Do you think she's really ill?'

'I think she may not have long to live — a few months or a year.'

I felt him stiffen. 'You're sure she isn't just saying that to get her own way? Mother is pretty ruthless, you know.'

'She's changed. She's changed towards me. I believe her illness has made her think deeply — and she wants to see you badly. She says she has something to tell you.'

'I was never sure, you know,' he said, and there was an odd, wistful note in his voice. 'I always felt that she didn't really like me — that she somehow resented me.'

'Why should she? You were her firstborn, her only son.'

'I didn't imagine it,' he said harshly. 'I felt it from the first, when I was just a child at her knee. . . . It was something in the way she looked at me. As if. . . . '

'As if what?'

He shook his head and laughed ruefully. 'I've no idea. I've never know what she was really thinking. She shows so little emotion.'

'But you love her, don't you?'

'Yes, I suppose I do. Whatever she is – she's my mother.'

'Then you will go and see her?'

'I'm not sure. I need time to think about it.'

'But, Harry. . . . '

'Don't nag me, Kate. Go to sleep now. I've told you, I'll think about it.'

'Oh, Harry, this is so peaceful,' I said. 'I could stay here for ever.'

We had spent the day gliding along the river past the backs of the colleges, and now we were sitting on the grassy banks of the River Cam eating a delicious picnic of cold chicken, fresh crusty bread and wine. I sighed, stretching out on the tartan wool rug we had spread on the grass and closing my eyes.

'I've always liked Cambridge, that's why I chose to study here instead of Oxford.' Harry leant over me, tickling my face with a blade of grass. 'What do you want to do now, Kate?'

'Can't we just stay here forever?' I asked dreamily.

He smiled and bent to kiss my lips. 'Lazybones,' he said, a hint of mischief in his eyes as I gazed up at him. 'I thought we might go shopping. I want to buy you a ring.'

'A ring?'

'Yes. As a symbol of my love.'

'I don't need symbols, Harry.'

He took my hand, pulling me to my feet. 'I want you to have it, Kate. I want to give you things. I'd like to lay the world at your feet.' He smiled and my heart somersaulted. 'Come on, it will be fun.'

I caught the hint of excitement in his voice and laughed. 'Yes, it will. We can visit that antique shop near King's College and buy something for the cottage, too. Something that will be just ours.'

'I'd like to pop into the bookshop on the corner of Trinity Street,' he said. 'I went there often when I was in college; they say it's one of the oldest in the country – it's been there for centuries.'

'You can buy me a book of poems and read them to me,' I said.

Harry smiled, seeming happy as we packed the picnic basket and rug into the punt. 'There's a jeweller's shop near the Magdalene

Bridge. I bought a brooch there for Mother once. I think we might find an antique ring there, Kate. Would you like that?'

'Yes, I'd love it.'

We returned the punt to the quay where we'd hired it and climbed the steps opposite the college, turning into Bridge Street. The shop itself was a very old building, with white plastered walls and blackened oak beams inside. It had been built in the fifteenth century, the owner told us, though for most of its history it had been a private house.

'And what sort of a ring were you looking for?' the shopkeeper asked, looking at us curiously. 'Would it be for an engagement?'

'No.' Harry glanced at me. 'I was thinking more of a lover's token – the kind of thing that was given as a promise of love centuries ago.'

'Ah. . . . ' Bright, beady eyes sparkled behind a pair of gold-rimmed spectacles. 'I think I may have just what you want, sir.'

He went into a room at the back of the tiny shop, coming back with a large black velvet box. When he opened it, I saw three rows of rings. The top line consisted of solid gold rings engraved and twisted into a knot; the second row were heavy bands of gold with three or five diamonds in a row – gipsy rings, he called them – but the bottom row caught my eye immediately. There was a variety of pretty cluster and band rings with different coloured stones.

'I've never seen anything quite like them,' I said.

'These are love rings,' he explained. 'The first letter of each stone is used to spell out a message. Ruby, emerald, garnet, aquamarine and diamond – Regard. And this one spells dearest – do you see?'

'That's exactly what I wanted,' Harry said. 'Do you like it, Kate?'

'It's beautiful,' I said. 'May I try it on, please?'

'Certainly. It looks as if it might fit,' the man said.

I slid the pretty cluster ring on the third finger of my right hand. It had an engraved gold band and the word ALWAYS inside it. It fitted me perfectly. I showed it to Harry and he nodded.

'We'll take it. Keep it on, Kate.'

'An excellent choice,' the shopkeeper said, beaming. 'It's early Georgian, you know. A very special ring.'

'It's for a special person,' replied Harry, taking out his wallet and laying several large white five pound notes on the counter.

We left the shop. Outside, I looked at Harry. 'That was a wonderful idea. I had no idea that rings like this existed. Everytime I look at it I shall read its message and think of you.'

He smiled, taking my hand and kissing it. 'When you do I shall know. Wherever I am, I shall know you're remembering this time. Now let's do the rest of our shopping – then we'll have scones and jam for tea.'

'Lovely.' We linked arms and I laughed, feeling ridiculously happy. 'I want a toasting fork, Harry, and a footstool – and we'll buy a rocking chair. One of those old wooden-seated ones with smooth seats that have been worn into a comfortable shape by constant use.'

His eyes lit with amusement. 'Trust you to know exactly what the cottage needs. I can see us now, sitting in front of the fire on cold winter evenings – me in the rocking chair, with you perched on the stool toasting crumpets.

The picture he'd painted was one of sheer bliss. For a moment it shimmered in my mind in all its glory, then quite suddenly it faded. I shivered as a cold chill went down my spine.

'What's wrong, Kate?'

Harry looked at me in concern. I couldn't say that I'd had a premonition that our idyll would never become reality. Instead, I smiled and squeezed his arm.

'It's not as warm as it was,' I said. 'Let's find that antique shop – then we can have our tea. I'm starving.'

'Already?' Harry laughed down at me. 'After the food you ate this morning? At this rate you'll soon need to let your clothes out instead of taking them in.'

'Beast!' I cried, poking him in the ribs. 'I was going to buy you a tobacco jar and a pipe rack, but now I'll think about it. I'm not sure if you deserve it.'

'I don't smoke a pipe, Kate.' He tried to keep his lips straight but they wobbled.

'That doesn't count. It goes with the cottage – and one day, when you're very old, you might take it up.'

Harry's eyes caught fire. 'Oh, Kate,' he said, his voice cracking. 'I do love you so.'

'We'll light a fire,' I said as Harry carried in the rocking chair. 'I want to make some toast.'

'Impatient Kate!' he cried. 'It isn't cold enough for a fire.'

'Yes, it is. Anyway, it doesn't matter.' I put my arms about his waist. 'Let's have our fire tonight, darling.'

'If that's what you want. I think there are some logs in the shed.'

'I'll crumple some paper,' I said. 'Fetch the logs, Harry.'

He shook his head but went outside. I began to crush some old newspapers and arrange them in the grate. Within a few minutes Harry was back.

'The logs seem a little damp,' he said. 'They'll probably smoke.'

'That doesn't matter.' It was as if someone had just stepped on my grave. 'I'm cold. Use the bellows to get it going if you have to.'

It was illogical and foolish, but I was desperate to have that fire now. I had a terrible feeling that time was running out for us, and I wanted to prolong the coming night. I felt that if only I could hold back the darkness with the flickering flames of my fire, then perhaps I could stop whatever it was that was going to happen.

He set light to the paper and a thin grey smoke began to curl up the chimney. The logs were damp and despite valiant attempts with the bellows and me blowing at the smouldering wood, all we got was a miserable little fire that refused to throw out any heat.

'I'm afraid you won't get your toast tonight, darling,' Harry said.

'Never mind. If you're cold, we'll go to bed. I'll keep you warm.'

He was smiling as he reached out for me, and I clung to him, trying to subdue my fear. We'd been so happy these past few days. I was afraid of letting go; afraid of what the future might bring. I kissed Harry feverishly, my hands moving urgently in the nape of his neck.

'Yes, take me to bed,' I whispered. 'Make love to me. I want you so much. So much. . . . '

I was awake long before Harry. I lay looking at his face, thinking how peaceful and relaxed he was now. He hadn't had a nightmare for five nights. From what he'd told me about his dreams, I knew that it was a tiny miracle. Such terrible dreams had haunted him – dreams of suffocating beneath the dead body of his friend and then the horror of seeing Bob's brains spilled out, half his head gone. It wasn't any wonder that Harry hadn't been able to sleep.

As I watched him, he opened his eyes and smiled up at me. He reached out to touch my face, stroking my cheek and then my shoulder and my breasts.

'You're so lovely, Kate,' he said. 'You know that you've cured me, don't you? Five nights without the dream. I feel like a new man.'

I bent my head to kiss him. He put his arms around me, pulling me down so that I was lying across him, his hand stroking my back. I nibbled at his earlobe, then our lips met in a kiss that stoked the fires burning inside us. Each time we made love it was better and better, our bodies perfectly in tune now so that we were aware of each other's needs without speaking. As Harry rolled me beneath him in the bed, I felt myself being lifted and carried away on a rising tide of desire. I had no weight, no substance. I was all sensation, all lightness, like the sea-spray spending itself against the distant shore, until I dissolved into nothingness and became a part of the man who had transported me to this earthly paradise.

Afterwards, as I lay with my head on his shoulder, licking the droplets of sweat from his skin with the tip of my tongue, he made a sound of contentment deep in his throat. Glancing up, I saw that he was smiling.

'I think that we should go to Brockmere now,' he said. 'I'll stay one night for Mother's sake.'

'I know that will please her.'

'While we're there I'll talk to Father,' he said. 'We know your birth date. It should be possible to establish whether or not your mother lied about him being the father of her child. If, as you say, she wasn't carrying you when she ran away, they would've had to see each other again after she was married.'

'Yes, I realize that,' I said. 'We can only hope, Harry.'

Icy fingers of fear curled about my heart. Harry seemed so confident now, but what if we proved beyond doubt that we did have the same father? Would it send him back to that tortured world of grief and guilt that had haunted his dreams?

I slipped from the bed, wrapping a robe around my naked body. 'I'm hungry,' I said. 'Stay there and I'll bring you breakfast in bed.' I smiled at him, hiding the fear inside me. 'We'll have one more morning, darling. Then we'll go. . . . '

CHAPTER TWENTY-TWO

It was a lovely spring day; the spring of 1918. Emma's spirits rose with every step she took, her skin warmed by the sun that was amazingly bright in an azure sky. The climate of France suited her so well and she felt healthier and happier than she had for a long time. She had begun to make clothes for other people again, and she found it much easier than working long hours in a café. It had brought her other benefits, too. She was making friends again, the kind of friends she had had in England. She could hold up her head once more.

It had taken a long, long time, but at last they were going to release Marc into her care. She was going to take him home, home to the small cottage she had rented several months ago. Smiling, she thought of the garden she'd worked so hard to fill with scented flowers: scented because Marc took great pleasure in the smell of things, never failing to notice if she'd used a new soap or perfume. A small frown creased her brow as she recalled something the Mother Superior had told her a few days earlier.

'Marc's sight may never be fully restored,' she'd said. 'But there could be an improvement in his right eye. We don't really know why he can't see more than just a hazy outline. It could be something behind the eye. We just don't know.'

'You're worried about what might happen if his sight returns? But he seems so normal now. So much better. . . . ' Remembering the agony of those first months, when Marc had begun to understand what had happened to him – the rages, the cold silences and the tears – she was suddenly quiet, her face grave as she said, 'We can only pray for him, Mother.'

'Yes, my child, we can pray.' The gentle nun smiled at her. 'At least he has you.'

Now, Emma's smile returned as she saw Marc standing on the terrace, his manner that of a man who was impatient to leave. Her doubts were stilled as he reached before him, feeling for the stone pillar, showing his insecurity. He had some vision, enough to know the colour of her dress, but he couldn't see her coming . . . he couldn't see his own face in a mirror. There were no large mirrors in the

249

cottage. Emma had had them all taken away. She meant to protect Marc, to save him the agony of knowing that his face was destroyed.

She stood watching him, smiling. It was going to be all right. He needed her. It was going to work. She began to run towards him.

'Marc,' she called. 'Marc, I'm here. . . . '

He held out his hands and she caught them. His face – that tortured, twisted mask of a face with its lashless eyes and the red slit for a mouth – was incapable of showing emotion, and yet she felt the welcoming gladness in him as he returned the gentle pressure of her hands.

'Emma,' he said. 'I thought you would never get here.'

Sudden hot tears blinded her eyes and a surge of gratitude swept over her. In Marc she had found a reason for living. She had been given a second chance of happiness; her love for him was fragile and tender, almost maternal. She knew that she would never again feel that all-consuming passion she'd known for Paul, echoes of which lingered on like the bitter aftertaste of too much wine. No, her love for Marc wasn't like that, but it had eased the ache inside her. Now she wanted only to spend her life caring for him; he needed her so desperately, was so reliant on her. And she needed that. She smiled as his fingers curled around hers, surprisingly strong and firm after all the months of pain and suffering.

'Are you ready, Marc?' she asked softly. 'Are you ready to go home?'

CHAPTER TWENTY-THREE

A strange dread was growing inside me as Harry's car drew up outside the house. I could sense the tension in him and I tried to smile, wanting to make this visit easier for him.

'We don't have to stay overnight if you don't want to. We can leave after dinner.'

'I'll manage,' he said grimly. 'I've got to face it sometime; it might as well be now.'

I got out of the car, shivering as a chill wind whistled about my ears. Someone had left the house and was coming towards us. It was Prue and, as I looked at her face, I knew something had happened.

'So you managed to get here at last,' she said, giving her brother a hard look from eyes that were red-rimmed from weeping. 'Well, it's too late. She's dead, Harry. She asked for you constantly, but we couldn't find you. . . . ' Her eyes turned accusingly to me. 'You could have telephoned, Kate. Your hotel said you'd cancelled – where the hell have you both been?'

'At the cottage Grandfather left me, not that it's any of your business.' Harry's face was white with shock. 'I'm sorry Mother's dead – but it couldn't have made much difference if I'd been here.'

'No difference?' Prue's face twisted with disgust. 'She was calling for you. She wanted to tell you something important. She had a hard time of it, Harry – and it was your fault.'

'You don't understand, Prue. . . . ' I began.

Her eyes flashed with contempt. 'I understand perfectly. I know exactly what you. . . . '

'Shut up, Prue!' Harry's tone was so agonized that she looked startled, lapsing into silence. 'If you say another word I shall leave right now.'

'You can't do that; the funeral's tomorrow. What would people say?'

'I don't give a damn what anyone says!'

Harry walked past her and into the house. She looked at me, startled.

'Harry hasn't been well,' I said as he disappeared from sight. 'It's

251

shell shock, Prue. A lot of the men suffer from it. Sometimes it changes their characters completely.'

'So that's why he's been refusing to come down.' Her face crumpled. 'I'm sorry I was so awful just now. It's just that. . . . ' She choked on a sob. 'Mother and I didn't always get on, but I loved her – and now I'll never have a chance to tell her. . . . '

'I understand, Prue,' I said. 'I'm sure she knew how you felt.'

'Did she?' Her mouth tightened. 'Anyway, I'm sorry I took it out on you.'

'It doesn't matter. Just try not to quarrel with Harry – please? He's been through a terrible time, you know.'

'That's what Mother always said; she said we should make allowances for him.' Her face creased with grief. 'It was so wretched watching her, Kate, knowing that she wanted him.'

That old jealousy was in her eyes again; it was something she couldn't quite hide. She resented the fact that Harry was the favoured child; the son and heir, while she was only a daughter.

The house was unnaturally silent. I sensed a curious emptiness, almost as if the very building were mourning its mistress. I gave myself a mental shake; I couldn't afford to be sentimental. Harry needed my support if he was going to get through the next few hours.

He was in the green drawing room, standing staring into the fire, a whisky glass in his hand. He didn't turn his head, though he must have heard Prue and I enter. As I watched, he lifted the glass to his lips and drained the contents.

'Father's in his room,' Prue said. 'He hasn't come down since. . . .' She choked on a sob. 'Shall I tell him you're here?'

Harry turned slowly to face us, and even I was shocked at the bleak expression in his eyes. 'No, not yet. He'll have to come out tomorrow.'

Prue nodded. She stared at her brother, obviously at a loss with this new Harry. 'I'll just let Mrs Bates know there'll be two extra for dinner, then.'

Silence descended after she'd gone. I was afraid to speak for fear of touching a raw nerve. Harry was in a world of his own, staring blindly into space as though he couldn't bear to face his own thoughts, then he moved to the sideboard, refilled his glass and drained it in one go. He picked up the decanter again.

'Is that wise?' I regretted the words immediately.

'Don't nag me, Kate. I need it.' He turned to me then and I saw his anguish. 'I killed my friend – now I've murdered my mother.'

'Harry!' I cried, starting towards him. 'Don't say such terrible things. Don't hurt yourself. Bob's death was an act of war, and your mother had a heart condition. Even if you'd been here, it would still have happened.'

'How can we know? You heard what Prue said; she was fretting over me.' His mouth twisted in a bitter mockery of a smile. 'Don't make excuses for me, Kate. I can live with what I've done, but I need a drink. Now, with or without your permission, I'm going to have another.'

Hearing the sarcasm in his voice, I felt as if he'd struck me. My tender, passionate lover had vanished and in his place was a man I hardly knew.

'I was only thinking of you, Harry.'

'Then don't!' He slammed the glass down hard, staring at me with an icy coldness. 'Don't treat me like a child, Kate. I won't stand for it.'

I looked into his eyes and flinched. This wasn't the man I loved. It wasn't his fault; I'd seen violent swings of moods in patients before and I understood – but that didn't stop it hurting.

'I wasn't,' I said quietly. 'Get drunk if it makes you feel better, Harry. I'm going up to change.'

As I walked from the room, I heard him call my name. I didn't look back. If I stayed we would quarrel, and that would do neither of us any good. Harry needed time to adjust to his grief.

I felt my own share of guilt as I went upstairs. Lady Selina had begged me to bring her son back to Brockmere, and I'd spent the last six days indulging my senses – but how could I have known she would die so suddenly?

I was brushing my hair when Harry knocked and then walked in from the adjoining room. He gave me a rueful look as I put down the brush and turned to him.

'Are you still speaking to me, Kate?'

'Of course.'

'I wouldn't blame you if you weren't,' he said, coming closer and beginning to fiddle with the dressing-table pots. 'I'm sorry for what I said.'

'It was as much my fault as yours. I didn't mean to interfere. . . .'

'Of course you did.' He smiled wryly. 'You were perfectly right. Getting drunk won't solve anything.'

I stood up, moving to slide my arms about his waist. 'I'm so sorry about your mother. We ought to have come sooner. . . . '

'It wouldn't have changed anything. In a way I'm glad I came too late. I don't think I could've borne a dramatic bedside scene. I suppose that makes me a moral coward.'

'You're so hard on yourself.'

'Sweet Kate.' He took me in his arms, giving me a hard swift kiss. 'Forgive me for hurting you. Sometimes I. . . . '

I placed my fingers against his lips. 'Hush, my love. We've had these few days of happiness. Whatever happens, remember that.'

He smiled sadly and nodded. 'We'd better go down. Prue will wonder where we are.' He pulled a face. 'At least she's given us convenient rooms – do you think she's worked things out?'

'I imagine she was just being thoughtful,' I said. 'Let's go and make our peace with her, shall we?'

After dinner, Harry went for a walk and Prue disappeared somewhere. I found her in the library, looking at the large, leather-bound bible in which the Redfern family tree was listed. She turned with a smile as I came in, beckoning to me to look.

'There's your mother's name, Kate,' she said. 'There's Grandfather's and his wife. . . . '

The names went back over many years, and there were cousins and uncles as well as the direct line. I looked at her face.

'You really care about all this, don't you?'

She nodded, looking a little self-conscious. 'It's the family,' she said. 'Not so much the land or the money, but the family. It's important that the family goes on.'

'Is it?'

'Yes.' She looked at me directly. 'Harry has to marry,' she said. 'You do see that, don't you?'

'I . . . yes, I see.' I turned away from her.

'I'm not saying this to hurt you, Kate. I'm really not. It's just that the family has to go on. . . . '

I woke with a start, lying tense and still as I listened in the darkness to the noise coming from the adjoining room. Hearing the cry again, I knew what had woken me. Harry was having the nightmare again. He'd been late returning from his walk and his room had been empty when I came up; I'd lain awake listening for him for ages but I must have fallen asleep. Throwing on my dressing gown, I hurried through the connecting door. Harry was fast asleep, his arms and legs thrashing wildly as he struggled in the grip of his dream. I bent over him, shaking his shoulder.

'Harry! Harry, wake up.'

It took several seconds to bring him out of the nightmare. His skin was beaded with sweat, and he seemed exhausted as he lay looking up at me.

'Was it very bad?'

'About the same. Did I make much noise?'

'I'm not sure. It woke me, but I'm a light sleeper.'

'You were fast asleep when I looked in. I wanted to get in beside you.'

'Why didn't you?'

'I didn't want to wake you.'

'I'll get in with you, then.'

'I was hoping you might.' He opened the covers invitingly.

I snuggled up to him, nuzzling his shoulder. 'You taste so good, sort of shrimpy.'

He turned towards me, his hand beginning to stroke my breast. 'Hungry, Kate?'

'For you, yes.'

He laughed huskily and bent over to kiss my lips, then my throat and my breasts. I lay back, letting him do as he liked but making no effort to help him.

'Lazy little devil,' he murmured. 'Are you just going to lie there?'

'Why not? I feel like being pampered.'

'If that's what you want. Open your legs, then.'

I obeyed and he slid down the bed beneath the covers. As his tongue began its delicate work, I gave a cry of protest, half pulling away. He held my legs apart, flicking at the sensitive mound between my thighs. It was the first time he'd made love to me this particular way and after the initial shock, I found it gave me an exquisite pleasure that was quite different from anything else we'd done together. I began to writhe as the sensation became almost unbearable, moaning loudly.

'I thought you came in here to stop me making a noise?'

'Beast,' I muttered. 'I hate you, Harry.'

'No, you don't,' he said, sliding his body up over mine so that he looked down into my eyes. 'You love me, and you love this as much as I do.' I gasped as he suddenly thrust into me hard. 'You're so wet and hot; it's good, isn't it, Kate? It's good for you, too?'

'You know it is.' My hands tangled in his hair, pulling his head down to mine. 'It gets better all the time.'

He chuckled softly, moving with a slow, sweet rhythm that had me arching to meet him. 'Lie still, my impatient one. You're in too much hurry. I want it to last.'

'I can't stand it, Harry . . . Harry!'

I was panting, out of control. My nails clawed at his back as I climaxed over and over again, my legs curling over his back as he continued with his relentless assault on my senses. Then at last he gave a moan and collapsed against me. I closed my eyes, exhausted.

'I thought I was going to die. You're insatiable.'

'I know. Good, isn't it?'

'Wonderful. I'm so happy.' I opened my eyes, reaching up to stroke his cheek. 'Will you still make love to me like that when I'm sixty?'

'I'll do my best. Don't forget, I'm older than you.'

'Poor old man. I'll have to help you out.'

'Oh, Kate,' he said. 'You always make me laugh. I love you so much. I think I'd die if I couldn't have you now.'

He was so intense that I shivered, suddenly afraid. 'Don't, Harry. Don't say it. Don't think it.'

He rolled onto his side, taking me with him. 'It's going to be all right, darling. I know I've been behaving badly, but it's being here in this house. We'll stay for the funeral and then we'll go back to London – and we'll talk about the future. . . . '

Helen visited, bringing her eldest child, a charming little girl who looked just like her. She was a wonderful mother, managing the child without needing to scold or shout.

I remarked on it and she arched her brow. 'Practice makes perfect, my dear – but I really thought you would have had one of your own by now. I know what you're doing is wonderfully brave and all that, and of course Selina was so proud of you. . . . '

'Was she?'

'Oh, undoubtedly. She never stopped singing your praises.'

'There was a time when I thought she didn't really like me.'

'That must have been right at the start.' Helen looked thoughtful. 'She often told me how much she was looking forward to having you back after the war – and to seeing her grandchildren growing up at. . . . ?' Helen stared at me as I went white. 'What have I said?'

'Lady Selina,' I choked. 'She couldn't have mentioned me and her grandchildren in the same breath. You must have it wrong, Helen.'

256

Helen frowned. 'No, I don't think so. I thought you and Harry . . . I'm so sorry, Kate. I seem to have put my foot in it.'

'It's not your fault,' I said. 'I'm sorry, Helen. I can't explain.'

I left the room hurriedly before I betrayed myself.

It rained throughout the funeral, drumming relentlessly against the roof all the time the Vicar was speaking. The church was packed to capacity, full of Lady Selina's friends and local people. She had been well liked and respected.

Prue was crying as we drove home, and I felt a tight knot in my chest. Harry's face was strained, but he managed to speak politely to all the relatives and friends who came back to the house.

'Only a little longer,' he whispered as we snatched a few seconds alone. 'They'll soon be gone.'

'You're doing well,' I said, smiling at him. 'I love you.'

'Oh, Kate,' someone said behind me. 'Come and tell us about yourself. Selina was so proud of you, you know. When do you go back to France?'

I moved away to talk to one of Lady Selina's oldest friends, my eyes roving round the room. Sir Gerald seemed to be his usual self. If he was still grieving, he hid it well. Prue was with her husband; she seemed to be drinking rather a lot and she looked pale and drawn. I sensed that she and Michael were having a difficult time. The atmosphere was tense and I was relieved when the guests began to leave.

'We're going to read the will now,' Sir Gerald said, appearing at my side. 'You'd better come. Selina has mentioned you, my dear.'

'Do we have to?' Harry asked tersely. 'We trust you to see to things, Father.'

'I would prefer it if you were all present. Besides, I need to talk to you, Harry – and I can't do that until after the lawyers have gone.'

Harry shrugged and glanced at me. 'I'm afraid there's no help for it, Kate.'

We all filed into the library. There was a lot of throat clearing before the lawyer began reading. At first it was all small bequests to servants and friends, then he glanced up, an awkward, apologetic look on his face.

'I'm not sure if you're aware of the terms of your wife's will, Sir Gerald. It is a little unusual.'

Sir Gerald frowned and nodded. 'I'm aware. It was her wish. Please continue.'

257

'Very well. To my daughter Prunella, I bequeath the sum of ten thousand pounds. To Kate Linton, I leave certain items of jewellery which have been set aside for her and one thousand pounds. The remainder of my jewellery goes to my daughter. The rest of my estate is left in trust for my son Harry, the income only to go to my husband, Sir Gerald Redfern, until such time as Harry marries. The capital will then pass to my son to be used as he desires.'

'No!' Harry ejaculated. 'I don't want that. The money should go to Father.'

'We'll discuss this in private, Harry.' Sir Gerald stood up, looking at the solicitor and his clerk. 'Thank you, gentlemen. We shall let you know if we wish for your advice in the near future.'

The lawyer understood that he was being dismissed. He nodded and then looked at me. 'Your bequest is being held at my office in London, Miss Linton. There is a sealed package. My instructions were that you should call for it in person.'

'Thank you.' I thought it a little odd that he hadn't brought the package with him, but perhaps he hadn't expected me to be at Brockmere.

Gathering his papers, he left, and silence descended in the library as Prue went to see him out. Feeling tense, Harry went to pour himself a drink before turning to his father.

'Surely something can be done? Mother shouldn't have put you in such an awkward position.'

'It was her money. She had a perfect right to do as she pleased.' Sir Gerald cleared his throat. 'I can't deny it's awkward. What with the war and one thing and another, the estate is hardly paying its way. Of course, I'll have the income until you marry.'

Harry glanced at me, then squared his shoulders. 'I have to talk to you about that. . . . ' He drew a deep breath. 'You see, I've – Kate and I have wondered if there might be some mistake about your being her father. Her mother lied to her several times – it's possible she also lied to you. How can you be sure Kate is your daughter? She must have been sleeping with her husband. . . . '

'Harry, please listen. . . . ' Sir Gerald looked at us apologetically. 'I'm sorry to hurt you both. I wish I'd told you at the very beginning, but. . . . '

'But you must have met her again, after she left Brockmere,' I said, my eyes accusing. 'After she was married.'

'Yes.' His eyes dropped before mine. 'I wanted to tell you, but you wouldn't listen.'

'Tell me what?'

'Richard was my friend before he met Emma. He told me himself. . . . He couldn't be your father, Kate. It wasn't possible.'

'I don't understand you.' I stared at him, my nerves screaming at him to stop what he was saying.

'Richard Linton couldn't have children.' In the silence that fell, I could hear the beating of my own heart. 'It was because of an illness in childhood. He was able to function as a normal man but the doctors had told him he would be sterile.' Sir Gerald saw the shock in my eyes and his own were sad. 'I'm sorry, Kate. Believe me, I wish it were otherwise.'

'Then you're definitely my father. . . .' Until that moment I hadn't realized how much I'd been counting on Lady Selina's hints that there was a way of proving it wasn't true.

Harry saw the distress I couldn't hide. He turned to face his father. 'You'll have the income for as long as you need it,' he said. 'I'm not likely to marry now, am I?' His voice was harsh with bitterness. 'I'm leaving now – and I doubt if I shall ever come back.'

As he turned to stride from the room, I heard Sir Gerald's harsh intake of breath. His face was stricken and he looked as if he might collapse.

'Kate,' he said brokenly. 'I never meant to hurt you – either of you.'

'I know,' I said. 'Excuse me. I have to go after Harry.'

I ran from the room, seeing Harry walking up the stairs, and I called to him. He heard me but didn't stop. I ran after him, catching his arm as he reached the top.

'Where are you going, Harry? You aren't leaving without me?'

He looked at me then, and his eyes were dead, blinded to everything but his own pain. 'There's no point in pretending any more, is there? We both know the truth now, Kate – we can never marry.'

'That doesn't change anything. We agreed we would go away. . . .'

'No!' He cut in harshly. 'I thought I could but I can't. I saw your face just now. I know what it would do to you, Kate. I can't drag you down. You think it doesn't matter, but in time it would. You'd begin to resent me, to hate me for what I'd forced you to become. We would never be able to keep it a secret. People would find out; they'd whisper and then we would have to move again.'

'None of that matters,' I said, tears sliding down my cheeks. 'You can't leave me, Harry – not if you love me.'

'It's because I love you,' he said, his hands clenching at his sides. 'Let me go, Kate. Let me go – before it's too late for us both.'

I saw the look in his eyes and I couldn't speak. He smiled slightly and his lips moved soundlessly, thanking me, then he turned and walked away, leaving me to stare after him.

Prue looked at me, her face strained. We were standing in the morning room and upstairs my cases were packed.

'I had to talk to you before you went,' she said. 'I want to tell you how sorry I am, Kate. No, really I am. There was a time when I was jealous of you, but I'd give anything if you and Harry. . . . '

'Please don't!'

'But I must tell you,' she said, and something flickered in her eyes.

'I don't want to hear this.'

'You don't know what I'm going to say.'

'And I don't want to,' I cried. 'Don't worry, I shan't stand in his way. I shan't try to stop Harry finding someone new. I – I hope he does. . . . '

A sob rose in my throat and I fled before the tears could fall.

I'd known Harry wouldn't be at the cottage before I went there, but I had to be sure. Telephone calls to his lodgings had drawn a blank; he'd left no forwarding address. Perhaps it was best that way, best that it should end now, but the thought that I might never see him again was unbearable.

Sitting alone in the familiar rooms that had so recently been my paradise, I felt despair sweep over me. The nightmare had become reality and my life was one long haze of pain: haze, because there was in those first days a feeling of being in a dream. My mind was, I believe, protecting me from a grief too terrible to bear. I knew now that I was Sir Gerald's daughter; that there could be no mistake.

Rocking in the chair that Harry had bought for me, I looked at the love token on my finger and tears stung my eyes as I remembered the day he'd placed it there.

'When you wear this I shall know you're thinking of me,' he'd said.

'Oh, Harry,' I choked. 'We had such a short time of happiness, my love. Wherever you are, forgive me. Forgive me. . . . '

I thought about what Sir Gerald had told me after Harry left Brockmere, of how he'd fallen in love with my mother when she was still a child of sixteen. They had been lovers before she ran away.

'I was in love with her,' Sir Gerald had said. 'But I respected my wife, Kate. I was grateful to her for bringing a fortune to Brockmere. . . . '

She hadn't been carrying me when she fled from Sir Mortimer's cruel threats. It was only after she was married that I was conceived. She had betrayed the man who had given her his name; I think that made me angrier than all the rest. Bitterness began to fester inside me as I thought about what my mother and her lover had done. Because of their sin two lives had been ruined. I hated them both – my mother and my father. I hated them with a fierceness that frightened me because it was so ugly.

Rocking alone before the empty fireplace, I admitted at last what I'd fought against so long. I'd lost Harry. It was over. . . .

I felt no guilt. If a sin had been committed it was against Harry and me. Our love was sweet and good. Fate had conspired to thwart us. I wasn't ashamed of what we had done. My grief was because I could never be with my lover again.

'I love you, Harry,' I said out loud. 'I'll always love you. No one will ever make me ashamed of that love.'

Brushing the tears from my face, I realized that it was time to leave, time to go back to France and take up the threads of my life.

It is said that time is the great healer, but I believe that work is a more powerful ally. Work, work and more work. In the next few weeks I found relief in working until I was too exhausted to think, too weary to feel anything but a deadening numbness.

'What's the matter with you – do you want to kill yourself?' Sandy demanded when I collapsed onto my bed one evening. 'You've been on duty for eighteen hours. And don't tell me you were needed; we're all needed, but most of us have the sense to take our breaks. In another four hours you'll be back on your regular shift.'

'Then stop asking silly questions and let me sleep,' I said. 'Nurse Brody was off sick again. I stood in for her – then we had three urgent cases brought in.'

The hospitals were still overflowing with wounded men: we had French, Australian and American soldiers besides our own British troops on the wards. Fighting was still fierce, the Germans making determined attacks at what they thought of as weak spots in the Allied lines. In May they had tried to break through at the River Aisne, pushing the French back as far as the Marne and to within sixty miles of Paris. But then, with the assistance of an American division, the line held and consolidated. By the beginning of June the battle was almost over, though repeated attacks were made against the British on the Montagne de Bligny. The hill was captured on the 6th of that month, but a daring counter-attack regained it. The fierce onslaught had ended in failure for the Germans. Yet a few days later they began an offensive against Pétain, an action which led to heavy French losses and another stalemate. Although the wounded were still coming in in great numbers, the mood amongst the men was optimistic. It was felt now that the Allies had the advantage. The great German war machine was at long last faltering.

Such was the situation when I returned to my duties in France. I heard whispers of a new offensive against the enemy. Men who had heroically taken the brunt of one attack after another spoke hopefully of turning the tide. The whispers were as yet only a dream, a feeling in the guts of men who had sensed victory even though they were still reeling from the punishing attacks of a still powerful enemy, but there were signs of hope. Jerusalem and Baghdad were in Allied hands. In Italy the Austrians were at bay. The tide had not yet turned but its fury was abating. Not that the fighting was any less fierce. It went on as before, and the wounded flowed into the field hospitals, but the mood was different. We could all feel it and it gave us hope.

As the days and then weeks passed, I found relief in my work. There was a certain satisfaction in living only for the care and comfort of others. I had managed to subdue my own pain. It was still there, of course, but tucked away in a private corner of my heart. I wouldn't let myself think of Harry – at least, only now and then when I lay sleepless on my bed. I was deliberately blocking out all my memories, living only for the moment. My life had been cruelly shattered, but I would learn to live again.

'My God! You look like death warmed up.'

Sandy spoke as she came into the room we were now sharing. Recently, some of the nurses had gone back to England, and we'd been able to swap our tent for the relative comforts of a farm cottage. I glanced at my friend, hesitating as I wondered whether to tell her the truth, then decided against it. I might not be able to keep my secret for much longer, but I was determined to stay at work for as long as I could.

'I'm fine,' I said defensively. 'Just a bit tired, that's all.'

Sandy stared at me doubtfully, seeming as though she wanted to say more, then she shrugged. 'I've had a letter from Jean Butts,' she said. 'She and Tom are getting married – did you know?'

'Yes. He's out of hospital and getting on well. They're going to live with her mother. I wonder what Mrs Butts will think of that? She always used to say that the only heroes were dead ones.'

'She'll probably resent having the poor devil foisted on her. Tom was regular army; he won't stand much chance of getting work now, will he? No training for anything but fighting and a cripple. . . . '

'Surely someone will – oh!' I caught the back of a chair as a wave of faintness swept over me.

'You're as white as a sheet.' Sandy frowned. 'You're in trouble, aren't you?'

I bit my lip, not meeting her eyes. 'What do you mean? I'm just a bit tired, that's all.'

'You're going to have to slow up soon, you know. If you're not careful you'll kill yourself – and the baby.'

I sat down on the edge of the bed, my legs suddenly like jelly. 'How did you know? It doesn't show, does it?'

'No.' She came towards me, concerned and sympathetic. 'It's something you sense. My mother had eight children. It's a look in the eyes, something special. I thought I was right but I didn't like to say anything.'

'You haven't told anyone else?'

'What do you think I am?'

'Sorry. It's just that I want to work as long as I can.'

'Will he marry you?'

'No. He – he can't.'

Sandy's eyes flashed with anger. 'Men! They're all the same. I know there's a war on but it doesn't give them the right to use us like that.'

'You don't understand. He loves me; he would marry me if he could.'

'They all say that.' Her mouth twisted with bitterness. 'You haven't thought it out, have you? What are you going to do when they throw you out of nursing? They will, you know. It doesn't matter how much you've done for the cause. You'll be disgraced, something to be hidden out of sight as if you'd got an infectious disease.'

I gave a shaky laugh. 'It won't be that bad, surely?'

'I've seen it before. If I were you, I'd leave now, before it begins to show.'

'Perhaps you're right, though I wanted to go on working for a

263

while. I'm not desperate for money; I have a legacy, but it's going to have to last me a long time.'

Her eyes narrowed. 'Won't your family help you?'

'I can't tell them.'

Sandy hesitated. 'I could lend you some money if you like?'

I shook my head. 'That's kind of you, but I'm all right for money. I suppose it's the loneliness I'm dreading. I'd rather stay on for a bit if I can.'

She stared at me, then, 'You haven't thought of – well, getting rid of it? I know a doctor who might. . . . '

'No!' I cried before she could continue. 'Don't say it, Sandy. I can't – I won't do it.'

'I just thought in the circumstances. . . . ' She shrugged. 'Please yourself. Do you want to read Jean's letter?'

'Yes, please.'

I took it from her, trying desperately to control my trembling hands. Sandy obviously thought I should get rid of my baby by means of an illegal abortion – a baby who would be born to the stigma of illegitimacy. I wondered what she would say if she knew the truth. My child would not only be born out of wedlock, it would be the fruit of an incestuous love – a love that was evil in the sight of the world. But she would never know. No-one must ever know. I intended to bear my child, but for that child's sake I must keep silent. I must lie if need be. No one must ever know the name of its father!

Some women endure hell in the first months of pregnancy; I was lucky. For two weeks I felt wretched, then the nausea and faintness passed and I began to feel really well. My skin bloomed, and although I gained some weight, I didn't look as if I was having a child, not at first. I managed to keep my secret from everyone but Sandy.

She was wonderful, a true friend. She did everything for me that summer and early autumn. We had shared the chores, but now she did all the cooking and cleaning. She bought me food, scrounging extra eggs, milk and butter, and saving all her sweets because I'd developed a craving for chocolate.

'You spoil me, Sandy,' I said one evening early in September when I came off duty to find yet another cooked meal waiting for me.

'Someone has to look after you,' she scolded. 'Look at the shadows under your eyes. How much longer are you going to continue working?'

264

I ran my hand over my stomach, feeling the mound beneath my uniform and blessing the cumbersome skirts. 'It doesn't show yet, does it? I thought I might give in my notice at the end of the month. The way things are going now it does look as if the war is almost over.'

She placed a finger to her lips. 'Don't say it, don't even think it, in case it's just a fluke.'

I laughed, knowing what she meant. A huge offensive had been mounted in the utmost secrecy. Throughout August the Allies had driven forward all along the line, successfully pushing back the enemy, but an increasing resistance late in the month had shown that the Germans were making their stand and holding their line along the Somme to Peronne. The Allied forces had made progress but the outcome was still uncertain.

'Oh, don't, Sandy.' I crossed my fingers. 'Surely it must be the end at last? I know we're not supposed to talk about what's going on, but they say this latest manoeuvre will trap the Germans, prevent them from getting back home to reinforce and. . . . '

We heard a knock at the door and Sandy went to answer it while I enjoyed the nourishing meat pie she'd cooked especially for me. I looked up as she came back, an envelope in her hand.

'It was Nurse Brody. She brought this over for you.' Sandy frowned. 'It's marked urgent, Kate.'

'Oh. . . . ' I felt a sinking sensation as I recognized the handwriting. 'It – it's from Sir Gerald.' I laid it on the table in front of me, staring at it as if it might explode.

'Aren't you going to open it?'

'I'm not sure I want to read it.'

'You can't just leave it, Kate.' She hesitated, then, 'Do you want me to read it for you?'

I shook my head, reaching for the envelope. 'I suppose I'd better read it.'

I tore the flap back, taking out the single sheet of paper with trembling fingers. At least he'd kept it brief, I thought. I scanned the first few lines, half rising to my feet as a protest broke from me.

'No!' I cried. 'It can't be – I don't believe it!'

The world was spinning crazily around me. I took a step towards Sandy and then fell forward as everything went black.

CHAPTER TWENTY-FOUR

'It's so quiet without the guns,' Marc said. He stood with his arm resting on Emma's shoulder, enjoying the scents of jasmine and musk roses borne on the air of a warm autumn evening. It had rained earlier and everything had a new freshness about it. 'Do you think it's really over at last?'

'In the market this morning the talk was all of the Germans' surrender,' Emma replied. 'It seems to be over – who can tell?'

She felt a slight stiffening in him as though his body had tensed, and she turned her head to look at him. These days she was responsive to his every whim, his every change of mood. She did everything he wanted without being asked, caring for him as though he were a beloved child. She believed that he appreciated her for it, that in his way he loved her. Staring into his face, she thought that his right eye flickered and she sensed that something was bothering him. Touching her cheek to the hand on her shoulder, she asked, 'What is it, Marc? What's wrong?'

For a moment he didn't answer, then the words came, harsh and abrupt as they often were when one of his moods was on him.

'Will you go?' he said. 'Now that it's finally over, will you go home, Emma?'

She smiled slightly, recognizing the fear that never quite left him, no matter how often she promised to stay.

'Go where?' she asked softly. 'I don't want to leave you, Marc. But even if I did, I've nowhere to go. This is my home now, here with you.'

'You could always go to him.' The words were cruel and bitter on his tongue, but she understood and forgave him.

'Paul doesn't want me,' she said. 'It was over long ago . . . long before we met. Please believe me; I'm happy here. I don't want to go anywhere.'

He caught her hand, holding it so tightly that she was aware of pain. 'I'm so afraid,' he muttered. 'Afraid that you will grow tired of caring for a blind, mutilated. . . . '

She hushed him with two fingers against his mouth. 'I love you as you are,' she whispered. 'Believe me, Marc. Your face isn't so terrible;

266

it feels much worse than it looks.' The small lie couldn't hurt him; he would never see himself. 'I want nothing more than we have this minute. Believe me, darling.'

His eyes stared blankly into the distance, his face an emotionless mask. Only the pulse working in his throat betrayed his inner conflict.

'Forgive me, Emma. I trusted a woman once; it's difficult to do so again.'

She was silent, leaving him to his memories. They had never spoken directly of the girl who had hurt him so badly; it was accepted between them, a part of Marc's past. He had his memories and so did she.

'There's nothing to forgive,' she said, and took his hand to lead him towards the door. 'It's growing chilly now; we should go in.'

'Who was she?' Emma asked Jacques the question she could never ask Marc. 'Who was the girl who hurt him so badly?'

'Her name was Antoinette,' he said, frowning. 'I've never met her, but I believe she's very pretty.'

'What did she do to him?'

'They were to be married,' he said. 'Then she met someone else – a man with money. . . . ' He shrugged his shoulders expressively. 'She wrote Marc a letter after he joined the army. By the time he could get leave she was married.'

'Poor Marc. He must have loved her very much.'

'Oh yes,' Jacques said. 'She was the only girl he ever loved. There was only Antoinette for Marc. . . . '

'Are you still in pain?' Emma bent over Marc as she placed a hand on his brow. 'The fever seems to have gone now.'

He looked up at her from the bed. His sight was changing, gradually becoming less blurred in the right eye. He could see her now. It was as if she were obscured by a mist, but he could see the shape of her body and her hair. In the sunlight streaming through the bedroom window, it looked red.

'Is something wrong, Marc?'

Emma stared, sensing a difference in him. It was so difficult to know what was going on behind that expressionless mask.

Marc hesitated. If he told her he thought his sight was coming back, she might leave him. She had sworn that she would never leave him while he needed her, but if he could see. . . . He needed her.

He was afraid of being alone with his nightmares, afraid of being able to see.

He was not a fool. Emma had told him that his face wasn't too bad, but he knew she was lying to comfort him. He might not be able to see, but he could feel. He could feel the ridges and puckering on his face. Sometimes when Emma was out, he would go to her dressing-table upstairs and take out the little hand mirror she kept in the top drawer and hold it in front of him, trying to see his face. He imagined what it must look like, and he knew that no woman could really love him. Emma stayed with him out of pity. If she ever guessed that his sight was gradually returning, she would go.

He closed his eyes as he felt the pain again, striking behind them. Something was moving again. He could feel it and the pain was almost unendurable.

'No, nothing is wrong,' he said. 'It's just this damned headache again. . . . '

'So it's over at last, then.' The fruit-seller tipped apples into Emma's basket. 'The Armistice will be signed any day now, Madame.'

'So they say.' Emma sighed as she paid for her purchase. She was tired and her head ached. She'd been up half the night with Marc; he'd had one of his attacks of pain, the worst since the early days at the hospice. 'Yes, thankfully we can look forward to peace now.'

'How is your poor friend now, Madame?'

'A little better.' Emma lied, wanting to get away.

'His cousin is such a pretty little thing,' the woman persisted. 'You were glad to see her, I expect?'

'Cousin?' A cold chill ran down Emma's spine. 'What are you talking about? Marc has no cousin.'

'She was asking for him in the village just this morning. . . . ' The woman stared as Emma turned, walking and then running back towards the road that led away from the market, back to the cottage. 'Madame! Your change. . . . '

Emma heard her but didn't look back. A terrible premonition had her in its grip and her heart was beating wildly as she hurried home. Marc had never mentioned a cousin; she was almost certain that he had none. If a girl had been looking for him . . . it had to be her! The girl who had betrayed him once before; the girl he'd loved so much that her desertion had almost destroyed him!

Emma was running now, her breath coming in great gasps. She was afraid of what might happen if Antoinette saw Marc before she'd had a chance to speak to her. A chance to warn her not to express revulsion when she saw his face.

She had to get back to Marc. The cottage was just ahead of her. She drew a great sobbing breath, and then as the door opened and a girl came rushing out, she knew that she was too late.

As she drew near, the girl paused for an instant, her eyes meeting Emma's in a look of sheer horror.

'You fool!' Emma screamed at her. 'What have you done? Why did you have to come here? Why?'

'I. . . . ' The girl shook her head and ran on.

Trembling with fear and anger, Emma hurried on to the cottage. She opened the door, depositing her basket on the scrubbed pine table in the large kitchen. Where was Marc? Usually he sat in his high-backed chair by the fire waiting eagerly for her return.

'Marc?' she called. 'Marc, I'm back.'

The silence terrified her. She went through to the tiny parlour with its bright chintz curtains and polished walnut sideboard, catching the scent of the late roses and dried lavender. She always kept the house full of flowers for Marc; flowers that he could touch and smell. Their scent mingled with the bowls of pot-pourri and the smell of beeswax. Marc was not in the parlour.

'Are you upstairs?' she called.

He didn't answer but she heard a slight sound, as of a caught breath. It was unusual for him to attempt the stairs alone; they were too steep and too dangerous for him. They always went up together, her leading with his hand on her shoulder to steady himself.

'Marc. . . . '

She went slowly up the narrow staircase, her heart thumping. Something was terribly wrong! She knew it, felt it instinctively. That girl had done or said something to upset Marc. . . . At the door of their bedroom she halted, her blood running cold as she saw him sitting in front of the dressing table, staring into her hand mirror.

He was actually looking at himself! In that moment Emma knew that he could see . . . he could see the horror of his own face, the monster that he had become. She could sense the shock and disgust he was feeling, the terror that must be in his mind. Oh, God, why hadn't she been here when it happened? She moved slowly towards him, the pity and pain mingling as she realized what he was going through. And then he turned towards her and she saw the dark hell in his eyes.

'Why did you lie to me? Why didn't you let me die?'

Marc's sight was still distorted but he had heard Antoinette's screams of horror, and he could see a blurred mass of crimson welts in the mirror. It was all he needed to see. Antoinette's unthinkingly cruel words were echoing in his ears. He hadn't needed to see clearly to know that she was staring at him in horror. He had seen her through a mist, but as she reached for her she had backed away, gagging and gasping as the vomit rose in her throat. And he had known that he was a monster. In his agony, he turned on the woman who had helped him, wanting to hurt her.

His bitter, accusing words hit Emma like a thunderbolt, making her gasp and recoil. In his agony, he was blaming her, striking out blindly in his rage and pain.

'Marc. . . . ' she whispered. 'I don't understand. It doesn't matter . . . your face doesn't matter. . . . '

His laughter cracked, lashing at her. 'It mattered to Antoinette,' he cried. 'I saw the revulsion in her eyes. I saw the horror and disgust – and so I came to see for myself.'

Emma's tongue moved over dry lips. 'Your sight,' she croaked. 'When . . . how?'

'Just after you'd gone,' he lied. He couldn't admit that it had been returning slowly for weeks. He couldn't admit to his fear of being alone. 'It was as if something moved suddenly. There was a blinding pain and then I could see shapes as if through a mist, and gradually the mist cleared. I sat in the kitchen, trying to adjust to what was happening. It seemed like a miracle, then I heard someone at the door and thought it was you. . . . Antoinette stood there. She was so beautiful . . . so very young and lovely and I thought, but then. . . . '
He drew a hard, painful breath.' And then I saw the look in her eyes. . . . ' He hadn't but he had known how they must have looked. He didn't need to be able to see to recall every line of Antoinette's face.

'Marc . . . darling,' Emma pleaded. 'Please listen to me. She doesn't matter. I love you. . . . '

He made a harsh sound of rejection in his throat. She would leave him anyway. What was the point? 'You. . . . ' He spat the word out as if it tasted foul. 'What are you to me?' Reaching out, he took Emma by the shoulders, his fingers gripping her, bruising her. 'Nothing. You are nothing!' he cried. 'I loved her – Antoinette – and because of you, because of your selfishness, she saw the monster you nurtured.' His anger blazed out once more. 'Why did you lie to me? Why didn't you let me die?'

The unfairness of it held her silent. She stood like a rag doll as he shook her and then cast her to one side, falling against the sharp edge of the dressing table to lie whimpering and retching, hardly aware of Marc's own agonized cry as he ran from the room.

Dazed, bruised, her thoughts in confusion, she lay without moving. Everything she'd worked for, everything she had salvaged from the wreck of her life had been destroyed in one careless moment by a thoughtless girl . . . a girl young enough to be her own daughter. As the irony of it struck her, Emma's lips cracked in a mirthless smile. That girl could almost have been Kate, she thought, the bitterness twisting inside her. Even when she tried to be unselfish, her intentions were misunderstood and rebounded against her. Why was it that Kate inspired devotion from her men, while she was used and then tossed aside like a despised and broken toy? What was it about her that. . . .

And then from downstairs in the parlour came the loud, terrifying sound of a single pistol shot.

CHAPTER TWENTY-FIVE

'I'll be sorry to lose you, Mrs Matthews. If you want to come back when. . . . ' The kindly face of my employer was pink with embarrassment as he avoided looking at my swollen belly. 'I know it's not what you're used to, but the customers like you and . . . well, this war has a lot to answer for.'

'It's very kind of you, Mr Young,' I said, feeling wretched as I saw the sympathy in his eyes. He believed I was a widow, as in a way I was. The man I loved, the man I would surely have married if fate had been kinder, was missing in action, believed killed. It was this that Sir Gerald had written to tell me, the news that had caused me to faint and made me realize that it was time I returned to England. It was as if Harry's death had brought me to my senses, making me more aware of the child I carried inside me. For that child's sake I'd bought myself a wedding ring and told my employer – the owner of a quiet, refined tea shop – that my husband had been killed in France. He believed me implicitly. I hated the lies I was forced to tell, but I had no choice. It was all part of my plan to disappear. A new name and a new life: I owed it to Harry's child. Now I smiled at the owner of the little tea shop. 'I'm not sure yet what I'll be doing, but I'll remember what you've said.'

'Take care of yourself. I hope you'll have a – well, you understand, I'm sure.'

'Yes. Thank you.'

Emerging into the chill of a crisp November evening, I walked slowly, turning up my coat collar to keep out the bitter cold. I was in no particular hurry to get back to the drab little room I'd rented in a modest house just off London's Haymarket. It was always chilly and the smell of cooking permeated throughout the house. My land-lady cooked meals for those of her lodgers who could afford them, but many were like me, living on a small income, and preferred to prepare our own food.

I still had some of the legacy my mother had left me, but I was being careful. After my child was born I thought I might find a small house somewhere in the country. Perhaps I could train to be a teacher, but I would need money to live on in the meantime. There was always the thousand pounds and the jewellery that Lady Selina had left me, of course, but I was reluctant to approach the solicitors in my present condition. I didn't want anyone at Brockmere to know I was carrying a child. Perhaps later, after the child was born, I might claim the money and the package Lady Selina had so particularly wanted me to have.

As I turned into a little side street, the smell of hot pies made me feel hungry. I decided to buy a meat pie and take it home for my supper.

Suddenly, my thoughts were abruptly shattered. A man had just come out of a bookshop a few yards ahead of me and, as the light from inside fell across his face, something made me turn away. I crossed the road hastily, not wanting him to see me. Keeping my back turned towards him until I heard the roar of a car engine, I caught another glimpse of his face as he drove off. It was Paul de Bernay! My heart did an odd little somersault, and I was still breathless as I went back to the other side of the road and into the pie shop. Thank goodness he hadn't seen me!

'Good-evening, Mrs Matthews,' the shop-keeper said cheerfully. 'Your usual, is it?'

'Yes, please,' I replied, smiling. 'It's cold tonight, isn't it?'

'We'll have snow before long, I shouldn't wonder.' He wrapped my purchase in newspaper and handed it across the counter. 'Have you heard the news then?'

I shook my head. 'I haven't read the paper this evening.'

'There's revolution in Berlin. The Germans are finished. We've beat them good and proper!'

'Is it certain?' I asked. 'Is the war really over at last?'

'The paper doesn't say it's signed and sealed, but it's only a matter of time now.'

I closed my eyes for a moment, feeling light-headed. 'I can hardly believe it. It's wonderful.'

As I went back out into the street, tears were slipping down my cheeks. The war was over; the long struggle had resulted in a clear victory for the Allies. For a moment I was filled with elation, then it suddenly drained away, leaving me empty and alone. What did it matter to me that there would soon be peace? I would still be alone. It was too late. Harry was dead. I would never see him again.

My head went up and I brushed the tears from my face. I was determined not to give way to self-pity and despair. I was alone but I would not be alone for long. Soon I would have Harry's child.

The bells were ringing wildly. I could hear them in my room even though the window was shut. I pushed up the bottom half of the sash window and looked out. People were rushing out of their houses and shops. At first I couldn't hear what they were saying, then I caught a few of the words and I understood what it was all about.

The war was finally over. The Armistice had been signed!

I watched for a few minutes, then I felt an urge to join in the celebrations. As I went downstairs, my landlady came out of her front parlour. She was crying and laughing at the same time, wiping her plump cheeks on a corner of her apron.

'It's over,' she said. 'Have you heard what they're saying, Mrs Matthews? The war is over!'

'I know. I heard the bells.'

I went out into the street. I could hear what people were saying clearly now.

'We've beaten them. We've done for the bastards at last!'

'Have you heard the terms of the Armistice?' One man laughed harshly. 'Foch ground their faces in the dirt – ruthless, that's what he was.'

'Plenty good enough for the bloody Boche!'

Pamphlets were being handed round, and someone thrust one into my hand. It was dated 11 November 1918. I scanned it briefly before handing it on to a man who was eager to see it for himself.

'They're to evacuate all invaded territory at once,' he read aloud. 'All arms to be surrendered in good condition. All Allied prisoners to be given up immediately – but not ours. My God! This goes on forever. We've bashed 'em, lads. We've done for the damned Germans!'

His sentiments were echoes by others, but the general mood was one of elation, not bitterness. People were happy. You could see it in their faces. There were so many people on the streets by now that it was impossible to change direction. I felt myself carried along with them, caught up in the excitement, my heart beating madly.

Trafalgar Square pulsated with the joy of the crowds. Everyone wanted to be there. People were singing, 'God Save the King,' joining hands in an ecstasy of relief, as if they needed to reach out in their joy and touch someone, perhaps to be certain that they were not dreaming. Others were crying – rich women in their furs, girls straight out of factories and shops, still wearing their turbans and aprons. It was a strange feeling to be caught up in such an excess of national fervour, but I wouldn't have missed it for the world.

Suddenly I was snatched up in the arms of a young sailor. He was a complete stranger and I felt a start of surprise, but then he laughed and kissed me.

'Beg your pardon, Mrs,' he said, grinning. 'I couldn't resist it. Don't tell your old man, will you?'

I smiled and shook my head. His words had brought the sting of tears to my eyes. I no longer wanted to be a part of this happy crowd. I turned, pushing my way through, trying to get away. It was almost impossible to move. Everyone else was pushing forward. I began to panic. I felt as if I couldn't breathe. My heart was thumping and my head was being crushed by an iron band. I had to get away. I had to sit down. Everything was going hazy.

'Please let me through,' I said. 'I feel ill. I must sit down. . . . '

'Let the lady pass,' someone said. 'She looks proper queer.'

I pressed my hand to my head, realizing what a fool I'd been to get trapped in such a crowd. It wasn't very sensible in my condition.

'She's going to faint,' a voice said near me.

'No, she isn't,' another voice said. 'I'll take care of her.' As I glanced up in surprise, the man smiled at me. 'Come on, Kate. Hold on to my arm and I'll get you out of here.'

'Paul?' I said wonderingly. 'Is it really you? How – I mean, where did you come from?'

'I've been following you for some time,' he said, frowning. 'I almost lost you for a while – but we'll talk later, when I've got you out of this.'

I nodded, not speaking as I clung to his arm. My head was spinning and I felt sick. Without Paul I might have fallen and could easily have been trampled on by the crowd. Not that they meant me any harm; they were good-natured but boisterous, parting only in response to Paul's repeated demands. It seemed ages before we were finally clear of the crush. I breathed a sigh of relief as we found ourselves in a little side street that was almost empty.

'That's better,' I said. 'I can breathe now. It was so stupid. I thought I was going to faint.'

'Thank God I was there.' He looked at me in concern. 'How do you feel now? My car is parked a few streets away – can you walk or shall we find somewhere to sit down?'

'I'd love a cup of tea,' I said, smiling shyly at him. 'You said you were following me, Paul – what did you mean?'

'Exactly that.' A wry look entered his eyes. 'Well, it was obvious

275

the other evening that you didn't want to see me. I was reluctant to intrude, but I felt you might find the crowds too much.'

I blushed as he took my arm and steered me across the road to a small café. 'So you did see me the other night. I didn't think you had.'

'I wasn't absolutely sure.' Paul glanced at my face. 'Then I saw you again this morning. I'd been back to the bookshop to collect something I'd ordered. When the bells started to ring everyone rushed out into the street. I was about to get into my car when I caught sight of you. I followed you on an impulse.'

We were shown to a table in the corner of the café, and Paul ordered tea and hot buttered toast. I unbuttoned my coat and sat down. There was no way of hiding my condition now, and I believed he'd already guessed.

'I'm very glad you did,' I said. 'Thank you for rescuing me.'

'It was my pleasure.' He glanced at the ring on the third finger of my left hand. 'I didn't know you were married, Kate.'

'He was killed in France.'

'I'm very sorry. I had no idea.'

I looked down at my hands, twisting the wedding ring nervously. 'I – I would rather not talk about it.'

'Of course not.' As I glanced up, he smiled. 'When is the happy event?'

'In two months, give or take a few days.'

'Will you be going home to Brockmere for the birth?'

'No.' I stared at him, my face white and stiff. 'I'd rather you didn't tell anyone you've seen me – anyone from Brockmere.'

'If that's what you want.' He wrinkled his brow, staring at me oddly, as if he'd just noticed the slightly dowdy clothes I was wearing. 'Is anything wrong, Kate? Are you in some kind of trouble?'

'No, of course not. I – I quarrelled with Sir Gerald, that's all.'

'I see.' He looked at me thoughtfully. 'I'm sorry. Is there anything I can do for you? If you need money I. . . . '

'No!' I cried sharply. 'Thank you for asking, but I don't need help. I can manage.'

'I'm sure you can.' His eyes were serious. 'That was clumsy of me, Kate. I know you've always preferred to keep your independence.'

Some of the tension drained out of me. 'I didn't mean to be so sharp, Paul. I'm fine. I can manage, really.'

'I know.' He smiled at me. 'You look very well.'

'I look like a woman who is shortly to give birth.'

'You're beautiful, Kate. That will never change.'

'Thank you, Paul.' I laughed. 'It's nice to be complimented, even if it is a little white lie.'

'Didn't your husband ever tell you you were beautiful?'

'I – I can't remember.' My eyes fell before his. 'This is very pleasant. Are you staying in England long this time?'

'I have some official business in France,' he said. 'Unfortunately, I must leave tomorrow – but I hope we can meet when I come back in the new year? Will you give me your address so that I can. . . . '

'No!' He looked startled as I blurted out my refusal. 'I'm grateful for what you did for me today. It's nothing personal. I simply want to be left alone.'

'But that's ridiculous,' he said. 'Everyone needs friends. Even if you won't let me give you money, I can help in other ways.'

I pressed a table napkin to my lips, then stood up. 'Thank you for the tea. I'm going now, Paul. Please don't follow me.'

He caught my wrist as I tried to pass him. For a moment we looked into each other's eyes. 'I thought we were friends? You said you'd forgiven me.'

'I have and we are.' I sighed, feeling too tired to argue. 'Please let me go, Paul.'

'If that's what you want, Kate.'

He let go of my wrist and I walked out of the café.

Christmas came and went. I spent most of the time alone in my room, though I joined Mrs Bailey and her other lodgers for a special dinner.

Now that the war was over the talk was of a new beginning; there was to be full employment and prosperity for everyone. A general election had been held in December and Mr Lloyd George and his Liberals had won the majority of seats, forming a coalition with his Conservative colleagues, the Labour party having decided to withdraw. It was the first election in which women had been allowed to vote, though only those over the age of thirty, but it was a historic occasion – and one that would have pleased Lady Selina very much.

During the past few weeks, I'd written several letters trying to find myself a position as a housekeeper in the country, but so far I'd had no success. It seemed that prospective employers weren't eager to take on a widow with a young child. It looked as if I would have no alternative but to claim the inheritance Lady Selina had left me.

I debated whether to do it at once or after my child was born.

Perhaps I could have it sent round – yet I seemed to recall the solicitor saying I must call for it in person. Perhaps after all it would be best to wait. I wasn't so very desperate for money. I could manage for a while longer.

The ache in my back was getting worse. I shifted uncomfortably in my chair, looking at the clock on the mantelpiece. It was nearly ten o'clock; I ought to stir myself. I needed to go shopping for food, but the effort was almost too much. After a week of activity, when I'd been unable to settle for more than a few minutes at a time, I felt tired and reluctant to move. Yet I knew I must go out if I wanted something to eat. As I got to my feet the pain suddenly struck, taking my breath away. I clung to the back of the chair, willing myself to keep calm. The moment for which I'd been waiting so eagerly had arrived. I'd planned for it and I knew exactly what to do. The bag I was to take to the infirmary was packed and ready. I had only to put on my coat and walk downstairs. Mrs Bailey or one of her lodgers would get me a cab. There was no need to panic.

I breathed deeply. The pain had gone for the moment. Putting on my coat, I picked up the small tapestry cloakbag and went out into the hall. I was sitting in my landlady's front parlour drinking a cup of tea when the next pain struck. She clucked in distress as she saw my face go white.

'You poor thing,' she said. 'Just sit there quietly while I see if they've got that cab for you yet. How long is it between pains?'

'I'm not sure. About twenty minutes, I think.'

'You'll not be in labour long then,' she said. 'My sister was just the same, hardly knew what it was all about. Now me, I had a terrible time with my first. In labour for ten hours I was. I thought it would kill me. Still, I mustn't frighten you. You'll probably have it easy.'

I smiled wryly as she went out. The pain I was already experiencing was agonizing. I did not expect to enjoy the next few hours.

'He's beautiful, Mrs Matthews,' the nurse said as she placed the child in my arms. 'Quite perfect in every way, even though he did give you such a bad time.'

I shook my head, a great wave of love flowing over me as I gazed at the red and wrinkled face of Harry's son. 'He is beautiful, isn't he?' I smiled up at her. Until that moment I hadn't allowed myself to consider the possibility that my child would be anything but

278

normal, that he might suffer from the close blood ties of his parents. Now I could laugh at the very idea.'I knew he would be of course; he's just like his father.'

'You mothers!' The nurse pulled a face. 'You're all the same. And now I suppose you would like to see your husband? He's been waiting outside with the biggest bunch of flowers I've ever seen.'

'My. . . . ' For a moment my heart lurched. 'I don't have a husband. I'm a widow.'

Her face fell. 'Forgive me. I took it for granted. . . . You have a visitor and I assumed. . . . '

'It doesn't matter. Will you ask him to come in please?'

'Yes. I'm very sorry, Mrs Matthews.'

She walked quickly from the room I shared with two other newly delivered mothers, neither of whom happened to be in their beds at that moment. So I was alone when Paul walked in, carrying a large bunch of expensive hot-house flowers. He stood just inside the door for a moment, then came to my bed.

'I thought it must be you,' I said.

'I've just left a very embarrassed nurse,' he said with a laugh. 'She thought I was your husband.'

'An easy mistake to make – when you bring me flowers like these!'

'Only the best for you.' He laid them on the table beside me. 'Are you comfortable here? Wouldn't you prefer a private room?'

'No, thank you, Paul. I like being with the other mothers. This is just right. I was lucky; all the beds in the main ward were full when I arrived. They call this the annexe.' I picked up the flowers and inhaled their perfume. 'Lovely – but how did you know where to find me?'

'Your landlady was very helpful.'

'So you did follow me home that day!'

'No. I had an agent of mine make inquiries while I attended to – to some private business in France. I arrived back only this morning.' He arched his brow. 'Did you really imagine that I would let you disappear, Kate? I'm sorry if you're angry, but I can't pretend to feel remorse. I know you have to find somewhere more suitable to live, and I shall make it my business to see that you have somewhere decent to bring up your child. Please don't refuse me; I want to do this for you. It's the least I can do.'

'You don't owe me anything, Paul. What happened – it wasn't your fault; it was my mother's.'

An odd expression flickered in his eyes. 'Don't judge her too harshly, Kate.'

'You don't understand,' I said bitterly. 'You have no idea of the pain she caused me.'

'Oh, I think perhaps I have,' he said quietly. 'Please trust me, Kate. Let me help you. For the sake of your child, if nothing else.'

For a long moment I stared into his eyes, then I looked down at my son. He was sleeping and he seemed so small and vulnerable. Suddenly I was remembering things my mother had said to me. Because of her pride and bitterness she'd refused to be helped, preferring to struggle on alone. As a child I hadn't been aware of our poverty, but now I knew there was a better way of life. Did I really want my son to be cared for by strangers while I worked long hours to provide the necessities of life? Was I willing to sacrifice everything for pride?

I glanced up at Paul and then I smiled. 'I don't know why you should want to do this for me, but it would be churlish to refuse. I can only say thank you.'

'Then it's settled,' he said smoothly. 'We shall take one day at a time, Kate. It's your life. You're free to do exactly as you please. Just trust me.'

I nodded. He was keeping something from me. I sensed it but before I could put my feelings into words, the nurse came in.

'Shall I take him now, Mrs Matthews?' she asked, looking at my sleeping son. 'It's time for your rest.'

Paul smiled as she took the baby from me. 'Have you decided on a name?'

'Perhaps Richard . . . I'm not sure.'

'A good choice,' he said, but I saw the look in his eyes and knew that he hadn't forgotten that Richard Linton was not my father. 'Would you like me to register the birth for you?'

'No!' I said quickly. Too quickly. His brows went up and I blushed. 'I'd like to do it myself.'

'As you wish.' He picked up his gloves. 'I must go now, Kate, but I shall come again tomorrow – if I may?'

'Of course. I'll look forward to seeing you.'

'You won't forget your promise to trust me?'

'No, I won't forget.' I watched as he walked from the room, then lay back against the pillows, feeling sleepy.

Paul took me to his flat overlooking the river. It was just the same as it had been when we'd had lunch there during the war, except that one bedroom had been converted into a small nursery.

'I've taken a suite of rooms in a hotel,' he said, smiling slightly as he saw a flicker of doubt in my eyes. 'It will suit me well. As you know I come and go often. I have to go back to France for a few days now; you'll be doing me a favour by living here.'

'It's beautiful, Paul – and all those things for Richard. I don't know how to thank you.'

'You just have.' He turned away to gaze out of the window. 'I'm a wealthy man, Kate. Quite rich enough to indulge myself now and then. What I've done so far is very little.'

'In your mind, perhaps.'

He turned to look at me then. 'I would like to do much more, but I shan't press you. I've engaged a woman for you. I'll pay her wages and she will cook and clean for you. If you wish, she will take care of Richard while you go out – it's up to you.'

'That wasn't necessary. I don't mind housework.'

'You've worked hard for a long time, Kate. Give yourself a chance to recover your strength. Believe me, I shall be gaining more from this arrangement than you.'

'That's nonsense,' I said and laughed. 'But I'm going to accept your generosity, Paul. I have to decide what to do with the rest of my life and I do need time to think.'

'That's all I ask,' he said quietly. 'That you give yourself time. . . .'

'You're very generous. Perhaps more generous than I deserve.'

'Ah no,' he murmured. 'Just be happy, Kate. I hope you will allow me to call now and then?'

'You must feel free to visit whenever you please. It's your flat, after all.'

'For the time being it's yours, Kate. I shall only be a guest in your home.'

'Then you will be welcome whenever you come.'

CHAPTER TWENTY-SIX

She was alone again. Marc was dead, his head blasted open by the pistol he'd fired into his mouth. The horror of finding him like that when she'd finally summoned the courage to go and look had sent Emma fleeing into the chill of the grey November day. She'd run to the village, sobbing, hysterical, refusing to return to the cottage with the priest and the doctor. Even after Marc's funeral she'd sent a young boy to fetch her things, knowing she couldn't face the echoes of that last terrible day.

People had tried to be kind to her. They brought her small gifts of food and asked her to make clothes for them, but she had lost the will to work. She was too confused to think clearly.

Her sleep was haunted by spectres with hollow eyes and skeletal fingers that pointed accusingly. In her nightmares, she seemed always to be running between rows of mouldering gravestones, from which the bodies of her parents, Richard, and Marc rose up screaming and clawing at her as they tried to drag her down with them.

And then there was Kate. Always when she thought she had escaped the others, Kate was waiting for her with her white, stricken face and huge accusing eyes.

'You lied to me!' the girl cried. 'You stole my happiness. You destroyed my life.'

'No!' Emma cried as she woke, shivering and cold with fear. 'No, Kate. Please, no. . . . '

Always the trembling would go on until she reached for the brandy bottle she kept in a cupboard beside the bed. Swallowing, gulping the fiery liquid that stung her throat, she felt the shudders subside. That was better. Now the ghosts were banished, but she mustn't go to sleep, because if she did they would return.

'You can't go on like this, Madame.' The doctor looked at her reprovingly as she stared up at him wearily from the unmade bed with its stained sheets. 'You must have food – and someone to look after you. Your landlady thought you were going to die, that's why she sent for me.'

'She shouldn't have bothered,' Emma replied, closing her eyes to shut him out. 'Please leave me alone. I just want to be alone.'

'Why don't you go to the nuns?' He frowned down at her. 'You must be properly looked after or you will die. Is there someone we could send for?'

'No one. I don't want anyone.'

Emma turned her face into her pillow as he left the room. What did it matter if she died? At least then she would be free of the nightmares that haunted her. . . .

She was aware of a cool hand on her brow; the coolness was a blessed relief after the heat of the fever. Opening her eyes, she looked up into the gentle face of the woman who bent over her.

'You're better at last,' the soft voice said. 'God be praised. I thought we'd lost you.'

'Where am I?' Emma struggled to sit up, but the weakness overcame her. 'Who brought me here?'

'We were told you were in need,' the nun replied. 'It is our vocation to care for those who need us. You were very ill, Madame, but now you will be well.' She smiled. 'Soon you will be well enough to receive your visitor.'

'My visitor?'

Emma's eyelids fluttered. She was too tired, too weary to wonder what the nun meant. It was a mistake, of course. No one would want to visit her. No one even knew she was alive. . . .

The nun fussed round her as though she were a child, fluffing out her freshly washed hair and plumping the pillows. Emma sighed, too weary to wonder what was going on and wishing that they would simply leave her in peace.

'So, now you're ready to see your visitor, Madame.'

A tiny shiver ran down Emma's spine. 'Visitor?' She stared, suspicion and fear mingling. 'Who is it?'

The nun smiled and left the room. Looking round, Emma took in the cool simplicity of her surroundings; the walls were white-washed and bare apart from a wooden cross above the door, yet she noticed now for the first time that there was a carpet on the floor and a comfortable chair by the window, and she realized that she wasn't in the hospice itself. This was one of the rooms the nuns reserved for special patients. But she had no money to pay for such favours. Surely the nuns knew that? Even as she pondered the question,

Emma heard a man's voice in the corridor outside. She knew that voice! Tingling with anticipation, she stared at the door, hardly believing what all her senses were telling her. And then it opened.

'Hello,' he said and smiled at her. 'You're looking very much better than you did when they brought you in, Emma.'

'Paul. . . . ' Her mouth was dry and her heart was thumping. 'How. . . . '

'How did I know you were here?' A smile played over his mouth. 'I never really believed you were dead, Emma. I suppose I didn't want to believe it. I felt guilty because of the way we parted, and I needed to know more so I inquired discreetly about the woman who was buried in your name. I discovered she had a friend and the friend fitted your description. Then I had an agent of mine look for Emmeline Dubois, and I discovered it was you; I've known of your whereabouts for some time. You seemed to be managing very well so I didn't interfere, but as soon as I heard you were ill I had you brought here.'

'So – so you're paying for this room.' She stared at him, feeling the old longing stir deep inside her. It was as strong as ever, buried but not dead. 'Why?' she asked. 'Why, Paul? Why did you bother?'

'Don't you know?' His smile was gentle as he sat beside her, reaching for her hand. 'I was always fond of you, Emma. Besides, I feel responsible for what happened.'

She stared at him, torn between pleasure at seeing him and resentment. 'I don't want your pity, Paul,' she said bitterly. 'I'm not Marianne. You don't have to feel guilty about me.'

He frowned, checking the anger her words roused. After all she'd been through, she had a right to feel resentful, and he knew that he had been motivated by guilt at the beginning, but now he had other reasons for wanting to help her. He smiled ruefully, playing with the hand that had clenched against him.

'Please don't hate me, Emma,' he said softly. 'I thought that perhaps we could be friends. . . . '

'Friends?' she echoed bitterly. Staring at him, remembering, she was tempted to scream to him, to tell him to get out of her life, and then he smiled – that old, enchanting smile that could always enslave her – and her heart missed a beat. Perhaps there was still a chance? Still a little of the old feeling left between them – and she wanted him so! 'Yes,' she said slowly, allowing a flicker of hope to enter her heart. 'I'd like that, Paul. I'd like that very much.'

'Good.' He squeezed her hand. 'This is what I'm going to do. . . . '

'Please,' she said, stopping him with an agitated flutter of her hand. 'Please, Paul – tell me about Kate. . . . '

'Kate?' His eyes probed and questioned. 'Are you sure you're ready, Emma?' As she nodded, his smile became warm with approval and she knew she'd said the right thing. 'Yes, I can tell you about Kate. . . . '

Emma glanced round the cottage, the disappointment almost choking her as she tried to hide it from Paul. He wasn't going to take her to the château this time; he'd made that clear from the beginning, but she'd hoped for something they could share occasionally, when he had time to visit. Although comfortably furnished, the cottage was small and she knew Paul would never have chosen it if he'd intended to spend time there himself. It was merely a sop to his conscience, she thought bitterly; she was his pensioner, another burden . . . like Marianne. The thought made her laugh harshly, anger churning inside her. Fool! Fool to think that he might really care! But then she was smiling as he looked at her, skilfully hiding her true emotions as she thanked him.

'It's wonderful, Paul,' she said, her eyes wide and apparently innocent. 'How clever of you to find it for me.'

He frowned, uneasy as he sensed something hidden. With Emma you could never be quite sure. You never really knew what she was thinking. Would it have been better to tell her of his plans from the start? Yet he wasn't ready to confide in her yet. She could ruin everything if she chose.

'You wouldn't rather go back to England?' he asked with a lift of his brows.

She shook her head, turning away to hide the surge of anger that was so fierce it surprised even her.

'No,' she said slowly. 'The climate suits me here, Paul. Besides, there's nothing for me in England now.'

'Kate is there,' he said, his tone betraying his slight impatience to her sensitive ear. 'She's alone now, Emma.'

She fought for control, smiling easily as she turned. 'I should like to see her, Paul – if she could forgive me for the terrible things I've done.' Her gaze lifted to his. 'It never occurred to me that she might fall in love with Harry. I thought of her as a child. You must believe me.'

'Children grow up,' he replied coldly. 'It was cruel and unnecessary, Emma.'

'Was it?' she asked, and lowered her gaze so that he shouldn't see the sudden blaze of fury. 'Yes, perhaps you're right. Ask her for me, Paul. Ask her if she will forgive me – will you, please?'

'Yes, of course.' His look was immediately warm with approval. 'And now perhaps you could answer a question for me?'

Her spine tingled and she sensed that it was important to him. She nodded. 'If I can.'

'It's about Kate's father,' he began, and faltered. As she looked into his face, she knew. She knew exactly what he wanted to ask and why. . . .

CHAPTER TWENTY-SEVEN

The first few months of 1919 were truly a time of peace for me. England seemed to be returning to normal. There was a sense of activity as men and women worked together to bring the new prosperity everyone longed for, and in those early days it did seem that things were getting better.

There was some protest from the army. The Government's idea had been to bring home skilled workers first, those men most needed in the drive for economic recovery, but this caused a great deal of discontent. It was Mr Churchill's suggestion that release should be on the basis of first in, first out, that finally solved the problem.

Cocooned in my own little world, I took little interest in politics. I had my child, Mrs Johnson my housekeeper – who also brought me respectability – and Paul. I seldom went very far. On mild spring days I would go for a walk along the towpath, pushing Richard's pram and stopping to feed the greedy ducks who squabbled noisily over the scraps of bread I threw them. When it was cold or wet I stayed indoors, reading or listening to the gramophone. Paul bought me new records whenever he visited, also books, flowers and a present of some kind for Richard. He had placed a clothes allowance at a fashionable modiste for me, and he insisted that I made full use of it.

'You spoil us,' I said each time he brought Richard a new toy. 'I can never repay you for your kindness.'

'I need no reward. Except to see the smile in your eyes.'

'You're so good to me. . . '

'Please say no more. All I want is to make you happy.'

And so the months drifted by. If I'd thought about it, I suppose I should have known that my peaceful life was unnatural. I should have been prepared for change. Yet until the day of my twenty-second birthday, I was content to drift on without giving much thought to my situation. That morning Paul arrived with several small gifts wrapped in silver paper. I opened them with pleasure, thanking him for the huge flaçon of French perfume, soft leather gloves, flowers and chocolates.

'Tokens,' he said, his eyes bright. 'Mrs Johnson will look after

Richard today. I'm taking you out – first to buy your present, then to lunch.'

'But you've given me so much already,' I protested.

'Please don't deny me the pleasure. You stay in too much. Look at the sunshine. It's a glorious day and your birthday. It should be a special day.'

His enthusiasm was catching. Suddenly I felt excited at the prospect of going out with him. 'You'll have to wait while I change,' I said.

I put on one of the new gowns Paul had provided for me. It was white, with a tight-fitting bodice and a sculptered neckline that emphasized the whiteness of my throat and showed off the pretty locket my mother had left me. The material was light and filmy and there were pretty ribbons at the wristbands. There was also a wide-brimmed hat with white feathers to go with it. I glanced at myself in the mirror, feeling a thrill of pleasure as I saw how well I looked. The woman reflected in the smoky grey glass of an antique mirror was a stranger to me. Her eyes held a hint of sadness but also of mystery. Her hair was thick and it shone with health. Whoever she was, she certainly wasn't the innocent Kate Linton who had gone to live at Brockmere in the summer of 1913. The last summer before the war. The last summer of innocence. . . .

'Who are you?' I asked of my image. 'What kind of a woman are you now?'

I'd been so naïve that first summer at Brockmere. I realized now that it was the last time I was really innocent. Before the war everything had seemed so simple. It was another world, a different kind of life. Nothing would ever be the same again, for me or for anyone who had lived through that period. There had been too much suffering, too much pain. Men had come back from the fighting with twisted limbs and scarred bodies; women had lost their husbands and lovers – I wasn't the only girl to have borne an illegitimate child, though unlike many I'd been able to hide my shame. In the eyes of the world I was a respectable widow with a housekeeper and a child. It was a safe, secure world that I'd created for myself and I was a little afraid to step outside it, but Paul was waiting.

He smiled as I emerged from the bedroom, his eyes seeming to dwell hungrily on my face. 'You look beautiful, Kate. You were always lovely, but now there's something special about you.'

'I was wondering who I am, Paul,' I said, slightly breathless as I

saw the glow in his eyes. 'You once said that there was another Kate
– do you think she's finally here?'

'I think perhaps she might be,' he said softly. 'Are you ready?'

'Yes, I think so.'

Richard was sleeping peacefully as we left. I knew Mrs Johnson
would look after him, but I felt a few pangs. I'd hardly left him since
he was born.

'He'll be fine,' Paul said as I looked back towards the window of
his room.

'I know.' I glanced at him as he got into the car beside me. 'Can
you always read my mind that easily?'

'Not always.' His mouth quirked. 'But it isn't hard to know what
you're thinking where Richard's concerned.'

'Are you saying that I spoil him?'

'Undoubtedly.' Paul laughed as I looked indignant. 'Why shouldn't
you? Just don't make him your whole life. You're still young, Kate.
Live for yourself.'

'I'm happy as I am.'

'You mustn't shut yourself away from life.'

'Is that what I've been doing?'

'You know it is.' He glanced at me and then back at the road. 'I
know you've been badly hurt, but you mustn't be afraid to let yourself
feel again. I've been down that road, so I know what I'm talking
about.'

'It isn't that. You don't understand.'

'Then tell me.'

'I will . . . soon.'

'I'm sorry. I didn't mean to scold you. This was meant to be a
happy day.'

'It will be.' I looked at him. 'I will tell you, Paul. I promise.'

'Let's forget it, shall we?' He smiled. 'What shall I buy you today?
I want to give you something you've always wanted – something to
make your eyes light up the way they do when you're really happy.'

'I can't think of anything. I have so much already.'

'Then I'll have to buy you something I want you to have.'

'Could I stop you if I tried?'

'No. I'm a man of iron when my mind's made up.'

'Don't I know it!' I laughed and sat back in my seat, relaxing.
'Surprise me, then. I promise I shan't say a word.'

His eyes gleamed with amusement. We drove in silence for several minutes, then he pulled into the kerb outside an expensive jeweller's shop.

'This is where you intended to come all the time, wasn't it?'

'I cannot tell a lie. I was hoping you would leave the choice to me.'

'Wretch!' I took his arm as we went in. 'I suppose you know exactly what you want?'

Before he could reply a man in a dark suit and shiny black shoes descended upon us. His smile of welcome and the deference in his manner left me in no doubt that we were eagerly expected.

'Ah, Monsieur de Bernay,' he said. 'I have everything ready. Perhaps you and Madame would like to step into my office?'

We were ushered into a small room at the back of the shop. There was a thick carpet on the floor, an impressive desk, three elegant elbow chairs in the Chippendale style and a huge safe in the corner. It was from the depths of this safe that he produced a black velvet box, lifting the lid to reveal the first layer of exquisite jewellery. Diamonds, rubies and emeralds sparkled against the softness of the velvet. He lifted the bracelets one by one, spreading them before me.

'These are the ones you preferred, sir,' he said, and lifting the next layer from his case, 'and these are the matching collars.'

'Choose whatever you like, Kate,' Paul said. 'I wasn't sure which stone you would prefer.'

'Oh, Paul,' I gasped. 'I can't . . . I mean these are so. . . . '

'You promised not to say a word. I thought the sapphire and diamond set would set off your eyes, but perhaps the rubies are better quality.'

The sapphire and diamond bracelet was a single strand of large oval-shaped stones in a simple setting; the necklace was the same, except that it had a large, pear-shaped drop. I'd once seen a picture in *The Tatler* of the Princess Mary wearing something similar, and I thought it very lovely – as was the princess herself, who had been the much admired and respected pin-up girl of the forces during the war.

'Perhaps you would rather have the emeralds – or just diamonds?'

I'd never seen such magnificent jewellery. Some of it was so ostentatious that I would never have dared to wear it, but the simplicity of the sapphire and diamond set appealed to me. I liked it and thought it was probably the least expensive of all.

'I like the sapphires,' I said hesitantly. 'If you're sure. . . . '

A look of satisfaction passed between the jeweller and Paul. Too late I realized that I'd been deceived by the apparent modesty of the design.

'A wise choice, Madame,' the jeweller said. 'These sapphires are of the finest quality, as are the diamonds.'

'We won't take them now,' Paul said. 'You can send them to the address I gave you earlier.'

'Yes, Monsieur, of course. I shall see to it personally.'

'Good.' Paul took my arm. 'Come, Kate. I've a table booked at the Ritz for one-thirty.'

'The Ritz Hotel. . . . ' I swallowed hard as Paul looked at me. 'How lovely.'

It was the last place I wanted to go; it held too many memories. Yet I couldn't spoil Paul's pleasure by telling him that.

The cream and gold dining room was busy when we were shown in, almost every table occupied. We were led to a secluded corner that was half hidden by a large potted plant. It gave us the advantage of being able to see into the room without being too much on display ourselves.

'This is the table you requested, sir?' the head waiter asked uncertainly. 'There is another by the window if you would prefer it?'

'No, this is exactly what we want.' Paul held the chair for me. 'Shall we have champagne, Kate?'

'Why not?' I smiled up at him. 'You're determined to spoil me, aren't you?'

'Why not?' he echoed. 'It gives me great pleasure. I've had little opportunity of late to indulge myself.'

As the waiter left us to peruse the menu, I glanced across at Paul. 'I can hardly believe that when we first met I disliked you.'

'Oh, you did. You made your hostility very clear,' he laughed.

'I was a stupid child.' I wrinkled my brow. 'Do you think that's why my mother left me behind?'

'She may have had reasons of her own.'

'What do you mean?'

He shook his head. 'Not now, Kate. Don't let's spoil things.'

I was puzzled by something in his manner. There was a hint of guilt in his eyes, as though he was consciously keeping something from me.

'You say it gives you pleasure to spoil me, Paul – are you lonely? I've always thought of you as having many friends.'

'There is a certain kind of loneliness that exists even – or particularly – in the midst of a crowd. I've known that feeling, Kate. I have, as you say, many friends. If my life is not as fulfilled as it might be, there were reasons. . . . reasons that for the most part no longer exist.' His eyes were serious as he looked at me. 'These past few months have been special for me. You must know how I feel about you?'

I had felt it for a long time, but hadn't wanted to admit it to myself, because it would mean committing myself to the future.

'Yes,' I said, choosing my words carefully. 'I – I suppose I have known for some time, Paul. I'm not sure what to say. I. . . . '

'You don't have to say anything, yet,' he interrupted. 'I'm not asking for more than we have – not yet. . . . '

'Kate, Kate Linton! It is you!' Paul was interrupted in turn by an elegantly dressed woman who suddenly swooped down on us. 'Forgive me for disturbing you, but I was so excited when I spotted you,' she gushed. 'Everyone said you'd simply disappeared without trace – and here you are dining at the Ritz. It's just too amusing for words!'

A chill went through me as I stared into the smiling face of Helen Forrest. She had put on a little weight since our last meeting, but she looked confident and happy. Paul had risen to his feet. He was shaking hands and murmuring something polite.

'How pleasant to see you – would you care for a glass of champagne?'

'I should simply adore it,' Helen said, her eyes sparkling behind the little net veil of her smart hat. She pulled on black leather gloves. 'Unfortunately, I have an appointment and I'm already late – but I must see you again, Kate. I want to hear all your news, and I've a great deal to tell you. Where have you been hiding yourself all this time? You naughty girl! We've all been so worried about you. Now you must give me your address. I insist.'

For a moment I could only stare at her as she snapped open her handbag and took out a little notebook in a silver case, looking at me expectantly. It was what I'd dreaded, the reason I'd taken such care to stay away from anywhere I might accidently bump into someone who knew me. My heart was thumping wildly and for a brief second I felt as if I might faint. Then I knew that there was no escape; I gave her the address of the flat and she wrote it down carefully with a tiny silver pencil.

'Oh, I know it well,' she said. 'A charming location – perhaps I could call one day?'

'Of course,' I said. 'I would be delighted to see you. How are

Philip and the children?' There was nothing else I could possibly say in the face of her obvious glee at seeing me again.

'Disgustingly healthy,' she said. 'I'll be glad when we can pack the boys off to prep school. I'll be in touch soon. You can't imagine how happy I am to see you – and looking so well and so elegant!'

As she moved away, Paul looked at my strained face. 'I'm sorry, Kate,' he said. 'I've been a damned fool. I should have realized there was a reason for the way you've been avoiding all contact with your family. Please forgive me.'

'You couldn't have known Helen would be here.'

'Do you want to leave?'

'No.' I lifted my head proudly and smiled at him. 'It's my birthday and we came here to celebrate. I'll have the lobster salad and strawberries to follow, please.'

His frown cleared as he saw the sparkle in my eyes. 'Bravo,' he said. 'Whatever is troubing you, we'll face it together. I promise you.'

'You may change your mind when I tell you,' I said. 'But that can wait for later. . . . '

I laid Richard in his cot and went back into the big, airy sitting room that overlooked the river. Paul was relaxing in an armchair by the window. It was still light and he hadn't bothered to switch on the lamps. For a moment I stood on the threshold, just watching him. He was reading a magazine that I'd bought which had published excerpts from many of the poems from the war, including pieces by Edward Wyndham Tenant and Mr Laurence Binyon, whose verses, entitled *For the Fallen*, written for Armistice Day, had been set to music by Elgar. There were many other poems by soldiers that told of love, hope and despair. The poetry of the Great War that had wrecked so many, many lives was strangely poignant and soothing to read now that we had peace.

Paul got to his feet and stood looking at me awkwardly. 'Has Richard gone off now?'

'Yes. He's fast asleep, but he was a long time. I think he may be cutting his first tooth.'

'That might explain the crying.' Paul moved at last. 'Would you like a sherry?'

'No, thank you. My head's still swimming from all that champagne – you have one, though.'

I sat down in the chair opposite Paul's. He poured himself a whisky and came to sit down again, placing the glass untouched on the table beside him.

'You said I mustn't hide from life,' I said. 'I think you may be right. I've been trying to run away from the truth. Not for my own sake but – but to protect someone else.'

As I paused, he frowned. I could hear the ticking of the little gilt clock on the sideboard and the sighing of the breeze in the willows. 'You don't have to tell me any of this,' he said. 'I know all I need to know about you.'

'I don't have to but I think I must.' I breathed deeply. 'I'm not married, Paul. I never was. The name I'm using belonged to someone I knew briefly. We spent one night together during the war.'

'Is that all?' He looked relieved. 'I guessed that you weren't married a long time ago.'

'Did you? How?' I smiled; I ought to have known that Paul wouldn't be shocked. He had never been one for convention.

'You showed no grief when you spoke of your husband. Knowing you, I was sure he didn't exist. You would never have been so casual if you'd lost a husband you'd loved.'

'I did like David Matthews a lot. If he'd cared to take advantage of that night we spent together, he might have been Richard's father – but he isn't. I had too much to drink and he was too honourable to touch me.'

Paul's frown returned. 'Why did you take his name?'

I got up and walked to the window, my back turned to Paul as I fought for the strength to go on. It was even harder to tell him than I'd expected. Perhaps even he would find the truth too much to accept.

'Don't tear yourself apart, Kate. It isn't necessary. I don't care who Richard's father was.' I heard the chair move as he came to stand beside me, and I flinched as I felt the touch of his hand on my shoulder. He turned me gently to face him. 'I love you. Don't you see that nothing else matters?'

'Paul, I. . . . '

He took me in his arms, bending his head to kiss my lips. For a moment I stood stiffly, resisting him, then I felt my knees tremble and suddenly I was clinging to him, returning his kiss with a passion that matched his own. We drew apart at last, looking at each other in wonder.

'Marry me, Kate,' he said. 'I'm free to ask now. Marry me. I'll adopt Richard. He'll be our son. There'll be no need for. . . . '

294

'Free to ask. . . . ' As I looked into his eyes and saw the remembered grief, I understood and I knew that the time for truth had come. 'Richard is Harry's son,' I said quickly. 'You have to know that, Paul.'

'You didn't have to tell me.' A faintly mocking smile entered his eyes. 'How could it have been anyone else? I know you, Kate. I knew long before you told me.'

'Then why. . . . '

He sighed deeply. 'Because I too have a secret. I've wanted to tell you, but I was afraid of what it might do to you.'

'I don't understand, Paul.'

'I wanted to tell you, but you seemed so wrapped up in your own safe little world. I can't keep it from you any longer, Kate. You have to know – your mother. . . . '

'My mother's dead.' I stared at him, an icy band seeming to squeeze my heart. My head was pounding and there was a dreadful crushing sensation in my chest. 'She is dead, isn't she, Paul?'

He took both my hands, holding them tightly as I began to tremble. 'Emma is alive. She's living in France, in a small house I bought for her. . . . '

'A house you . . . you knew she was alive. Why didn't you tell me?' My cry was sharp with accusation, reflecting the pain I felt inside.

'I wanted to. You must believe me. . . . '

His words were very faint. The thudding at my temples was unbearable. I could hardly see his face. As he came towards me, I instinctively retreated. The ground beneath my feet seemed to shoot up and then I fell.

I lay on my bed, looking through the open curtains at the moon. The sky was curiously light, almost white and translucent. My eyes felt prickly but I hadn't cried. I felt very strange, as though my mind was detached from my body. A body that ached from a grief that was a physical pain. Yet I wasn't conscious of pain as I lay watching the moon. I seemed to float, weightless, a soul in search of peace.

'Kate, are you awake?'

'Go away,' I said, wanting to hold on to that elusive peace. 'I need to be alone for a while.'

'I'll be here when you need me. We have to talk.' He paused but I didn't answer. 'I love you, Kate. I didn't mean to hurt you.'

'Soon. We'll talk soon, Paul.'

He went away and I turned my eyes back to the moon. My mind

was filled with so many memories, too many for me to be able to sort out the confusion of half-remembered words, a smile or the touch of a hand against my cheek. I seemed to hear the whirr of a sewing machine and the hiss of the gaslamps. I smelt the hot, soapy tang of the back kitchen washdays and listened to the sound of shouting from next door. The scent of my mother's perfume seemed to linger in the air, making the pain suddenly twist inside me. All at once the numbness left me and I was aware of the pain, and of the anger.

Lies, lies and more lies! It seemed that everything I'd trusted or believed in was false. Even now I didn't know who to trust. Everyone I'd ever cared for had lied to me. Except Harry. He'd also been the victim of those wicked lies. And because of them he was dead – because he couldn't bear the agony of knowing that our love was forbidden. I was certain that he had gone back to his unit in the hope of death, that he had invited it.

I had to know the truth about my mother. Paul was right. We must talk. Yet even he had lied to me. He'd known she was alive and he'd kept it from me. I got slowly to my feet, pausing to splash my face with cold water before going through to the sitting room.

Paul had only a small lamp burning. Like me, he'd been staring out at the night sky. He turned as he heard me moving behind him, and I saw by the expression on his face that he too was grieving.

'You were right,' I said. 'We must talk. I have to know everything.'

'Yes, of course. I never wanted to hurt you. You must believe that.'

'I do. I know you care for me.'

'Thank you for that, Kate.'

'Tell me about her,' I said. 'Is she really living in your house in France?'

'In the house I bought for her. She owns it. I've also given her an income that is hers for life.'

I sat on the edge of a chair, tense and suspicious. 'Why should you do that? She left you, didn't she?'

'I help her because I feel responsible. Besides, I've always liked Emma. If I'd been free when we first met, I might have married her. She has been ill, Kate. I had to do something for her.'

'Why didn't you tell me all this when we discussed it during the war?'

'Do you think I would do that to you? I didn't know for sure that she was alive then, though I suspected it. I traced her a few months before the war ended.'

'You should have told me on Armistice Day.'

'I didn't know what to do. You were obviously in trouble. I was afraid of creating more problems for you. And then there was the legal side of it. Emma took the name and papers of a woman she'd befriended. It took some sorting out. . . . '

'So that's how she did it.' I stared at him, tasting the gall in my mouth. 'Why? She must have known how much it would hurt me.'

'I asked her that. I was very angry with her.'

'What did she say?' My nails curled into the palms of my hands. 'All these years and she's never once – why does she hate me?'

'She doesn't hate you, Kate. She wanted you to be free and she thought you would cling to the past while you believed she was alive.'

'How could she?' I leapt to my feet, pacing the room. I felt feverish, my mind reeling as I struggled to come to terms with what Paul had told me. It was almost too much to comprehend – that a mother could do something so deliberately cruel to her own child! 'How could she think that her death would set me free? I've never ceased to grieve for the way in which. . . . ' Suddenly I realized the depths of my mother's betrayal. 'She was never ill. It was put on to make me agree to go to Brockmere so that she could go with you alone. . . .'

'Yes.' Paul got to his feet as he saw the stricken look in my eyes. 'Don't break your heart, my darling.' He tried to take me in his arms, but I moved out of reach. He looked hurt but I couldn't have borne him to touch me at that moment.

I felt battered and bruised, as if I'd been severely thrashed. I wanted to cry but my eyes were hot and dry. It might have been better if I'd been able to weep, to cling to Paul and let him ease the agony inside me.

'The legacy,' I said dully. 'That was from you, wasn't it?'

'Yes.' He looked at me pleadingly. 'I wanted you to have something. . . . '

'Don't!' I tore the locket I'd believed was from my mother from my neck and threw it on the floor. 'I hate her – I hate what she did to me.'

'You shouldn't judge her too harshly, Kate. You know how hard her life was. For years she'd worked like a slave to support you both, never having the things or the laughter she craved. There was no money for expensive clothes or jewellery, no time to enjoy herself. She felt that her life was slipping by, that it would soon be too late, even though she was still an attractive woman.'

'I can understand why she went with you,' I said. 'And I can sympathize – but to lie to me, to let me think she was dying. Then to send proof of her death that was the cruellest thing of all.'

'I think she understands that now, Kate. She regrets what she did – she wants to see you.'

'No!' I cried. 'I won't see her. I'll never forgive her. I can't.'

'Never is a long time.'

'Why should I see her?' I stared at him. 'What has she ever done that I should feel pity for her?'

'She doesn't want your pity, Kate. She wants – she needs your forgiveness.'

I laughed harshly. 'She hasn't needed it for years – why now?'

'She has been through a terrible time.' Paul frowned. 'She told me some of it, but I sensed there was more. She drinks, Kate. She almost died of it a few months ago.'

I stared at him, feeling something, some small remnant of remembered love, catch at my heart. 'She must be very unhappy.'

'Yes,' he said quietly. 'If you won't see her, Kate, will you at least write to her – try to forgive her if you can?'

'I don't know,' I said. 'I shall have to think about it.'

'And what about us?' he asked. 'Are you going to marry me?'

I raised my eyes to his, seeing the entreaty there. 'I don't know, Paul,' I said. 'I just don't know . . . you'll have to give me time.'

The letter from Lady Selina's solicitor was delivered just two days after I'd seen Helen at the Ritz. She hadn't wasted much time! It was addressed to Miss Katherine Linton and it asked me to collect the package she'd left me at my convenience, or state when I would be at home to receive it personally.

I decided to leave Richard with Mrs Johnson. I could take a cab and then walk through St James's Park to the lawyer's office. It was a nice day and I could ask the solicitor for advice. If I elected to invest my inheritance in a small country property, he might act for me.

I was uncertain of the future. Unless I married Paul, I couldn't go on living at the flat, and I still wasn't sure how I felt about that. When he'd kissed me, I'd responded more than willingly; I might even be a little in love with him, but could I believe in him after his deception? Could I ever love him as completely as I had Harry?

Reaching the solicitor's office, I was shown upstairs by a clerk and asked to wait in a comfortable room. After about five minutes a man came in, carrying a small package. It was tied with string and heavily sealed with red wax.

'Miss Linton?' he inquired tentatively. 'Do you remember me? We have met once before.'

'Yes, I remember you. I'm sorry I haven't been in touch before. I was in France for a long time.'

'I know. Mrs Forrest gave me your present address. We act for her husband and she knew we were anxious to trace you.'

'So that's why she was so insistent.' He looked puzzled and I shook my head. 'It doesn't matter – I ought to have come a long time ago.'

'I hope you will be satisfied with our stewardship of your money, Miss Linton. In the absence of your instructions, I took the liberty of investing it for you – I now have fourteen hundred pounds at your disposal.'

'That's more than satisfactory, sir. Will you keep it for me a little longer, please? I may wish to buy a cottage in the country, and I shall need someone to act for me.'

'I should be delighted.' He beamed at me. 'Now, I must ask you to sign for the package. Lady Selina was most insistent that it should be placed directly into your hands.'

'Isn't that a little odd?'

'She had a good reason, depend upon it. Lady Selina knew her own mind, Miss Linton. I've carried out her instructions exactly.'

'Yes – despite my shocking bad manners in not coming to see you.' I smiled as I rose to my feet. 'Thank you very much, sir. I'll be in touch with you about the money when I decide what to do.'

Paul was waiting for me when I returned to the apartment. I went into the bedroom to take off my hat and coat, slipping the package into a drawer. He looked at me anxiously as I came out again.

'Perhaps I shouldn't have come?' I was silent and he moved towards me, his manner so hesitant that I was moved despite my anger. 'Kate, forgive me,' he muttered brokenly. 'I know I was wrong but. . . . '

Suddenly the ice melted around my heart and I went to meet him. He sensed my change of mood and his arms opened to enfold me. I lifted my face for his kiss, feeling the warmth flood through me.

'Oh, Kate,' he muttered. 'I've been in agony. I thought I'd lost you.'

'I was angry,' I said. 'But when I saw you just now, I realized how much I'd missed you. I don't want to live alone for the rest of my life. . . . '

'Then you will marry me?'

I looked up at him. For a moment I hesitated, still reluctant to commit myself; then common sense took over. Harry was dead: nothing could change that. I might not love Paul in the same way as I had loved Harry, but there was a strong physical attraction between us. I had felt something that first time he kissed me, and rejected it because it frightened me, but I'd been a child then and now I was a woman.

'Yes, Paul,' I said at last. 'Yes, I will marry you. . . . '

CHAPTER TWENTY-EIGHT

Staring at the letter on the table in front of her, Emma felt the need for a drink. She'd been fighting the craving for days, knowing that if she once gave in it would take over. And then she would lose all hope of ever getting Paul back. He'd made his disgust at her weakness for strong drink quite plain during his brief visits, and because of that she'd fought the craving and the nightmares. It was a slender thread of hope she'd clung to, but it was her lifeline and without it she knew she was finished.

The letter was from Kate. She'd recognized the handwriting at once, but had been afraid to open it. Knowing how badly she must have hurt her daughter, she was afraid of her hatred and her anger. Kate must be bitter about the way her life had been destroyed. She would never be able to forgive her.

Walking to the cupboard in the corner of the room, Emma took out a decanter of brandy and looked at it. She withdrew the stopper and then replaced it, gathering her courage. It was ridiculous to be afraid of a letter. Returning to the table, she picked it up and tore open the envelope while her nerve held, scanning the first page.

As she'd expected, Kate's first words were angry and reproachful; then, as she read on, the tone changed, becoming wistful and a little plaintive. Emotion caught at Emma's throat. She felt the sting of tears. What had she done? What had she done to the girl she had once loved so much? Through fear and jealousy she'd destroyed her own daughter's life. Mixed emotions warred in Emma as she fought the battle inside her. At times she'd come close to hating Kate, but deep within her there was still a tiny remnant of the love she'd had for her. It had always been mixed with resentment, somehow, resentment at the responsibility that had been thrust upon her after Richard died. That resentment was still there, but coupled with a desire for forgiveness, a need to be loved. Kate had always loved her. She was perhaps the only one who had ever truly cared for Emma.

Emma took the brandy and poured it down the sink. She was going to stop wasting her life. She didn't quite know how she was going to get through the lonely nights, but somehow she would manage. But first there was something important she had to do.

She'd spoilt Kate's life, but perhaps it wasn't too late. Perhaps there was a way of making amends.

CHAPTER TWENTY-NINE

Paul had telephoned to say he would be delayed. I laid Richard to rest in his cot, having rubbed his sore gums with a little soothing jelly. As I replaced the jar in my dressing-table drawer I suddenly saw the package from Lady Selina. It had lain there forgotten since the night I'd found Paul waiting for me. We'd been so busy making plans that I hadn't given it a thought. Taking it out, I cut the string and broke the sealing wax. Inside was a letter and a diamond brooch, also two smaller pearl brooches. The diamond brooch was very large and in the shape of a star, obviously valuable, but I couldn't see why Lady Selina should go to such lengths to make sure I received it safely. She had left far more valuable jewellery to Prue. It must be the letter that was important.

I sat with it in my hands for several minutes, feeling very nervous, then, making up my mind, I broke the seal. It was stupid to be afraid of a letter. Reading the first few lines, I began to tremble. It couldn't be true! It just couldn't!

'No! Oh my God, no!' I cried, then I began again, reading more slowly.

'My dear Kate.' The words were blurring on the paper as I fought my tears. 'If you're reading this I'm dead, and it is likely that my secret will be shared by only one other person – you. I believe you are strong enough to make your own decision. I've done what I thought right, but perhaps you will think differently. I leave the final decision to you. Do what you believe you must, Kate. The facts cannot be altered, but you must choose, now that you know. . . . '

My thoughts were suddenly suspended as I heard someone knocking at the door, a loud, insistent knocking that made me tingle with alarm. Leaving the letter lying on the bed, I got up and went through to answer the door,.

The woman who stood there had her arm raised to knock again. Shock went through me, leaving me speechless and rigid, unable to move or speak. She looked older and her cheeks were heavily rouged, but there was no mistaking her identity. We gazed at each other in silence, both obviously feeling a little dazed, then at last she spoke,

'Hello, Kate – won't you invite me in? I've come a long way to see you.'

Taking a deep breath, I stood back. 'Hello, Mother,' I said, sounding unnaturally calm. 'You had better come in, then.'

'Is Paul here?' she asked, looking a little wary.

'No – but I'm expecting him later; he was delayed on business.'

'He's such a busy man, isn't he?' Her voice carried a hint of irony.

'Yes.' I glanced at the decanters on the table and then remembered what Paul had told me. 'Can I get you a cup of tea or coffee?'

She laughed harshly. 'I see Paul has told you about me, Kate. No, thank you. I don't want anything. I shan't take up much of your time. I just came to tell you something, then I'll go before Paul gets. . . . '

Anger surged through me. 'How dare you?' I cried and she looked startled. 'All these years . . . all those lies – and you can't take time to sit down and talk to me!'

Something flickered in her eyes, then she smiled oddly. 'Not because I don't want to, Kate,' she said. 'I wasn't sure you would want to talk to me.'

For a moment anger, grief and bitterness warred against a very different set of emotions and I couldn't speak; then as she hovered, obviously about to leave, I knew myself defeated. Tears sprang to my eyes, running silently down my cheeks.

'Damn you!' I muttered fiercely, brushing them away. 'Of course I want to talk to you – you're my mother.'

'Oh, Kate. . . . ' She turned aside for a moment. I hesitated, then went to the sideboard and poured us both a glass of sherry. She took it gratefully, draining the glass but shaking her head as I offered another. 'Thank you, but I'd better not. I'm trying to ration myself.'

I looked at her as she sat in one of the ebony elbow chairs. 'Paul said you were ill a few months ago. He – he told me about Marc. I'm sorry.'

'It was my own fault,' she said with an expressive shrug. I lied to him and he couldn't accept the truth. If I'd been honest from the start it might have been less of a shock for him.' She looked up then. 'You'd think I'd have learned by now, wouldn't you?'

'Why did you lie to me?'

She smiled wryly. 'Surely you know by now? I was frightened, Kate. Frightened that Paul would compare us – you were so fresh and young and lovely. He was already halfway to being in love with you, even then. If you'd come with us, I knew he would gradually turn from me to you – and I was madly in love with him. I still am. . . . '

I stared at her as silence fell between us. 'Is that why you've come?' I asked at last.

'To beg you to give him back to me?' Her mouth twisted deprecatingly. 'I'm not that much of a fool; I know I've lost him. I lost him a long time ago – perhaps from the moment he kissed you in the kitchen. . . . ' She broke off and looked over her shoulder as a pitiful wail came from the bedroom.

'That's Richard,' I said. 'He's cutting a tooth. Excuse me, I ought to. . . . '

'May I?' she asked, her eyes suddenly pleading. 'Please, Kate?'

I hesitated, then inclined my head. Even as she went into my son's bedroom, I felt a prickle of fear – she wouldn't harm him, would she? A moment later I was ashamed as she came out, carrying him carefully in her arms. Miraculously, he had stopped crying. She smiled at me, her eyes very bright.

'My grandson,' she said proudly. Then, with a little frown, 'You called him Richard – why?'

'I'm not sure. Memories, I suppose.'

'Because you wanted to believe that Richard was your father?'

'I know he isn't. Sir Gerald told me it was impossible.'

'Because of that childhood illness?' she inquired and I nodded. 'Richard went to a specialist after we were married. He was told that it wasn't impossible; it wasn't likely that he would have children, but it wasn't impossible.'

'So I could be his daughter after all?' I gave a harsh laugh as she acquiesced. 'How odd that you should tell me now – when it doesn't matter any more.'

'Kate. . . . ' She looked at me awkwardly. 'Are you in love with Paul? I mean really in love with him – the way you were with Harry?'

I didn't answer at once, then I met her eyes and she saw the truth. 'I do love him. . . . '

'But you would choose Harry if you could?'

'I don't see the point of this.'

'Please – answer my question, Katie. It's important.'

305

'No!' Paul's voice from the doorway was sharp, agonized. 'Don't answer her, Kate. She's only trying to drive a wedge between us.'

Her eyes went to his face and she turned pale. For a moment I thought she would faint and I took Richard from her arms. She hardly seemed to notice; her mind was focused only on Paul.

'That's unfair, Paul,' she said at last. 'I just want Kate to know the truth.'

'No!' he cried. 'If you do this, Emma, I'm finished with you. I shall hate you until the day I die.'

She smiled then, a smile full of sweetness and sadness. 'I know that, Paul,' she said. 'But I have to do this for Kate. I'm sorry. . . .'

'Do what?' I asked, going through to lay Richard in his cot and coming back to confront them. 'What is this all about?'

'It's about you,' my mother said. 'It's about what you want from life.'

'She wants to marry me,' Paul said, slipping his arm about my waist possessively. 'Tell her, Kate. Tell her you don't want to hear this. It can only hurt you.'

I sensed the tension between them and it puzzled me. I drew away from him, looking at my mother. 'Go on,' I said, through lips that were almost too stiff to move. 'Tell me – tell me about Harry. I want to know.'

She glanced at Paul and trembled, then she steadied herself and turned back to me. 'I'm not sure whether or not it matters to you, Kate, but. . . . Harry is alive. . . . '

I swayed as her words struck me. Shocked and breathless, I could only stare at her. My gaze went from her face to Paul's and I saw the anger and despair in his eyes.

'You knew,' I whispered. 'You knew and you didn't tell me. . . . Why?' But even as I asked, I knew the answer.

He had not told me, because he was sure that once we were married I would never have left him for Harry. Even knowing what I now knew, I could not have put him or myself through the shame of a divorce. It wasn't a secret he could hope to keep for ever – he must have been on edge when we saw Helen in the Ritz, realizing that at any moment she might tell me. She had said that there was something I should know, but she hadn't contacted me so perhaps she had changed her mind. Philip probably told her it was not her business to pry into my life. I was angry with Paul for not telling me the truth. Yet he had believed that I could never marry Harry, so perhaps he had only meant to save me pain.

'Why didn't you tell me?' I asked again. 'How long have you known?'

'Only a few months. . . . '

'A few months!'

'It couldn't make any difference,' he said, his eyes pleading with me. 'He's your brother. . . . '

'No,' I said quietly. 'That's just it, he isn't.'

'He might be,' my mother put in quickly. 'I was never really sure.'

I shook my head and her eyes widened. 'It doesn't matter if Sir Gerald is my father or not. Harry couldn't be my brother, because Sir Gerald wasn't his father. . . . '

I could hear the clock ticking as the silence settled over us. Paul's face was frozen, his eyes like black ice. My mother looked incredulous and a little frightened, as though she'd just realized the full implications of what she'd done.

'How do you know?' She was the first to speak, breaking the spell. 'Did Selina tell you?'

'She left me a letter with her solicitor,' I said. 'I opened it this evening – just before you arrived.' A harsh sound of disbelief issued from Paul's throat. 'It was in the drawer; I'd had it since – since the night I agreed to. . . . ' My voice failed and I couldn't go on, looking at Paul in mute appeal.

He moved at last, pouring himself a stiff whisky. 'The night you agreed to marry me?' he asked, and his tone carried the sting of sarcasm. 'A promise you now intend to break, I suppose?'

My legs felt weak. I sat down, shaking, my head whirling. 'Please, Paul,' I whispered. 'I'm so confused. I don't know what to think.'

'Don't you?' His bitterness flared. 'Then let me spell it out for you, Kate. You promised to marry me; you're wearing my ring and we've published our intention in *The Times*. You can either keep your word or jilt me; the choice is yours.'

'That isn't fair, Paul!' My mother leapt in to defend me. 'You knew Harry was alive; you should have told her.'

'What interests me is how you knew?' He looked at her coldly.

'You told me yourself.' She laughed shakily as he denied it with a curt toss of his head. 'But you did, Paul. You were so anxious to discover the truth of Kate's birth. It couldn't have mattered to you unless Harry was still alive. I knew he had to be – so I rang Gerald and asked him. Oh, I didn't say who I was, of course. I pretended

307

to be a friend. Gerald was most obliging. Harry's living at Brockmere. Apparently, he limps a bit and he was ill for a time, but. . . . '

'And you couldn't wait to use your knowledge to destroy me?' He spoke quietly but she flinched. 'How you must hate me, Emma.'

Her eyes flickered but she refused to drop her gaze. 'No, I don't hate you, Paul. I owed this to Kate, don't you see? Just as you owe her the chance to make up her own mind.' Her voice was barely a whisper and I saw how much it was costing her to defy him. 'I'm sorry. I know you won't believe me, but I love you.'

'Damn you!' he cried, and turned to me, his eyes angry. 'Well, Kate, I'm waiting.'

I rose to my feet, meeting his eyes. 'I can't give you my answer yet,' I said quietly. 'I have to see Harry first. I have to talk to him. Please, Paul. Please understand.'

For a moment I thought he would deny me, then, quite suddenly, the tension drained out of him and I saw a flicker of self-mockery in his eyes:

'But I do,' he said. 'That's the trouble, Kate. I understand only too well. . . . ' His eyes became distant and cold, colder than I'd ever seen them. 'Since you wish it, I suppose I can only agree to let you go. . . . '

Paul had gone now. Mother looked at me, seeing the distress I couldn't hide.

'Did I do right?' she asked, catching her breath as I hesitated. 'Please, tell me – was I right to come? You do believe that I did it for your sake?' I could see that it was important to her that I should believe her and I smiled.

'Yes,' I said and opened my arms. 'Yes, I believe you – and no matter what happens now, you were right.'

She closed her eyes as the relief washed over her, surrendering herself to my hug. 'Thank God,' she muttered, 'I'll go then. . . . '

'No!' I caught her hand and held it firmly. 'I shan't go down to Brockmere until tomorrow. Stay here with me this evening. There are so many things I want to ask you – so much to talk about.'

She looked at me doubtfully, then she smiled. 'Yes,' she said. 'I want to tell you, Kate. I want to tell you everything – and then perhaps you may begin to understand. . . . '

We had spent the evening talking. In the spare room my mother lay sleeping, Richard in his cot beside her. She was pleased that I'd named him for the man she'd married. I smiled as I remembered her pet name for him . . . Froggie. . . . Somehow it made him come alive for me in a way he never had before. I was glad that she had loved him, even though her selfish behaviour had hurt him. But I understood that selfishness a little better now; I understood and I forgave.

I'd tried to sleep but I was too restless. Sitting by my window in the light of the bright moon, I took out Lady Selina's letter and looked at it. Just a few hours ago I had felt angry and cheated that it had come too late; now it was as if a small miracle had happened. Recalling all those mysterious hints Harry's mother had given me, I understood what she'd been trying to tell me and why she'd called so desperately for her son as she lay dying. A secret like this must have lain hard on her conscience. I knew how difficult it must have been for her to confess her guilt in this letter. She was a proud woman and the secret she'd been forced to keep all her life must have been like a hair shirt, pricking her remorselessly. She'd caused Harry and me much grief by her stubborn refusal to tell her husband the truth, but the choice must have torn her apart.

I began to read once more.

'The choice must be yours, Kate. Only you can decide whether Harry should be told the truth. I've kept it to myself for so many years. If you tell him he is not Gerald's son, I believe he will feel honour-bound to renounce his inheritance – and I'm sure you know how much Brockmere means to Harry. It would have been easier to tell the truth than to live with this lie on my conscience all these years, yet how could I destroy the pride and love Gerald felt for his son – his only son? Believe me, Kate, I've agonized over this so many times. Especially since I realized that you and Harry cared for each other. Perhaps I should've confessed my secret then, but I was reluctant. I was afraid of all that it would mean. It is only since my illness that I. . . . '

I folded the letter and slipped it into my writing case. Now I understood all the things she'd told me. She had loved Harry's father very much, and because he had been slowly dying of an incurable illness, she had given way to the temptation to make love with him. For a girl with Selina's principles that must have been a momentous decision. Then, when she knew she was carrying her dead lover's child, she had panicked and married a man she did not love. She had spent the rest of her life paying for her mistake. She had kept her feelings in check for so long that even her beloved son believed she did not truly care for him. I understood that she had found it impossible to tell us the truth, and only when she realized she was dying did she become convinced that she must confess.

Tomorrow I would see Harry and then. . . . What then? I wasn't sure what I should do. I cared for Paul and I knew that I owed him a great deal. If I broke my promise to him I would be condemned as heartless by a critical world. But Harry . . . Harry was my life, my other self. Without him I would never be complete.

Sighing, I stared at the moon. Whatever I did, someone would suffer.

CHAPTER THIRTY

She stood on the pavement outside his hotel, trying to make up her mind whether or not to go in. He had been so angry when they parted, but she needed to see him once more, even if it was for the last time.

Gathering her courage, she went into the lobby and asked for him at the desk.

'Is Monsieur de Bernay expecting you, madam?'

'Yes. He's waiting for me,' Emma lied.

She knew the desk clerk was watching her as she stepped into the elevator and asked for the top floor. No doubt he would telephone Paul's suite and let him know she was on her way up.

Pausing at the door, she wiped the palms of her hands with a handkerchief and drew a deep breath. She didn't expect him to welcome her with open arms, but she wanted to part as friends. She wanted to be able to see him sometimes. Taking a deep breath, she knocked once.

The door opened immediately. Paul stood on the threshold, glaring at her.

'What do you want?'

She stared into his cold eyes and knew she ought not to have come. It was useless. He would never forgive her. He believed that she had deliberately destroyed his relationship with Kate. She knew it and yet she still couldn't stop herself pleading with him for understanding.

'Please, Paul,' she whispered. 'You have to believe me. It was best that she should know. I did it for Kate's sake – and, in a way, for yours. If she had discovered the truth after you were married. . . . '

His eyes darkened with anger and she saw that he knew she was right, but was not prepared to admit it. He turned away from her. 'You did it because you were jealous,' he said coldly. 'You were always jealous of Kate.'

She knew that for a moment, when she had read Kate's letter, there had been a surge of terrible jealousy, a desire for revenge, but in the end she had been driven by a far stronger emotion – a mother's love for her only child. She had wanted to make up to Kate for some

311

of the damage she had done. He had to believe that. It was important to her.

'Please, Paul,' she whispered. 'Please believe. . . . '

'Get out,' he said without turning round. 'I don't want to see or hear from you again.'

She gasped, feeling as though he had punched her in the stomach. She had never thought he could be as unyielding as this. For a moment she stared at his back, then she smiled, her head high as she walked to the door.

'I won't ask again,' she said proudly. 'I'm sorry, Paul. I really did love you. God help me, I still do!'

Then, opening the door, she went out of his room, down the stairs and out of the hotel into the street.

She spent two days wandering the streets of London, thinking, remembering, regretting. She was not yet forty but she felt she had already lived several lifetimes. Where should she go from here, and what should she do?

Memories haunted her. Not all of them were sad. She remembered the early days with Froggie. How young and foolish she had been then. It had been good with Paul, too, at the beginning. She had experienced more than many women did in the whole of their lives.

Sometimes she lingered outside a pub, tempted to lose herself in the forgetfulness that strong drink brings. Once she sat in the gardens of a riverside inn and ordered a glass of shandy. She stared straight ahead, not really aware of what was going on around her. She was smiling slightly, remembering the way Froggie had danced attendance on her, bringing her a posy of snowdrops he had searched for for hours. . . .

'May I buy you a drink?'

Glancing up into the eyes of a young man, Emma shook her head. 'No, thank you,' she said. 'I was just leaving.'

She walked away, her heart beating very fast. She had so nearly given into the temptation. She had been down that road too often . . . and yet what else was there?

She stood looking down at the muddy waters of the River Ouse, wondering what had made her come back to Ely of all places. She had walked past the house in Willow Walk, standing outside to stare at it until a woman came to the window and twitched the curtains angrily. Smiling to herself, she walked on until she reached the

Cresswells, a favourite haunt of Kate's when she was young. It was deserted now, the wind whipping the water into little waves. Staring down at the water, Emma felt herself drawn towards it, drawn by something deep within her. The river called to her, promising forgetfulness. Embraced in its cool arms she would find peace, and an end to the emptiness inside her. She would no longer have to remember anything.

The wind tugged at her wide-brimmed straw hat. She took it off, staring at it as she remembered the day Paul had bought it for her. A surge of almost unbearable pain went through her. Then, on an impulse, she threw the hat into the river. It landed neatly on the surface of the water and was soon bobbing merrily downstream. It would carry her away, too, if she wished, down to the cool, dark peace her soul craved. . . .

CHAPTER THIRTY-ONE

Bates was waiting for me at the station. Mrs Bates had taken my call earlier, sounding surprised but pleased to hear from me.

'Well, bless me,' she said. 'Sir Gerald will be pleased, miss. I'll tell him you're coming down, shall I?'

'Yes, of course. Thank you.'

Bates took my bag, an inquiring expression in his eyes as he looked at the child in my arms. I nodded encouragingly and held Richard up for him to see.

'His name is Richard,' I said proudly. 'He's six months old and he has one tooth.'

'He's a fine-looking boy.' Bates glanced at my ringless left hand. 'It's good to have you back, Miss Kate.' His voice carried no hint of censure.

'It's good to be back,' I said. 'How is everyone?'

'Not so bad.' He frowned as he led the way out to the car, signalling to the porter to follow. 'It seemed a bit strange when the last of the convalescents moved out, empty like. Then Mr Harry came home and started to put things right. We've had builders in repairing and decorating and there's three new maids; the gardeners are up to strength – oh, and Mr Harry has bought a new stallion.'

'It sounds as if things are back to normal?' I felt a sinking sensation in my stomach. If Harry had taken up the reins at Brockmere, would he want to give it all up for me? Had I even the right to ask?

I got into the car, wondering if I'd been right to come after all. Perhaps Harry had learned to forget me? Glancing out of the window, I looked at the familiar scenery as we drove through St Ives. Apart from the damaged spire of All Saints' church, into which an aircraft from the RFC station at Wyton had crashed in March 1918, it all seemed the same. . . . The old bridge over the river with its arches, and the chapel, which had once also served as a toll house, and the steam mill built in 1854, that was converted into a printing works in 1902. Serene and beautiful, the little market town seemed to slumber on, untouched by the passage of time. A lump came to my throat as I remembered so many happy days spent there during that last summer before the war, and I hardly listened as Bates chattered on, telling me bits of news about the estate. It wasn't until we were nearly at the house that he said something that caught my full attention.

'I suppose you know that Miss Prue is living at Brockmere again? She and her husband have separated.'

'No, I didn't know.' I frowned. 'When did that happen?'

'A few months after her ladyship died. There was a bit of trouble,' he said, clearing his throat. 'I'm not a gossip, miss, but I thought you should know – Miss Prue, well, she had an affair with one of the officers staying here and her husband. . . . There was a terrible row and she's been behaving a bit oddly ever since.'

'I see. Thank you for telling me, Bates.'

He nodded, making no further comment on the subject. 'Rosie will be pleased to see you. She came in to see to your room personally.'

'Rosie is here?' I was pleased. 'That's marvellous.'

We had drawn up outside the house. Rosie came rushing out to greet me. She was a little plumper, but otherwise exactly the same, her face wreathed in smiles of welcome.

'It's so wonderful to see you,' she cried. 'We've been that worried about you!'

'I'm sorry I didn't write,' I said. 'I'll explain later.'

'You don't need to.' She smiled and took a peek at Richard. 'He's beautiful – I'll put a cot in your room. We've still got Mr Harry's. . . .'

Rosie's look was significant, and I knew I didn't need to tell her who was my son's father. She had prepared a large airy room for me; it smelt of polish and there were bowls of fresh flowers everywhere.

She looked at me as I laid Richard in the cot she had fetched from the nursery. 'Are you going to stay now?'

'I don't know,' I said. 'Perhaps, after I've spoken to Harry.'

She nodded, her eyes serious. 'He's at the stables. Sir Gerald had a meeting – and Miss Prue went shopping. They'll all be back for tea.'

I was thoughtful for a moment, then, 'Are all my old clothes still here, Rosie?'

'Yes.' She was surprised. 'I put them in the wardrobe.'

'My breeches, too?'

'Yes, but. . . .' She frowned and stopped.

'But what?' I asked. 'Don't you think they'll fit me?'

'It isn't that,' she said awkwardly. Her eyes dropped as mine probed. 'Mr Harry – you might find he's changed. . . .'

'What do you mean?'

315

Her gaze lifted then. 'He has moods, Kate,' she said, speaking to me as a friend. 'He read about your engagement and – and he's hardly had a civil word for anyone since.'

'I see.' I bit my lip. 'Thank you for telling me, Rosie. But it makes no difference. I fancy a ride – if you'll keep an eye on Richard for me?'

'Of course,' she said and smiled. 'I'm glad you've come back. He may not know it, but he needs you.'

Rosie left me to change, promising to pop in regularly to see that Richard was still sleeping. I found my old riding breeches and put them on. They still fitted me; I didn't look much different from the old Kate, the one who had sneaked out to go riding in the park with Harry.

My heart was beating wildly as I slipped out of the house and walked in the direction of the stables. I felt as if I was sixteen again, and I glanced over my shoulder, almost as if I expected to be caught and punished.

Reaching the stableyard, I halted abruptly as I saw the two men deep in conversation. Supposing I'd made a mistake in coming here? Supposing Harry didn't want to see me? I was suddenly afraid. I hesitated, wanting to run away, back to the safety of the house, and then it was too late. Harry turned and saw me.

For a moment he stared at me hungrily, his eyes leaping with excitement; then, as I took a hesitant step towards him, his expression changed. I watched the colour drain from his cheeks and saw the line of his mouth harden with anger. My heart sank. He didn't want to see me. He had never looked at me that way before, almost as if he hated me. The groom had sensed his mood and melted away, disappearing into the background.

'Harry,' I said, keeping my voice as light as I could. 'It's wonderful to see you – you look very well. . . . ' I broke off as I saw the flash of fire in his eyes. My legs were so weak that I thought they would give way beneath me.

'Why have you come?' he asked bitterly. 'Damn you, Kate! Can't you leave me in peace? Why didn't you stay in London with him?'

'Please, Harry,' I whispered. 'You have to listen to me. There's something I must tell you. . . . '

'What can you tell me that I want to know?' he demanded, his voice grating harshly. 'That you have a son? That you're going to marry the father of your child? I already knew, Kate. I've known for weeks – since Helen saw you with de Bernay at the Ritz.' His mouth

316

twisted with contempt. 'You could at least have let someone know where you were. . . . '

He was so bitter. He wasn't even going to give me a chance to explain.

'No, Harry,' I said, fighting for control. 'You're wrong. I couldn't tell anyone. I had to keep my secret – our secret. . . . ' My throat tightened and I couldn't go on.

He stared at me, disbelief in his eyes. 'What are you saying?' As I gazed at him in mute appeal, a look of horror came into his eyes and he held out a hand as if to ward me off. 'No,' he said harshly. 'No, I don't believe you. I don't believe you, Kate.'

Hearing the absolute denial in his voice, I knew that I had been wrong to come. I had thought only of my own feelings, my own gladness that we could at last be together. It had never occurred to me that Harry would deny his son.

'Please listen to me,' I said. 'There's something you don't know. . . . '

'I don't want to hear,' he cut me off abruptly, his face hard. 'It's over, Kate. I've made a new life for myself here. I've made my choice and this is what I want – I'm going to be married myself.' His eyes glittered as I stared at him. 'Do you remember Clare Brockley?'

Harry thought Richard was Paul's child. He didn't want to hear the truth. He had shut me out of his life. We could be together now as man and wife, but it was too late. I was too stunned and hurt really to take in what he was saying. All I knew was that he didn't want me. He wasn't even prepared to listen to me. He had stopped loving me. I backed away, the pain twisting inside me, then I turned and ran.

'Kate. . . . ' I heard the cry but I didn't look back.

Tears blinded my eyes as I reached the safety of my room. I blinked as I saw Prue standing near the dressing table, her back towards me. She had been looking at something and she flushed as she turned and saw me. I realized that my writing case was lying on top of the table. Rosie must have unpacked my things and put it there.

'Hello, Kate.' Prue looked at me challengingly.

She was wearing what looked like loose divided trousers made from a silky material with a long, straight top tied round the waist by a vivid sash, and her hair had been cut very short. She had bound an embroidered band around her forehead in a very Bohemian style, and she had a long cigarette holder between her fingers. As I stared in surprise, she put it to her mouth and drew deeply, blowing a little smoke ring and laughing at my expression.

'Don't look so shocked,' she said. 'I told you things would be different after the war, didn't I?'

'You – you look so different,' I said. She looked as if she had at last found her true self. 'It suits you, Prue.'

'So I'm told.' She arched her brow. 'I'm an independent woman now – or hadn't you heard?'

'Someone did mention it. I – I'm sorry about Michael.'

'Are you? I'm not.' Her lashes flickered. 'He wanted children, you see – and I can't have any. I did try to tell you after Mother's funeral, but you wouldn't listen. Anyway, we decided a divorce was the best thing. I'm staying here until it's final, then I shall live in London. I have friends there.'

'Is that what you want?' I looked at her, feeling guilty. By right Prue was now the heir to Brockmere. 'I thought you liked it here?'

She shrugged her shoulders. 'It will never be mine, will it, Kate?' She seemed to wait for my answer and when there was none, shrugged. 'Anyway, I like living in town; it's more exciting. I've met a man. . . . ' Her eyes danced with amusement. 'He's a concert pianist, Kate. He thinks I should take up music seriously. I'm thinking of following his advice.'

For a moment I was surprised, then I realized she had changed. When we first met she had been a rather awkward, self-conscious girl, a little jealous and resentful of her brother. Her first taste of unrequited love had made her spiteful, and she had wanted to hurt Harry when she followed us to the boathouse that day, but since then she had been through the trauma of her mother's death and the break-up of her marriage. I knew her inability to have children had been a serious blow to her, but now I saw that it had all somehow combined to make her stronger. She had discovered her true self and, in doing so, she had found contentment. Prue knew what she wanted out of life.

'I'm glad you've found someone,' I said. 'You were always very good at playing the piano. I think you should go ahead and do whatever you like.'

'So do I,' she said, and laughed.

I hesitated, then walked to the dressing table and picked up my writing case, putting it on the bed. She watched as I began to take things from the drawers and wardrobe, puzzled.

'What are you doing?'

'I'm leaving. I should never have come.'

'Why on earth not? This is as much your home as Harry's – or mine.'

'Harry doesn't want me here.'

'That brother of mine doesn't know what he wants. He's been impossible since he heard you were going to marry Paul. . . . ' Her eyes were bright. 'I suppose you are going to marry him. You haven't changed your mind?'

There was an air of expectancy about her. 'I'm not sure what I'm going to do,' I said. 'Why – are you still interested in Paul?'

She laughed and shook her head. 'I'll never break my heart over a man again,' she said. 'There are far more diverting things to do.' She drew deeply on her cigarette. 'Surely you'll wait and speak to Father before you leave?'

'No, I don't think so,' I said. 'I'll write and arrange a meeting somewhere else. Now, I must pack. . . . '

'I'll tell Bates you want a lift to the station then.'

'I could ring for a taxi.'

'Don't be silly, Kate,' she said. 'And you can't leave before tea. I simply won't allow it. For one thing, I haven't been introduced to that baby.' Her eyes flicked towards Richard's cot. 'What's his name?'

There was an air of confidence about her now. I saw echoes of Lady Selina in her, though I knew she would never believe it. In a few years she would be just as forceful as her mother had been. I rather liked the new Prue, and I knew I couldn't refuse her.

'Richard,' I said, sighing as I realized how foolish it would be to run away. 'All right. I'll stay for tea – and I'll talk to Sir Gerald.'

She smiled, a flicker of triumph in her eyes. 'You won't regret it,' she promised, and went out.

Prue and Sir Gerald walked to the car with me, Prue reluctantly releasing Richard into my arms at the last moment.

'I'm sorry Harry's being such a bore,' she said. 'I went down to the stables to look for him before tea, but he's gone off somewhere.'

'He didn't want to see me.'

'He's a fool,' Sir Gerald said gruffly. 'I wish you would stay a little longer, Kate.'

'I'll let you know when I'm settled,' I replied, smiling as I kissed his cheek. 'Perhaps you can visit me?' He promised that he would and I nodded. Having made my peace with my mother, it was time to get to know my father.

'You mustn't just disappear again. I want to see my nephew from time to time – where are you going?' Prue asked. 'Back to London?'

'No. . . . ' I shook my head. 'I need to be completely alone for a while. I'm not really sure where to go.'

She took a key from her pocket and handed it to me. 'This is to Harry's cottage. You stayed there once, remember?'

'I couldn't. . . . ' I felt a quiver inside. 'Besides, no one's been there for ages.'

A little smile played about her mouth. 'I've been tidying it up recently. Harry wants to sell it. Use it for as long as you like, Kate. He never goes near it.'

I hesitated, remembering the peace and welcoming atmosphere of the cottage. Prue sensed my hesitation and pressed the key into my hand. I looked at her.

'You won't tell Harry where I am? Please. You must promise me.'

'Cross my heart and hope to die,' she said, her brows arching. 'Trust me, Kate. Just trust me. . . . '

EPILOGUE

And so I came to the cottage, the place where Harry and I had been happy. Here for a short while we had lived in a paradise of our own, and the memories were all around me. It was as I sat in the rocking chair that Harry had bought for me that the tears finally came and with the tears came memories. Bittersweet memories that would haunt me all my life, but there was also acceptance. I knew now that I could never marry Paul. I loved him but not in the way I had loved – still loved! – Harry. Knowing that, I realized that I must set Paul free – free to find someone who would truly love him. We had all been caught in the web of lies my mother had woven, but at least for Paul there was still a chance of happiness with someone else. For me there was nothing . . . nothing but my child. Perhaps it was enough. It would have to be enough, because I had written to Paul, teling him of my decision. It had been painful and I knew it would hurt him, but the alternative might have been even more painful for us both. When I'd believed Harry dead, I'd thought it could work, but now I knew it would not. I loved Harry and I always would, even though I knew he no longer cared for me.

I stayed at the cottage a week, and then I knew I was strong enough to begin anew. I would go away somewhere; I'd come to terms with my memories; I'd forgiven my mother, now all I had to do was to learn to live again.

I packed my things and went down to the corner of the road to ring for a taxi. I would go back to London for a few days while I made arrangements to buy a house in the country somewhere – somewhere far away from Brockmere and Harry – perhaps somewhere in Cornwall or Devon. I thought I might like to live by the sea, and it would be good for my son. Picking up Richard, I kissed his face and held him to me.

'We'll be happy together, darling,' I whispered. 'I'll never leave you. I promise.'

I loved my son. He was all I had, for I knew I would never marry. I should always love one man – a man who no longer loved me.

Hearing the doorbell clang urgently, I went to answer it, expecting my taxi. When I saw who stood there, I gasped and stepped back, my heart racing.

'Why have you come?' I asked.

'Why didn't you tell me, Kate?' he countered, and as he smiled my heart turned over.

'Tell you – tell you what?' I turned away, holding Richard to me, not wanting him to see my face.

He came into the cottage, dominating it. I retreated to the fireplace, keeping a distance between us. I was trying not to hope for the impossible and my legs felt like jelly. Why had he come?

'Prue told me you were here,' he said. 'She read your letter, Kate – the letter Mother left you.'

'Oh. . . . ' I swallowed hard, turning to face him. 'So you know then.' He knew the truth about his mother, but that couldn't matter to him now. He was going to marry someone else.

'I know that Sir Gerald isn't my father,' he said, frowning. 'When I asked him about it, he said he'd suspected it long ago but he wouldn't hurt my mother by asking for the truth.' His mouth tightened. 'She has a lot to answer for, Kate. I can't believe that she let us go through all that agony when she knew it was unnecessary.'

He hadn't had time to think it through as I had. He didn't understand how difficult it must have been for a woman like Selina. I asked him how much Prue had told him, and then I realized that she hadn't taken it all in. Probably I'd come in before she'd finished reading the letter. I explained that his mother's lover had been ill.

'She let him make love to her, because she knew it would make him happy,' I said. 'It only happened twice. Then, after he was dead, she realized she was having a child. Gerald Redfern had asked her to marry him several times, and in a panic she agreed. She knew she ought to tell him the truth, but if his father had known. . . . '

'Grandfather was a tyrant.' Harry nodded, his face grim. 'But she could have said something later – when she knew we were in love.'

'In the beginning, she thought Brockmere meant more to you,' I said, laying Richard back in his cot. 'She was thinking of you and the grief she might cause – to you and her husband. Was she wrong, Harry? How do you feel, knowing that you aren't Sir Gerald's son?'

'You can ask that, Kate?' He laughed harshly. 'Don't you know what this means to me – the agony I've lived with, thinking that you and I. . . . ' He took a step towards me, his hands gripping my shoulders painfully as he looked down into my eye. 'My God, Kate – don't you know how I feel about you?'

322

My knees were beginning to tremble. 'You said it was over,' I whispered. 'You said you were going to marry Clara Brockley. . . . '

'I talked a lot of damned nonsense,' he said. 'Don't remind me, Kate. I was a bloody fool and I've been in agony ever since, sulking, refusing to go home because I couldn't bear to be under the same roof with you – couldn't bear to be near you and not hold you in my arms. . . . ' A shudder ran through him as he reached out for me. 'Forgive me, Kate,' he said pleadingly. 'Please. . . . '

I held back despite the clamouring of my senses. 'Richard is yours,' I said, my eyes meeting his, searching. 'There has never been anything . . . Paul and I have never. . . . '

'I know.' Harry smiled ruefully. 'That's where I went, Kate, to find him. He told me that I was a bloody fool – and he was right.'

'Oh, Harry,' I choked, still afraid to believe that he was here and it was going to be all right. 'And you don't mind about Brockmere?'

'Sir Gerald says he'll leave it in trust for Richard – ' Harry grimaced. 'He says that all he wants is for us to be together.'

'And what does Prue think of that?' I asked. 'You know she was always jealous of you; she always wanted Brockmere herself.'

'That's the funny side of it,' Harry said. 'She couldn't care less, Kate. She really couldn't. It's as if knowing that I'm not the heir has released her from whatever it was that haunted her when we were young, and she wants Richard to have the estate, because she can't have children of her own. All Prue really cares about is that the family should go on at Brockmere – and no matter who your father was, you do have Redfern blood in you. She's relying on us to have lots of children she can spoil whenever she comes to visit.' He grinned in his old confident manner. 'She tore me off a strip for going off the way I did and said it was a good thing she'd always been nosey – she asked me to apologize for her to you, for reading your letter, but I said you wouldn't mind in the circumstances.' He took a step towards me, looking down at me intently. 'Not that it would have made any difference. I would have come looking for you once I'd pulled myself together.'

'I might not have been here,' I said, hearing the honking of the cab outside. 'I was about to leave.'

'I would have found you.' Harry smiled and went to the door. 'I'll pay him off, shall I?'

He was gone only a few seconds. When he came back, the smile was gone. I stared up at him, sensing that he was holding something back.

'What is it, Harry?' I asked. 'Something's bothering you – you're not still thinking that Richard is . . . ?'

He put a finger to my lips, then bent his head to kiss me. For a moment I clung to him as the passion flared between us. I was breathless as he let me go, but his eyes were bleak and I felt anxious.

'Tell me,' I said. 'You mustn't keep anything back, Harry. Not now. . . . '

'I hate to have to tell you this,' he said, taking my hand to hold it tightly. 'But . . . they think Emma may have drowned herself in the river at Ely. . . . '

For a moment my blood ran cold. I stared up at him, then I shook my head in disbelief. 'No, I don't believe it,' I said. 'They haven't found her body, have they?'

'No. . . . ' He looked at me unhappily. 'Someone – his name was Eric Potter or something like that . . . does that ring a bell?'

'He was our neighbour,' I said. 'Go on, what did he see?'

'It was all in the local paper – he saw her standing outside the house where you lived, then she walked down towards the Cresswells – and later on someone fished her hat out of the river. They've been checking the banks and reeds for a couple of days. . . . '

'They won't find her,' I said. 'Because she isn't dead.'

'How can you be sure?' He looked concerned. 'I don't want you to be hurt like you were the last time.'

'I shan't be,' I said confidently. I smiled and reached up to kiss his lips. 'I know she isn't dead, Harry. She's alive and one day she'll turn up out of the blue, wondering what all the fuss was about.'

He touched my cheek. 'As long as you're not hurt again.'

'She can be selfish and thoughtless,' I said as he pulled a face of disapproval. 'But she's my mother, Harry. It's as simple as that. Besides. . . . ' I smiled at him. 'Nothing can hurt me now.' A surge of sheer joy went through me as I moved towards him, lifting my face for his kiss. 'Come on, darling – let's go home. Home to Brockmere. . . . '

She was sitting in a train somewhere in the middle of Austria. In her purse were ten English pounds, a few francs and one hundred Austrian schillings. She had left everything Paul had given her behind; the future was precarious, but she'd never been happier. It was the great adventure; the beginning of the rest of her life. She wasn't so very old, and she could still look attractive if she wanted to, but that wasn't important. What mattered was that she was free, free of the pain and the memories. Truly, gloriously free at last.

In her hand was a postcard addressed to Mrs Kate Redfern. Smiling she drew a picture of a large fat frog with a king's crown on its head on the blank side. She looked at it thoughtfully for a moment, wondering if it was enough, then, nodding, she put it into her bag for posting later.

Kate would understand. . . .